COLD
SHOULDER

Lynda La Plante

JOVE BOOKS, NEW YORK

This work was originally published in different form in Great Britain by Macmillan London, a division of Macmillan General Books, in 1994.

This Jove Book contains the complete text of the hardcover edition. It has been completely reset in a typeface designed for easy reading and was printed from new film.

COLD SHOULDER

A Jove Book / published by arrangement with
Random House, Inc.

PRINTING HISTORY
Random House, Inc. edition published March 1996
Jove edition / September 1997

The Putnam Berkley World Wide Web site address is
http://www.berkley.com

ISBN: 0-515-12128-2

A JOVE BOOK®
Jove Books are published by The Berkley Publishing Group,
a member of Penguin Putnam Inc., 200 Madison Avenue, New York,
New York 10016.
JOVE and the "J" design are trademarks
belonging to Jove Publications, Inc.

PRINTED IN THE UNITED STATES OF AMERICA

10 9 8 7 6 5 4 3 2 1

Also by Lynda La Plante

BELLA MAFIA
ENTWINED
FRAMED
PRIME SUSPECT 1
PRIME SUSPECT 2
PRIME SUSPECT 3

FOR THE LATE

ROY LA PLANTE,

A GENTLEMAN

ACKNOWLEDGMENTS

I sincerely thank Susanne Baboneau, Gill Coleridge, Esther Newberg, Patty Detroit, the real Lorraine Page whose name I borrowed, Hazel Orme, Clare Ledingham, Liz Thorburn, Harry Evans of Random House, and my wonderful American editor, Susanna Porter. To everyone at the Pasadena Police Station and Sheriff's Office, thank you for your time and expertise. But above all my thanks to a very admirable lady who brought me the story of her life.

COLD
SHOULDER

Los Angeles, California, April 12, 1989

It was dark, the alley lit only by neon flashes from the main street; not a single bulb above the many exit doors leading into it remained intact. The boy was running. He wore a black bomber jacket, a bright yellow stripe zigzagging down its back; shiny black elastic knee-length pants; and sneakers, flapping their tongues and trailing their laces.

"Police officer . . . freeze."

The boy continued to run.

"Police officer . . . freeze."

Halfway along the alley, the boy sidestepped a trash can like a dancer. The flash of a pink neon light gave an eerie outline to his young body, and the bright zigzag stripe appeared like a streak of lightning.

"Police officer. Freeze!"

The boy turned, in his right hand the stiff, flat metal of a 9mm pistol, and Lieutenant Page unloaded six rounds from the long-barreled .38. Bam-bam-bam-bam-bam-bam. The boy keeled over to his right, in a half spin, his head jerked back, his arms spread, his midriff folded, and he fell face forward. His long dark floppy hair spread over his gun arm, his body shuddering and jerking before he was still.

Lieutenant Page approached him, automatically reloading

the .38. The hoarse voice of Sergeant William Rooney barked
out to back off, to put the gun in the holster. Pushing past, his
wide ass hid the body as he squatted down on his haunches.

"Get back in the patrol car, Lieutenant."

Page did as requested, snapping the shoulder holster closed.
The car doors were open. A crowd of people, hearing the
gunshots, had started to press forward. Two uniformed officers
barred the entrance to the alley.

Sergeant Rooney was sweating as he carefully wrapped the
weapon before easing it away from the boy's bloody fingers.
He stared at the young dead face, and then walked slowly to
the patrol car. Leaning inside, he displayed the weapon, cushioned in his snot-stained handkerchief. "This the weapon,
Lieutenant?"

The 9mm pistol was a square, flat silver Sony Walkman.
Inside was an old Guns N' Roses tape. Axl Rose had been
blasting out, "Knockin' on heaven's dooowarrr . . ."

Page turned away. Rooney's fat face was too close, sniffing
like an animal, because he knew, and he could smell it. "Get
back to base—and fucking sober up."

The locker room was empty, stinking of feet and stale sweat;
the vodka was stashed under a tote bag. Just feeling the cold-
ness of the bottle gave Lieutenant Page's jangling nerves instant relief. Page leaned on the sink, not even attempting to
hide the bottle, drinking it like a man in a desert until it was
empty. Suddenly the sink was slippery and the floor uneven,
moving, shifting, and the long bench against the nearest wall
was a good, safe, secure place to hide beneath.

Fifteen minutes later, Sergeant Rooney kicked open the
door. "Lieutenant? You in here?" His fat feet plodded down
toward the washbasins. "Captain wants you in his office.
Now!"

She was hunched against the wall beneath the bench, her
skirt drawn up, one shoe on, one off, knee poking through
ripped tights. Her head rested on one arm, the fine blond hair
hiding her face. The other arm was spread wide across the
floor. Rooney tapped her upturned hand with the toe of his
black crepe-soled shoes. "Lieutenant!"

He bent down slowly, and yanked her hair roughly away
from her face. She was unconscious, her lips slightly parted,

her breathing deep and labored. A beautiful face, the fine blond eyelashes like a child's, the wide prominent cheekbones, and perfect straight nose almost enhanced by her flushed pink cheeks. Out cold, Lieutenant Lorraine Page was still a class act. Rooney stood up, then with his foot pushed her arm closer to her body. She moaned and curled up tighter. He wandered over to the washbasin, picked up the empty bottle, then returned to Captain Mallory's office.

"You find her?"

"Yep! She's out cold on the floor, bottle must have been in her locker."

Rooney stood it on the captain's desk and just shrugged his shoulders. "She's a lush, been coming down for a while. I thought she was in control, I've talked to her. . . . She always had an excuse—you know, marital problems, et cetera, et cetera . . ."

Captain Mallory stared out of the window, then sighed. "Get her out of here, will you? Get her badge, her gun, and tell her to stay out of my sight."

Lorraine didn't even empty her locker: it was done for her, everything stuffed into the regulation tote bag. The key was taken, along with her weapon and badge; hardly able to focus, she scrawled her name on the official sign-out document. She was helped from the station, still too drunk to comprehend what was happening. Rooney had gripped her by the elbow, pushing her roughly through the corridors. The zipper on her skirt was half undone, her slip showing, and if Rooney hadn't held her tightly she would have fallen more than twice. He even banged her head, as if she were a prisoner, warning her to dip low to get into the rear of the car. She had laughed, and he had slammed the patrol car door so hard the vehicle rocked.

"You think it's funny? I hope you can sleep at night, Lieutenant. Sleep as deeply as that kid you took out. Now get her the hell out of here. . . ."

As the car drove out of the station parking lot, it was early morning, but Lorraine had no idea of the time or how long she had been drunk, she didn't even see the mother of the dead boy, weeping hysterically, being brought in. All she had been told was her son had been shot while escaping from a drug bust.

Two weeks later, Lieutenant Lorraine Page was officially out
of the precinct. No disciplinary action was taken. She lost her
pension, her career, but her forced resignation was quietly
glossed over and it never reached the press. Tommy Lee
Judd's family never knew the name of the officer who shot
their fourteen-year-old son six times. At the inquest it was
stated that the boy had ignored three police warnings to stop.
He had been charged with crack dealing two years previously,
but the statements from his probation officer that he had been
clean for the past six months were glossed over. His death was
recorded, and the record filed away. No one mentioned that
he had had no weapon, and had been mistaken for another
suspect—or that the officer who opened fire had subsequently
been released from all duties and was no longer attached to
the force.

In fact, Lieutenant Page might never have existed, and, as
word got around, no one who had worked alongside her spoke
to her again. She was given the cold shoulder. She had betrayed their badge, her rank and position: she had been drunk
on duty, and a fourteen-year-old boy had died. They closed
ranks—not to protect Lorraine, but to protect themselves.

Twelve years' service, two commendations, and a service
record that any officer, male or female, would have been proud
of, were over. No one cared to find out what would become
of ex-Lieutenant Lorraine Page.

After the shooting, when she had been unceremoniously
dumped outside her apartment's entrance, she had stumbled
inside and collapsed onto her bed. The building was incongruously in a very prosperous area, considering Lorraine's job.
Situated in old Pasadena and overlooking the Arroyo, an array
of Jags, Mercedes, and Range Rovers was parked in the white-
marked parking zones of the condo's private parking lot; not
a Ford or a Honda was in sight. Anyone who entered the
private terraced housing estate was checked by their own security. Mike, Lorraine's husband, knew she was on night duty
and was not expected to return until mid or late morning, so
he had already dressed and fed their two daughters, and driven
them to school. He did not witness the return of his wife or
see the state she was in. While Lorraine slept through the rest

of the morning, their baby-sitter, Rita, picked up the girls and brought them home, where she checked the details of Lorraine's duty times. According to the schedule, Lorraine was due for two days' leave and should have returned home by now. Rita would have stayed to make the girls their lunch, but little Julia, age six, was calling "Mommy, Mommy," as four-year-old Sally began collecting her toys to play with her mother.

"Is your mommy home?" Rita asked, surprised Lorraine had not called out or acknowledged her before then. She often slept during the day when she was on night duty, but she usually left a note to say she was home. The girls had opened her bedroom door and discovered her.

"Yes, in bed," piped Julia.

Rita tapped on the open door and peeked into her room. Lorraine was lying facedown, her head beneath a pillow. "Mrs. Page? Is it okay if I go on home now?"

Lorraine eased away the pillow. "Yeah, yeah, thanks, Rita."

Julia climbed up on the bed. She had already delved into her toy box, bringing out puzzles and something that made a pinging sound that cut like a knife through Lorraine's blistering headache.

"Mommy, can we go to see the puppets?"

"Mommy, I want pee-pee." Sally pulled at the duvet.

"Mommy, can we go to see the puppets?" Julia repeated, as Lorraine slowly sat up.

"Mommy, I want pee-pee *now*."

Lorraine had to hold on to the edge of the bedside table to stand upright. She took her younger daughter into the bathroom and helped her up onto the toilet. "I not got my panties down," the little girl howled.

After a good belt of vodka she found in the freezer, she was less jumpy and strung out. Once she'd settled the girls in front of the TV, Lorraine had another few nips of vodka with three aspirin so she could bathe and clean herself up. By the time Mike returned from his office, the kitchen was in order, their bed remade, and Lorraine, with her face made up, looked presentable. Wearing a long cotton wrap, she was checking the fridge for what she could cook for dinner when she heard the front door slam and Mike's usual, "Hi, honey, I'm home." He dumped his briefcase and, smiling, came to stand behind her, slipping his arms around her and cupping her breasts in his hands.

"We got time for a quick one before they come?"

Lorraine eased away from him. "Who?"

He returned to the table and picked up his briefcase. "Donny and Tina Patterson. I said we'd eat here and then go to the movie. Rita said she could baby-sit."

She closed her eyes.

"You haven't forgotten, have you? I wrote it down, it's on the board."

"Fine, okay. Did you buy some groceries?"

Mike pursed his lips. "You said you'd pick up dinner on the way home from work this morning."

"I'm sorry, I forgot. I'll go get something now."

"Don't bother," he snapped, and went into the bedroom. She followed.

"It's no bother, for chrissakes, it'll take me two minutes. I'll get dressed and—"

He began to loosen his tie. "Send out for something. There's a list of takeouts by the phone. Just call one of them. . . ."

"Anything you don't make a list of, Mike?"

He glared. "Yeah, and you know what that is. I haven't slept with you for a month—you want me to start putting that down? Like, when it suits you?"

She walked out, not wanting to get into an argument as the two little girls hurtled into the bedroom to fling themselves at Mike. He swung them around, tickled them on the king-sized bed to their delight. Then he picked them both up and carried them to the bathroom, bathed them, combed their hair, and put them into their pajamas. They were tucked into bed, each with her own special doll, when he returned to the kitchen. Lorraine was sitting with a mug of black coffee.

"You want to say good night to them?"

"Sure." She got up and bumped into the edge of the table, and gave a little smile. As soon as she was gone, he checked the freezer. One look at the bottle was enough.

"Did you call for some takeout?"

Lorraine was cuddling Sally. He repeated the question and she sighed. "Yes, some pizzas are coming any minute."

"Pizzas?" he said flatly. Donny Patterson was his superior in the law firm, so Mike had wanted something special, but he went to set the dinner table. He could hear Lorraine reading to the girls, who were giggling loudly—she was good at funny voices. He took out the best cut glasses and the best mats and even gave the cutlery a quick polish. Then he went into the kitchen and began to make a salad. He was neat and methodical as usual, carefully slicing each tomato, washing the lettuce and the celery.

"You going to get dressed?" he called out, one eye on the clock. When he walked into the bedroom, Lorraine was lying on their bed, eyes closed. He opened the wardrobe and began to choose a shirt, a pair of slacks. He took great pride in his clothes, which were expensive, stylish, proof of his newfound success. He was hoping to be made a partner in the firm, and knew it was in the cards.

"What you working on?" she asked, stretching her arms above her head and yawning.

"It's the Coleridge case. It looks like he'll divorce his wife without too much aggravation, and it's more than likely he'll get custody of the children."

"Really?" she said, without any interest, as she watched him holding up a shirt against himself.

"Do you like this shirt?"

"Yes."

"What are you going to put on?"

She swung her legs over the side of the bed. She didn't feel like seeing anyone, let alone going to a movie or having dinner with two self-important, wannabe-wealthy middle-class snobs. "Oh, maybe the Chanel or the Armani. I dunno, Mike, and I've got a headache."

"You want an aspirin?"

"Nope—maybe I'll take a shower."

He held her close. "The Pattersons are important to me, sweetheart, okay?"

She kissed him and rested her head against his shoulder. "I'll be a good girl, promise."

He touched her cheek. It never ceased to amaze him that she could arouse such passion in him. He loved the way she looked, her tall slender body. "You okay? Did you have a bad night?"

She pressed her face into his neck. Did she have a bad night? The painful blurred memory physically hurt, and she moaned softly, a half sob which he took to be confirmation that she wanted him. He began to slide her robe off her perfect shoulders, kissing the side of her neck.

"I better change." She stepped away from him.

"What's the matter, Lorraine?"

She sighed, shaking her head. "Nothing, Mike. I guess I'm just tired."

He heard the shower running and slowly got dressed. As he reached for his cuff links, he saw the photograph of Lorraine and her former partner, a dark, tousle-haired, moody-looking guy. Lorraine always referred to him by his last name, Lubrinski. Since his death, she had been different, unapproachable. Mike had tried unsuccessfully to get her to talk about it, but she seemed reluctant even to hear Lubrinski's name. Mike had not said a word when the silver-framed photograph appeared after the man had been shot. He had tried to persuade Lorraine to take a few weeks' leave, but she refused. Instead, he knew, she had asked for more overtime and specifically night duty.

Lubrinski's laconic half smile seemed to mock him, yet he was sure there had been nothing between them. She had admired him, Mike knew that. He had seemed shy, hardly speaking on the few occasions Mike had met him.

Lorraine came out of the shower, wrapped in a towel with another around her wet hair. "You want some aspirin, sweetheart?"

"Yes, I do, thanks."

She sat down on her dressing table stool, opening one of the drawers to take out her hair dryer. It felt leaden in her hands. All she wanted was to lie down and sleep. Mike handed her a glass of water and two aspirins. He kissed the top of her head; her hair fell in a soft pageboy that flattered her heart-shaped face.

"I'll maybe get a partnership soon," he said, as he sat on the edge of the bed. "It'll mean a lot more money and you not having to work."

She slowly rubbed foundation cream over her cheeks, a small dollop on her nose. "When will you know?"

"Well, this Coleridge case is good for me. He's an influential guy—he's even said he'd recommend me to his friends."

"All getting divorces, are they?" He laughed as she dipped the thick brush into the face powder and dabbed it over her face. "I thought you wanted to specialize in criminal law, Mike."

"Yeah, I did—maybe I still do, but it's good to get a grounding in all aspects. Besides—"

"Divorce pays better, doesn't it?"

Mike's expression was sharp. "Is that such a bad thing? Don't you like this place?"

"Yes, of course I do."

"Well, I'll be making a lot more soon. Next we'll have a house in Santa Monica, right on the beach."

"Oh, business is that good, is it?"

He laughed again. "It'll take a few years, but Donny seems to think I'll go places. When I look around here, it's hard to believe what we came from." He slipped his arms around her. "And I'll never forget how I got here. If it wasn't for you . . ."

She smiled, now brushing on a light blusher. Those days when he was studying day and night, when he worked at any odd job he could get, those days felt like a long, long time ago.

"We'd have more time together, too, sweetheart."

Lorraine put down the brush. "You mean if I was at home with an apron on and a casserole in the oven?"

"I don't think you'd ever be that, sweetheart, but you know we should think about it and also, maybe, about a trip somewhere. When will you know about your next vacation so I can work it out with Donny?"

She carefully outlined her lips, and caught her pale blue eyes staring back at her. They looked so tired. "I'll check on it as soon as I can."

Mike leaned across to take a comb from the dressing table. She continued to carefully outline her lips, watching him. He was unaware of her scrutiny as he ran the comb through his thick dark brown hair, then peered closer into the mirror to check his hairline. She even caught his small almost congratulatory smile, as his hair was definitely not receding. Mike was not exactly your "Marlboro Man," but he was in good shape and worked out regularly, playing a lot of tennis, so he was always tan. He was a very attractive man, she admitted, although probably more so to himself of late than to her. He was looking too groomed for her liking, and as if to confirm what she was thinking, he opened a bottle of cologne and splashed some into his cupped hand. She didn't like the bit-

tersweet smell he had begun to use; it wasn't effeminate, it
was just sharp to her nostrils, but she didn't mention it. And
just thinking about it reminded her of Lubrinski and the way
he had described Mike once, just joking, saying Mike had a
floral aroma and, grinning, asking if perhaps that was why he
was failing with women—no floral bouquet.

The doorbell rang and Mike charged out, leaving the air
heavy with his Forest Flowers. It was the pizza delivery. She'd
better get a move on. She heard him on the phone, confirming
with Rita what time she was to come over. Mike the methodical! Upwardly mobile Mike was so different nowadays, she
seemed to be losing him.

Lorraine stared at the blurred picture of Lubrinski. She
touched his face with the tip of her finger. His face seemed to
crease into a smile—but that was impossible; he'd never smile
at her again. Lubrinski was dead; he had died in her arms.
Sometimes she felt as if she were dead. Nothing seemed real
anymore; this apartment, all the new appliances Mike had
filled it with, all the new furniture. Mike had organized the
move down to the curtains. She had liked their old place even
if you did have to lug the stroller up and down three flights
of stairs. She missed the neighbors. Sometimes Mike's energy
drained her, and lately she was always tired. She never spoke
to anyone in the building and didn't even know who lived on
their floor.

The doorbell rang again and she could hear Mike welcoming
the guests. Still she sat, unable to muster enough energy to
join them. She pulled out the bottle from the bottom drawer
of the dressing table. Just a few sips, that's all she needed.

Donny and Tina were chatting in the kitchen while Mike
uncorked the wine. Tina Patterson looked as if she were heading out to a premiere rather than the local cineplex. She kissed
Lorraine on both cheeks and Donny gripped her hands tightly
in a firm "trust me" handshake. Mike ushered everyone into
the dining area and proceeded to pour the wine. He was doing
everything—seating his guests, bringing in big platters of
pizza, apologizing for the informal dinner, explaining that Lorraine had only just come home from duty.

She sat sipping her wine. She couldn't look at the pizza: its
bright colors made her feel like vomiting. They discussed the
Coleridge case. Donny constantly gripped Mike's shoulder in
another "trust me" gesture that irritated Lorraine, just as she

found Tina's delicate hands with their red-painted nails annoying. They made clicking noises on the plate as she picked up a minuscule slice of pizza, popping it into her collagen-enhanced lips. "To look at you, Lorraine, you'd never know you were a cop, it's just amazing."

Lorraine forced a smile as Mike reached over and held her hand. "I'm so proud of my wife. You know, she's been commended for bravery twice."

He sprang up from the table, went to the side cabinet, and returned with two framed photographs. Lorraine in uniform with President Reagan and in a group picture of the year's most decorated officers. "Lorraine caught the killer of that little girl, you remember the one that was found in a drain? The caretaker had done it, she was the one who caught him."

Tina made the right noises, shaking her head and rolling her eyes—with admiration, Lorraine supposed. She drained her glass; she needed another drink. "I'll put some coffee on," she said, leaving the table. She took out the vodka from the freezer and drank from the bottle. She had only just slipped it back when Tina appeared carrying the dirty dishes. "Men's talk in there. Can I help?"

Lorraine laughed. She was feeling better, eased by the vodka and wine. Tina began to stack dishes in the dishwasher.

"Do you get involved?"

"Pardon?"

"When you do these murder investigations, do you get involved?"

"Yes. I can't help it." Lorraine was fixing the coffeemaker. Her hands shook and she spilled the ground coffee over the counter. She brushed it off and onto the floor.

"Does it affect you?" Tina asked, running the dishes under the tap. "I always know when Donny's on a tough case—he's so moody. He works out at a gym to get rid of the anxiety, you know, but . . . that case with the little girl . . . That must have been terrible."

Lorraine reached for a tray. "She was only six, her name was Laura Bradley. She'd been raped, tortured, and she had a face like a little angel. Yes, it hurt me."

Tina tried to think of something adequate to say in response but couldn't. Lorraine had suddenly slumped into a chair as if she were exhausted, her head bent forward, hiding her face.

"You okay?" Tina asked.

"I still see her face, always Laura's face. I don't know why . . . don't know . . ."

Lorraine gave a long heavy sigh as if she had a great weight on her shoulders, and then leaned forward, resting her head in her hands. Tina hovered a moment before she walked out; she still could not think of anything to say.

Lorraine continued talking, unaware Tina had left the room. "For a while afterward, I got possessive about the girls, scared they'd be picked up. It never leaves you. You think it'll go away but it never does. Something somebody says or asks makes it all flood back and . . ."

Lorraine looked up, expecting Tina to still be there, but instead heard her voice in the next room.

"Okay, you guys, no more business, this is movie night. We're just gonna enjoy ourselves."

There were so many previews before the movie that Lorraine excused herself, saying she wanted to go to the ladies' room. She needed another drink. She figured if she just slipped out to the nearest bar and had a quick one, she could be back before the film started.

When she hadn't returned halfway through the movie, Mike went to look for her. He called Rita to see if she had gone home; she hadn't. Back in the cinema, he told the Pattersons that Lorraine sent her apologies but had felt ill, and rather than spoil their evening had gone home. It was after eleven when Mike got back. He checked Lorraine's duty schedule; he knew she was on a two-day break, but he called the station anyway in case there'd been a change. He was put through to Bill Rooney.

After the call, Mike paced the apartment, sat in the kitchen, then in the living room flicking the TV from channel to channel, waiting. He checked the girls. He waited until he fell asleep on the sofa. He was woken by shrieking laughter. He got up and crossed to the window.

Lorraine was standing on the sidewalk outside, paying off a taxi. Two people were inside it. He watched her drop her purse and fall against the wall before she reeled into their building. A couple of lights from neighboring houses came on and people stared from their windows. This was a very security-conscious area, and Mike could imagine their disgust when they saw the drunken woman stumble into the building.

The front door was open as she walked from the elevator. She took a deep breath and, with a fixed smile, peered inside. Mike grasped her by the elbow and drew her into the kitchen. He kicked the door closed. "Where've you been?"

"Oh, I hadda do something."

"What?"

"Just interview somebody." She was trying to keep her voice from slurring; her eyes were unfocused. He pushed a cup of coffee toward her. "I'm tired."

"Drink it and sober up."

She rested her head in her hands. Mike drew out a chair and sat opposite her. "I know, Lorraine."

"Know what?"

Mike told her he had spoken to Rooney. She sighed, looking away, and shrugged. He leaned over and gripped her hand. "I know about the shooting. Why didn't you tell me?"

She tried to pull her hand away. He wouldn't let go. "Why won't you talk to me?"

She pushed him off and hunched up, clasped her hands together. He had to lean farther forward to hear her. "There's nothing to say, Mike."

He got up and paced the kitchen. "What do you mean, nothing to say?" He wanted to slap her. "You were drunk on duty and you're telling me that you have nothing to say about that?"

She gave a soft laugh. "No complaints."

He gripped her hair and drew her head back. "You killed a boy, Lorraine." She made no effort to release herself and he shoved her forward, disgusted. "You shot him."

She nodded.

It was impossible for Mike to know what she was thinking; her eyes were glazed, and she seemed to be half smiling.

"You're out, don't you understand? You're off the force. *They've kicked you out!* Rooney told me they took your badge."

She shrugged again. "Well, that'll make you happy, I'll get some nail extensions and some jumbo rollers and make myself into a Tina clone. That what you want, Mike? Is that what you want?" Her face was ugly with rage. He turned on her, equally angry.

"Jesus Christ, aren't you ashamed? At least have the decency to show some remorse!"

She turned away, her whole body trembling. "Don't, please don't do this, Mike. I am trying so hard to hold myself together, I am trying, please don't think for one second I don't know what I've done. If you could just put yourself in my position, just . . ." Her voice became inaudible as she muttered to herself, and he sighed because he couldn't, not for a second, put himself in her position. One moment she would appear to have no remorse, the next she was so vulnerable, so obviously in need of comfort, but he felt incapable of knowing what he should do or say.

"Oh, Mike, Mike, I'm bleeding inside. I don't know what to do or what to say to you, to anybody, because I am hurting so much, I am hurting. Lubrinski's dead you know, you know that?"

"What?" he asked, still unable to hear her clearly. He couldn't decipher her slurred words, and in exasperation he told her to go to bed. He had to repeat it.

She bumped against the doorframe, and fell facedown on the bed. Mike didn't bother to undress her. He was almost out of the room when she said something, muffled by the pillows. She was repeating it, over and over. "I don't remember, I don't remember, he's dead, he's dead."

Mike never heard the plaintively whispered, "Don't go." Instead, he sat in his study until dawn, compiling notes for his case. The next morning, Mike called Rita to take the girls to their school. He bathed and dressed them and packed their little lunchboxes with sandwiches and cookies. Lorraine remained in their bedroom. He showered in the guest bedroom and when he came out he saw she was in the kitchen, sitting at the table, a glass of whiskey in her hand. He dressed for the office and then joined her, sitting down opposite. She held up the glass. "Hair of the dog."

"What are you going to do?"

"You mean work?" she asked.

"No. Will you be on trial or what?"

"I don't know."

"I blame Lubrinski. You haven't been the same since you started working alongside him."

"Lubrinski's dead, for chrissakes."

Mike watched as she refilled her glass. Suddenly he sprang

to his feet and yanked away the bottle. "That's enough."

She held out the glass like a child asking for more. He snatched it. "It's nine-thirty in the morning. How long has this been going on?"

"What going on, Mike?"

Holding the bottle, he almost felt in need of a drink himself.

"I just wanted something to relax me. I've been kind of tense lately."

He was speechless; she sounded almost flippant, as if the terrible events surrounding her termination from the police force could be dismissed just because she was tense! Her drunkenness glossed over as easily as the boy she had killed. He shook his head.

"I don't have a problem, Mike. It's just . . . lately things have gotten to me."

He felt even worse, as if someone had punched the air out of his lungs. Lorraine looked at her bare feet. "I feel all strung out and I can't remember what happened the other night."

He swallowed: could it be possible that she was blanking it out of her mind? Is that what she was doing? If it was, he wouldn't allow it to continue. He took a deep breath to keep his voice steady.

"You killed a kid, Lorraine. They've taken your badge. You're out, don't you understand?"

"Oh." She said it lightly, still staring at her feet.

Mike was still fighting to keep his voice under control, but it was getting harder by the second. It was as if she was playing some kind of game with him.

"I'm gonna talk to Rooney again. I don't know if they're pressing charges."

"You've talked to Rooney, have you?" she asked.

"Yes," he snapped. "I told you last night. How the hell do you think I know about it? And what do you think Donny is gonna say about this if the press gets hold of it?"

"Donny?" she said, confused. "What's he got to do with me?"

"He's got a lot to do with me. I'm in the middle of a big case right now. How do you think it's gonna look if they find out my wife not only opened fire on a kid but was drunk on duty as well?"

She rubbed at her neck. "It's none of their business."

Mike closed his eyes. "No? You think the press won't have a field day with this?"

She took out a cigarette, hands shaking. He watched as she tried to light it. She inhaled deeply. "You remember that day, Mike?" She looked at him, tilting her head to one side. "Best day of my life. You'd just qualified and . . ."

She laughed, dragging on the cigarette again. She was making his stomach churn—it was as if everything he said to her wasn't getting through. And then she made him want to weep.

"I knew by the expression on your face you'd passed the bar. But I didn't say anything, I knew you wanted to tell me yourself, and you acted so casual, wondering if I was off duty that night. Nothing special, you said, just thought that maybe we could have a quiet dinner someplace."

Mike's eyes filled with tears as she laughed again.

"We hadn't been able to afford dinner out for so long, but you kept up the act until we got to the restaurant. It was Bianco, remember that little Italian bistro with the red-checkered tablecloths?"

She got to her feet like a dancer as she mimicked the maître d' ushering them to a private little booth with the candles lit, the wine on ice, and a small bouquet of roses tied with a blue ribbon.

" 'Mrs. Page, you are now married to a qualified lawyer,' and you lifted the glass, and you were crying and I was crying and I loved you so, I was so proud. I loved you with my entire soul and never thought anything could ever come between us. So what happened, Mike? I feel as if I don't know you, as if I'm drifting in some kind of sea. I hate what you're becoming and I've gone along with it, never felt I could say anything to you, but it's all changing between us. You want success more than you want me."

Mike poured himself two fingers in the tumbler she had used and drained it. It was as if someone was pulling the rug out from beneath his feet. Suddenly everything he had been striving for was ragged at the edge. He sat down, cradling the glass in his hands. "Nothing has changed between you and me, nothing. I love you. I have always loved you. Okay, maybe I've had to put in more hours lately, but then so have you. You know I wanted you to give up work, you think I didn't notice the strain you were under, but you'll never talk to me about it."

She knelt down at his feet and wrapped her arms around him. "I want things to be the way they were when we both had nothing."

"You had your career. It was me that had nothing," he said petulantly.

"But you know why, don't you? I worked hard so we'd have a home and you'd have your chance."

He leaned over and kissed her forehead. "Maybe you haven't noticed that I'm earning good money now—you haven't needed to work for years and you're missing the girls growing up." She leaned against him and he slipped his arm around her. "Whatever happens, we'll come through this together."

They went to bed and made love for the first time in ages. That evening, Lorraine began to prepare dinner, even putting candles on the table. Then it started, the panic. It swamped inside her, beginning, as always, with fast flashes of faces. Lubrinski, then Laura Bradley, and now the boy. A boy running with a yellow stripe down his jacket. All she could think of was to get just one drink; then the panic would stop and the pictures would blur into oblivion. Just one drink would do it and she'd be all right. She went on with the dinner, having just one more, then another and another. Mike didn't come home until after midnight. He saw that the table had been laid for some special occasion; the candle wax had melted over the cloth. In the kitchen he found two wine bottles and the Scotch bottle, all empty in the trash can with the remains of dinner.

Lorraine was asleep, still in her dress. He didn't wake her, not even to tell her that Donny had offered him a partnership. He pulled the quilt out from beneath her and laid it gently over her. He checked on his daughters—they were both sound asleep. He went around the apartment and threw every liquor bottle he could find down the garbage chute. Not until he slid into bed next to her did he see that Lorraine was cradling the picture of Lubrinski in her arms. When he tried to take it from her she moaned and turned over. Maybe there had been more to their partnership than he had realized. Maybe they had grown apart . . . so many maybes.

He closed his eyes and remembered that night as clearly as Lorraine had, that dinner at Bianco's. How excited he had been booking the table, arranging for the flowers and wine to be ready. He turned toward her curved back, gently stroking it.

She had never looked more beautiful; she had worn her blond hair down to her waist in those days, and when she was on duty she would braid it into a neat roll at the nape of her neck. He had always loved when she came home from work, the way one of the first things she would do was unbraid her lovely silky hair. Often he would brush it out for her, it was always a signal that now they were on their own special time. It was also often a signal for them to make love. He wanted to cradle her in his arms now, wanted to make love to her right this moment, but she remained turned away from him, Lubrinski's picture still clasped in her hands. He wondered if Lubrinski had made love to Lorraine, and by the time he did eventually drift into a restless sleep, he was sure that he had. It was easier to blame someone else for the failure of their marriage than accept the possibility that he had changed.

The next morning, Lorraine was up early, cooking breakfast for the girls. Mike could hear her laughing and talking. By the time he went into the kitchen, they were ready for school.

"I'll drive them," she said. "You haven't had breakfast yet!"

He snatched up his car keys. "I'll drive them, okay?"

"When will you be home?"

"I'm in court today, so I'll be late." He walked out without kissing her goodbye, slamming the front door.

She was making the bed when he called. He'd made her a doctor's appointment.

"You did what?"

"Listen to me, sweetheart, he's somebody you can talk to, friend of Donny's—"

Lorraine interrupted, "I don't need a goddamned shrink, especially not some asshole friend of Donny's. There's nothing wrong with me that a few days' rest—"

Mike was adamant, not wanting to sound angry but unable not to. "Yes, you do, Lorraine, listen, don't hang up—"

Her voice was icy, calm and controlled. "No, Mike, I don't need anybody, I am not sick, okay? That's final. I'll see you tonight."

Lorraine made no contact with the station. She checked the newspapers for articles on the case, scanning the pages as fast as she could turn them, afraid to read about herself but at the same time wanting to know the outcome. When she did find a brief article about the shooting, it made no mention of her part in the death of the young boy, and that just made her feel worse. She was afraid, too, to be seen on the street, and for the next few weeks she led a double life. When Mike left in the morning she did some housework and ordered in groceries. When Rita brought the girls home, she played with them, read to them, and cooked dinner for Mike. He knew she was drinking but she denied it and he never saw her with a glass of alcohol in her hand. He had no idea that she spent her days sitting in front of the television with a bottle of vodka, keeping herself at a sustained level. Mike hid from himself that she was drinking consistently, partly because it meant less tension between them. He asked Rita to tell him if she ever saw Lorraine drinking, especially in front of the girls.

It was only a few weeks later that Rita called him. It was a Saturday, Mike had only gone into the office to do a few extra hours on a case but had become so immersed he had forgotten the time. Lorraine and he had promised the girls they'd go out for a picnic in the afternoon. "You'd better come home, Mr. Page. I don't know where she is—she left the girls by themselves—anything could have happened. I only dropped by as I was passing, she never called me or nothin'."

Mike drove like a madman back to the apartment. The children, he discovered, had been alone for most of the day. After Mike had calmed them, he asked Rita to stay with them and went out in a blind fury to find his wife. After searching in vain for three hours, he called home. Rita was in tears: Lorraine was back, she was drunk, unable to stand upright. A cigarette dangling in her hand, she apologized when he got back to the house, telling him that she had had an important meeting. She seemed barely to hear him when he talked to her, and if he touched her she screamed senselessly at him. Then, as if terrified of something or someone, she begged him to hold her tightly.

The next morning, shamefaced, she promised him he would never see her like that again. Never again would she touch a drop.

Mike coped as best he could. He instructed Rita never to leave Lorraine alone with the girls, to stay until he got home.

But the situation grew worse. Time and again he confronted her with empty bottles he found hidden around the apartment. She would swear she hadn't had a drink and even accused Rita of planting the bottles.

Mike was at the breaking point. He tried to understand Lorraine's frame of mind by putting himself in her position—she had shot an innocent boy and had lost the job she had always been so proud of—but all he felt was shame and guilt, of which she showed none. When he tried to talk to her about it, she seemed more intent on blaming her failure on his success.

No matter what he said she twisted it against him. If he had any guilt about those years when she had kept him and the children, it was soon dispersed by her venomous onslaughts. She exhausted him; night after night, he would dread coming home, afraid he'd find her ready for a fight. At other times, she would kneel at his feet and beg his forgiveness, pleading for him to carry her to bed. And yet throughout these agonizing weeks she seemed incapable of tears.

In the end, Mike himself went to Donny's doctor friend. He needed to talk it over with someone. The doctor warned him that unless Lorraine sought help Mike would be dragged down with her. He encouraged him to leave her and thus force her into seeking medical help. But Mike's own guilt and his awareness of how much Lorraine had done for him held him back. When his daughters became scared of their mother, though, Mike made one last attempt.

Lorraine finally agreed and, quiet and sober, she accompanied him to the doctor. She spent two hours in his office, talking first with Mike present and then alone. After the appointment she had appeared almost triumphant, admonishing Mike for wasting money. There was, as she had said to him over and over again, nothing wrong with her.

Mike returned the following day and was told that Lorraine had insisted that she was perfectly all right and able to cope with no longer working. She had refused to have a blood test.

But the drinking continued and the rift between them grew deeper. Lorraine adamantly refused to admit anything was wrong: she had her drinking under control. She was becoming sly; she would dress well and appear sober, but rarely managed to leave the apartment. Mike continued to find empty bottles hidden away.

Six months after Lorraine had left the force, he filed for

divorce. He refused to make her move out of the apartment, and signed it over to her with the contents. She protested when he insisted on custody of the girls but otherwise seemed not to care that he was leaving. He gave her five thousand dollars and promised three thousand a month in alimony. She was strangely elated when he brought the papers for her signature, which made him suspect that she didn't believe he would go through with it. But she signed with a flourish and smiled.

"You do understand what you've signed, don't you, Lorraine?" Mike asked quietly.

"Yes."

He gripped her tightly. "I'm leaving and taking the girls, but call me if you need me, and I'll do whatever I can to help. You need help, Lorraine, all I want is for you to acknowledge it." He felt terrible. She helped him pack, kneeling to lock the suitcase. She was wearing a pale blue denim shirt and her feet were bare. Her hair shone as she bent over the cases. Mike wanted to hold her, to make love to her. This was madness.

The Pattersons came to help with the suitcases. The girls, clasping Tina's hands, thought they were going on vacation. It had taken only the afternoon to get everything packed and out, such a short time after all the years they had been together.

"Tina's going to take the girls in their car. Do you want to say goodbye to them?" Mike asked.

"No. I don't want to upset them." She heard her daughters asking if they were going to see their granny and why was Mommy staying behind? She heard Tina reassuring them that Mommy would be coming to see them. She heard Donny call out that everything was in the car. She heard Mike say he would be out in a few minutes. She heard Rita saying goodbye to Julia and Sally, her voice breaking as if she were crying. Rita had known them since they were babies.

Mike walked into the kitchen. Lorraine turned toward him and raised a glass. "Just milk."

He leaned on the table. "I don't want to go, Lorraine."

"Doesn't look that way to me." She tried to smile, to shrug it off as if it were nothing, but her eyes betrayed her. She couldn't quite make the nonchalant sarcasm work.

"I love you."

She tossed her hair away from her eyes. "I love you, too, Mike."

There seemed nothing left to say. He crossed to her, reached out, and held her in his arms. She rested her head against his shoulder, the way she always had. He could smell lemons, a clean, sweet smell of freshly washed hair, and he tilted up her face and kissed her. She had the most beautiful clear blue eyes he had ever seen. She seemed to look straight through him, yet her lips had a soft sweet smile.

"Promise me you'll get help?"

"I'll be okay. Don't worry about me, Mike."

Donny Patterson sat in the car. He watched Mike walk slowly down the path, looking as if he was crying.

"You okay, partner?"

Mike got into the car and blew his nose. "I feel like such a prick. She doesn't seem to understand what just happened."

Donny put his arm around his friend. "Look, buddy, I been through this three times. It's not easy, but, Jesus, now that it's over you're gonna feel such relief. She's got problems. You tried every way to help her, Mike."

"Maybe we'll get back together," Mike said.

Donny gripped Mike's knee. "Christ almighty. When are you gonna face facts? She's a drunk and she was dragging you down with her. If she won't get help, you're gonna have to forget her, act like she's dead. Believe me, it's the best way. Say to yourself she's dead, be a hell of a lot easier."

Mike nodded. His heart felt like lead. He closed his eyes. "I loved her," he said softly.

Lorraine sat on the sofa, flicking the TV from channel to channel. There was no need now to hide the half-bottle of vodka that lay beside her. She could do what she liked, she was on her own. She didn't deserve anyone's love or respect, she knew that. She was deeply ashamed that she didn't have the guts to slit her wrists. Or was it because she didn't deserve to die so easily? She was her own judge and her own jury. She had to be punished.

Lorraine finished the vodka and went in search of more. She looked around the bedroom, seeing the open wardrobe doors, the empty hangers where Mike's clothes had hung, and backed out of the room. She discovered another bottle hidden in the kitchen and had drunk most of that before she wandered into the children's room. She was humming tunelessly. She got into Sally's tiny bed, holding the bottle to her chest. She could smell her daughter on the pillow; it was as if the little girl was kissing her face, she felt so close. She reached over to the other bed for Julia's pillow and held it to her cheek. She snuggled down clasping the pillows. "My babies," she whispered, "my babies." She looked drunkenly at the wallpaper, with its pink and blue ribbons threaded around children's nursery rhymes. Little piggies, little rabbits, and funny flying elephants. Two little beds for her two little angels.

She could feel a lovely warm blanket begin slowly to cover her body, a soft pink baby blanket, like the one tucked around her when she was a little girl, like the one she had wrapped around the dead child's body. She felt her chest tighten with panic, her body tense. She could hear him now. Lubrinski.

"Hey, how ya doin', Page?"

"I'm doin' okay, Lubrinski," she said aloud, startled to hear her own voice. "I'm doin' fine, partner." She frowned. Who was screaming? Some woman was screaming, the terrifying sound going on and on and on, driving her nuts. She rolled out of bed and ran from the room. She tripped and fell to her knees until she was crawling on all fours into her bedroom. The screaming continued. She heaved herself up and caught sight of a figure reflected in the dressing table mirror. She clapped her hands over her mouth, biting her fingers to stop the screams. It was her. She was the woman screaming. The terrible sweating panic swamped her.

It was Lubrinski's smiling face looking up at her from the dressing table that finally calmed her. She snatched up the photograph. "Help me, Lubrinski, for chrissakes help me."

"Sure, honey, take a shot of this, then what say you and me go and rip up the town? You wanna hit the bars?"

"Yeah, why not, you son of a bitch?" Lorraine gave a tough, bitter laugh, and felt herself straightening out as the panic subsided and she was back in control.

That was the first night Lorraine went out to drink alone. She phoned for a taxi and instructed the driver to go to Sunset and Curson, a known hangout for hookers just on the east border of West Hollywood. On that first night, Lorraine was still reasonably steady on her feet and sober enough to move farther afield than any local bar, not wanting any embarrassing encounters with any of her old Pasadena colleagues. She knew most of the West Hollywood bars and clubs, even the whores, because Lubrinski had taken her to them. When they came off duty together or had a tough assignment and needed to ''come down,'' they would hit these places, and for the same reason she chose them that first night. Tixie's, Golden Slipper, Two Dimes, Glory Hole, Max's—the list of small, dark bars and clubs was endless, and within a few weeks Lorraine had revisited most of them.

She was never sure how she returned home, but thanks to her local Dial-a-Cab she always managed to wake up there in the morning. Some days she would drink in the apartment, all day, passing out before she could call her taxi. It got so she was never completely sober; she'd wake up to a drink and order a taxi to make trips to the local grocery store, liquor store, and the bank to cash checks, always using Dial-a-Cab. All the drivers got to know her, and got to know that the lady tipped well. Half the time they would have to open her purse and count out the fare money for her since she couldn't, and they all nicknamed her ''Keep the change.'' She truthfully believed at this stage she would come through it all, there would be a way out. She was still looking good, still bathing and changing, even sending her clothes to the laundry, but she was up to two bottles of vodka a day, and that was before she went out to the clubs. Soon the trips to the grocery store were bypassed because she never felt like eating, and when she did she would simply open a can of soup or baked beans as the whole process of cooking herself a meal was too much aggravation. Drinking became her sole preoccupation, and she liked company, so the trips to the bars and clubs continued. Every night she hit Sunset Boulevard and moved from one stool to another the length of Fairfax Avenue to La Brea. She never knew who she ended up drinking with, she didn't give a damn, and they didn't seem to mind when she called them Lubrinski. A lot of Lubrinski look-alikes came and went, and there were many more drunken nights when she didn't care if Lubrinski was with her or not. All she cared about was getting another drink to keep her away from the terrified woman who screamed. Drunk, the pain was eased; drunk, she didn't miss her babies; drunk, she was happy and comforted; drunk, she had friends—drinking was all that mattered.

Lorraine's downward spiral began the night after Mike left her. It was a long road she traveled, searching for oblivion.

And it was frighteningly easy. Lorraine became easy prey, people were real friendly in the bars, but they used her and stole from her. Dial-a-Cab stopped doing business with her because although she continued to pay and was still known as "Keep the change," she could also become very aggressive and sometimes violent, accusing them of stealing. Other times she was sick in their taxis. So she used other, less scrupulous companies. And when even the possibility of meeting up with old colleagues didn't mean anything to her anymore, she started to drink locally. She'd end up in sleazy back parlors of run-down joints run by Hispanics or African-Americans in the Orange Grove section of Pasadena. Sometimes she would take a group of these so-called friends back to her apartment. When Lorraine had drunk herself into a stupor, they'd leave with anything they could carry out. Her neighbors complained but she paid no attention. When the money was gone, she sold the furniture, and then the apartment, and everyone in the immaculate Green and Green enclave sighed with relief. She was gone.

Lorraine felt happy because she thought the screaming woman would leave her, would stay behind in the apartment. It was good to have a big stash of money, never to worry where the next bottle came from, but when the screaming woman followed her to the run-down room she rented, she moved on; she had to keep running from the woman whose terrible screams frightened her so much and dragged her down so far. She could take the fights, and the taunts of prostitutes and pimps. Hell, she'd arrested many of them. They pushed her around and spiked her drinks. But drunk, she didn't care. Drunk, the screams were obliterated. Drunk, the men who pawed her meant nothing. Drunk, she could hide, feel some comfort in slobbering embraces, in strange rooms, in beds where the screaming woman left her alone. There she felt safe, secure in the knowledge that she was slowly killing this woman who would not leave her in peace. She was never sober long enough to understand that the woman she was so intent on running away from was herself.

ONE

She had almost died that night. The hit-and-run driver had probably not even seen her, and Lorraine couldn't remember a thing. She had been taken to the hospital with head injuries. The following weeks were a blur, as she was moved from one charitable organization to another; she had no money left and no medical insurance. Eventually she was institutionalized and preliminarily diagnosed as schizophrenic. To begin with, she was not thought to be an alcoholic because so much else was wrong with her. She had severe abscesses on her shins, a minor venereal disease plus genital herpes, skin abrasions, and was in poor physical condition from lack of decent food. She weighed only 105 pounds and as she was over five feet eight, she looked like a walking skeleton. Her body was pale, almost bluish, but her hands and face were tanned from living on the street. Eighty cigarettes a day had left her with a persistent heavy cough. She contracted pneumonia, and for a few days it was doubtful that she would live. When she pulled through, the hallucinations, screaming fits, and vomiting made the doctors suspect severe alcohol withdrawal symptoms.

A string of psychiatrists and doctors interviewed her and prescribed various medications. Two weeks after the accident, she was transferred to the nightmare of L.A. County USC

Medical Center—with no insurance there was no other place that would or could take her. The wards were full of L.A. County's worst cases, the dropouts and no-hopers. Drug-crazed kids, deranged old ladies, suicidal middle-aged women—every fucked-up female soul who walked the earth seemed to be marooned in the same wing with Lorraine. They added chronic alcoholism to Lorraine's list of ailments. Her liver was shot, and she was warned that if she didn't give up drinking she would be dead within the year. Eventually she was transferred to the White Garden Rehabilitation Center.

Rosie Hurst was working as a cook at the center, one of those women who worked for the rehabilitation program in order to participate in it. Rosie, a plump, sturdy woman with short, frizzy permed auburn hair, was a recovering alcoholic with six months' sobriety. She worked hard and was as friendly as she could be with the inmates, a there-but-for-the-grace-of-God attitude never far from her thoughts. Some of the saner inmates were allocated menial jobs in the kitchen, and that was how Rosie got to know Lorraine Page.

Lorraine didn't want to live. She had been waiting to die, wondering hazily why she wasn't already dead, and then musing that, perhaps, she was. And this was hell. It wasn't such a bad hell—the drugs made her more relaxed—but God, she longed for a drink. It was the only thought that occupied her dulled senses. Her mouth was thick and dry, her tongue felt too big, and she drank water all day, bending down to the small fountain in the corridor, hogging it, mouth open, hand pressed down on the lever for the water to spurt directly into her swollen mouth. Nothing dulled her thirst.

"How long you been an alcoholic?"

Rosie had been watching her in the corridor. Lorraine couldn't say because she had never thought of herself as an alcoholic. She just liked to drink.

"What work did you do?"

Lorraine could not recall what she'd been up to for the past few years. All the weeks and months had merged into a blur, and she could hardly distinguish one year from another. Or the bars, dens, seedy, run-down clubs where she had been drunk alongside girls she had once picked up and locked away. They had liked that. And the pimps she had hassled and booked in her days as a Vice Squad trainee liked being able to sell her so cheaply. She was known to go with anyone, as long as they kept her supplied with a steady flow of booze. Hotels, bars, dives, private parties . . . Lorraine would be cleaned up and sent out. It didn't matter how many or who they were, just as long as she made enough money for booze. She had been arrested, not just for hooking but for vagrancy, and released, pending charges, but had never made her court appearance. She had simply moved on to another bar, another part of town.

At the time of the hit-and-run accident, Lorraine had reached rock bottom. She was so far down in the gutter she couldn't even get a trick, so no pimp wanted her attached to his stable. So many truckers, so many different states, she was unaware she was back in L.A. She owned only what she stood up in, had even sold her wedding ring. She was such a wreck that the prostitutes didn't want her hanging around them. She was even out in the cold from the street winos, because she stole from them. She had become incapable of caring for herself or earning a few cents for food.

No one remembered her as Lieutenant Page—that was all so long ago. The human flesh trade moves on and changes fast. Most of the young vice cops who saw her falling down in the streets had no idea who she was.

No one cared, not even Mike or her children. Mike had tried often, over the years, to help her. He heard from her occasionally on the girls' birthdays and at Christmas, but she was usually incoherent on the phone or else just asked him for money. The calls stopped when Mike remarried and moved to a new house. The children settled into a new school, a new life. They no longer asked about their mother; they had a new, better one. Lorraine made no attempt to contact Mike again, almost relieved that she had at last severed every tie. Mike stopped her alimony payments and gave her a settlement. She never contested it, unaware that accepting it meant she lost even visitation rights to her daughters.

Only Rosie, because of her own problems and her open friendly nature, wanted to help Lorraine, so thin and pale, with that strange waiflike blond hair that hung in badly cut, jagged edges. Her fingers were stained dark brown with nicotine, and she had lost a front tooth. She also had a strange way of looking at people, her head tilted as if she were shortsighted, an odd, nervous squint, made more obvious because of a nasty scar running from her left eye to her prominent cheekbone. The shapeless regulation blue hospital gown hung loosely on her skinny frame. She wore overlarge pink slippers that flopped at her heels as she walked.

Rosie and Lorraine worked side by side, helping to dish out food and make up trays. As the weeks passed, Rosie realized there was more to Lorraine than appeared on the surface. She never had to be told twice which inmates required a special diet but always passed out the food to the right women.

"You must have had a job once. How old are you?" Rosie was trying to make conversation.

"I guess I must be around thirty-six. D'you have a cigarette?"

Rosie shook her head. She'd given up smoking when she gave up booze. "I used to work on computers. What sort of jobs did you do?"

Lorraine was delving among the food scraps in the trash can, looking for a butt end. She gave up and dried her hands. "Rosie, you wouldn't believe me if I told you. I'll go an' see if I can steal one."

Rosie watched as she shuffled over to Mad Mona, who really was out to lunch but always had a closely guarded pack of cigarettes. She watched Lorraine searching Mona's pockets, pretending to tickle her, and then the screaming started as she caught Lorraine with her precious pack. But Lorraine got one, and came back puffing like an asthmatic on an inhaler.

"Do you have any family?" Rosie asked, as Lorraine leaned against the door, eyes closed, relishing her smoke.

"Nope."

Rosie remarked that she had a son somewhere, but hadn't seen him or his father for years. She busied herself at the sink, and was about to resume her conversation when she saw Lorraine had gone. Rosie took off her overall and went to collect her wages, a pittance, considering the number of hours she put in, but she was only part-time, and most of the staff were Mexican. Probably they were paid even less. She smiled at the receptionist as she buttoned up her baggy cardigan. "I'll see you in a couple of days."

The receptionist nodded. "It's gettin' warmer now. You won't need that on."

Rosie shrugged—she had arrived so early that there'd been a chill in the air. She asked how long Lorraine was being kept in the ward.

The receptionist checked on the clipboard behind her. "Oh, she's due to be released. May not be here when you come back Thursday. The doctors haven't signed her out yet, but she's down to leave. Has she been okay in the kitchen? You know the way they are—steal anything . . ."

Rosie's shopping bag suddenly felt heavy: the chops and half-chicken she'd taken along with the sugar, potatoes, and carrots meant she'd be fired if she were caught. She hurried off, saying she wanted to catch her bus.

Lorraine, however, was still a resident when Rosie returned two days later. She looked even paler, and coughed continually. Rosie smiled warmly and said she was glad she had not left.

Lorraine shrugged. "Yeah, I guess it's nice to have someone here that speaks English."

Rosie chuckled, and as Lorraine moved on down the corridor, Rosie could hear her persistent coughing. According to the receptionist, she had developed a fever, so they were keeping her for observation. Rosie was concerned but didn't have time to talk since she had to prepare lunch. But just seeing Lorraine leaning against the corridor wall, as if she needed it to prop her up, made Rosie feel a strange compassion; there was something about Lorraine. She reminded Rosie of some kind of wounded bird, the ones that immediately make your heart go out to them because you want to help them, and you take them home in a cardboard box with every intention of making them better, feeding them milk with an eyedropper, and then they make you feel hopelessly inadequate because they won't feed, they just fade away. Lorraine was fading before Rosie's eyes, but it was not until later, when they were washing up, that she could ask Lorraine how she was. She seemed reluctant to talk and didn't bother helping Rosie with the trays, more intent on guarding her position at the water fountain. Her need for alcohol was becoming more desperate each day; she craved sweets and nicotine, stealing treasured hoards of chocolate bars and cigarette packs from the unwary.

With no money and no place to live, Lorraine decided she'd

have to turn to Rosie, who might have somewhere she could stay—and something worth stealing. That was her sole motive for talking to Rosie. Lorraine wanted a drink, wanted money, wanted out of the crazies' ward. All Rosie wanted was a friend, and Lorraine was the pitiful little bird needing to be fed and cared for.

"You know, I could help you—if you want to help yourself. If you tell me, say, 'Rosie, I want to help myself,' then I will do everything in my power to help you. I'll take you to my meetings. . . . We have counselors, people you can really talk to, and . . . they'll help you get work. You're an intelligent woman, there must be something you can find . . ."

Lorraine had given her that odd squinting look, smoking a cigarette down to the filter. "Yeah. Maybe I could get my old job back."

"What did you do?"

"I was a cop."

Rosie chuckled, rolling out pastry. She jumped when Lorraine came up close behind her, so close and so tall she had to lean over.

"I am arresting you on the charge of molesting that pastry, Rosie. Anything you say may be taken down and used in evidence against you . . ."

Rosie laughed, and Lorraine tickled her, just like she tickled Mad Mona. Far from naïve, Rosie was beginning to suspect that Lorraine was after something. She wondered what it was. She dropped heavy hints that she was broke just in case Lorraine had thought otherwise and was after money. . . .

Lorraine had been found on April 11. Now it was the fourteenth of May and she was given her marching orders. While she waited for Rosie to arrive, she cleaned the kitchen. Then she helped Rosie all morning, but it was quite late before she mentioned that she was leaving. To her surprise, Rosie told her she already knew. "I've been thinking about all the things you've been telling me, Rosie. And, well—you're on. I'll come to one of these meetings 'cos I want my life back." Her voice was hardly audible. "I'll tell you a secret. I really was a cop, a lieutenant."

Rosie looked up into the pale face. "Is that the truth?"

Lorraine nodded. "Yeah. Look, can I crash on your floor

until I get a place of my own?'' She figured if Rosie knew she had been a cop she would trust her. It worked.

Rosie gave a wide grin, concealing her hesitancy. "Sure you can, but it's not much of a place. Do you have a lot of stuff?''

Lorraine lied, telling Rosie that her belongings were with a friend she didn't want to see because she was another drinker—and she wanted to stay clean.

Rosie understood, knowing it was a mistake for a drinker to return to old friends and old habits.

"Okay. You can stay at my place.''

At 4:00 on the afternoon of May 15, Rosie waited for her outside the hospital. Lorraine was wearing an odd assortment of clothes. Nothing fit—sleeves too short, the skirt waistband hanging around her hips. She carried a clean set of underwear in a brown paper bag, and seemed even taller, thinner, and stranger-looking than she had in the safety of the rehabilitation clinic. Someone had given her a pair of pink-framed sunglasses, the lenses so dark they hid her eyes, and most of her scar. Seeing her in the bright crisp May sunshine, Rosie had severe doubts about taking her in. She wished she had not been so friendly, wished Lorraine did not or had not reminded her of some silly bird. She was, Rosie knew without doubt, a lot more trouble than any small feathered creature you could stick in a cardboard box.

"It's a lovely day,'' Lorraine said without enthusiasm.

"Yes, it is,'' Rosie said flatly, as they headed for the bus station.

Lorraine was silent on the long journey to Pasadena. She didn't like going back to her home territory, but there was no place she could think of that she'd rather go.

"You know Pasadena at all?'' Rosie asked staring from the window.

"Nope.''

"Well, I live in what used to be a real nice area, part of the old Pasadena, lotta trees, and they're real old, see the trees?''

Lorraine nodded, staring at the massive trees spreading their branches across the road. She had a memory of her apartment, of Mike, but she shrugged it off. Better to lie, say she didn't know Pasadena, rather than admit she'd actually worked as a police officer there.

"Most of these houses have been taken over by Hispanics

or Blacks. This is the Orange Grove area, only a few more stops, then we get off.''

Lorraine nodded. The heat inside the bus was oppressive, she felt tired out, and Rosie's continued travelogue was beginning to get on her nerves.

"I live on Marengo. Cops made it a no-parking zone during the day and we had drug dealers parked bumper-to-bumper every night. Now it's real quiet and residents are allowed to park there in the day, but the whole area's kinda run-down.''

Lorraine nodded. She could feel the sweat begin to trickle down her neck, and wiped her face with the back of her hand. The bus was filling up since it was almost rush hour, and it seemed to lurch to a stop at every corner. Lorraine sighed when Rosie nudged her as they passed some bars with their windows boarded up.

"See? These places get robbed over and over and the cops do nothin', that's why a lot of 'em got bars up. 'Round this place come dark, you get the drunks, and once the sun goes down they start out sellin' their drugs to kids, lotta crack sold 'round here.''

Rosie suddenly stood up, nudging Lorraine again. "Next stop is Orange Grove, might as well push our way to the front.''

Lorraine was glad to have Rosie—even felt a strange desire to hold her hand, afraid she would lose sight of her, and at the same time glad she did not live anywhere near her old apartment in the better part of town.

As they were walking along toward Marengo Avenue, Rosie maintained her travelogue monologue, mostly because she couldn't think of anything else to say. She wafted her hand toward a liquor store. "There was my downfall, too close to the apartment. Now I stay this side of the avenue." She pointed to a grocery store. "I shop there and live just along the avenue. It's very convenient. Might as well buy a few things, you wanna come in with me?''

Lorraine nodded. Even from this distance she could see the liquor section in the grocery store. Her body broke out in a sweat, her mouth felt rancid, and she kept licking her lips. As she stood at the counter next to Rosie, who was buying bread and salads and coffee, she felt like screaming. Her eyes constantly strayed to the bottles: she wanted a drink so bad she felt faint. Rosie was having a friendly exchange with the Mexican owner of the store. She turned to introduce Lorraine but he moved on to another customer before she had the chance.

Rosie ushered Lorraine back out into the sunshine. She was sweating herself by now and a little embarrassed about her apartment. It was not that large; it was by any standards very modest . . . well, if one wanted to be truthful, it could be described as a little bit on the squalid side. Part of Rosie's constant chatter was out of nerves, she had never had anyone stay with her.

"It's number two twenty-three," Rosie said, nodding farther up the street. "It's a blue house, set back from the road. One time it must have been real nice. Now you can see all the houses with iron bars or boarded-up windows, sad, used to be a real nice area."

Lorraine stopped and cocked her head to one side. "Rosie, it sounds like you're making excuses. I don't care if you live in a two-by-four hut. Right now I have nobody and no place, so I am just happy we met, okay?"

Rosie nodded, then beamed. Sometimes her round, pretty face was like a plump child's. The sweat had made her frizzy auburn hair form tight little ringlets around her forehead and the nape of her neck. She had a habit of blowing air upward, in fast short puffing sounds, acting as her own fan, but she was still sweating profusely as they arrived at number two twenty-three. The two-story house was very run-down and broken up into numerous apartments. The old sashed windows had all seen better days; in fact, the whole property looked in need of restoration—some windows broken, others boarded up. A group of kids playing on the front steps stared insolently at Rosie as she passed them.

"Little bastards, all of them. I hate their mother, she's a real whore. Not that I have anythin' against Hispanics, don't get me wrong, but she plays her radio sometimes so loud I dunno if I got mine on or it's hers."

Rosie occupied an apartment on the top floor, and Lorraine guessed that what was more than likely the fire escape seemed to be the way to her front door.

"Here we are, now, you go up ahead. It's so narrow, this staircase, I'm always stumbling down . . . watch how you go, the fifth step is loose. It's wood, crazy considerin' this used to be part of the fire escape, but the landlord is a cheap son of a bitch."

Lorraine laughed—so unusual for her that Rosie looked up at her questioningly, but Lorraine just shrugged. It had amused her about her own assumption regarding the fire escape and then for Rosie to immediately say that was what it had originally been built for. And it was pretty dangerous as some of the boards were not only loose but rotten.

Rosie unlocked the screen door, then her front door. As she pushed it open a cat screeched and dived out between Lorraine's legs.

"That's Walter. Go in, you first."

Rosie's tiny apartment was stiflingly hot, even with the blinds down. She turned on the air-conditioning, which droned noisily. There was a living room and one cramped bedroom with a tiny bathroom attached. The kitchen was a messy corner of the living room. Rosie busied herself unloading the groceries, pointing out the couch for Lorraine to sleep on, bringing sheets and pillows.

"Now, do you want some tea, or coffee, or something cold? I think I've got chilled Coke—or lemonade?"

Lorraine leaned back against the sofa, rolling an ice-cold Coke can across her forehead. She was still desperate for a real drink. She gulped at the Coke, draining the can quickly.

Rosie held up a pack of cigarettes. "I thought you'd be needing one, so here." She tossed it over. "Now you clean up and run a comb through your hair, and then we should go, the meeting's due to start in about an hour."

Lorraine closed her eyes and sighed. "Maybe I'm a little too tired today."

Rosie loomed over her. "Today is when you really need to go, and I can arrange that you go every day for the first few weeks."

Lorraine managed a weak smile and hauled herself to her feet, crossing through Rosie's dusty bedroom into the small bathroom, which was crammed with jars of creams, tubes, and a vast array of worn toothbrushes and half-squeezed toothpaste tubes. Old tights were hung up to dry, large faded panties and a grayish bra pinned on a piece of string, so large Lorraine stared in disbelief.

She ran the water and bent down to drink it, gulping it down, then she splashed her face and reached for a threadbare towel. She looked at herself then, really studied herself, no drugs and stone-cold sober for the first time in years. The image that stared back was of a stranger. Her eyes were puffy, washed out, red-rimmed, and her nose had small, white-headed spots at each side. She caught sight of her yellowish, stained teeth, the gap in the front. The scar stretched her left cheek slightly, an ugly reminder of a past she wanted to obliterate. She traced the outline of her cracked, swollen lips and then ran her hand through her thin hair. Strands of it came away. It looked as if someone had hacked it haphazardly, any way but straight. Maybe she'd even done it herself, she couldn't remember. There were not just days or weeks or months she couldn't remember but whole years.

Rosie rapped on the door. "What are you doing in there?"

Lorraine took a deep breath. "Just washing. Won't be long." As she dried her hands she gazed at the stains along her fingers, the nails jagged, bitten, and dirty. Everything about her was hideous: she was revolting, she disgusted herself, she *was* disgusting. And deeply angry. She didn't know this person. Who was she?

Rosie looked up from the sofa as Lorraine came out of the bedroom and smiled. "You ready?"

Lorraine looked around for the pink-framed sunglasses. She pushed them on, as if to hide behind them. "Thank you for taking me in like this. It's very good of you."

Rosie, searching for her keys, wafted her hand. "I made a vow, because somebody helped me out when I was down. I promised that I'd help someone else if I could. I guess that person is you."

Lorraine sat at the back of the meeting, hands clenched, face hidden behind the sunglasses. The old church meeting place was on Walnut Street. The other people there had greeted her with such warmth that she had wanted to run out of the building. Gripping her hand, Rosie had found her a seat. She was introduced only as Lorraine. Nobody gave their last name unless they wanted to. As the meeting began, Lorraine was able to get a good look at the others. None looked in bad shape, though a few had a lost air about them, as they sat with their heads bowed or stared into space. Slowly she began to pay attention to those who told their stories.

One woman recalled how she had not known who she was for fifteen years, because those years had merged into one long, blurred binge. Now she was smart, and positive, and proud that she had been dry for four years. She had met someone who had given her love and stability. Soon, she hoped, she would have the confidence to tell him that she was an alcoholic. He had been so embarrassed for her when, sober, she had tripped over a loose stone and fallen flat on her face. She laughed then, saying that she hadn't had the heart to tell him she had been facedown on the floor more often than she had been upright. She grew emotional, lifting up her arms as if she were at some Baptist church meeting. Lorraine sighed with boredom. "I'm standing upright now, and I intend to remain this way, just as, when I get a little stronger, I will tell him that I am an alcoholic. Hopefully he will come to one of our meetings so he can fully understand my illness and that I believe, at long last, I am in recovery. I want to recover—just as I know I will always be an alcoholic. I am an alcoholic. Thank you for listening to me, thank you for being here. God bless you all . . ." She burst into tears and many people clustered around her, hugging her, congratulating her.

Lorraine remained at the back of the hall, embarrassed by the show of emotion. She was glad when the meeting ended, refusing to hold other members' hands as they prayed together for strength and guidance. Rosie, on the other hand, was very into it all, her eyes closed, clutching the hands of two elderly women.

Later, back at the apartment, Rosie was full of enthusiasm and energy. "Those meetings saved my life. Some people have been going for ten or fifteen years. When you face what you are it doesn't stop. You will always be an alcoholic. One drink, and you're back at square one. What you've got to understand is that you have an illness, and it can kill you. If I hadn't stopped drinking I'd be dead now, as would most of those people there tonight."

She set the table, splashed water into glasses, clanking ice cubes. She was sweating even more than usual from the heat of the stove. Even at seven in the evening, the air-conditioning was so halfhearted that the temperature in the apartment was nearly eighty degrees.

Lorraine played with her food, drank three or four glasses of water. Rosie reached over and scraped the remains of her meal onto her own plate, plowing through the leftovers as if she were starving. Her mouth bulging with food, she waved her fork in the air: "Now, what are we going to do about finding you some work? You don't have any money, right? As soon as we've finished supper, we can catch a bus, go to another meeting across town, see if maybe anyone has any work, just to tide you over, nothing too strenuous. There's meetings going on in West Hollywood every day, morning, lunchtimes, and evenings . . .''

Lorraine couldn't face another meeting, let alone another bus ride. "Maybe I could just sleep now? I'm really tired."

Rosie nodded—maybe she was pushing it. Instead, she chatted incessantly, about her job as a computer clerk in a banking firm. She took out her family albums, displaying her parents' home, her ex-husband, the son she hadn't seen for five years. She talked until her eyes drooped from tiredness. "I lost so much, Lorraine, but I'm hoping to see my son soon. My ex said that I could have a day with him. I want him to get to know me as I am now. The most important thing is that I take every day on its own, I count every day as precious, because it's a new day without a drink." Lorraine smiled, but she was longing for Rosie to leave her alone. She yawned in the hope that Rosie would take the hint and go to bed, but she went on for another hour, delving into the pages of her beloved AA manual as if it were a bible, reading snatches aloud.

At last she stood up and wagged her fat finger at Lorraine. "I am responsible," she said. "Keep on telling that to yourself: I am responsible." She went into her bedroom and closed the door.

Lorraine flopped onto the couch with relief. She lay there for about fifteen minutes, listening to the air conditioner, the cat lapping its milk . . . and all she could think about was how she could get a drink without Rosie finding out. Eventually she drifted into sleep. She slept without pills, without alcohol, a deep, dreamless sleep.

Lorraine was awake before Rosie, and started brewing coffee. It was only five, and still reasonably cool. She felt hungry, too, and ate some bread and cheese, followed by a bowl of muesli. She'd had four cups of coffee and five cigarettes before Rosie appeared.

"Good morning, coffee's made . . .''

Rosie grunted, poured some, and returned to her room. Lorraine sat by the window, smoking. A new day. Would she make it without a drink? Could she make it? Most important, did she want to make it? She didn't answer the last question—for the moment at least she was too aware of the rich smell of coffee, and that it was a beautiful day.

Rosie was not at her best in the morning, and got annoyed when Lorraine went to take the first shower. She stayed in the small bathroom for a long time, scrutinizing herself. Scars covered her thighs. Small round marks like cigarette burns were dotted all over her white-bluish skin. Her feet shocked her: they looked like an old woman's, reddish toes and heels all blisters and corns, with hideously long toenails—she was surprised they hadn't been cut at the hospital. She scrubbed herself almost raw, using up all the hot water. She oiled and massaged herself with Rosie's lotions, cleaned her teeth gently, and creamed around her mouth so her cracked lips felt less painful. Finally, she used Rosie's shampoo and hair conditioner, and then began searching the cabinet for nail scissors and a manicure set.

Rosie was seething. Lorraine had been in her bathroom since half-past seven and it was now almost nine. When she emerged, swathed in Rosie's towels, Rosie pushed past her and banged the bathroom door shut.

"Well, thanks a bundle!" She stormed out. "You've taken all the hot water! Now I gotta wait an hour, maybe more. I always have a shower in the morning."

"Sorry," Lorraine muttered. The floor shook as Rosie thudded into the living room.

"Would you come in here a minute, please!" Rosie boomed.

Lorraine sighed with irritation and peered into the room. Rosie, like some irate drill sergeant, stood in front of the couch with her hands on her hips.

"Okay. This is not a hotel. It's not the goddamned hospital. When you get up in the morning put your bedclothes away, and it'd be a nice gesture if you tried washin' a dish when you used it. This is my home. It may not look like much but it's all I got an' I work my butt off to keep it."

Lorraine watched as Rosie dragged her sheets and pillow from the couch and hurled them toward her. They landed at her feet. She was picking them up when the floor shook again and Rosie thrust a dirty ashtray under her nose. "And all this smoking—it's not good for me. Please try and cut down or at least open the window and wash out the ashtray.''

Lorraine couldn't have gotten a word in if she'd wanted to. Rosie slammed into her bedroom and two seconds later charged out again, demanding that Lorraine go back in and clean the bathroom.

''It was a shit hole when I went in there!'' Lorraine screeched. ''You like it so fucking much, you clean it!''

Rosie glared. ''No fucking way! Get the vacuum out of the closet, and clean up in there!''

Lorraine sat down and rubbed her hair with a towel. ''I've just gotten clean, I don't want to get all dirty again.'' Before she could make any further excuses Rosie charged to the closet, yanked open the door, and dragged out an old-fashioned Hoover. Lorraine continued to rub her hair, looking on as the fat body wobbled under the pink nylon nightgown, and then she caught sight of Rosie's extraordinary bedroom slippers, like boats, but with the face of Pluto on one and Mickey Mouse on the other. The faces were old and food-stained and Pluto was minus one ear.

Lorraine almost laughed out loud at the sight of Rosie's immense bottom as she bent over to fit in the plug. Lorraine grinned at her. ''I can see you haven't had that out for a while, you should run it over the carpet in here. It's full of cat hairs. Are you working at the hospital today?''

Rosie switched on the vacuum cleaner and glowered. ''No, I am not,'' she shouted. ''Why? So you can have a good rummage through my things? I only work part-time, in case your memory fails you. Mondays and Thursdays.''

Lorraine nodded, uncertain what day it was, and fazed by the change in Rosie's personality. Rosie continued to complain, bellowing above the machine's roar, which made Lorraine's head ache. Peace came when Rosie departed for her shower, but only for a moment: more loud thuds emanated from the bedroom as she dressed. Closet doors squeaked, drawers banged open and shut, until Rosie appeared with an armful of clothes which she tossed onto the floor. ''Here, something might fit. If it doesn't, throw it out. I dunno why I kept these old things, maybe because I hoped I'd shrink. . . . Help yourself.''

Lorraine looked through the odd assortment of garments, all in dreadful colors and a mixture of sizes, ranging from a ten to a sixteen. Nothing fit. A few items were vaguely clean, but there were no shoes or underwear. Finally she chose a print dress three sizes too large and tied a belt around her waist. At least it would be cool. She put on her panties from the day before, turned inside out. She had no bra, no stockings or tights. She looked around for the brown paper bag she had brought from the hospital, but couldn't remember where she had left it. Her hair was dry now, and she tied it back with an elastic band, then folded the rest of the clothes and put them into a black plastic garbage bag. She tipped the contents of the kitchen trash can into the bag, and carried it outside for collection.

Finding herself outdoors in the beautiful sunny morning, Lorraine headed directly to the deli at the end of the street, as if drawn by some invisible force. She stood in the street staring in the window with all the bottles on display. The windows were barred, and she threaded her fingers through the meshing, longing to go inside. She didn't have so much as a cent, so unless she robbed the place, there was no way of getting a bottle. Reluctantly she walked back to Rosie's, climbed up the wooden staircase, then hesitated. She could hear Rosie talking on the telephone, and she sat on the steps to listen.

"Well, I was hoping since I've got a few days off this weekend if we could make it Saturday? I can get the bus over . . ."

The call went on for a while longer, then Lorraine heard the thudding footsteps, and a door slamming. She went inside and opened the fridge. Rosie appeared, dressed in a white blouse and circular flower-print cotton skirt. Her frizzy hair was wet, and she was tugging a comb through it.

"Water was still cold! And you had the last Coke yesterday. I'm not a charity, you know. Now, we'd better see which meeting you go to." Rosie began making a series of phone calls and talked at length to someone whom she described as her sponsor. Eventually she hung up.

"Jake figures I shouldn't be your sponsor, but since I've taken you on, I'll give it a try. Anytime, day or night, if you feel the need for a drink, or someone to talk to, then you just tell me. Have you wanted a drink this morning?"

"What do you think?"

Rosie sighed irritably, and warned Lorraine that she did not have enough money to ferry them both to meetings all over

L.A. "Don't you have any money at all?" she barked.

"No, but I'll manage . . ."

Rosie pushed past her into the tiny kitchen area, mixed cereal and fruit in a bowl, and began to munch noisily. Slowly, the warm, friendly Rosie began to surface. She complimented Lorraine on how she looked, and started counting dollars from her purse. Lorraine watched, trying to work out how much money it contained. As soon as she had a chance, she would steal it and get the hell out of the apartment.

"How about social security? Can you claim any benefits?"

Lorraine shrugged. Said she couldn't remember her number, but declined to admit to Rosie why she didn't want to—the skipped bail, court appearances, debts . . . If she tried to apply for financial assistance she'd be arrested. Rosie gulped her coffee and began to make a long list, chewing the end of an already gnarled pencil.

"Okay. We got enough here for a few days, but we'll look around for jobs, see about taking you down to Social Services to see if they can trace your number and maybe you'll get some cash. Not that you can live on what they dole out, I know, I'm on it—"

"We? I can manage on my own."

"No, you can't. I can't go off to the hospital and leave you, well, not until I can trust you. So here's some suggestions . . ." She had jotted down waitress, cleaner—mostly menial jobs— and then listed all the addresses of AA meetings. Lorraine wondered idly if all this effort was to help Rosie stay on the wagon, never mind herself.

"I thought you said you were something to do with computers. Can't you get a decent job?" Lorraine inquired.

Rosie looked up. "Oh, sure. I can get into any bank and they'll make me head cashier! I lost my job, my respectability. I've got no references, not even a driver's license—they canceled it. I thought you'd know that—if you were a cop like you said. If you were, why can't *you* get a decent job?"

Lorraine began to chew at her nails. She'd finished the pack of cigarettes; now she craved not only a drink but a cigarette, too. She suddenly felt tired, and yawned deeply. It was as if she had been up for hours, which indeed she had, but it was still only ten o'clock.

"Can I use your toilet?"

"You don't have to fucking ask me to go to the john, for chrissakes!"

When Lorraine didn't show for fifteen minutes, Rosie went to check on her. She was curled up on her bed, deeply asleep, her hands cupped under her chin. Rosie studied Lorraine's sleeping face, and realized that she must once have been beautiful. You could still see glimpses of it: in repose, Lorraine's face lost its hardness. Her mouth was closed, so you couldn't see the missing tooth, and the deep scar was hidden by the pillow. For the first time Rosie really wondered about Lorraine's past, still certain that the cop line was just that, a line.

She crept out of the bedroom, then searched through Lorraine's belongings. Nothing. The brown paper bag was empty of any personal mementos. No letters or cards, no makeup—and the plastic purse they had given her was empty, she hadn't lied about that. But Rosie was sure she had lied about having no family; a girl who had been as attractive as Lorraine must have had someone—had maybe even been somebody.

Rosie let Lorraine sleep for almost the entire day. She read, made some calls, cooked lunch for herself. Food was one of the few pleasures she had left in life. At four o'clock the phone rang. She snatched it up, afraid it would wake Lorraine.

"Hello, is this you, Mommy?" The high-pitched voice tore at her heart. At last he had called. It was her son.

"Yeah, it's me. How you doin', Joey? We gonna meet up? I kinda thought maybe this weekend?"

"I can't, I got a big game, I'm on the second division basketball team, and so I can't. I gotta go now."

Rosie started to panic. He was going to hang up. She wanted to tell him she would drive across L.A. to see him play, but she stuttered, "Wait, Joey, what about you gettin' a bus out here to me? I can meet you at the station, Joey? You still there, Joey?"

"I'm goin' to Florida. Me and Dad are movin' there, we got a place to rent and everything."

"Florida?" Rosie screeched.

There was an ominous silence. She could hear Joey whispering. "Is that woman goin' with you, Joey? Is . . . put your dad on the phone. Joey, you hear me? I wanna speak to—"

Rosie was shaking, she knew that cheap bitch was there,

knew she must be putting her ten cents in. Her hand clenched around the receiver as she heard her son calling his father, and then the phone being put down. "Hello? Hello?"

Her ex-husband came on the line—she could even hear his intake of breath as if he was preparing himself to speak to her. It always got her so mad, the way he talked to her, all calm and coming on like he was a shrink, or as if she were ten years old.

"Rosie?"

"What's all this about Florida? You never said anythin' to me about Florida, takin' my kid to Florida."

"Rosie, just calm down."

"I'm calm, for chrissakes. I'm angry, too."

"When we're settled we'll write. This is a good job for me, a lot more money." The voice was smooth, saying each word too slowly.

"I wanna see Joey. I'm not interested in what you earn— you never paid a cent to me, anyway."

There was the sound of heavy breathing and then he repeated slowly and painstakingly that as Rosie had not been awarded visitation rights, let alone custody, she had little say in where Joey lived. That was up to him and he was making the best decision for his son's welfare and if she didn't like it then she should hire a lawyer.

"Oh, yeah? And where do I get that kind of money?"

"You got it to buy booze, Rosie. Maybe you're stewed right now—you usually have been in the past when you've called. It's been six months since your last call and Joey doesn't wanna know, Rosie. It's not me and don't think it's Barbara either, he—"

"You bastard."

Again the heavy breathing. "Rosie, I'm sorry, let's not be like this. We'll write, we'll be in touch. I'm hanging up now because I don't want to get into an argument. I'm hanging up, Rosie."

She looked at the receiver as she heard the line go dead and replaced it gently on the cradle. She patted the phone with the flat of her hand, wishing it was her boy's head. She didn't even know how big he was now, it had been such a long time. . . . One day, she told herself, she'd hold him in her arms and he would forgive her. She felt so empty she wanted to cry, for all the lost years.

Wrenched from a deep sleep, Lorraine woke up, heart pounding. There had been a violent crash, as if the front door had been knocked down. Music blared out, the volume on maximum. She sat up, and eased herself off the bed. She didn't recognize the screeching, confused voice. Then the sound of breaking glass topped even the music.

Lorraine pushed open the bedroom door, and gasped. Rosie was reeling around the room, falling into furniture, drinking from a quart bottle of bourbon. She leered at Lorraine, and waved the bottle. ''You wanna drink? Come on in, sit down, have a drink with me!''

Lorraine watched, incredulous, as Rosie crashed into the kitchen, smashing glasses as she attempted to get one from the cupboard. She swore and kicked at the jagged pieces. Her eyes were unfocused, her face bright red and sweating. She swayed as she poured and held out a half-full tumbler. ''Have a drink, skinny!''

Lorraine was about to take the glass when the front door opened. She had no idea who the short, squat man was who knocked the glass out of Rosie's hand, snatched the bottle from her, and began to pour the contents down the sink. Rosie screamed and lunged at him with a punch, missed, and fell into the closet. Mops and brooms tumbled around her as she slumped on the floor, weeping. Her sobs came louder as he ran water into the sink, making sure every drop of liquor was gone. Rosie's head fell forward onto her chest and her breath came in terrible, heaving rasps.

''Help me get her into the bathroom and *turn that fucking music off!*'' Lorraine did as she was told, and between them they dragged Rosie into the bedroom, then the bathroom, by both arms, like a beached whale, and inched her into the base of the shower; then the man turned it on full blast. When Rosie finally came to, she began to vomit. The man held her head up, getting soaked himself in the process. He snapped out instructions for Lorraine to find more towels and a pillow. When the vomiting subsided he turned off the water, stuffed a pillow under Rosie's dripping head, and stood up. ''She'll sleep it off now.''

Lorraine followed him into the living room. He was attempting to dry himself with one of the kitchen towels. "You started her on this binge, huh?"

Lorraine shook her head. He began to brew coffee, and found some cups, treading warily over the broken glass. "What brought it on, then?"

"I dunno." She folded her arms. The smell of the bourbon hanging in the air made her swallow because it smelled so good. "You got a cigarette?"

He tossed over a squashed pack, and rubbed his shoulder. "She must weigh a ton. I'm getting too old for this—she's put my shoulder out before now, and my back. Once she knocked me out stone-cold. So, if you didn't bring the bottle in, did she get it herself?"

Lorraine lit the cigarette and pocketed the packet. "I don't know. I was asleep."

"Oh, yeah?" he sneered. "Sleeping one off, were you?"

Lorraine was annoyed by his aggressive, punchy manner. His neck was short, his greasy black hair thinning, even his hands were pudgy. "You her boyfriend or something?" she asked.

"Her what? You kiddin'? Need a bigger man than me to take that rhino on. I'm her sponsor, but I dunno for how much longer. They called me from the liquor store—little arrangement we have, saves them from one of her visits. You get her started, did you? Then she went for a bottle? After she's finished one bottle she's only after the next. Those bars they got up may have kept them safe from the riots, but they wouldn't from Rosie." He helped himself to coffee, and poured some for Lorraine. "I'm Jake Valsack."

"Lorraine."

Jake eased his ample backside onto the sofa. "Well, you made it through a night, did you? And . . ." He looked at his watch and smiled. When he smiled, his face changed from something that resembled a chimpanzee into a cute pixie. "You been dry almost a whole day. We'll go to the meeting— she won't come round for a while yet."

Lorraine had no desire to go to another meeting, so she said she'd stay with Rosie. Jake hooted with laughter. She was getting increasingly irritated with him.

"So, Lorraine, what kind of work did you do before drinking?"

She crossed to the kitchen and poured more coffee. "I was a secretary."

He swiveled around. "So you can type, huh? You got a job? Rosie said you'd need one."

"You going to give me one?"

Jake hooted again. "What you think I am—nuts?"

Lorraine sat on the sofa arm. "So what did *you* do before drinking, Jake?" she inquired sarcastically. He looked up at her from round, dark eyes—he really was a dead ringer for a chimpanzee.

"I was a doctor. Still am a doctor only I can't practice anymore. Now I help run a clinic for junkies and alkies and anybody who needs help, like Rosie."

Lorraine looked away, for she could read the pain in those animal eyes. Maybe Jake could see something similar in her own, because he seemed to relent. He opened his wallet and passed over a card. "You can call me on that line. I know somebody who needs a little clerical work done, could earn you a few bucks—or you can work for me. I'm a glutton for punishment. We need as many helping hands as possible, but there's no money in it."

As she pocketed the card, she felt Jake's cigarettes. She didn't dare bring one out in case he asked for them back. He stood up and glanced at the broken screen door. "Tell Rosie I'll come around and see her in the morning."

Lorraine watched his stocky figure strut off down the road. Then she searched for Rosie's handbag. She was opening the purse when she heard moaning from the bathroom. Rosie was trying in vain to stand up. Lorraine looked at her, in no way disgusted by the spectacle: she'd seen and been in a lot worse states herself. "I guess I just tied another one on, didn't I?"

Lorraine laughed. "Yep, you sure did. Your pal was here—Jake."

"Was he? Well, are you gonna stand there gloating or are you gonna help me get up off the fucking floor?"

Lorraine tried to pull her up but fell forward on top of her. Rosie felt like an immense wet blanket. Eventually, after much tugging and heaving, Lorraine managed to get her into a sitting position, where she held her head in her hands and groaned. Lorraine poured a glass of water and held it out. Rosie gulped it down, and then demanded another. She drank four full glasses before she rested back against the shower. "Did you say Jake was here?"

Lorraine nodded, and Rosie began to cry, guilty and morose. She sobbed and sobbed, a jumbled, incoherent stream of adoring phrases about the chimpanzee man, blowing her nose and wiping her eyes.

"First thing tomorrow morning, Rosie, I'm going to go see if I can find a job. Did you hear me?"

Rosie hauled herself slowly to her feet. "Sure. Do what you like."

"Can I take a few dollars? You'll probably be asleep when I leave," she called from the living room.

"Sure, honey, if there's any left. I dunno how much I spent. . . ." Rosie dragged herself unsteadily to the chair by the telephone and sat down. "I'll wait awhile, then call him. I need to talk to him. I'm sorry, but I guess you'll do better without me. I knew I'd make a lousy sponsor. Jake was right about that." She leaned back with her eyes closed. "You must be proud of yourself. You didn't have a drink with me, did you?"

"Nope, guess I didn't." Lorraine quickly went to bed to avoid further conversation. In the morning she made a pot of coffee, emptied Rosie's purse, and walked out.

She had no intention of seeing Rosie again. She felt almost lighthearted, a strange new confidence in herself: she had not taken a drink. She might have finished the bottle if Jake hadn't walked in when he did, but, as it was, she had not had a drink.

She walked the streets for hours, relishing her freedom and the possibilities offered by the dollars in her purse. The May sun was bright but not too hot, though she could feel the heat of the sidewalk through her cheap secondhand shoes. So she stepped onto the grass, enjoying its softness beneath her feet. She soon realized she'd walked a complete circle when she found herself back on Marengo, remembering from her station days that it was one of the worst drug areas of Pasadena. Still, the feeling of being in control of something as simple as her own feet, of walking steadily, made her confidence jump a tiny notch higher. She looked up to the big old trees, their branches just budding, and smiled; it was as if she had not really seen for a long, long time. She took off the elastic band from her hair and shook it loose. It smelled of lemons, just like the old shampoo she used, how long ago? Lorraine reached the corner, and stopped to light a cigarette. Tossing the match aside, she inhaled deeply and let the smoke drift slowly out of her mouth. She sucked again at the cigarette, watching the lit rim of tobacco move up the white paper before she exhaled. She didn't want to think about the past, about what or who she had been. Today was what? Wednesday. She frowned, trying to remember the date, calculating back to her release from the clinic. It was the seventeenth of May, she smiled to herself. It had been a long time since she had been able to recall what day of the week it was, much less the date, and at this moment she had no reason to think how important this date would become.

A car crawled to a stop just ahead of her. She'd seen it out of the corner of her eye even before it passed: a dark blue sedan. She could even describe the driver: linen jacket; blue open-necked shirt; short blond thinning hair; round, rimless glasses; and a wide, wet mouth. That was what she focused on as he leaned out of the window. He smiled, running his thumb around his shiny wet lips as he asked if she needed a lift anyplace. Lorraine stepped closer, inclining her head, showing him her profile so that the jagged scar couldn't be seen, keeping her lips half closed. She didn't want to scare him off, didn't want him to see too much of her teeth—or lack of them. She was an old hand at this and knew that if he was a cop he would try to get her to name a price. She bent lower, down to his level.

"You lost?" She said it softly, her hand reaching out to the door handle. "You need me?"

He stared at her as if sizing her up, then looked past her both ways before he jerked his head. "Get in."

Lorraine opened the passenger door and climbed in beside him. He drove off fast like they always did, acting macho. Acting stupid. He said quickly, licking his wet lips all the time, that he wanted oral, he wanted it public. Did she understand? Lorraine leaned her arm along the back of the seats, but as she touched his neck, he jerked away. He didn't want to be touched, he said, he hated being touched. He kept on driving, passing every car on the highway until he wheeled into the parking lot of the Glendale shopping mall. The ground level was not too full—just a few people staggering to and from the store with bulging bags of groceries, their hatchbacks open wide as they loaded up. The place didn't look like it was doing great business, but then it was only midafternoon.

The sedan's tires screeched as he sped across the parking lot, heading for a vacant area on the far side, slightly hidden around a corner from the main section. Lorraine had already seen two security guards wandering around and was getting edgy; this guy wasn't fooling when he said he liked it public.

He had hardly switched off the engine before he unzipped his trousers. Lorraine put her hand out. He swiped it aside. "I told you, I don't want you to touch me!"

"Okay, chill out, man, want me to talk dirty, you like that? That what you want?"

His body was tense, his hands clenching and unclenching.

"No, I think you want to be sucked off, right here, like with maybe someone close enough to catch you at it, that's exciting, isn't it, bad boy? You're a very bad boy, aren't you? Well, you got lucky because that's my specialty. I give the best head. Come on, you want to ask me for it, yes? That's what you want, isn't it?" His lips twitched, his eyes darting around the parking lot. She kept her voice low, whispering, making sucking sounds, and he closed his eyes. "Like I said, I'll make you feel good, real good, and this is a real public place, but we got to sort out my dough. Can we sort that out? Yeah?"

He looked out of the window, getting more excited as a few customers stashed away their groceries, their voices echoing against a concrete building. He loosened his belt, as if he hadn't heard her, pulling at his pants. "Just do it, bitch."

Lorraine's back pressed against the passenger door and her right hand felt for the door handle. If he played games, she was out. "Twenty dollars."

A woman with her husband and two kids parked directly opposite them. As they headed toward the exit, Lorraine's john started to jerk himself off, his mouth stretched in a weird wet smile of pleasure. His erect pink penis burst up from his open fly and he began to pant, leaning his head back, as his left hand flicked the switch for his seat to recline.

Lorraine tried again. "Twenty dollars."

He lost his erection and gave a half sob. She swore, realizing he was one of those half-a-minute stand-up-for-America and then the weeping impotent syndrome.

Fumbling in his wallet, he took out a thick wedge of bills,

peeled off a twenty, and tossed it at her. "See what you can do for it, bitch!" He reached over and grabbed her by the hair, forcing her face onto his pink flaccid worm. Lorraine could smell him, smell his trousers, even the cotton of his blue-striped boxer shorts. His hand on the back of her neck was grasping her hair as he pressed her farther down onto his crotch.

Was it the sweet lemon smell of her freshly washed hair? Or that she was stone-cold sober? She knew exactly what she was being paid to do, she'd done it plenty of times before. But never sober. Facedown between a john's legs, having just been paid twenty dollars for a midafternoon blow job in a parking lot, the ghost of Lieutenant Lorraine Page resurfaced and fought back for a tiny fraction of respectability. She couldn't suck him off.

"I'm sorry. You can have your twenty dollars."

He held on to the back of her head, forcing her down. She pushed up with her hands trying to free herself. He was much stronger than she was and, leaning over the seat toward him, she was vulnerable, incapable of getting away. He was able to hold her down with only one hand, and her head was partly wedged under the steering wheel. She heard the click of the glove compartment being opened but couldn't see what he had taken out. She forced herself to relax, to try to get into a better position so she could move off him, but he still had a tight grip on her hair.

The first blow stunned her for a second—it glanced off the back of her scalp—but he had hit her with such force that he had automatically released his hold on her. She pushed upward with all her strength, propelling herself against his chest. He slipped back in his reclining seat, and it was then she saw the claw hammer. As he tried to raise it to strike her again, she knew he could kill her if he wanted.

Lorraine twisted her face up toward his, and bit into his neck. She held on ferociously, her teeth breaking the flesh. He screamed, now more intent on getting her off than on using the hammer, but she wouldn't release her bite.

A family loading their groceries looked over to the sedan with its windows steamed up, but the screaming made the woman push her kids inside their car. She even shouted for her husband not to go across, but he ignored her, and as he reached the driver's door, he called out: "You all right in there?'' He turned back to his wife, who gestured for him to walk away, but he bent down, his hand tentatively reaching for the handle on the driver's door. "You all right in there?" he repeated.

As he opened the door, Lorraine fell out, face forward onto the cement, almost knocking him off his feet. The family started to shriek as they saw the back of her head covered in blood, and blood streaming from her mouth.

The sedan jolted backward, dragging Lorraine with it—her dress was caught on the reclining seat lever. The man who had come to her assistance made a grab, almost had the driver by his sleeve, but then he, too, fell, as the car swerved to make a turn. The door slammed shut, and with burning rubber tires the blue sedan shot across the lot toward the exit.

The woman was bending over Lorraine as she struggled to stand. At her feet was the wallet: it must have fallen from the john's jacket in the struggle. She snatched it up. "He tried to rob me, he stole my bag and—"

The woman shouted for her husband to call the police, but Lorraine shook her head. "No, no, it's okay—I've got my wallet. I'm fine really—"

"But you've been injured, look at you."

Lorraine backed away from their concerned faces. She touched her head. "It's nothing, I'll report it to security. Thank you very much."

By now the woman's husband had run back to them, red-faced and shaking with nerves. "I'll get the police. Are you okay?" The woman suddenly became suspicious of Lorraine, and caught her husband's arm. "Get in the car, just leave her. She said she doesn't want any help. Get back to the children!"

He looked from his wife back to Lorraine, who managed a half smile. "I'm okay, thanks for your help."

Still, he hesitated, but his wife called him again, and as he hurried across to her, Lorraine could hear the shrill voice. "Can't you see what she is? Didn't you see her face? She's a whore, she was probably trying to steal from him. Just get in the car! Report her to security, hurry up." They continued to argue, and as they drove out he stared back at Lorraine, confused and shocked.

In the ladies' room Lorraine soaked a handful of paper towels and held it to the back of her head. She had lost a shoe, her dress was bloodstained, and she couldn't stop the flow of blood from the back of her scalp. Her mouth, too, was bloody, and she panicked. Had he hit her in the mouth? But it wasn't her blood, it was his, from the bite she had given him. She was shaking now, her legs jerky, and she had to sit down on the toilet seat to stop herself from fainting.

With trembling hands she opened the wallet. A driver's license with a photograph—but not of the man inside the car. There were odd ticket stubs and dry cleaning receipts, and more than three hundred and fifty dollars. She folded the money, and stuck it into her panties. Then she stuffed the wallet into the trash can. She remained at the washbasin for another fifteen minutes, using more towels soaked in cold water as a pad. When she had recovered enough to make her way slowly into the store, she crossed to the public phones. She still felt dizzy and faint as she ordered a cab to pick her up at the main entrance. She was about to give him Rosie's address but said instead that she wanted to go to Orange Grove. Lorraine hardly had the strength to get out of the cab and she had to ask him to continue down the road to Marengo.

The driver watched her stagger slightly, wearing only one shoe, as she headed across the street—it was not until he got back to his garage that he found his seat was bloodstained and he started cursing. Jake, who had returned to check on Rosie, was watching the display from the apartment window. He heard Lorraine stumble on the missing step of the fire escape. Thinking her as drunk as Rosie had been, he still helped Rosie carry her upstairs. When he spotted the wound on her head he insisted Lorraine go to the hospital. She refused. She didn't want any hospital or police reports—she was fine. And she had not had a drink.

The wound was still bleeding freely, so reluctantly Lorraine agreed to go with Jake to his old clinic to have it stitched. By the time they arrived she was subdued. She lay on the couch as a doctor examined the gash. Because she was with Jake, the doctor didn't question her story, but Jake doubted her claim that the wound had been caused by her falling on a loose piece of sidewalk. It looked to him as if someone had struck her from behind; if the blow had landed an inch farther up, her skull could have been shattered. She'd been lucky.

Lorraine returned home with Rosie and Jake, her head bandaged and her hair cropped. Rosie put her in her own bed, and gave her the sedatives and antibiotics the clinic doctor had prescribed. Once she was asleep, Jake began to quiz Rosie. "What did she tell you that you think is lies, Rosie?"

Rosie shrugged. "Oh . . . just that she used to be a police officer."

Jake smiled, his eyes concentrating on unscrewing the hinges of the damaged screen door. "Well, that may be fantasy, of course. I think she's a whore and that's why she didn't want to go to the police. Someone nearly killed her today, though. But my worry is you—because you are my main concern, Rosie dear, and you were doing so well before she came on the scene."

"She didn't have anything to do with me tying on a load, Jake. That was thanks to my husband."

Jake squinted at the hinge. "Maybe, but you're vulnerable right now, sweetheart, and it won't take much to make you fall off the wagon. How long has she been dry? Not long, right?"

Rosie knew he was right and that he meant well, but she couldn't keep calling him just for social reasons—even though she had every right to call him when she was in trouble. "I get lonely, Jake. I need a friend."

Jake held up the new hinges. "Who am I to say what you should or shouldn't do? I'll have to come back and fix this tomorrow. These aren't the right screws."

Rosie sighed and looked toward the bedroom. "I think we'll be okay, for tonight anyway. It'll take my mind off things, looking after her."

Jake put on his jacket. "Up to you, but keep your eye on her. I don't trust her."

He had made no mention of Lorraine's reaction when he had seen the thick wad of notes fall out from under her skirt. Her expression was angry and when he asked about the money she had told him to mind his own business; it was just her savings. Jake was sure she had a police record, he could tell by her face: that hardness. She must be as tough as any man to have taken such a crack and still be able to walk around, but he decided it wasn't his business. He'd seen a lot of drunks with their heads cut open, maybe they survived because the amount of alcohol in their bloodstream acted like an anesthetic. Well, that was his theory.

Rosie started to make some chicken soup, even though it was a warm evening outside—almost into the eighties. She was feeling a little wobbly herself and had almost eaten the entire pot before taking a small bowl in to Lorraine. She had been awake for quite a while but kept her eyes closed, wincing as Rosie collapsed onto the bed. Her head ached, a sharp nagging pain that pressed into her eyes.

"Soup," barked Rosie, holding up the bowl and a large spoon. Lorraine smiled. It was the last thing she would have thought of asking for on a warm clammy evening, but once she tasted the first spoonful, it hit the right spot—as her mother always used to say. She took the spoon from Rosie and fed herself, dunking the fresh white bread into the remains, and finally wiping the bowl clean.

"I'd offer you some more but I made a pig of myself," Rosie admitted as she took away the bowl.

Lorraine snuggled down. "I'm full and it tasted so good . . . and I don't mind you sleeping with me—you'll never fit on that sofa out there."

Rosie laughed. "Well, thank you very much! I thought I'd take the cushions off and put them on the floor. I'd kick you out, but Jake said you should watch it, you know, not roll around or bang your head. I'll manage out in the living room— but only for one night."

Lorraine listened to the plodding feet moving around. Her hand had slipped into her panties to feel the money. She was afraid that maybe Jake had mentioned it to Rosie. It was still there, and it acted as a comforter. She had more than three hundred dollars, enough to get away from Rosie.

The bedroom floor shook as Rosie reappeared with some hot chocolate, slipped the mug onto the bedside table, turned on the night-light, and straightened the duvet. It was the caring that did it, simply being tucked in like when she was a little girl, that made Lorraine's heart ache.

"Rosie . . . you still there?" Lorraine whispered.

"Yep, hovering like a hot-air balloon. Don't forget to take your antibiotics."

Rosie watched Lorraine slowly raise herself on her elbow, her face twisted in pain. "You want an aspirin?"

Lorraine nodded, and Rosie got two tablets and held the mug of hot chocolate to her lips. Lorraine felt the thick sweet liquid slip down her throat.

"I'll be right outside if you need me."

Lorraine flushed. "Rosie, I, um . . . well, I guess I do want my life back, and if it means going to those meetings, well, then we'll go together.''

Rosie nodded. ''I should fuckin' hope so. G'night, sleep tight. Tomorrow you're back on the sofa.''

Lorraine gave a soft laugh, and nestled down. She hadn't heard the sound of her own laugh for so long that it warmed her now, and made her feel good, as did the soft duvet and big, squashy pillows. She tried to calculate how long she had been sober, since being picked up at the roadside. It was, she estimated, about five weeks, and she had not had one drink. Could she . . . did she really want to stay on the wagon? The money was a hard lump in her panties. She eased it out and tucked it under the pillow, keeping her hand on it, feeling drowsy, wondering vaguely why the driver's license had a different picture from the guy who had picked her up. The car was probably stolen, she told herself, the wallet must have belonged to its real owner. She sighed deeply as she recalled the incident. The claw hammer kept in the glove compartment. Very convenient. The position he had forced her into on his lap, the reclining angle of the seat . . . as if he had done it before? Jake had said she was lucky to be alive, another fraction of an inch higher and he would have cracked her skull open. If she hadn't bitten his neck she'd be dead. She knew she had marked him—the bite was deep. Should she call the LAPD in the morning, or contact someone at her old division, give them an anonymous tip? Describe the attacker? She yawned, maybe. Maybe she should just get some sleep, take it all day by day like Rosie said, but it unnerved her that she was even capable of thinking in that direction, like there was still some of the cop left inside her when she was damned sure that person was long dead and buried. In the end she drowsily just put it down to one of the problems of being sober. She never even thought about the nightmare screaming woman, she had not returned—not yet.

Rosie pulled the cushions off the sofa, turned the TV set down low, and, from her reasonably comfortable position on the floor, propped herself on her elbow to see if there were any more game shows scheduled. She used the remote control to move from channel to channel, paying only a moment's attention to the local news item that showed the photograph of

Norman Hastings, whose body had been discovered in the trunk of his dark blue sedan. He had been beaten to death with some kind of hammer. His wallet was missing. Anyone with any information regarding the dead man was asked to contact the local police, and a number was flashed on the screen. Fifteen minutes later, she switched off the TV and settled down, with a regretful sigh. Tomorrow was another day, another meeting when she would have to admit she had slipped. She began to recite the twelve AA traditions. She rarely got beyond the sixth or seventh, and tonight was no exception. By the third she was sound asleep. ''The only requirement for AA membership is a desire to stop drinking.''

TWO

The news bulletins about the discovery of Norman Hastings's body were repeated on the early-morning television shows, but now included footage of the abandoned blue sedan and a further request for anyone who had seen him or his vehicle to come forward. The officer heading the murder inquiry at the Pasadena Homicide Division was Captain William "Bill" Rooney.

Soon after the morning news, Rooney's department received a phone call from a Don Summers. He was not 100 percent certain, but he thought he had seen the blue sedan in the Glendale shopping mall parking lot the previous afternoon.

Rooney did not get around to questioning Summers until the following day. He doubted if Summers's evidence could help, since he could not be positive that he had seen the exact car, and had not made a note of the license plate number. Neither had he had a clear view of the driver, only the woman who had been in the vehicle with him. Rooney was able to ascertain that at the time of Summers's possible sighting of the blue sedan, Hastings, according to the autopsy report, was already dead. Rooney also had details of the dead man's missing wallet, and knew that it contained a few hundred dollars, which Hastings had withdrawn from his bank on the morning of his death. He suspected that robbery was the murder motive as they had failed to come up with any other reason. Hastings appeared to be a happily married man, well liked at his job and without enemies or anyone with a grudge against him. Also, Hastings's car had been found in another shopping mall, the Plaza, a much larger, more upmarket mall than the one in Glendale, so it was quite possible Summers was mistaken.

Rooney did not review Summers's call-in statement until he had further evidence from Forensic and the full autopsy report. Although the interior of the sedan had been cleaned and no prints found—not even those of the dead man—Forensic had discovered two further blood samples: one on the driver's seat, the other on the inside of the glove compartment. What prompted Rooney to question Summers personally was the woman's shoe found rammed beneath the front seat. It did not belong to Hastings's wife.

Rooney sat with Mr. and Mrs. Summers as Summers repeated his statement of how he had seen the blue sedan parked, heard the man screaming, and gone to investigate. He was now more sure that it was the car in the photographs shown to him by Rooney. His wife was convinced that if it was not the same car, it was the identical model and color.

"Okay, now, can you tell me about the woman? The one you stated was in the car?"

Summers gave a good description. Tall and thin, she was wearing a bloodstained, flower-print dress. She was injured, her mouth was bleeding, and he thought she had a head wound. She was also clutching a purse. She had told him the man had tried to rob her. Summers's wife interjected that she had thought it was a lie, because when they offered to call the police or for some assistance the woman had refused, insisting that she was all right.

Rooney asked for a more detailed description of the woman. Summers was hesitant but his wife wasn't, recalling the thin, wispy, badly cut blond hair, that the woman was about five feet eight inches tall but exceptionally thin and sickly looking. She remembered remarking to her husband that the woman might be a prostitute.

"What made you think that?" Rooney asked.

Mrs. Summers bit her lip. "I don't know, just something about her, a toughness. She was very rough-looking, sort of desperate—and, of course, she was covered in blood."

"That doesn't mean she's a whore," said Rooney.

Don Summers glanced at his wife. "Maybe she wasn't. All

I can say, and I got a closer look than my wife, was that the woman was terrified—and she was really hurt, blood all over her dress.''

Rooney showed them the shoe found in Hastings's car and they said they believed that the woman had been wearing only one.

''We need to find our Cinderella,'' Rooney joked, but the Summerses didn't find his comment amusing. They were over-awed by the massive new Pasadena police station, a high-tech palace, the computerized holding cells below. The vast new complex prided itself on its modern amenities—all the cells were glass and nicknamed ''pods'' by the officers, as each cell could hold up to twenty-five people. There was a computerized locking system, all gates patrolled and watched from panels via television monitors. Other signposted areas identified medical examination sections, fingerprint areas, interview rooms in the basement. Occupying the entire first floor was a massive, tiled central lobby opening onto three chromed elevators. Even the staircase was tiled, as were the various floors containing the community relations section, reference section, neighborhood crime task force, patrol and field officers section, then a large traffic section and the main supervisors' offices. In fact, the building was so modern and spacious it made Rooney feel uncomfortable. Lorraine had never even seen what her old precinct had turned into. Not that she would have felt like Rooney—she would have applauded the improved facilities. Rooney on the other hand hated so many soulless corridors, rooms, and sections, so many clerks. The old days, when a guy could pass a pal in the narrow, paint-peeling halls, have a chat, smoke a cigarette, were over. Nearly every office had NO SMOKING signs; some officers had even stuck them on their computers. Only Captain Rooney continued to work in a haze of cigarette or cigar smoke, his office door closed as the new laws required. The truth of the matter was that he didn't quite fit in with the new highfliers who surrounded him, but retirement was looming shortly. He figured the Hastings murder would be his last case and he hoped to crack it fast, get a good retirement bonus, and then be put out to pasture. He was un-sure about life outside the police, which had been the only world he had known since he was eighteen. And the prospect made him uneasy, but then so did the new station.

By the time Rooney returned to his office there had been

another call in connection with the Hastings homicide. This time the caller was anonymous and refused repeated requests to divulge her name. She did, however, give a detailed description of the man she thought was driving the car belonging to the deceased: around 180 pounds; possibly about five feet ten, though she wasn't sure; blue eyes; rimless gold-framed, pink-toned glasses; straight nose; thick-lipped mouth; wearing a linen jacket and shirt. She described a bite wound in his neck that would be visible above shirt-collar level, close to his jugular. It would be deeply inflamed as the teeth had broken the skin and drawn blood. Furthermore, the man was in possession of a claw hammer, which he kept in the glove compartment.

Rooney looked at the duty sergeant's notes. ''She said all this over the fucking phone?''

''Yes, Captain. Then she hung up.''

''So, you or whoever took the call got a trace on it? Shouldn't't've taken more'n a second with all this newfangled equipment.''

The call had not been traced, partly because it was felt to be a ''joke'' call, and it had also come through to the wrong department. Rooney plodded back into his office. He waved the anonymous statement at his lieutenant, Josh Bean. His blond crew cut and preppy tortoiseshell glasses, his neatly pressed uniform and smooth, mild manner were qualities Rooney couldn't come to terms with. Bean was the new breed, the educated desk-chained college graduate, one who had never smoked anything and was always complaining about having to be a passive smoker. Bean, in other words, was a needle in Rooney's side. Now he let it rip at the overneat lieutenant.

''You fuckin' read this? Whoever she is she wants him caught—she's even described the weapon. What's odd, though, is that the only thing she seems unsure of is the guy's exact height. Everything else—clothes, hair, glasses, mouth, even his weight—she gives it all. But not her name! And the stupid sons of bitches didn't trace the call, that's what's wrong with this place, too many bastards in too many different departments and no one making connections.''

Bean took a look at the statement. She hadn't given the car's license plate number, he mused, as Rooney deposited his overweight frame into his precious old leather swivel chair behind his desk.

''I bet that Summers woman was right,'' Rooney said,

thinking out loud. "She was a whore, that's why she doesn't know how tall the guy is. Maybe he never got out of the vehicle, just picked her up on the sidewalk . . ."

Bean cautiously nodded agreement. Rooney always unnerved him, gave him the impression he loathed having to work alongside him, so he was always a little tentative. "Unless both the Summerses and this caller got the wrong guy. Maybe he just drives a blue sedan."

Rooney leaned on his elbows and gave a doleful look at the pristine Bean. "Possibly, but it's the hammer, a claw hammer. If you read Forensic on the type of weapon used to kill Norman Hastings, they say: 'A blunt-edged hammer-type head, one inch in diameter, with a claw section one and a quarter inches long.' " He sifted through his files until he found the Forensic photographs of the dead man, closeups of the blows inflicted to his skull, cheeks, and chin. If the anonymous caller was telling the truth, they were looking for a killer with a big bite taken out of his neck.

Rooney looked at Bean and grinned. "This shouldn't take long then, should it? We got Dracula out there now—but at least we can check all Hastings's associates. No bite, we'll eliminate them."

Lieutenant Bean frowned, unsure if Rooney was joking. Suddenly he barked at Bean to get cracking.

"I thought you were kidding, for chrissakes!"

Rooney picked at his bulbous nose. "Fuck off. We got to take that call seriously, it's too detailed not to. Go on, move it! And, by the way, the shoe we got could also be the whore's. The Summerses sort of thought she had only one shoe on, but they weren't certain."

"Right. I'll take the shoe with me—get everyone to try it on, maybe find the owner." Bean was joking but Rooney looked about as amused as the Summerses had been by his Cinderella crack. He kept on working, flipping through the file, yawning. Something was nagging at him—the description? Was it too pat? Some kind of hoax? But the fact that they had found bloodstains in the glove compartment where the anonymous caller claimed the man kept the hammer was just too close a coincidence. Rooney guessed the caller was the woman the Summers couple witnessed leaving the car, and that Mrs. Summers had been correct. She probably was a whore, but he kept his thoughts to himself; he wasn't going to give the starched college kid a hint, let him get it for himself.

Rooney stared from his office window at the elaborate Plaza Mall. No witness had come forward to say they had seen the man who left the sedan there, no one had seen some guy with a bite out of his neck, and the Plaza was a busy mall with a lot of exits and a hell of a lot of people using the arcade and the parking facilities. Granted, the sedan had not been parked on ground level but on the upper story, which was never as full. It was only because night security became suspicious that they were contacted, and that was not until hours later. Rooney sniffed; would the same man have used one mall to attack this possible woman witness and then driven to a second mall, all the time with a body in the trunk? He sighed; he'd had a lot stranger cases—bodies dumped in a lot of places, but for him, a shopping mall was a first.

Lorraine had the worst headache she had ever known. No hangover had been this painful. She was dizzy if she stood up, if she moved she felt sick—she had vomited the first time she sat up. Thanks to the antibiotics and the aspirin, however, the splitting pain behind her eyes eased a fraction. She had made the phone call then, while Rosie was out getting ice from the grocery store. She had been brief intentionally, as she didn't want a trace made—it showed how long she had been out of the force that she didn't know they could make an immediate check if required; she was lucky they had not taken her call seriously. She was back in bed when Rosie returned.

The torn old sheet crammed with ice was soothing, but there was no way she could get up and go to the AA meeting. Rosie was uneasy about leaving her alone, but needed to go to the meeting herself. Lorraine just wanted to be left alone. Her whole body ached, but the pain across her eyes was torture, so bad she couldn't even think of a drink, let alone getting up to pour one. All she wanted was for the pain to go away.

She remained in Rosie's bed for more than a week. It was now May 28—eleven days since her injury. All Lorraine could think about was getting herself fit enough to leave; she still had to be helped to the toilet, for even that small amount of movement exhausted her. She found any noise unbearable—

no TV, no radio. She could eat, though, and Rosie waited on her hand and foot. She enjoyed being needed; it occupied her mind and, like Lorraine, she was hardly giving a thought to booze.

Two more weeks went by. Jake dropped by a few times to see how Lorraine was coming along, and like Rosie, he was getting quite fond of her. Sick as she was, she didn't complain and often made him laugh. Her pain was obvious, however, and more than once he told Rosie that if Lorraine's condition did not improve she should be taken to the hospital.

Finally, in mid-June, a month after the attack, the headache subsided and Lorraine was able for the first time to walk around the apartment by herself. That afternoon, Jake took out her stitches. The wound had healed well, but he was doubtful about his prowess as a hairdresser. Lorraine had almost a crew cut at the back of her head and crown while the front was long and jagged. It gave her a boyish look, and she made them laugh when she tied a ribbon around the front strands to keep them from flopping in her eyes. She read a lot, magazines at first, because even flicking through the newspapers gave her a headache, but gradually she began to plow her way through Rosie's spartan collection of bodice-ripping blockbusters.

She kept the money stashed beneath the mattress. Sometimes she had qualms of guilt when Rosie paid for everything, but didn't know how she could hand out money if Rosie believed she was broke. Afraid of being questioned too closely about its source, she decided against mentioning it. And Jake made no reference to it either.

Finally she saw a way around it. Late one afternoon, when Rosie returned home from work, Lorraine presented her with fifty dollars. "You can be proud of me, Rosie. I went over to my friend, then to a pawnbroker's. Here, this is for you. I sold off my things."

Rosie looked at the money and then back to Lorraine.

"So who's the friend?"

Lorraine lied, and she was very good at it, looking directly at Rosie. "She's a girl called Sonja, a drunk, even offered me a drink. I don't want to see her again, just like you said, Rosie, stay away from old friends, they'll drag you down."

Rosie nodded, satisfied. She had no idea that Lorraine had never left the apartment, but she did remark that it was time they discussed the sleeping arrangements. She assured Lor-

raine she didn't want her to leave, it was just that Rosie needed
a good night's sleep in her own bed. That night, Lorraine
moved back onto the sofa. The weather had become very warm
and with no air-conditioning in the small apartment apart from
a dilapidated box stuck on the window ledge, the heat built up
from the day and seemed to Lorraine to get even hotter at
night.

Two months had passed since Lorraine had last touched
alcohol, and more than four weeks since the attack. Curled up
on the uncomfortable sofa, she began to plan what she should
do next. On the positive side, she was sober. She had no craving yet; would it develop as she regained her strength?

Money she did have, more than three hundred dollars. It
seemed like a fortune, but she knew it wouldn't last long. She
wanted to move on, but the question was: where to? And what
would she do? Two more days and it became obvious, not just
to Rosie but to herself, that she could no longer hide out in
the small apartment. Rosie was already hinting that the fifty
dollars had been swallowed up in groceries.

Lorraine felt incapable of making major plans for her future;
it was the immediate that occupied her. Marooned in the apartment she watched a lot of TV and could follow the murder
inquiry. The news showed an artist's impression of the woman
seen in the blue sedan, which she found almost amusing; it
bore no resemblance to herself, and Lorraine felt no guilt in
not making further contact. The police were making inquiries
to all the cab companies, trying to ascertain if anyone answering the blond woman's description had hired a cab that
afternoon. They had drawn a blank at all the hospital emergency rooms. It seemed no one apart from the Summerses had
seen either the woman or the deceased's blue sedan on the day
of his murder at either of the shopping malls. Lorraine's phone
call was becoming more and more important to the investigation.

Jake, now a frequent visitor, was disturbed by her inertia.
In an attempt to motivate her, he suggested that, if she was
interested, his dentist friend could do something for her teeth.
They needed treatment badly, and the missing tooth didn't help
her looks. If she could find thirty dollars or so, he said, she
could get it capped.

"Know a laid-off dentist, too, do you, Jake?"

Jake laughed, but she was right—his friend was AA and only just starting to rebuild his practice.

For days after her first appointment, Lorraine was in agony. But the end result was two front teeth capped, all her cavities filled, her gums cleaned, and the rest of her teeth bleached. Her mouth was swollen and sore, but the exercise had been a success. She used the lie about selling off her belongings again, and paid the thirty dollars. She now had only to give a doleful look to Rosie, "Sonja, went to see Sonja. She's a really bad lush but I didn't have a drink." She also gave Rosie another twenty, adding that now she had nothing more to sell or pawn.

With what she told Rosie was the last of her money, Lorraine went to the local hair salon to have her hair streaked, cut, and blow-dried. Jake's pitiful attempt at styling had limited her choice—the back was so short where the scar was still visible—but the salon did a reasonable job, making the back and sides even shorter and the front into long bangs, which accentuated her cheekbones, while the highlights gave color to her lusterless hair. She was by no means transformed into a beauty: her nose was crooked from where it must have been broken, and the white jagged scar on the left side of her face remained. Nevertheless, a new, more confident Lorraine was emerging.

Rosie was astonished and full of admiration as Lorraine presented herself, and Jake was equally complimentary in a backhanded way. He had whistled, then said, "Honey, you must have been a looker!"

Rosie became a little envious. Nothing she could do to her frizzy mop would ever change her looks—and it rankled that Lorraine could afford an expensive haircut yet not pay a cent toward the rent. Money was short, and Rosie's salary plus her benefits was hardly enough to keep herself, much less two.

It also irritated Rosie that although she went to AA regularly, Lorraine made excuses to stay in the apartment and read. Eventually she had to make it clear that she was not a charity, and it was time Lorraine got off her ass.

But Lorraine was scared to leave the safety of the apartment. Even Jake's presence was comforting. He was always so dependable and calming. She still made no mention of her hidden stash: it was her only security and it meant that she could, if she wanted, go on a whopper of a binge. The idea of drinking remained an avenue of escape for her, but she no longer woke up with booze on her mind. Far from it: some days she relished the simple pleasure of waking up and knowing where she was. But then that was quickly replaced by fear—fear of being let loose and alone.

Lorraine never hinted at her inner turmoil. To Rosie and Jake she appeared confident and composed. She was meticulously clean, often taking two or three showers a day, scrubbing her body until it felt raw. She examined her teeth and gazed at her face in the mirror, studied her scars, as if she were trying to find out who she was, and where she had been the past six years.

She drank bottled water all day and ate so well that her skin took on a freshness and her fingernails grew. She sat for hours polishing and filing them, totally preoccupied with herself. She never did any housework, looking on as Rosie changed sheets and went alone to the laundry. Not once did Lorraine cook or do dishes; she ate whatever Rosie banged down in front of her, and ignored the heavy hints about outstaying her welcome.

Finally, Rosie turned to Jake. She wanted him to ask Lorraine to leave.

"I thought you liked her?" he mused.

"I did, I do, but she just takes from me, Jake. And I'm not just talking about money. She uses all my hot water, all my things, and now she doesn't even talk to me, never says thank you, just sits looking at herself, cleaning herself. Sometimes she reminds me of my goddamned cat. She's got to leave, she's driving me nuts!"

Jake came by when he knew Rosie was out. He tapped on the screen door and let himself in. Lorraine was sitting by the window, reading. She looked up, acknowledged him, then returned to her book. "We got to have a little chat," Jake said, sitting on the sofa. Lorraine didn't look up. He crossed his fat legs. "I know you're maybe scared of leaving here, you feel safe, feel like you're getting back to some kind of normality. But it's an unreal normality, Lorraine. This is Rosie's home, and she's broke—caring for you and herself . . ."

Lorraine snapped the book shut. "Okay. I'll leave."

"You don't have to do that, but you got to get a job, put some money into the housekeeping, help out around the place. Then, when you've found your feet, maybe you can get a place of your own."

Lorraine stared at her manicured fingers and looked out of the window. "I don't know about that . . ." She turned to him. Her eyes were washed-out blue, wide apart, without expression. He couldn't tell what she was thinking. "It's been a long time since I worked, Jake. You know—with sane people . . ." She half smiled. "Maybe I'm not ready to take on any responsibility. I'm kind of living day to day, but I hear what you're saying, and I'll leave."

"Where will you go?" Jake asked.

She shrugged. "I don't know. I'll make out. What do you care?"

"I care a lot—especially after all that dental work you got done! Hate to see you go and start the rot again, because if you walk out of here with no purpose you'll be back on skid row before you know it."

She sighed; she felt tired and it hurt to think. She ran a finger along the scar at the back of her head. "Skid row. That where we met?"

Jake bristled. "Listen, honey, I was a drunk but I never ended up on no skid row, I never sunk that far down."

"Joke, it was just a joke. . . . Look, Jake, I'm real tired, so if you don't mind leaving . . ."

He got up and went to the kitchen. "I'll make us some coffee." He saw the way her face tightened. She wanted him to leave, he knew, but he hadn't finished. "Let's talk some more, Lorraine, throw a few ideas around. Like I said, you got to find a purpose."

She picked up the book again. Jake walked over and snatched it away. "You can fuck around with Rosie, Lorraine, because she's weak and desperate. She needed you in some sick kind of way—it took her mind off her own problems. But now you got to put something back, d'you understand?"

She smirked at him. "Why don't you put something back, Jake? Give her a screw, she needs that more than anything else! I'll bet she hasn't been laid in five years."

He could have slapped her sullen face, but he didn't. He just held the steady gaze of her washed-out eyes. "You been screwed lately, have you? Remember it?"

"I've had enough to last me a lifetime."

"I bet you did. A lot of drunks whore for booze—that what you did?"

"Fuck off."

Jake gripped her skinny wrist. "I fuck off—and you're fucked. You need Rosie, you need this place, because it's all you've got—but you're using her. I'm just trying to help. You're already helping yourself. I knew you had some dough but I kept my mouth shut. I know how you paid for your teeth and the haircut but I reckon it's your business."

"Right, it is," she snapped.

"You look a hell of a lot better than when you first arrived—and you can keep on looking and feeling better—but you have to want a future!"

Jake had to hand it to Lorraine: she still didn't give an inch, still showed no sign of what she was feeling. She did, however, drink the coffee he made and even though she didn't speak to him again, she seemed to listen, chain-smoking his cigarettes, staring at the wall. Eventually he could think of nothing more to say. He wrote down a few contact addresses for jobs and went away, feeling depressed and disappointed. She didn't say goodbye or thank him for the extra pack of cigarettes he had left. Jake was a soft touch, he knew it, he always had been, and what was strange was that he still liked Lorraine—so what was a pack of cigarettes? By the time he walked to his car, he looked up and listened, because he could hear the sound of Rosie's vacuum. Maybe his little talk had made Lorraine think.

By the time Rosie returned, the apartment was tidier. Lorraine had, as Jake suspected, vacuumed and had also cleaned the kitchen. Rosie's bed was made, the bathroom was clean. Even the cat had been fed.

Rosie mumbled thanks and put down a grocery bag full of cans of Coke, oven-ready french fries, and a cooked chicken. She began cooking dinner as Lorraine watched television, shrugging in reply to anything Rosie said. They ate in silence, Rosie glancing at Lorraine while she sucked each chicken bone, eating with her hands, polishing the plate clean with her bread. Rosie shifted onto the sofa for a better view of the TV as Lorraine cleared the table and cleaned up. Not until she had dried all the dishes and put them away did Lorraine begin a conversation.

"Jake was here."

"Yeah, I know."

"I'll go an' see if I can get a job tomorrow, start paying some rent."

Rosie nodded. "Okay. You want to come to AA tonight?"
Lorraine hesitated. "Okay."

As before, Lorraine sat at the back of the church hall, playing
no part in the proceedings. As she checked over the list of
jobs she'd try for in the morning, her head throbbed. Then,
without any warning, the sweating began, and she slipped out
into the corridor, where she found the water fountain. She had
gulped down several mouthfuls before she was steadier and
her mouth stopped feeling like sandpaper. The fountain was
close to a large bulletin board: there were lists of contacts,
jobs, AA meetings, white elephant and garage sales. Lorraine
noted down an address for secondhand clothes.

Rosie appeared, looking concerned, but seeing Lorraine
squinting up at the bulletin board in that odd way she had,
writing down information, she relaxed.

Lorraine looked over to her. "I guess I'll need some clothes
for work. You want to come to a yard sale?"

It wasn't until they got there and Lorraine began to stack
up suits, shirts, shoes, that Rosie wondered how she was going
to pay. When she asked how much they'd cost, Lorraine lied,
telling her that the woman was practically giving away the
stuff since she was moving. She had actually paid a hundred
and fifty and was now down to less than a hundred bucks in
her stash. The fact that she had broken into it for something
other than booze, was, even though she didn't realize it, another step forward.

Rosie sat on the living room couch draining a can of Coke
as Lorraine inspected her new clothes, trying them all on, mix-
ing and matching. Her face wore a studied, concentrated expression. She muttered and nodded, running her hand through
her hair.

"Mmmm, nice, not bad . . . yes, I like it."

She felt jealous as she watched Lorraine parade up and
down like a model on a catwalk. The clothes were good, anyone could see that, tailored skirts and jackets, a particularly
nice cream silk shirt, and a black crepe one, tasteful walking
shoes and a pair of brown slingbacks that had never been
worn. "I doubt if you'll need that gear for the jobs Jake's got
lined up for you," Rosie pointed out, burping from the Coke.

Lorraine was looking at herself in the long wardrobe mirror.

"Maybe I'll try for a real job. There were quite a few listed at the meeting."

Rosie pouted. "Like what?"

Lorraine turned around. "Receptionist—got to look smart for that—nice and easy, sitting down all day. I might get lucky."

Rosie sniffed. "You might not."

Lorraine hardly slept. The sofa was uncomfortable at the best of times, but constant worrying about the next day made her toss and turn. She was sweating with the heat, which made her drink glass after glass of water. Four times she had to walk through the bedroom to use the bathroom, but she didn't disturb Rosie, who slept as always like a beached whale, snoring loudly. Lorraine's thirst seemed unquenchable. She finished all the Coke, all the bottled water, sweating and shaking, flopping up and down on the old sofa. Then it started—the craving. She badly wanted a beer. Would it be so bad to have just one?

She slipped into Rosie's old dress, and inched open the screen door. The need consumed her; she could think of nothing else. She got as far as the bottom step before she saw the patrol car moving slowly up the road, the two officers inside staring at the buildings as they cruised along. She watched for a few moments before returning to the apartment, where she looked out from the window as they passed on down the street. By the time they had disappeared she didn't feel so desperate. Still fully dressed, she got back on the sofa.

She had been expecting them. They must have contacted the cab companies by now, but because she had seen no sign of police interest, she had been too wrapped up in herself to give it a second thought. Now she remembered . . . but instead of focusing on the present, Lorraine recalled her own days in uniform.

The only female in the precinct, she hadn't even had a place to piss in private until they designated a toilet for her. Some joker drew a lady's figure with enlarged tits on one of the stalls in the men's room. She would do anything rather than go in there, and even when she had her own so-called stall, there was never any privacy, as there was always a cop leering nearby. Her partner would be furious because she was always asking him to pull over so she could run into a diner or coffee shop. It got so she wouldn't drink during the day so she didn't have to piss. They nicknamed her the Golden Camel, because no matter what temperature blistered the paint off the car, Rookie Lorraine Page never accepted a drink. Later, she sure as hell made up for it; she got so she could drink most of her colleagues under the table. It had started as an act of bravado, to show she was as good as any man on or off duty. She could hold it. And then she got a new nickname: Hollow Leg Page.

Half dreaming, half awake, Lorraine recollected times she had not thought of for years. What hit her hardest was the persistent humiliation to which she had been subjected. A woman in a man's world, a woman none of them wanted or encouraged to become part of their close-knit group. She had clawed every inch up the ladder—always proving herself tougher than any man. She was not better educated, she had no special qualifications, and if her father had not been a police officer she doubted she would have ever joined up. She'd enrolled almost as an act of perversity.

Lorraine had hated her father, because he had no time for her while he had doted on her brother, Kit. Whatever Kit had wanted Daddy made sure his precious son got. Kit was the pride of the family.

Lorraine's mother had been an alcoholic, a frightened, pathetic woman who drank in secret, who remained inside the house, afraid of her own shadow until she had drunk enough confidence to go out. To everyone's embarrassment, she would be picked up and brought home in a squad car by one of her husband's colleagues. She was never charged with being drunk and disorderly, whatever she did. If she stole money or became abusive, it was quietly glossed over, and she would be locked in her bedroom to get over yet another binge. Poor Ellen Clark. Sober she was regretful, apologetic, and weepy. Lorraine used to hide from the sound of her sobs by covering her ears with her pillow. When her mother was sober, the house would return to order and routine—until the next time.

Lately, Lorraine had not given her mother much thought. Now, she could picture her pale face, her white hands always twisting the thin gold wedding ring. Her red-rimmed eyes, her lank blond hair. Lorraine was the image of her mother: perhaps that was why her father had so little time or love left for her.

She never discovered what had started her mother's drinking. She used to search for the hidden bottles and, under instruction from her father, pour the contents down the sink. At first she always told him when she found the telltale bottles, but it seemed to Lorraine that the awful fights that followed were always directed at her, as if the blame was somehow partly hers. In the end, the pale, thin look-alike daughter protected her mother, and simply poured away the booze without saying anything.

Lorraine's mother died quietly in her sleep. She was only forty-two, and Lorraine thirteen, but from then on Lorraine ran the house. She cooked and cleaned up, waited on her father and brother. She would watch them leave for ball games, always together, like pals rather than father and son.

Kit was killed in a car accident. Two kids joyriding in a stolen car mounted the pavement and ran him down. That night Kit hadn't come home for supper, and her father got the phone call, just as she was about to serve him steak. She could smell it, all these years later, the steak, the mashed potatoes, and the mint peas. She knew it was something terrible because of her father's expression and the way he let the phone slip from his hand as he pressed his face into the old, flowered wallpaper. Then he punched the wall twice before he walked back to his chair and picked up his jacket.

"There's been an accident. It's Kit."

Lorraine was left alone with a father who never came to terms with his grief. He hadn't been affectionate before the accident, and afterward he showed her no warmth whatsoever. If he felt any pride in her being accepted into the police academy, he kept it to himself, and he was dead three weeks before she graduated.

Lorraine sold the house and prepared to move into an apartment. It had been while sorting through his belongings that she had found pictures of her mother. She had once been so beautiful, with a fragility that took Lorraine's breath away, but the sweet smile, even in her youth, was a little frightened. Lorraine burned most of the memorabilia, keeping only a photograph of her brother and one of her parents on their wedding day. She would have liked one of them all together, as a family, but there hadn't been one—there hadn't really been a family. Now she had nothing—not even a photograph of Mike or the girls. She pictured them in her mind, little Julia and sweet-faced Sally . . . and Mike. The feeling of loss swamped her.

She woke up as Rosie thumped into the kitchen. She felt

stiff from the cramped position in which she'd finally fallen asleep.

"I'm going to be late," Rosie muttered, in her usual raw early-morning mood. She stood shoveling in her cereal, milk trickling down her chin. Lorraine stretched.

"Will you feed the cat?" Rosie barked.

Lorraine joined her in the kitchen. "Do you think alcoholism is hereditary?"

Rosie rammed her cereal bowl into the sink. "If you came to a few more meetings you'd know, wouldn't you? They say it is. Why don't you read the leaflets I gave you?" She continued spouting as she returned to the bedroom, and Lorraine uttered a silent prayer of thanks that she had not gone out for that beer. Another day over, sober.

Rosie plodded down Marengo toward the bus stop by the liquor store. As she disappeared down the street, a squad car drew up opposite her house. Two officers checked the address and glanced over and up the rickety wooden stairs. The cabdriver had not been sure of the number he had driven the woman to, but he had known the street and the date his fare had called in. He had picked her up at Glendale Mall's main entrance, it was logged down, and she had first asked to be dropped at the Orange Grove intersection, then changed her mind and told him to drive up Marengo. His description of her matched that of the other two witnesses, Mr. and Mrs. Summers. He was able to add a few more details: the woman had a front tooth or teeth missing and badly bitten fingernails—he'd noticed them when she had paid the fare. She'd also told him to keep the change, which was only a dollar.

Lorraine examined herself: the suit jacket was a fraction too large, the skirt band a couple of inches too wide, but she bloused up the jacket, a safari-style fawn cotton, and with the cream silk shirt beneath, it looked good. She borrowed a pair of pearl stud earrings from Rosie's jewel box, and used her mascara, a little rouge, and powder and, as the lipsticks were all a violent orange, rubbed on lip balm instead. When she heard a knock on the door she hesitated: maybe she should have asked Rosie about the earrings. If she was back, she might get into one of her moods. She heard a second knock; knew it couldn't be Rosie, who would have used her key, and assumed it was Jake.

She stepped back in shock as the two officers lolled at the door. One remained outside while the second came in to "ask a few questions. . . ." She lit a cigarette and sat on the edge of the sofa, thankful she had cleared away the blankets and pillows.

"Do you live here?"

"Yes, I do."

"What's your name?"

"Laura Bradley. Actually I'm just staying here, I don't own this apartment."

"Who does?"

Lorraine gave Rosie's name. He asked for a description, and she said Rosie was dark-haired, Hispanic-looking, and in her late thirties.

"Is she fat?"

Lorraine half smiled. "No. Why? Has something happened to her?"

"No. Were you here early evening on the seventeenth of last month? That'd be May seventeenth, miss."

Lorraine nodded, frowning, doing a good cover job. She repeated the date as if trying to remember, then asked innocently. "What date is it today?"

"June twenty, miss. This was last month, seventeenth of May."

"I guess I was here, yes, think I was at home that night. Why?"

"Did someone else come here? Did a taxicab bring someone else to these premises?"

"No. Not that I can recall . . ."

The officer stood up, walked toward the bedroom, and pushed open the door.

"Just the two of you live here? Nobody else? Short, dark-haired man?"

Lorraine laughed. "No. It's a small place. Why are you so interested?"

The officer showed her a photograph. It was similar to the one she had seen in the wallet but much larger. Lorraine knew at a glance that it was the same man as on the driver's license—the owner of the wallet.

"Do you know this man?"

"No, I'm sorry. What has he done?"

"He was murdered, ma'am. Haven't you read about it? Local man."

Lorraine looked suitably shocked, then stood up. "Maybe he lived here before I came to stay—I can ask my friend."

The officer slipped the photograph back into his jacket. "Thanks. Truth is, we're only interested in tracing the woman—cabbie says she was dropped off around here." He relaxed, smiled at Lorraine. "Since you don't fit the description we must have the wrong place, but thanks for your help, been nice talkin' to you."

Lorraine followed the young officer to the door. "Was she murdered, too?" she asked innocently.

"No, but we think she may have known the man driving the deceased's vehicle. We have two witnesses."

"They saw her coming here?" asked Lorraine.

"No, we were told she may have been brought here by cab. We're asking everyone in the street if they saw her. She must have been hard to miss. She was covered in blood."

Lorraine opened the front door. "I'll ask Rosie when she comes home if she saw her. Do you have a number? Somebody I can call?"

The officer told her to contact her local station or sheriff's office and they would pass on any information to the department handling the homicide.

After they had gone, Lorraine leaned against the door. Her heart was beating so rapidly that she felt dizzy. She began to berate herself for being so stupid. She was not involved in any murder. All she had done was tip off the cops with the description of the man who picked her up. There was nothing to be afraid of—except that she had taken the wallet. But she'd gotten rid of it and nearly all the money was gone. They had not been new notes so she doubted they could be traced. Why was she worrying about something so inconsequential when the officers hadn't even recognized her as the woman they wanted for questioning? She ran her tongue over her newly capped teeth. She had come a long way since that attack, physically and mentally, and eventually she relaxed and congratulated herself on the way she had handled the cop.

She even mentally castigated the police for being so slow in finding the cabdriver who had driven her home that afternoon. If she had been on the case it would have been the first thing she'd have checked. She closed her eyes, trying to remember if he had driven off before she crossed the road. She was sure he had and then she remembered Jake and Rosie helping her up the staircase. Had he seen them? She was sure he had already driven off.

Satisfied she was in the clear, she left the apartment, her pace quickening as she walked toward the bus stop on Marengo. Nothing in her appearance resembled the woman the police had described: her hair was well cut. She looked elegant, though her shoes were too tight and she was without a purse, but she was more confident than she had been in years. She caught a glimpse of her reflection in the grocery store window as she passed and didn't even notice the rows of liquor bottles, so intent was she on admiring herself. It was another day, and she had moved on faster than she could ever have anticipated or believed possible.

THREE

Captain Rooney looked over the reports and statements from the various officers. They were, as he had half expected, of little use. It was already mid-June, Norman Hastings's body had been discovered on the seventeenth of May and they had, in Rooney's estimation, fuck all. The taxi driver had given them a bum address and nobody had located the bloodstained woman with only one shoe. She had disappeared—could even be dead. The Summerses had been questioned again to see if they could match the description of the man driving the sedan from the anonymous caller. He was similar, they said, but they were not too clear about the driver of the vehicle. When shown a photograph of Norman Hastings, they were sure that it was not him. Rooney doodled over his notebook.

He wondered again if they were looking for two killers, the man and the blond woman working together. They had killed Hastings and then had an argument, maybe they had come to blows inside the car at the shopping mall. The woman subsequently made the anonymous phone call describing her partner, husband, or lover. . . . But if that was so, she would have known the killer's height and could even have given his name, although that might have incriminated her, too. Rooney concluded that the woman was probably not involved in the murder and did not know the killer's name or height because she was, as he had first thought, a prostitute the driver had simply picked up. But what kind of nut picks up a whore with a fucking body in the trunk of his car?

The missing blond woman had become a vital witness to the murder of Norman Hastings. Somebody out there knew who she was. A man and a woman had helped her out of the cab. Rooney instructed his officers to step up the search for her, and called in the two officers Lorraine had met earlier.

He checked over all the statements they had taken. They were convinced that no one had lied. They thought the cab-driver might have been mistaken. "We saw only one blond woman, Captain, but she had all her teeth, her hair was short, and she was real smart, just staying with her friend. She didn't look like a whore or the type to know one."

Rooney told them to go back and question everybody again. Seeing them exchange covert, bored looks, Rooney snapped, "Get the cabdriver to go with you if you have to. Go on, get moving!"

The two men had just reached the office door when Josh Bean walked in. "You better look at this, Captain."

Rooney reached out his beefy hand for the internal fax sheet. Rooney looked up. "We'd better check this out. Looks like our missing girl."

He snatched up his jacket, told the two officers they could go off duty. If the new information panned out, they had just found their star witness and the search was over.

The run-down apartment block was a graffiti jungle. Burned-out rubbish littered the disused yard and every window was smashed. The Paradise Apartments billboard, showing palm trees and a seminaked girl sunbathing, was peeling and covered in daubed slogans. A lot of buildings around this section of East Fair Oaks and Colorado were going to be part of a big redevelopment. The apartment block was now being patrolled by a security company and makeshift fences had been erected around the grounds. Some sections of fence were broken down, but the big gates were usually locked.

The security guard was sweating, holding the lead of a snarl-ing dog that looked like a cross between Lassie and a pit bull terrier. Rooney overheard him explaining that he had first seen the car on his day shift, two days ago. He'd told the company it had been dumped but nobody had done anything about it.

Rooney stepped under the obligatory yellow tape to join the group gathered around the covered corpse. There were two patrol cars, lights blinking, and officers assembled to clear the area. Groups of kids were hanging around watching avidly. This wasn't unusual in the middle of the day as most of them never bothered to attend school for more than one or two days a week, if that. This was becoming known as crack dealer territory.

"Who found her?" Rooney asked as he approached the corpse.

"That kid over there, one with the red hat on, but he must have had help to drag her from the trunk of the car. That's been there for maybe two days, by the way—the car, dunno about the body." The young officer was sweating, it was almost ninety degrees, and the sun blistered down. Flies were everywhere.

Rooney stared at the kid, who was no more than six or seven and laughing as he pointed to the dead body, nudging his pals. The sweating officer continued. "I talked to the security guard, seems they stopped patrolling nights for a few days when they got short-staffed, and this was dumped about the same time. He says he told his company about it but nobody did anythin' about it." Rooney wrinkled his nose; the stench was disgusting. "Yeah, you said. Anythin' else?"

"She was in the trunk of a wrecked car, we think the kid dragged her out here, said he thought she was alive—but if she had any jewelry on her, she ain't got it now."

As he crouched down, Rooney took out his handkerchief to cover his face—the stench was of a decomposing body at least two days old, and with the heat, it smelled like longer. So much for the kid's story about thinking she was still alive. She was wearing a floral-patterned dress, with a belt and flat black shoes. Rooney checked them and noted they were the same size as the one they had found in Hastings's car. Her thin legs were bare, and one stretched out at an odd angle. Her arms were by her sides, the back of her dress undone. The thin blond hair was matted with dark congealed blood; a wound gaped at the base of her skull, so deep, he could see white bone. Slowly they turned over the unwieldy corpse. Her face had been hammered out of all recognition. Blood obliterated the brightly colored flowers that had once patterned the front of her dress. There was nothing Rooney could do; he couldn't tell if it

was their witness or not. His only option was to wait for the
report to come in, and for her to be cleaned up so he could
see her face.

"Any of her teeth missing?" he asked as an afterthought.

An officer peered down into the mass of blood hiding her
face.

"I can't tell, her nose has been flattened so bad."

Rooney plodded over to the kid, who, seeing the big, square-
shouldered man head toward him, was suddenly not quite so
cocky and self-assured.

"You move the body, did you?"

"Yeah, I was gonna do mouth-to-mouth, been learnin' it at
swimmin'."

"Have you? So once you dragged her out, then what did
you do?"

"Nothin'. I ran to the guard, told him, that's all I done,
honest."

Rooney drew the boy close and told him to turn out his
pockets, but he had nothing, no jewelry, and started to cry.

"Any of your pals take anythin' off the body?"

"No, sir, I swear, nothin', I done nothin'."

Rooney returned to his office with Bean. He opened a bottle
of Scotch, and even the lieutenant had a heavy hit. No matter
how many you see, it's always the smell that gets to you, stays
in your nostrils. The sweet, sticky, cloying smell of rotting
flesh.

"I think it's our witness. Cinderella," Rooney said flatly.
"Fuck it! Really needed to talk to her." He sighed.

"Yeah." Bean knocked back his drink. His eyes watered,
not being a drinker, but seeing the corpse had made him feel
very shaky. He hadn't seen that many and Rooney knew it.
He indicated the bottle for a refill and Bean shook his head.

"No, thanks, I'm okay."

"I sincerely hope you are, son, because we got a lot of work
to do."

Rooney looked up as his secretary peered in. A message
had come through from the city morgue: the corpse wouldn't
be ready for viewing until at least the following day, maybe
longer. Did he want to speak to the scene-of-crime officers?
Rooney jerked his head for Bean to go and do the legwork;
he had some paperwork to finish. Bean raised his eyebrow,
knowing Rooney always said that when he wanted to take off

for home. But he was wrong this time: Rooney spent the next hour making phone calls to different precincts. It was something one of the officers had said—or he might even have said it himself. She had been hammered in the face and at the back of the head. He wanted to know if anyone else had a similar homicide—weapon used probably some kind of hammer, that was all he had. . . . In reality, he spent more time shooting the breeze with old buddies, in no hurry for the facts. He knew he wouldn't get them straight off, if at all. Old files would have to be sifted through and checked out on computer. Probably wasting everybody's time, but he caught up on gossip, arranged a game of billiards, and agreed to have a drink with Colin Sparks, an old poker-playing pal he hadn't seen for six months.

Sitting on a bar stool in Joe's Diner, his fat ass bulging over the red plastic stool top, Rooney had downed two beers and a chaser by the time Sparks walked in, but promptly ordered another round and a fresh bowl of peanuts.

Sparks whacked him on the back, then handed Rooney a dog-eared file. "I'm late because I got interested in this! It happened before I got transferred—it's been around for four years. Dead hooker. Go on, read it."

Rooney grinned at the young, fresh-faced lieutenant and cuffed him like a father would his son. "Looking sharper than ever, Colin. How you keeping?"

"Fine, new baby on the way—everythin's good."

Rooney opened the file. He looked at the prostitute's face, her dyed blond hair scraped back from her head showing at least an inch of dark hair growth. Half-Mexican. Maria Valez, age thirty-two. The next page had a photograph of her body when it was discovered in the trunk of a wrecked Buick. Like the dead woman that afternoon, Maria's face had been virtually obliterated by heavy blows. There was an enlarged shot of the back of her scalp, showing the deep wound. Type of weapon, possibly a claw hammer. No witness, no arrest, no charges, case closed for lack of evidence, but authorized to remain open on file.

Rooney closed the file and tossed a handful of peanuts into his mouth. "Can I keep this? There're a few details on blood groups I'd like to check out with my case."

"Go ahead."

"Thanks." Rooney smiled and waved at the waitress for another round. "An' I'm gonna treat you to the best raw fish in Pasadena! You know that Japanese place? Serves good shark fin soup, you ever had shark fin soup?"

Rooney, well toasted, and Sparks, still fairly sober, left Joe's Diner to head for the Japanese restaurant farther up the road on Holly. Rooney's crumpled jacket flapped. The file was stuffed under his arm and he was sweating in the early-evening heat. He upped his flat-footed pace to get into the air-conditioned restaurant.

Lorraine emerged from the health club Fit as a Fiddle feeling like a washed-out rag. Her heels were blistered, her silk blouse creased, beads of sweat dripped from her bangs, and her hair was wet at the nape of her neck. So far she had applied for ten different jobs to discover either that the position had been filled, or that she didn't have the required experience. At Fit as a Fiddle she had snapped back at the Cher-with-muscles look-alike: "How much fucking experience do you need to pick up a phone and book an appointment?"

Cher had wafted a hand adorned with fake nails. "Maybe I was just bein' polite. You look like death warmed over for starters—and you're too old, okay? That real enough for you?"

Lorraine had slammed out and was about to throw in the towel and go home when she saw the whitewashed storefront with a handwritten sign in the window: STAFF WANTED. Lorraine checked the notes she'd taken from the help-wanted ads on the AA board. She squinted at the storefront; printed in fading letters was SELLER SALES. She figured she might have gotten lucky—maybe they'd just started advertising. She straightened her jacket, used the sleeve to wipe the sweat from her face, and walked to the door at the side of the store's front window. The buzzer sounded like a low fart. A moment later and she would have faced Captain Rooney as he and Sparks walked into the Japanese restaurant three doors down the street. As it was, she almost walked straight out of Seller Sales: there was no one in the reception area—just a counter, a bowl of wilting flowers, two posters for Gay Liberation, and a faded breakfast cereal ad. She looked toward a large makeshift screen dividing the shop front from the back room and could hear the tinny sound of a radio playing. She coughed, edged closer to the side of the screen. A man shot around it, covered in white paint. "Thank God! Come on, come on, hurry up. I'm Art Mathews. I've been getting desperate."

Lorraine hesitated, then she closed the door behind her, following Art around the screen and into the back room. He was about five foot four with a tight, muscular little body shown off by a close-fitting white T-shirt, skintight white jeans, white sneakers, and white socks. His dark eyes were too large for his face, magnified behind huge glasses—round, thin, red-framed bifocals—and made even more striking by his complete baldness. The room was cluttered with paints, trestle tables, stacks of canvases, ladders, and rolls of carpet. Art walked in small, mincing steps, sidestepping all the paraphernalia with a dancer's precision.

"Now the phone is somewhere, and the lists. Oh, Jesus, where did I put the lists? I'm so behind—and they said you'd be here hours ago . . ."

Lorraine looked around. "I think there's a misunderstanding."

Art stood, hands on hips, his little rosebud mouth pursed.

"I was wondering about the job on offer, printed in the window and—" she was interrupted.

"Seller thingy closed down months ago, I've taken the lease over. I'm opening an art and photographic gallery here tomorrow, would you believe it? My God, if you knew what I've been through . . . *where's the fucking phone!*"

Lorraine spotted it beneath a table. Art dragged it out, swore because it was off the hook, and sat cross-legged on the floor.

Lorraine watched as he arched his body in order to drag out a card from his jeans pocket, and punched out some digits.

"What are you here for?"

She coughed. "Receptionist." She tried again. "Salesperson."

He looked at the card, then back to Lorraine, his eyes darting like a demented frog's. He pursed his lips as his call was connected. "This is Mr. Art Mathews and I was promised a . . . hello? *Fucking answering machine!*"

He sprang to his feet. "I need someone to call my guest list, there's over a hundred people, and I need it done by tonight. I need someone here to help me open this up. I've got to get that paint on the walls, hang those canvases and photos. I called this shittin' agency for them to send someone, did they? Jesus Christ!''

Lorraine unbuttoned her jacket. "I'll do it. How much you paying?"

Art clapped his hands. "Ten bucks an hour—I love you. What's your name, darling?" She told him. "Right, Lorraine, here's the phone, grab a seat, I'll find the list and you start with the calls. I need to know how many are coming so I can order the wine . . ."

"Have they been invited already?" Lorraine asked.

"They have, dear, but not to this address. I had a problem with my last place. Now, if I don't open and show all these canvases and photographs, I'll be fucked—I'll lose my credibility and it's hanging on a thread as it is. Now sit yourself down and dial, sweetie. . . ." He alighted on a bulging Filofax. "Right, darling, here you go. Be charming, be cool, but get an answer."

Lorraine perched on the chair, took out her cigarettes and lighter, and studied the guest list, detailed in a neat fine scrawl, in pinks, greens, and blues with red stars drawn against some names. "Does the red star mean they're important?"

"No—just a good lay!" Art shrieked with laughter. He did almost a triple pirouette as the buzzer sounded in reception. He scurried out, flapping his hands at Lorraine. "Dial, go on, start dialing, and get *results*. . . ."

Lorraine could hear a lot of shrieking and raised voices, then Art returned with a massive floral display—and two extraordinary-looking transsexuals, carrying a basket of food, a crate of distilled water, and two more floral displays. "These are my dearest friends, Nula and Didi, they're going to help me. This is—what's your name again, dear? She's going to make all the phone calls and be Girl Friday."

Nula and Didi began to put down their supplies as Art moved to clear the back of the room. Lorraine smiled at them and continued to flick glances in their direction as she started making calls. They were both outrageous to say the least, but Nula—the one wearing a silky red wig down to her waist—was particularly startling. She had on a frilled off-the-shoulder bright yellow Spanish-style blouse, a six-inch-wide black stretch belt with an enormous buckle, tight Lycra orange pants that almost matched the red of her wig, and she was wearing high stacked heels, her toenails painted a dark plum red, matching her long fingernails. Her makeup was applied so thick it was shiny with sweat, but her thick lips were perfectly outlined with dark maroon pencil and pink lip gloss. Nula was even taller than Lorraine, and as she plucked the wig off her head, she revealed a classic male hairline that was receding to almost the middle of her scalp. She tossed the wig onto a table and opened a bottle of water.

"I'm Nula, are you thirsty, Luvvie?"

Lorraine nodded. Nula's voice was deep and rasping, and as she teetered across to Lorraine, pouring the water into a paper cup, she bent across the table, revealing heavy breasts.

"Water, water, Lorraine, yes? Did Art say you were called Lorraine?"

Lorraine nodded, taking the paper cup gratefully.

"I knew someone called Lorraine once, in high school. She was horrid—well, to me."

Lorraine turned to Didi, who almost outdid her friend Nula in her style of dress. But the effect was softened because Didi was very pretty: big wide brown eyes, an uptilted nose, and rosebud lips accentuated by a vermilion red lipstick. Didi was also much smaller than Nula, and rather plumpish, or curvaceous as she preferred to be described. Didi was not wearing a wig. Her dark hair was drawn back in a ponytail, snatched back from her young, round face. On her ears she had big gold-looped gypsy earrings, and she wore a pair of tight denim jeans cut off as shorts and a black stretch top that showed that, like her friend, she, too, had a very ample bosom. But unlike Nula's, her voice was high-pitched, almost feminine. She was intently sorting out tapes, and Lorraine noticed her hands were large and mannish but with long false nails, painted silver.

"Let's play some nice music." She smiled at Lorraine as she crossed to a ghetto blaster and slipped in a cassette. Lorraine expected some ear-shattering music to interrupt her calls, but was surprised by Didi's choice.

"This is Mahler's Symphony Number Nine, I just love it."

The volume almost restful, Lorraine smiled. Didi laid out a neat row of tapes, choosing each with studied concentration. She turned to Lorraine, asking in her whispering high voice: "Do you like opera?"

Lorraine nodded as Didi selected the next tape. She had never listened to opera in her life. She jumped as Art dived toward her and banged the phone. "Come along, dear, start working, busy, busy."

The pace at which Art and his two friends worked was astonishing. Nula and Didi whipped off their clothes and stacked shoes and pulled on old shirts and, barefoot, hurried around the room. They hardly spoke as they painted, neatly and rapidly, as if they had done it before. They had painted all the walls with a quick-dry rough white, swept the floors, stacked the rubbish, torn down the screen partitioning at the front of the store, and were now painting that area, using big rollers on sticks.

Lorraine remained at the table, making calls and listing acceptances and refusals. She now had her spiel down to a bare minimum: "Good evening, I am calling on behalf of Art Mathews's new gallery, Art's Place . . ." She gave the address, time of the show and mentioned that wine and canapés would be served from seven o'clock. Most said they would try to make it, but only twenty said they'd definitely be there.

The strains of Puccini floated through the room, and Lorraine downed two bottles of water as she continued her calls. Nula slipped her some homemade banana bread wrapped in a napkin, a little bowl of fruit salad, and some crispbread with homemade pâté. Her big hands were encased in bright yellow rubber gloves, and her shirt was covered in white paint splashes, but she had the friendliest wide and warm smile. Lorraine often caught Nula looking at her. She would give her a wink as she painted and cleaned, and Lorraine noticed that it was Nula who was doing most of the heavy lifting and carrying. Didi, the more feminine of the twosome, paid Lorraine hardly any attention. She was prissy, constantly asking Nula if her work was all right, and twice Lorraine saw Nula cross and kiss her, congratulating her like a child. When they did take a short break the three huddled together, admiring the gallery, discussing where the paintings and photographs would look best. Art occasionally leaned over Lorraine to see the list, but on the whole behaved as if she weren't there. It was almost ten o'clock when Lorraine made the last call to a Craig Lyall. The deep, rather affected voice inquired if it could speak to Art. She covered the mouthpiece. "Art, it's a Craig Lyall, he wants to speak to you."

Art passed his brush to Nula. His whiter-than-white outfit

was filthy, his round glasses speckled with paint. "This is he," he lisped into the phone.

Lorraine got up and stretched. Her back ached, and her mouth was dry again. She wandered toward the main room where Nula and Didi were unwrapping canvases and stacking them against the walls. Art hung up, came across, and put his arm around Lorraine. "Well, that, my dear, was good news. Sweethearts, Craig Lyall is coming." He peered up into her face. "You can go now but I insist you're here tomorrow. What on earth did you do to yourself? Car crash?"

Lorraine stepped away from him, her hand automatically moving to her scarred face. "Yes."

"You should have it fixed, dear. I know the best surgeon if you want his name . . ." Art put his arm back around her waist and gave her a little hug, beamed, then released her to dig awkwardly into his tight pants and take out a thin leather wallet.

Lorraine felt embarrassed as he counted out thirty dollars in ten-dollar bills, but she took the money and pocketed it fast. "See you tomorrow, then," she said, hovering at the doorway. All three smiled and Art accompanied her to the door. When he unlocked it, it started to buzz. He tutted, "I'll have to get this fixed."

Lorraine turned back to see him inspecting the faulty buzzer, his bald head shining in the streetlights. She intended to get a bus, and was heading toward the bus stop, when a car traveling in the opposite direction tooted its horn. Lorraine looked over and was relieved to see Jake at the wheel. "You want a lift?" he called. By the time she had crossed the street, Art had closed the door and returned to Nula and Didi.

Nula looked at Didi and nodded. "Tell him."

"Tell me what?" Art asked, his attention focused on the paintings.

"I think I've seen her before, though I can't put my finger on where. I've been trying to remember all evening. How did you find her?"

"She just walked in off the street. I thought she was from that agency I use, but she was looking for work at Seller Sales."

Nula studied her nails. "That's been shut for months."

Art said, "Didn't you like her?"

Didi shrugged. "I've just got this funny feeling about her."

Art wished they would pack up and leave, as he liked hanging paintings alone, taking his time to choose where each would go. "Isn't it time you two left?"

Nula gave a sarcastic, "Well, thank *you* . . ." and started to gather her stuff together. On went the wig, the makeup was freshened, and finally she grew another four inches as she clasped her shoes on. Didi was almost ready, giving a last look around. "It looks good—be even better when I bring some more knickknacks tomorrow."

Art kissed them both, almost tearful with gratitude. "You'll be here in the afternoon, won't you? Are you working tonight?"

They chorused "yes" and as he watched them walk off, arm in arm, they both turned and flicked their hips at him, laughing, only their rather broad shoulders giving away their former masculinity—at least if you were as nearsighted as Art.

As soon as they were out of earshot, their good humor act ended abruptly and Nula snapped, "I think you should have told him."

Didi pouted. "Why didn't *you*? It's always me. We'll have to work it out between us. If he finds out he'll go ape-shit, so we'll deal with it."

Left alone, Art took out a tiny square envelope from his jeans pocket and carefully laid out a half-inch line of crystal meth. This would see him through his all-night session. He snorted, blinked back tears as it burned his nostrils, then took a few deep breaths. No rush, nothing immediate like cocaine . . . he'd given that up. It would be a while before he felt any real benefit, so he placed the canvases around the room, then sat cross-legged in the center of his little white gallery to appraise each painting. They were awful and he knew it.

Nula and Didi, still arm in arm, headed into their apartment in a wondrous and outrageous building that perfectly suited them. They shared a large studio apartment in the famous Castle Green building. At one time it had been exotic, the palm trees and the Moorish-style opulence of bygone days still in evidence if a little worn down, the paint peeling. A lot of artists lived in Castle Green, a lot of oddballs, but not many as odd as Nula and Didi. Nula had changed into an even more overtly sexy outfit: higher stacked heels, tight leather miniskirt, and, as she was well endowed, showed off her tits with an outrageous, low-cut spangled bodice. She heard the door opening and turned from her makeup table. Didi dangled the car keys, then walked and stood over Nula at the dressing table.

"Nula, I need some more spirit gum, you know how I hate to take this off." Nula reached up for Didi's hand. "I know and I'll pick some up for you, promise. Will you just check my wig, darling?"

"Well, okay, but then leave me alone. You know I hate anyone seeing me like this."

Nula pouted at herself and dipped her fingers into thick moisturizing cream. She hated her big hands, which, even with nail extensions, looked too large and mannish. "Funny the way I keep thinking about her, that Lorraine. Do you think she's a prostitute?"

Didi teased Nula's wig. She was wearing a thick, curly redhaired one, the long straight one thrown to one side. There were lots of wigs of every shape and color, some on wig stands, others bunched up on the floor. "I suppose you could always ask her. She said she'd be there tomorrow. You look lovely, now go on, get out or I'll never be ready."

Left alone, Didi stared at her reflection in the mirror and then, using the tail end of her comb, began to ease the wig meshing from her face. Lorraine had been wrong about Didi having her own hair. It was a wig, a very expensive wig made from real hair, unlike Nula's synthetic crap. The wig was inched slowly away from Didi's face and gently eased back. She checked the meshing, knowing it would need to be cleaned later, and then carefully pinned it to an old cloth-covered wig stand she'd used in some show. She carefully pinned the meshing down, not wanting it to stretch or become wavy; satisfied, she began to remove her makeup. As she drew the tissues across her fine cheeks, she stared at herself, hated what she saw—her own wispy balding head was as bad as Nula's, but unlike Nula she hated to see herself without her tresses.

Half an hour later Nula was on their turf, on Sunset Boulevard, hustlin' her tricks, duckin' and divin' down to the cars that cruised past. Most drivers knew she and Didi were trannies—the area was known for it. Both had their own regular customers and both paid off a regular lookout. Curtis wasn't actually a pimp, more of a minder, but he took a cut of every trick and seemed to know how many johns came and went. But Nula and Didi paid up without argument. It wasn't worth the aggravation to protest. Besides, at times they were grateful for his tips, as he seemed to know in advance when the Vice Squad was in their area.

Tony de Savoy, nicknamed Curtis because he wore his hair like Tony Curtis used to wear his, strolled up smiling warmly. He kissed Holly, his special sweetheart, tapped her tight little ass for her to get moving, then turned to Nula.

"Hi, how you doin'?"

Nula shrugged. "Kinda quiet tonight. Curtis, you know a broad called—oh, I can't remember her name—Lorraine Page. Big tall blonde with a sort of beat-up face?"

"She's not one of mine, why?"

"I just met her tonight, remembered her from someplace."

Holly folded a piece of chewing gum into her baby-doll mouth and chewed hard. Curtis looked at the wrapper she had dropped. "Put it in the trash can, slut."

Holly pouted and bent down exaggeratedly to retrieve it, sashayed past, and flicked it into an overflowing trash can.

Curtis nudged Nula. "She's a looker, isn't she? And with a figure to match. Hey, Holly! Shake that tight ass."

Holly giggled and twisted, showing off her tits, then flounced off, teetering on her high heels, swinging her ass. Holly was heading down Sunset toward her territory. They never or very rarely crossed over. The johns knew where the transsexuals hung out, the whores; they all had their hustler territories marked out.

Nula saw the car cruising and took off as Curtis slipped a comb through his slicked-back hair. "See you later. You just missed a trick—nothing gets by my sweet Holly."

He laughed as Nula started to cross the road toward the john but Holly was ahead of her. "I'll be at the Bar Q," he called out as she sidestepped an oncoming car and gave the finger to the driver.

Nula watched Curtis stroll on down his territory, stopping to chat to his girls. Holly was starting to get into the john's car and Nula hurried across the road after her, giving a quick look back to see if Curtis was still watching. But he was chatting up two black chicks, laughing and still flicking his comb through his grease-mop hair.

"This is mine, Nula baby. He wants a real woman. See ya." Holly laughed as she got into the passenger seat.

Lorraine sat in Rosie's bedroom, telling her about Art and the gallery. She even gave her ten dollars toward the rent.

"So, will you go back for the show?" Rosie asked.

Lorraine pulled off her creased shirt. "Well, he wanted my phone number in case he has some more work, so I think I'll go."

Rosie bashed the pillow. "Put my earrings back in the box! And ask next time—they happen to be real pearls. About the only thing my ex-husband ever gave me . . ."

Lorraine made a show of removing them and replacing them. Rosie watched her every move, irritated yet again by Lorraine's confidence. She seemed to be getting herself back together, but instead of feeling pleased, Rosie felt jealous.

"Maybe I'll come with you."

"Don't go out of your way. What's the matter with you?"

Rosie sat up. "Nothing—but didn't you think I'd be worried? Jake was, too."

Lorraine unzipped her skirt. "Did you send him out to look for me?"

"Of course I did. I didn't know where the fuck you were— no note, nothin' to tell me what you were doing."

Lorraine stepped out of her skirt, and Rosie turned away, not out of embarrassment but with the shock of seeing just how thin and scarred Lorraine was. "What the hell happened to you?" she asked softly. "All those scars . . ."

Lorraine wrapped a towel around herself. "I got them when I was too drunk to feel I was getting them. Some of them are cigarette burns—maybe I did them myself . . ."

Rosie sighed as she heard the shower running. She'd meant to tell Lorraine, and Jake for that matter, that she'd lost her job at the hospital. It was nothing she'd done: they were cutting back on part-time staff.

By the time Lorraine emerged from the shower, however, Rosie was fast asleep. Lorraine turned off the light and went into the living room to turn the sofa into a bed. She sat, still wrapped in her towel, with the TV turned down low, smoking a cigarette. Another day without a drink—and a day when she felt she had done something positive. But what did it all mean, anyway? She closed her eyes as she leaned back. Was every day going to be like this? Tramping from one place to another looking for work? She got to thinking of how much Art and his two helpers had achieved in one evening. They had transformed that shitty little place, not into anything fantastic, but he was going to be able to open a gallery—maybe even make some decent money. What was she cut out to do? She wondered what Nula and Didi did, probably hooking she suspected. Then again, maybe not; they seemed pretty professional about painting the art gallery. Maybe they worked in another gallery or a nightclub. She'd liked them, Art, too, and the music—maybe things *could* get better. . . . Maybe the key was to do as Rosie and Jake said and take each day as it came, not try to think of any long-term goal, just another day—and one without a drink. She was so tired she fell asleep almost immediately, before any pictures of her past had time to squeeze across her mind. She had no way of knowing that her past would catch up with her the longer she remained sober. Old memories long forgotten would resurface to haunt her, like her dead brother's face. She had been able to deal with Kit, but there would be more, much more, and she was not ready for it. The closer the past inched toward the present, the sooner she would have to face what she had obliterated by drinking.

Nula met up with Curtis for breakfast. She hadn't seen Didi for hours, so presumed she had scored either a hotel john or an all-nighter. Curtis was edgy. He'd been looking for Holly and kept asking everyone who came and went if they'd seen her. Nula said she'd seen her score but not since. She could tell he was pretty coked up, so she downed her coffee, paid what she owed him, and took off. It was almost five-thirty and she was feeling strung out, worried that Didi hadn't turned up.

Didi was at home, lying supine with an ice pack on her head. Nula leaned over her, concerned. "You okay?"

Didi removed the ice pack to show a bruised eye. "What do you think? Look at me, I got a black fuckin' eye and my foot, I twisted my ankle when I got out of the car, it's all swollen up."

Nula brought more ice and wrapped it in a dish towel to place on Didi's foot. She was concerned: the bruised face could always be taken care of, but if Didi couldn't walk, that blew it for picking up customers.

Didi sighed, shifting the ice pack on her head. "Oh, I remembered where I saw that Lorraine . . ."

Nula was creaming her face. "Where?"

"AA meeting, we were both there, few days back."

"So, that's that then." Nula wiped the tissue over her chin, looking at the blur of grease and makeup removed from her stubble-free face. She touched the soft skin lovingly; the hormone pills cost a hell of a lot, but they were worth every cent just to feel her skin so smooth. Odd that she hadn't remembered Lorraine from the AA meeting. She was usually good with faces.

"I'm gonna look terrible for the opening," Didi moaned. "Art won't let me in, I'll look so bad—you know the way he is."

Nula looked at her. "I wondered where you'd disappeared to. I was worried, then I thought you might have scored. Curtis was strung out, lookin' everywhere for Holly."

"I couldn't walk, could I? And my face, Jesus Christ, look at my face. Forget being able to score anything looking like this."

"You'll be fine. I'll cover those bruises and your foot'll go down. I remember once I had a john punched me straight in the nose. I thought I was gonna die, two black eyes, but I got a nicer nose afterward. Wonder why she never had that scar fixed?"

Didi stared at her as if she were crazed and then eased the ice pack over her face. She started to cry but Nula said nothing. She put Didi's discarded clothes in the wardrobe with distaste. They were stained and would have to be laundered. Suddenly she saw the car keys on the dressing table and whipped around. She began to panic. Why had she brought the car keys back?

"Where's the car?" she asked and Didi slowly removed the ice pack. "What did you do with the car?"

"I just had to leave it outside, I couldn't walk back."

Nula swore. She could have slapped Didi, but instead she snatched up the keys and walked out slamming the door. Didi flopped back onto the pillows. Sometimes Nula really freaked her—she had no feelings. She cuddled down under the sheets, feeling sorry for herself. Then she felt beneath the pillow for the big topaz ring and slipped it on her finger. It made her feel better, more secure. At least she'd kept that safe, and now she'd gotten it she was going to keep it; it was hers.

The morning was bright and clear with the sun bringing a deep low orange glow that seemed to pinpoint the beige, highly polished metal of the Lincoln. A police car drew alongside it. The two officers noticed it because it was in a no-parking zone. That was the only reason they stopped. One officer got out and looked at the front of the car: he noted down the license plate and returned to his car. He glanced back, which was when he noticed the pink material sticking out from the trunk.

The car had not been reported stolen, but both officers walked over to it. One tried the doors. They were unlocked. He peered inside as the second officer pressed open the trunk.

She lay curled up on her side. One glance was enough. Her face was grotesque, beaten so badly that hardly a feature remained intact, and there was a gaping wound at the back of her skull. No one could have recognized her easily, but the tiny anklet she wore with a name engraved in gold letters made them think she was probably called Holly.

FOUR

Lorraine was up and cleaning the apartment before Rosie was awake. She put some coffee on to brew while she stacked and folded her sheets and bed linen. She had a plastic bag full of laundry ready to take to the laundromat, and was mentally compiling a list of groceries.

Rosie eventually surfaced, glowered, and established her usual early-morning gloom. Lorraine's hyperactivity served only to increase it.

"You want any laundry done?"

"Jesus! I don't know at this hour, do I?" Rosie banged open the cupboards as Lorraine started up the vacuum.

"Can you just *leave* that until I've had my breakfast?"

Lorraine picked up the laundry and walked out. When it had hit spin she took off for the nearest big grocery store. Everything was at a convenient walking distance from Rosie's place, she supposed that was the biggest plus. She could even walk to the art gallery if she felt like using up that much energy.

It had been a very long time since Lorraine had shopped or bothered to choose food. She wandered up and down the avenues of goods, and the effort of concentrating on what she wanted to buy became more and more difficult as the Muzak attacked her in one ear while a bubblegum voice belted out "sales of the day" in the other, enhanced by the high-pitched ping of computer cash registers, a clicking she couldn't identify, bells ringing from checkout people to floor manager as prices were asked, checkout girls screaming conversations, and the peep-peeping of each article as it was passed over the automatic price scanner.

It seemed to Lorraine that she was the only person aware of the sounds. She noticed all the other shoppers were moving like lightning—it seemed that their sole intention was to get from point A to point B at the fastest possible rate. Carts collided; there was heavy breathing from a customer if she took too long weighing food. Not until she got to the freezer section did it occur to her that maybe the customers were moving so fast in the grocery section because they had just suffered frostbite in the arctic temperatures of the frozen-food department. Nothing was familiar; had it really been that long since she had done something as ordinary as going to a grocery store?

No matter how hard she tried, Lorraine could not get the plastic bag open. Her tomatoes were still on the scale as she battled with the bag that, she felt sure, was only a single strip of plastic. "Excuse me, could you show me how to get this open?"

The pink-gingham-clad shelf stocker didn't look up from her task of stamping the canned peas, with what looked like a small machine gun. Now Lorraine knew what the click-click-click noise was and she waited until the gun had ceased firing before she wafted her unopened bag. "Is there a trick to this?"

The assistant stuffed her gun into her pocket, and without uttering a word took the bag, licked her forefinger and thumb, rubbed them over the serrated edge, shook it open, and returned it to Lorraine.

"Very hygienic. Thank you!" Lorraine turned back to her scales with the waiting pound of tomatoes only to discover someone else had tipped them out.

She bought salad, yogurt, fresh fruit, oranges for juice, some whole-wheat bread, cereal, and nuts. She was picking up some cherries when it started. She steadied herself, and pushed her cart over to the freezer section. Her whole body began to shake and she could feel perspiration breaking out all over. As she opened the ice-cream freezer, the gust of chilled air reminded her of the morgue and the first time she had had to take prints from a corpse. She had not shown any disgust, or emotion, but had clung to the fingerprint card and the black ink roller.

"Get the prints, Page, and bring 'em up to records."

Lorraine had lifted the stiffened hand. She was a black woman, about fifty. Lorraine didn't look at her face, but forced herself to concentrate on taking the prints. No sooner had she uncurled one dead finger than it recurled, the woman's hands tightening into fists. Lorraine was unaware that all the team was watching her, giggling like schoolboys as they saw her struggle. Eventually she had forced the woman's hand to lie flat, palm upward, but just as she began to roll on the black ink, it had taken on a life of its own, curling so tightly around Lorraine's fingers that she could not release them. The watching men broke up, and only one of them had the decency to feel sorry for her. He was not much older than she was, but the team had shown him the ropes—unlike Rookie Page: she was to be their entertainment. She watched as he hit the elbow of the deceased, which opened up the fist long enough for prints to be taken. She had laughed, treating it all as a big joke. But she'd had nightmares for weeks of being trapped by the dead in that hideous cold, viselike grip.

"Please shut the freezer doors," snapped a gingham-garbed floor manager as she marched past. Lorraine rested her head against the fridge door, as the sweating subsided, but her hands were shaking. She didn't understand why she had suddenly remembered that incident.

When Lorraine got home, Rosie was looking through the help-wanted ads, checking the possibles. By midafternoon, she had made a few calls, but found no work. She sat watching television and eating the nuts Lorraine had brought home. She paid scant attention to the announcement that a seventeen-year-old girl, Angela Hollow, nicknamed Holly, had been found brutally murdered.

Lorraine blew her hair dry, then rubbed moisturizer over her face and neck, and into her hands. She was sitting on Rosie's bed, smoothing cream into her fingertips when Rookie Lorraine Page appeared again. The rubber gloves she wore to examine a corpse always made her hands dry, and she kept lotion in her locker. The others teased her about it, but it wasn't just the dryness—it was the stench. No matter how fresh the corpse, there was a sickly sweet smell to it. Lorraine never wore perfume, so the moisturizer not only felt good, but smelled clean and fresh. As she massaged her hands, it started again. She was powerless to stop the memories.

They say your first homicide is the one you remember most clearly. Lorraine had been summoned to a domestic and her car had been first on the scene. The small house had looked so neat from the outside, so normal, so quiet that she and her partner had radioed back to base to double-check the address. A neighbor had called to say they had heard screaming and gunfire.

Lorraine tried the front door. It was open. The woman's throat had been slashed, as had her arms and chest. She was wearing a cotton shift, nothing else, and there was so much blood that the material was a bright vermilion. They found her husband in the front bedroom with his head blown apart, the gun still in his hand. Blood had sprayed over the walls and soaked into the blanket on the bed where he was lying. The third body, that of a twelve-year-old girl, was in the back bedroom. She had been killed by a single knife wound to the heart. She was tucked up in the bed, the covers up to her chin, one arm around a doll, as if peacefully asleep. Subsequently, they discovered pornographic material and videos of the child and the dead man. Lorraine never forgot viewing those wretched homemade films, just as she never forgot how innocent the little girl had looked with her doll. She learned from that incident never to judge by appearances: the family with no previous criminal record, the suburban couple with their respectable jobs, played out in secret a despicable game of perversion on their own child. It was a hard and brutal lesson for a twenty-year-old rookie cop. Worse followed, but sitting in front of Rosie's dressing table, the memory of that first suicide/murder came vividly back. Lorraine felt icy cold, as if she were standing in the morgue, as if the child's murder had just happened, as if the little girl was calling out to her.

Rooney stared at the body, moving around the stretcher, pulling at his nose. The hammer blows to her face had broken both cheeks, her nose, and the right side of her jaw. The wound to the back of her head would have killed her, as it had cracked open her skull. She had no other body scars, no new skin abrasions or bruising, and her fingernails were intact, but there was evidence of previous beatings. At seventeen years of age,

Angela Hollow, blond, about five feet seven, with a good figure, had three previous arrests for prostitution.

Rooney thanked the morgue attendant and returned to his office. Bean was waiting. He had interviewed Holly's pimp and four other girls who had seen her on the evening of her death. No one had seen the man who had picked her up, but one witness remembered the metallic beige car. They had not glimpsed the driver as he had been on the far side of the road. All they remembered was seeing Holly cross the road at about nine-thirty. She had not been seen since. Holly was picked up on Sunset but the car had been left over an hour's drive away, not far from Rooney's Japanese restaurant. He mused her name was Holly and they'd found her on Holly; he wondered if there was a connection, but doubted it.

Rooney looked through the statements and tossed over the file he had been given by his friend Colin Sparks. "Have a look at that, Josh. I want the blood group checked out against that girl we got and on the Hastings guy."

Bean left the office, but returned immediately with a lengthy internal fax. "You better look this over, it just came in."

Rooney nodded. "Angela Hollow. It's a fucking hammer again."

As he went out, Bean heard Rooney swearing. The fax sheets were the result of his previous evening's calls. Three more girls, in different areas over a period of seven years, had all been killed by hammer blows to the back of the head, and suffered severe facial injuries. All were hookers of different ages, their bodies left in the trunk of a stolen vehicle. No witnesses. Each case left open on file. Three murders, Angela Hollow made it four and Maria Valez five, the woman from the Paradise Apartments, still unidentified, six, and if the killer had also murdered Norman Hastings it was now seven. If they had all been killed by the same man, as Rooney began to suspect, he had better start gathering the evidence to link them together. He was now about to launch a multiple-murder inquiry. He pulled his pants up over his belly and peered at the street map on his wall. A few were obviously in and around the same area, his fucking territory, but others were not. He glared at the map and began to draw circles with a red felt-tipped pen.

Later that afternoon he got the first verification. The blood found inside the stolen Hastings car matched the retained blood sample from the murder case handed to him by Sparks. The killer of Maria Valez had left no other incriminating evidence behind, but Rooney made a note that she had, like the woman in Hastings's car, put up a struggle. According to the autopsy reports, she had clawed and scratched her assailant: blood samples had been taken from beneath her fingernails. None of the other women had had a chance to struggle: they had been efficiently killed by the blow to the back of their heads.

Rooney summoned Mr. and Mrs. Summers again, hoping they would not identify the corpse from the Paradise Apartments as the woman they had seen in the mall parking lot. If it were not her, then what they had witnessed in the Glendale shopping mall, the woman struggling in Norman Hastings's car, was a failed murder attempt, possibly by the same killer. It also meant that Cinderella was still alive and could be a vital witness—or accomplice.

As they had been throughout, Mr. and Mrs. Summers were eager to give every assistance. They had never been to a morgue before or played a part in any criminal investigation, let alone a murder inquiry. Rooney decided they should see the body together, and he accompanied them into the viewing room.

"Okay, she's behind the curtain. We can turn her around, get any side you want to see, right or left. You just take your time . . ." He pressed the buzzer for the curtain to be moved away from the window.

The dead woman had been cleaned up, her hair washed and combed, and they had also had her face repaired, covered and filled in by a qualified cosmetic mortician. A little trace of makeup served only to enhance the deathly pallor and her eyes were closed.

Mrs. Summers let out a gasp. She stepped closer, but her husband remained where he was, staring through the window. It was the husband Rooney concentrated on; he had been close to the woman for longer and had spoken to her.

"Yes," said Mrs. Summers.

"I don't know . . ." said her husband.

"It's her—look at her hair, it's the same hair."

"Maybe."

Mrs. Summers turned to Rooney. "I'm sure it's her."

Rooney nodded, then looked at Mr. Summers. "What do you think? We can turn her around if you like?"

"No, no, I think my wife is right. She's the woman I saw."

Rooney asked if he was positive that it was the woman he had tried to help in the parking lot the afternoon of May 17.

"Yes," Mr. Summers said firmly.

Rooney returned to his office. Bean was waiting for him: he had received confirmation via police records, and they now had an ID of the victim. The dead woman Mr. and Mrs. Summers had just identified was Helen Murphy, age thirty-nine, a prostitute, mother of three children, all in foster care. Murphy had been reported missing three weeks before she was found.

The Summerses' misidentification meant that Rooney and his team were no longer looking for Lorraine. Instead, they focused on trying to find a link between the dead women and Norman Hastings.

But Rooney was still not satisfied. He looked over the report and asked if dental records were available, remembering that the cabdriver had said the woman had a front tooth missing. Helen Murphy had false teeth. Rooney was anxious to bring the cabdriver in to view the body. He was not as positive as the Summerses: she was similar and had the same coloring, he said. Eventually, he agreed that it was probably the woman he had picked up. Rooney conceded that Helen Murphy was the woman from the Glendale shopping mall parking lot, which meant there would be no further visits to Rosie's address. That line of inquiry was now closed.

It was five o'clock when Rooney faced his team. He had requested extra officers and an incident room. They waited patiently as he shuffled his papers. "Okay, this is Helen Murphy," he began. "Prostitute, blond, age thirty-nine, body found in the grounds of the derelict Paradise Apartments. She had been dumped in the trunk of a wrecked car and had been there for approximately two to three days. A kid lifted her body out of the trunk of the car, he said, wanting to give her mouth-to-mouth resuscitation, which he'd been learnin' at swimming lessons! But we found nothin' on the kid, so if he did steal from her body we'll never know."

The men stared at the blown-up pictures. Next to appear were Angela Hollow and the stolen vehicle, then Maria Valez, and three more unidentified females. Lastly, there was a photograph of Norman Hastings and his car.

Rooney paused as the men murmured and made notes. "Okay. Obviously the Norman Hastings killing is different because he's male. Maybe the car was stolen and Hastings managed to see or catch the thief. Either way, he was killed with a similar weapon to that used on each of the others: a claw hammer. We know it's not the same weapon—some of the impressions taken from the women are of different dimensions, but all of them have been hammered in the face, and the claw section used for one blow at the back of the skull, near the base. When the victim is face downward, the claw hammer strikes and gets drawn upward, leaving, as you can see, one hell of an open wound."

Rooney waited as they took it all in, then began again. "The women are all prostitutes, all with records, obviously all blond. Never any witnesses. Nobody has ever come forward with any motive, and so far we haven't found a link between the women, apart from their line of business and the fact they were tall, blond, and—apart from the last girl, Angela Hollow, nicknamed Holly—all dogs."

Rooney continued for another hour, explaining the Summerses' part in the inquiry and Hastings's missing wallet. He concluded with the description of the man driving Hastings's stolen car. The man they were hunting, he pointed out, would have a bad bite mark on his neck, close to the jugular, according to Helen Murphy. He tapped the dead woman's face, presuming now that she was the woman to make the anonymous call to the station.

"Our first hammer killing comes in 1986, the next 1987, then 1988, 1991, which was Maria Valez, and the last two, Helen Murphy and Angela Hollow, plus Hastings, are all within months, if not days of each other. We've got a gap between 1988 and 1991, unless more come to light. Let's hope to God they don't—and let's give this all we've got."

One young, eager-faced officer asked where they were going to start and Rooney, unsure himself, snapped that as the victims were hookers, they should start by asking on the streets, in the brothels. To begin with, he wanted it kept low-key, and until they had more evidence, he wanted the press kept out for as long as possible.

· · ·

Rooney returned to his office feeling worn out and hungry. Bean got there ahead of him, and was waiting, his hands stuffed into his pockets, staring from the window down to the Plaza Mall. He jumped when Rooney barked out, "You feel like some Jap food?"

Bean didn't, but agreed to accompany Rooney, because he wanted to tell him he didn't think they should keep it from the press.

As they got into the car, Rooney gave him a sidelong look. "What's the problem?"

"Well, I don't think we should keep this quiet. We could have a multiple killer on the loose! Those gaps between the murders, what if our man was in prison?"

"Whoever the fuck he is, he's on the loose now."

"That's my point, Captain. He killed Norman Hastings, Helen Murphy, Angela Hollow within weeks of each other. Even if it's just hookers he's taking out, the street girls should be warned. I mean, they're not all from Pasadena."

As Bean expected, Rooney dismissed this. "We get the fuckin' press in on this, they'll blow it up all out of proportion. This way it's giving us time to make some headway, because we have fuck all, but—"

"A pretty tight description. Somebody somewhere knows a guy with a fucking bite out of his neck."

Rooney started the engine. "*That* we never put out, else we'll have Dracula and his uncle wastin' our time. . . . The guys on the street can put the word out to the whores, but you know as well as me, nothin' stops them. They'll keep on trading no matter who we say is out there." He turned the car and prepared to drive out of the police parking lot.

"Who do you think is out there, Captain?" Bean ran his finger around the neck of his tight-fitting shirt collar.

"Someone with a hatred of tall, skinny, blond whores—how the fuck do I know? You got his description, what do you think?"

"I dunno."

"Right, you don't know, nobody knows. They may give us all the psychological profiles from so-called professors, why he kills, what he gets out of it. But when you say: 'Okay, where do I find the guy?' they don't fuckin' know. The truth is, Lieutenant, they can pinpoint or direct us to a psycho, because he's obvious. But our man, he's not obvious; he's cool.

It looks like he's been getting away with it for years. It don't even run to a pattern because of Norman Hastings, who was a straight, decent guy.''

They drove out of the lot in silence. Then Bean sighed. ''Killer obviously has a thing about hookers. . . .''

Rooney snorted. ''So maybe his mother or his wife was one. Then you can say he's killing her. Bullshit. I hated my mother but that don't make me want to kill every square-faced, red-haired tyrant, now does it?''

He drew up outside the Kwoks Kwok and switched off the engine. He was beginning to wish he hadn't asked Bean along. ''That means he's just taking out his hammer whenever he feels like it. Now shut up, I'm hungry and I don't wanna talk about it.'' Rooney got out, locked the car, and caught sight of Art's Gallery. ''Christ, how did that spring up? It was an old real estate agency yesterday.''

He wandered over to look: inside were a lot of people rapping and drinking, arty types, not his sort. A cab drew up and more guests began heading inside. A good-looking coiffured man in a pale blue denim outfit paid off the driver, adjusted his shades, and followed his two tanned friends into the gallery as Rooney walked into his favorite restaurant. Art screamed out a welcome to his friend Craig Lyall and drew him into the throng.

Some time later, Jake arrived with Rosie and Lorraine. They pulled up and parked behind Rooney's car. Jake was wearing a cheap suit with a nylon shirt and wide flowered tie, Rosie a tent-type dress that accentuated rather than hid her bulk, various bead necklaces that clicked as she walked, and a pair of leather sandals. Lorraine had on the same fawn skirt, now pressed, her black crepe blouse, and the safari-style jacket draped around her shoulders. This evening she wore sling-back high heels, and appeared even taller and thinner than usual. Her makeup was as sparse as ever, and, as Rosie had refused to let her borrow the pearl studs, she had no jewelry. Art made a great fuss over her when she walked in, telling her she looked simply wonderful, and that her friends were more than welcome.

An attractive gay young man was drifting around with a tray of wine. Lorraine was about to accept a glass when Jake asked loudly for mineral water and she quickly withdrew her hand. The three of them stood a little self-consciously at the doorway to the main room, which was crowded with guests.

"Do you want to see the paintings?" asked Lorraine.

"Are there any?" Rosie couldn't see a single canvas as they edged farther inside.

Nula beckoned Lorraine and took hold of her hand. "Didi remembered where we'd seen you—at a meeting!"

Lorraine was puzzled, then she understood. She looked at her glass of water, noting that Nula had one, too. She asked about Didi and Nula told her about the twisted ankle. Nula was as outrageously dressed as when they had first met, and her perfume was overpowering.

"Oh, I'm sorry, after all her hard work, too. Have many pictures been sold?"

Nula shrugged. "I hope so. Art is broke, but then, aren't we all?"

Lorraine looked across at Rosie and Jake standing exactly where she had left them. "Come and meet my friends?"

Jake was polite, but Rosie stared, looking up at Nula with such obvious fascination that Lorraine felt uncomfortable, but Nula didn't seem to mind. She chatted on about the gallery, how much work she and Didi had done, and how marvelous Lorraine had been. "Were you an actress?" she asked Lorraine suddenly.

Lorraine smiled. "No, I wasn't."

"What do *you* do?" asked Rosie bluntly.

Nula cocked her head to one side and smiled. "Anyone who hires me, dear."

Rosie wasn't sure what she meant and didn't care, she was hot and her feet hurt. She caught Jake's eye. "Look, I don't think this was such a good idea, why don't we leave?"

Jake looked at Lorraine. "Okay by me. Lorraine?"

They were about to walk out when Art caught Lorraine's hand and drew her toward some of his friends. Rosie and Jake waited for ten minutes beside the car before Lorraine appeared. "You two go on, I'll stay for a while longer. Art needs me to help out a little."

Jake opened the driver's door and was about to get into the car when a big potbellied man walked out of the Japanese restaurant, accompanied by a fresh-faced younger man with a crew cut and glasses. The older man was deep in conversation while searching in his pockets for his car keys, yet he couldn't help but see Lorraine, who was only yards ahead of him. Jake saw the way Rooney looked, then looked again. He stopped talking in midsentence, as if surprised, or shocked. Jake couldn't make out which.

"Lorraine?" Rooney called out loudly.

She half turned and took a sharp involuntary step back, bumping into Rosie.

"It is you, Lorraine, isn't it?" Rooney stepped closer.

Jake noticed the way she straightened her shoulders, clenched her fists.

"Lorraine," Rooney repeated again. He couldn't stop staring—it was like seeing a ghost. Was it her? Or was he mistaken? Then she tilted her head, gave that sidelong look, and he knew for sure. He said emphatically, but flatly, "It's Lorraine Page." She gave a barely detectable nod and hurried back inside the gallery. Rooney watched her go, then stared directly at Jake and Rosie. "Evening."

Rosie heaved herself into the car. Jake slammed his door, still observing Rooney as he walked around to his own car.

"What was that all about?" Rosie asked.

Jake shrugged as Rooney drove away. "He's a cop, so is the guy with him. The big fat guy is Bill Rooney, a real mean shit."

Rosie was astonished. "My, I have never heard you talk like that!"

"Well, maybe there's a lot about me you don't know. I guess there is about your roommate, too. That fat prick busted me, maybe he arrested her, too. Looked like he knew Lorraine from someplace she didn't want to be remembered bein' in."

He drove a few yards, then stopped. "Maybe I should go back, see if she's okay. She looked kinda shook up." He was about to reverse when Lorraine walked out of the gallery with Nula as a taxi drew up.

Jake set off again. "You know any more about her? She ever mention some money she had? Remember that night she came back, when she said she'd fallen? She had a lot of money on her then."

Rosie looked out of the window. "She told me she sold off some things a friend was keeping for her, somebody called Sonja. Jake, I think I'm gonna ask her to leave. There's something about her—I dunno, but she's . . ."

"Tough?" said Jake.

"Yes, with a selfish streak, too. I mean, I kind of admire

the way she's getting herself together, but I know as much about her now as I did when I first met her. Sometimes I get the feeling she doesn't want anyone to know her.''

"That cop knew her. He knew her very well.''

Rooney turned off the ignition outside Bean's apartment. "She was picked up for prostitution. Last time they put her in a straitjacket, she was that crazy.''

Bean had his hand on the door handle. "She looked straightened out tonight.''

Rooney nodded. "Yeah, she sure as hell did. Tonight I didn't get that close a view, but she was one hell of a looker back then—never fooled around, well, not that I knew of. I think she even had a couple of kids, married to a lawyer, but whatever she was, she blew it. That lady sure as hell hit the skids.''

Bean opened the door. He was barely interested in ex-Lieutenant Lorraine Page, but Rooney seemed eager to continue. "Killed an unarmed kid.'' He shook his head. "Six bullets, emptied the fucking thirty-eight into him—and you know what sickened me? She was laughing, no kidding, meant fuck all to her. She was pissed—she was a lush. I kinda thought she must be dead by now . . .''

"Good night,'' said Bean, stepping out of the car. He wished he'd stuck to his guns and refused the raw fish Rooney had plied him with. He felt sick and it was either the fish or that weird Japanese beer he'd swilled it down with.

Rooney remained deep in thought. He could still picture her curled up on the washroom floor, skirt up around her thighs. That was the last time he'd seen her, so drunk she couldn't even stand. That half smile on her face had been the same half smile she had given him tonight.

Lorraine looked around Nula's strange apartment with its outrageously theatrical living room. She knew this old building. When she was on the force, it used to have some drug dealers living there. Now it had been cleaned up and was, she remembered, more of an artist's colony—Nula and Didi's taste certainly suited it. There were drapes and frills, mock leopard skin sofa and chairs, fur rugs, and huge paintings of nude female couples with male genitals displayed in provocative poses. Just as she was wondering idly if Nula and Didi had been totally transformed or if they still had their cocks, Nula came out of the bedroom. "Something terrible happened to a friend of ours."

A limping, sniffling Didi appeared, wearing dark glasses, dressed in a scarlet silk kimono, a clutch of tissues in her hand. She wore a tight turban wrapped around her head and no makeup. "She was a friend, only seventeen. They found her locked in the trunk of a car. She'd been hammered to death, not a feature left intact. . . . Now what pig-shit bastard could do a thing like that?"

Nula suddenly started sobbing loudly. "We saw her last night—I was standing an' talking to her. Holly was so cute, so nice . . ."

Lorraine listened as they wept and wailed. She didn't know who they were talking about. She tried twice to interject and ask if they'd like her to leave, but they seemed unaware she was in the apartment. Of the two Didi seemed more upset, and it was Nula who eventually turned to Lorraine. "I'm glad you're here, help take our minds off it, she was only a kid. . . . Didi, we gotta keep busy. Let's feed this babe— come on, get that apron on."

Didi nodded, blew her nose, and wiped her eyes without removing the glasses. "I must look terrible, I feel terrible, I feel naked without my hair on, but I just couldn't do a thing."

Didi scurried into the kitchen and Nula sniffed loudly. Her mascara had run and she spat on a tissue to wipe beneath her eyes. "I'm sorry, you must think we're crazies. But you know, it was the shock, knowing her and . . ."

Nula looked toward the kitchen. She leaned forward, tapping Lorraine's knee with her fingertip. "She'll be okay now. She's really upset, but I can always cheer her up. We're very old friends, been together for years—we met in a show. It's always good to have one good friend, know what I mean?"

Lorraine wasn't so sure. Nula's deep, gravel voice was sometimes hard to listen to, even more so now that she'd removed her wig like she'd done the first time they'd met. She was remarkably unself-conscious about the thinning hairline. Lorraine wondered if she knew how masculine she looked without her tresses as she watched Nula make trips back and forth from the kitchen to talk to Didi. Twice Nula came back and pulled a face at Lorraine, taking some more tissues in to Didi who was obviously still very tearful.

Didi cooked a delicious dinner and set a table with candles. Lorraine noticed she was the domestic one in the couple, fussing over which glasses they should use, which napkins and place mats, as slowly the initial shock of Holly's death subsided. Their conversation turned to their friend Art: the fact that he was a genius photographer, his boyfriends, his bankruptcy, his inability to stay in business.

Nula gestured to their apartment. "This was his, then he made a stack of bread and he *gave* this to us and even when he's been broke and desperate, he has *never* asked us to leave."

Lorraine nodded. The place was a nightmare, but that was just her taste, and she was enjoying the outrageousness of the pair, swapping stories, jokes about old times when they'd been dancers. They didn't speak of the present, but out came albums and old programs. Eventually they seemed to talk themselves into silence. The subtle music, playing throughout, was switched off, and Lorraine took her cue to leave. She stood up, smiling her thanks.

"How long have you been dry?" asked Nula, the question coming out of the blue.

" 'Bout two and a half months."

Nula laughed and told Lorraine that she had been dry eight years, Didi four. She looked at Didi, and then pursed her lips. They constantly interacted, exchanging sly looks, often picking up on each other's sentences. Didi shrugged and Nula cocked her head to one side.

"I suppose we should tell you we're whores—you've probably put two and two together anyway. We both drank to get the balls, if you'll excuse the pun—it takes a lot of guts to do what we do, and to do it in drag, and with a 'fuck you' attitude, know what I mean?"

Lorraine didn't but she nodded as they linked arms. Nula, head and shoulders taller than Didi, seemed to be almost protecting her. Didi gave a watery smile.

"It's just that we'd prefer you to hear it from us rather than anyone else—and we'd like to see you again. What we're trying to tell you is don't be shy about anythin'. We all been drunks, right? And we think we've got your number."

Lorraine was taken aback when Nula released her arm from

Didi and crossed to stand close, too close, slipping an arm around her shoulders. She was wearing the same heavy scent Lorraine had noticed in Art's gallery and, close to, it was overpowering.

"Listen, I got contacts who could put some work your way, straight, decent johns, all you gotta do is ask."

Lorraine did a neat sidestep, saying that she had some work lined up, and thanked them again. They insisted she take a cab home and Didi limped over to the phone and called for one to pick her up outside the apartment. She hadn't meant to sound so cool, be so distant, but they were touching on that hazy part of her life that remained unreal, the part she hadn't yet faced up to. At the same time, she couldn't help but feel angry that they seemed to know she'd been a hooker. Somehow she had felt that no one could or would suspect that.

Nula kissed her cheeks. "You come by any time, and keep it in mind, if you need cash to tide you over, we can always get you a few clients. Don't you be all shy, you just come out with it, you can be our friend, right, Didi?"

Didi nodded her head. "Yeah, and we got a lot of contacts."

"I'll think about it."

Lorraine was relieved to get away from them, from the cloying perfume. Yet they had, unknowingly, helped her over a hurdle she had dreaded. Seeing Bill Rooney again had been like a punch in the stomach, so totally unexpected that she had been unable to speak, or even acknowledge him. The humiliation of the meeting made her feel physically sick. The cab fare took the last of her earnings from the gallery but she didn't care. One thing she knew for certain, she couldn't turn tricks again. There'd been a lot of times in the past when she'd ended up looking like Didi after a night with a rough john.

Each step up to Rosie's apartment was an effort, and the last person she wanted to be confronted by was Rosie sitting like a Buddha watching a mind-numbing game show. Lorraine shut the door and headed for the bathroom. The television was clicked off, ominously.

"We got to talk."

Lorraine hesitated. "Yes, I know, but I need a shower first." The television clicked back on. When she returned to the living room, wrapped in just a towel, off went the television. "Just let me get a drink." Lorraine slammed the fridge shut. It was empty. "Thanks! Thanks a fuckin' bundle!"

Rosie smirked. "Now you know what it feels like!"

"So you did it on purpose? You big fat pig, I bought enough to last days—"

"Oh, yeah!" Rosie sniggered. "Well, who the hell do you think has been filling up that fucking fridge since you arrived?"

Lorraine turned on her. "Jesus Christ, I've *given* you money!"

Rosie pulled herself up. "An' I gave you a roof over your head, and my bed when you were sick. I fed you, washed you—and not once did you have the decency to say thank you!"

"So now you want me out of here, is that it?" Lorraine sighed.

"Why don't you get off your high horse and be real?" Rosie retaliated. "I'm honest with you, when are you going to level with me?" Her fat body quivered, her pudgy hands rammed onto her hips.

"Level with you about what?"

"Who you are for starters!" Rosie shouted.

Lorraine lifted her arms in exasperation. "You know who I am! I've fucking told you who I am! *I am Lorraine Page!*"

"That's not enough. I knew your name at the hospital. It's like I live with somebody I don't know, and I can't take it."

Lorraine lit a cigarette and closed her eyes. She sat on the edge of the easy chair. "Rosie, I can't tell you much because I don't know who I am. I am trying to find out who the fuck I am, so if I don't know, how am I supposed to tell you?" She got up and paced the room, taking long drags on her cigarette. "I look in the mirror and I don't know if this is the way I always looked. I see scars all over my body, and I don't know who put them there. I don't even know how I got this!" She pulled her hair away from the jagged scar on her face. "I got marks all over my body. I can see them, you can see them—but what about the ones inside my brain? There are whole years of my life missing, and sometimes I just don't know if I *want* to find out everything."

Rosie nodded, suddenly concerned. "How about tonight? You seemed pretty shook up." Rosie waited but there was no reply. "That man this evening, the fat guy, he said your name three times. Do you know who he was?"

"Yeah."

"So why don't you start telling me? No? Okay, I'll make it easier. He's a cop, Jake knew him. Now if you've been in prison, it doesn't worry me—just tell me, 'cos I'd like to know."

Lorraine gave a soft, humorless laugh. "You see, you didn't believe me. I told you back at the hospital, Rosie. I told you what I was."

Rosie stared as Lorraine sat down, rested her head against the chair, and closed her eyes. "I was a cop, Rosie. In fact, I was a lieutenant, and that fat man you saw tonight used to be my sergeant. His name is William—Bill—Rooney. He looked surprised, huh? Seeing me? Maybe because he thought I was dead, probably hoped I was . . ."

"Why did you leave?" Rosie asked.

"I was kicked out—because I was a drunk." In a low, expressionless voice she began to tell Rosie about her husband, her two daughters, the divorce, her husband's remarriage, his custody of the girls whom she had not seen for almost six years. "After the divorce I went on a binge. It kind of lasted until you found me. I sold everything—apartment, furniture. The car was taken because I was caught drunk-driving. I got off with a fine. I got away with a lot of things, I guess, for the next few years. I don't remember much of it, just that eventually all the money ran out and when I had nothing left to sell . . ." She coughed, a smoker's cough that made her body shake and her eyes run.

Rosie waited, watching as Lorraine lit another cigarette from the stub. "So, go on, when you had nothing else to sell, then what?"

Lorraine gave her that odd, tilted, squint look. "I sold myself, Rosie—to anyone, anything, anyplace, just so long as I got a drink. I worked for the pimps I'd arrested, and got drunk with the whores I'd booked. I ended up in shit holes, bars, and flophouses. And I hardly remember a day of it. I got arrested for whoring, I got picked up for vagrancy. By the time I was hit by the truck—when I was taken to the hospital—I think I had reached a sort of dead-end hell. That's it. That's who I am, Rosie. Now you're as up-to-date as I am."

Rosie began to make Lorraine's bed. It was a sickening story, but not one that she hadn't heard before: everyone she knew at the meetings, including herself, had a similar story of loss and desperation. What was different about Lorraine, however, was her complete lack of emotion when relating it.

Lorraine slipped into the freshly made-up sofa and sighed contentedly, laying her head on her arm. "I'm thinking . . ." she said softly.

"What about?" asked Rosie.

"Well, I'm not sure about bothering to get myself back together. Who am I doing it for? Be okay if I felt good, or if I felt I was doing it for a reason. But there's no reason."

Rosie stood, elephantine, in the bedroom doorway. "Maybe because it's your life. Or perhaps it's those two little girls." Lorraine said nothing, so Rosie continued: "My mother died when I was ten and there's a hell of a lot I would have liked to ask her—like who the fuck in my family did I inherit this fat from? My dad was skin and bone. And I'd like to know if she loved me. She took an overdose, you see, killed herself."

Lorraine propped herself up on her elbow. "You know, Rosie, sometimes I sort of loathe you, especially in the mornings, but if I forget to say thank you, then I'm sorry. I've got no one else who gives a shit about me, no other place to go. So thank you for being my friend."

Rosie blushed. "Good night, Lorraine."

Lorraine heard her move heavily into the bedroom, and then lay back staring up at the ceiling. Her daughters had had a new mother for five years, and they probably weren't even little anymore. They probably wouldn't want to see her. She didn't even know where they lived.

It hurt to remember, physically hurt, as if each memory was so tightly stored away she had to squeeze it out. It was strange, because instead of being able to conjure up her own daughters' faces, she saw only the little girl she had once been assigned to trace. Laura Bradley, six years old, who had last been seen waiting outside school for her mother. Lorraine, the officer in charge of searching the school outbuildings and cellars, had found Laura's naked body stuffed into one of the big air-conditioning pipes. Like a rag doll, so tiny, so helpless, yet her body had felt warm and Lorraine had tried mouth-to-mouth resuscitation. But nothing brought her back to life; even when she had felt the small rib cage lifting, it was not Laura breathing, it was Lorraine's own breath.

Lorraine got out of bed and began to pace the room. Why? Why was she suddenly remembering this child? Laura Bradley had been brutally sexually abused, her injuries so horrific that all the officers on the case were sickened; Lorraine recalled seeing even the big, blustering Bill Rooney weeping. Obsessed with catching the killer, she worked day and night and had no time to spare for her own daughters. She had shouted at her husband that the girls were never to be left alone for an instant, and made sure the baby-sitter was always waiting to pick them up from their nursery school.

She poured herself a glass of water. She remembered yelling in fury at Mike, "I'm trying to find Laura Bradley's killer. You may not think that is important, but you didn't hold her dead body in your arms. I did. And I will not sleep until I have that bastard locked away so my daughters and every kid in this neighborhood can be safe."

Mike had tried to make her rest, but Lorraine had kept up one hell of an investigation and she wouldn't let it go. From day one she had been suspicious of the school janitor and she kept up the pressure. Intuition told her she had the right man. Even her chief hinted that perhaps she should back off, but she refused, returning time and again to the scene of the crime and to the janitor's home, until, in yet another confrontation when she had shown him Laura Bradley's clothes, all her photographs, when she had interrogated him for more than six hours, she finally broke him. He admitted his guilt. She had been so proud, and she had been promoted. Laura Bradley could at last rest in peace.

Lorraine felt chilled now, remembering the visit of the young uniformed officer to Rosie's apartment, asking about the night she had returned after the attack in the parking lot, how she had substituted the dead child's name for her own. She had uttered it without a moment's thought. Now she realized just how often in that long-distant past she had placed her work above the needs of her own children and husband. Mike had been right. She had become obsessive. She had also become addicted to the adrenaline, the excitement, the tension, and the pressure—until she had found it impossible to relax.

She returned to bed and sat for a moment staring at the wall. Maybe Rosie was right, maybe she should try to contact them again. She would like to explain things to Sally and Julia, perhaps even ask for their forgiveness. Yes, her life *was* worth bothering about, even if it was just to make peace with her children and Mike. Feeling calmer, she turned off the lamp, snuggled down, and was asleep within moments.

This was the first time she had dealt with a part of her past without getting the shakes. She had gone over it in her mind and remained calm. Forced herself to hold on, remain distant from it. It was another step forward in her rehabilitation.

But to Rosie she had spoken about her past as if she was talking about another person, another Lorraine. She hadn't cried or, to Rosie, appeared to feel remorse or guilt. Instead, there was a cold confidence, a control that seemed to be getting stronger, as if she were divorcing herself from the past. What she was not doing, which Rosie had surmised, was facing the full reality.

Rosie knew how harsh that reality was. Unlike Lorraine, she couldn't sleep. Instead, she was mulling over what she had been told. At some stage in her own recovery, Rosie, like Lorraine, had asked herself if remaining sober, facing what she was and what she had lost, was worth all the trouble and the pain. Sober, she felt, she had nothing to live for. It had been Jake who had said her life was worth fighting for, for the sake of her son. She had tried to contact Joey, and she had felt really positive, but it had been a disaster. Rosie had been, and was still, unable to cope with the emotional strain of seeing her son, of knowing there was another woman he called mother. She could not cope with talking to her ex-husband, or seeing the new home he had made for himself and their boy. As it all swept over her once more, she began to feel guilty about opening up the same terrible emotional road for Lorraine.

She crept out of bed. If Lorraine was awake she would tell her that she should take more time before she tried to confront her lost family. She was wrong to push her, she wasn't experienced enough, and maybe this wall of control Lorraine was building around herself was good, and safer for her than allowing anybody like Rosie or Jake to break it down. But Lorraine was sleeping, one hand tucked under her chin, only the strange, jagged scar running from her eye to her cheek marring her look of innocence. She seemed peaceful, a half smile on her lips.

Rosie made a vow. She would not ask Lorraine to leave the apartment: it was important for her to have a sense of security. Lorraine was her friend. That settled, Rosie went back to bed, swiped at her pillow, and, within seconds, passed into a deep sleep.

FIVE

Lorraine tried again to find work, but it was not until the first week of July that she managed to get a job in a florist's shop. It was only short-term, replacing a sales clerk who was on vacation. She also did four nights at Art's gallery, since he stayed open until ten in the evening. He was rarely there, and she was often alone waiting for the odd customer. A number of paintings had been sold, but business was not exactly flourishing. Art was mostly out looking for new pictures, but whenever he saw her, he greeted her with affection.

The week was good because she was occupied, and with the little money she earned she bought two more outfits at a garage sale. Nula and Didi dropped in for chats, and always brought some homemade banana bread with them. Didi was no longer wearing dark glasses, but she was still limping, yet she refused to see a doctor. The two transsexuals admired Lorraine's taste in clothes and discussed secondhand bargains they'd bought. Because of their size they often found it difficult to get really stylish clothes, especially shoes. Lorraine was looking better and feeling stronger every day. Her sweats were less frequent and she had put on weight.

Rosie had rented a computer and printer and started doing clerical work at home. They began a routine of sharing the cleaning and laundry. Lorraine contributed toward the rent and groceries. It meant that at the end of the week, after she had bought her cigarettes and clothes, she had little left. But what was left, she saved.

When the florist job ended, Lorraine asked Art if he could use her for a few more hours. Since more paintings had been sold, and he had discovered a new artist, he took her on for two full days a week, plus the four evenings. There were so few customers she didn't know how the gallery paid for itself let alone paid her salary. On her way to and from work she had to pass Fit as a Fiddle, now called Fit 'N' Fast, and decided to join one of their classes. She only managed the first ten minutes of the step class before she felt her energy give way. However, she began to practice in the empty gallery with a stack of telephone books and slowly built up her strength, stepping up and down until her legs felt like jelly.

Every day Lorraine would use Art's telephone to try and trace her ex-husband. She called a number of Mike Pages, but so far she had been unsuccessful. He had disappeared. Rosie, using the telephone directory for her clerical work, noticed the pages folded down on the name Page. She surmised that Lorraine was trying to trace her husband. One evening as they sat watching TV, Rosie gave Lorraine a sidelong look. "So, you haven't found him yet?"

Lorraine was about to ask what she was talking about but Rosie nodded at the telephone directory.

"You don't miss much, do you, Rosie? Well, yeah, I've sort of been trying. I was gonna try the Bar Association: if he was still practicing, they would know his address, but I don't know . . ."

Rosie nodded, seemingly intent on the TV program. "Yeah, well, you take your time. You'll need to be strong, you know, and I'd just take it all a day at a time."

That night, as Rosie slept, Lorraine took out a scrap of paper. She'd lied, she didn't know why, she just didn't want Rosie to know she had found Mike. Mike Page was living in Santa Monica. She had not spoken to him directly, but to a secretary, who confirmed that he had two daughters, Julia and Sally. Before the secretary could ask her any questions, Lorraine had hung up.

It was a Friday evening, mid-July, boiling hot outside and just as hot inside, two weeks since Lorraine had found Mike's office number. She had put off getting in touch, always making the excuse that she didn't have enough money to get the bus

to Santa Monica—and she was still in need of better clothes.
She arrived home with a banana bread made by Didi and some
fresh fruit. She was flushed from walking. It had been a full
day of exercise: she had done a light workout with Hector, the
owner of Fit 'N' Fast, who had put together a beginner's program for her, starting with small weights to build up the at-
rophied muscles in her arms and legs.

Rosie peered up from a mountain of brown envelopes and
watched as Lorraine removed boxes and boxes of vitamins
from her bag. Hector had taken to giving them to her free
because most were samples. He had suggested she take vitamins E, C, D, and B12, and, with her past record of alcohol
abuse, zinc. They all knew about Lorraine's drinking problem—Nula had told them—but Lorraine didn't mind. It was
easier that everyone knew, and besides, as none of them drank
she was never tempted.

"I see we've been to the hairdresser—or did Hector turn
his muscular body to that, too?" Rosie smirked.

"No, I had it done near the gallery." She still had the short-
cropped cut, but she'd had new streaks put in.

Rosie licked a few more envelopes, slapping them down.
She didn't say how good Lorraine looked because she was
jealous. Lorraine was changing before her eyes. She was
lightly tanned from all her walking back and forth to the gallery, and whereas before she had seemed to shuffle, head bent
forward, shoulders rounded, now she was straight-backed and
looking fit.

Lorraine counted her money, putting some aside for Rosie.
Then she went into the bedroom and opened the crammed
closet. She took out her shoes, and stuffed the money inside
with the rest of her savings. She sniffed gingerly: Rosie's
clothes stank of body odor. She wished she had her own closet;
not that Rosie didn't shower—she did—but her weight and
the heat of the apartment made her sweat profusely.

"You comin' to a meeting with me tonight?" Rosie asked,
lolling at the door. "Only I got to deliver these so I thought
I'd maybe go straight from there."

"I said I'd go over to see the new paintings being hung."

Rosie pursed her lips. "Hector helping out, too, is he?"

Lorraine sighed. "Hector's gay, Rosie, okay?"

"Maybe he swings both ways—some of them do, you
know . . ."

"Rosie, don't start. Go mail your letters, I'll make some supper."

Rosie banged out and Lorraine went into the kitchen. She cleaned up, then sat down by the telephone. She knew it was after office hours, but she had the urge to make the call. Mike Page's answering machine was on. This time she heard his voice, which gave an emergency number where he could be reached. Lorraine jotted it down and waited a moment before she dialed.

"Hello."

The high-pitched voice was obviously a child's.

Lorraine hung up. She lit a cigarette and smoked it before dialing again. This time Mike answered. She had to swallow hard before she could speak.

"Mike, it's Lorraine."

There was a pause before he spoke.

"Well, long time. How are you?"

"I'd like to see you . . . and the girls."

Another long pause, and then Mike coughed.

"Yeah, I understand that, and it's fine by me. When do you want to come?"

Lorraine's hands were shaking. She couldn't answer. Mike asked if she was still there. "Maybe this weekend?" he said.

"You mean tomorrow?" Lorraine could hardly get her breath.

"Or Sunday, that'd be better." He suggested twelve-thirty. They could have lunch, maybe walk on the beach together.

There was another pause. Then Lorraine said, "Twelve-thirty Sunday, then," and hung up before he could say anything else. She stared at his address. Her mouth was dry. She mentally repeated every word they had said to each other. They had not spoken for so long.

She sat cupping a mug of coffee in her hands. She had finally done it. Slowly she calmed herself down. She'd be able to cope, she'd coped so far, and she was looking good. More important, she was sober.

Bill Rooney sat opposite his chief, Michael Berillo, leaning forward, which made his squat backside spread even more. Berillo was thumbing through the thick dossier of the case to date. Even flicking through documents he seemed to flex his muscles. He stood over six feet four inches in his socks, his muscular frame slightly top-heavy as his legs were relatively short. His broad shoulders slanted from his thick hairy neck. Rooney often wondered what it would be like to be that huge. Berillo could not walk past a mirror without glancing at himself. Rooney had also noticed that Berillo had recently changed his hairstyle, combing his black hair forward—and he'd had a quiet smile when he'd seen Berillo caught in the wind, raising his hand quickly to keep his hair in place, a man going bald and hating it.

Berillo came to the end of the thick dossier and flicked it closed, clenching and unclenching his fingers in and out of a fist.

"Nothin'. We haven't got a single witness—"

"But there was a witness, Bill."

Rooney nodded. "Yeah, but that was Helen Murphy. We figure he must have tracked her down again after the attack, right? And made sure the second time."

"But before she died, this phone call . . ."

Rooney nodded. "That's what we've been going on—all we've had—and it was a pretty good description."

"What about the bite?"

"By now it'll have healed, or scabbed over, I dunno."

Chief Michael Berillo did one of his glowers. No matter what hour of the day or night, he always had a dark five o'clock shadow. As he leaned back in his chair, his expansive chest almost burst the buttons on his sweat-stained shirt. "Any of this Helen Murphy's associates give you anything?"

"Nope. She was a real old dog, though, hard to believe anyone'd pick her up, let alone screw her, and most of the people we talked to don't have a lot to say about her. Nothin' complimentary—she was trouble with a capital *T*. She also moved around. We can't trace her husband—he's a trucker, nobody seems to know where he is—and she's got three kids in foster care."

"Irish?"

"What?"

The chief yawned. "I said, was she Irish? With a name like Murphy . . ."

"No, that's her husband and he's from Detroit. We talked to a woman she roomed with, and she said nobody had seen the husband for at least six or seven months. But we got him circulated so as soon as he's traced we'll question him."

The two men remained silent, each wrapped in his own thoughts.

"Six."

Rooney nodded. "Yeah. Six—seven if we attach Norman Hastings. We've interviewed everyone he worked with, everyone he knew. He's got—or had—a real nice wife and two kids, nobody seems to have anything against him. He was a well-liked, ordinary guy, played poker with a few pals, went to ball games, good steady worker, and—"

The chief banged his elbows on the desk. "No connection to any of these women. Did he pick up hookers?"

Rooney shook his head. "If he did, his wife didn't know it, and none of his friends did either. Unless they're lying."

The chief started to thumb through the massive dossier again—it represented the hours and hours of interviews and statements, the lists of officers assigned to the investigation. "Okay, we'll open it up further. Let's see if any other states have anything on record. Reason is, to keep this on the boil I'm going to need more. We got a hell of a lot of men with their thumbs up their asses, and we'll have to open it up to the press."

"Shit! You know what a circus there'll be once there's a whiff of a serial killer on the loose."

"You've had it all to yourself, Bill, and you've drawn a blank. We got a fucking maniac out there and I can't hold this back any longer. We'll get in a psychological profiler."

Rooney snorted, and the chief brought his huge fist down hard on the desk. "Get all the help you can, Bill, and get it fast. You and your team have to get some results soon; I can't let you sit on this—and you know it. Bring in Helen Murphy's husband. So far he looks like the only possible suspect and you need one."

"What's that supposed to mean?"

"You dumb? I'll have to bring in more than a fucking profiler. Don't you understand? I'm under pressure. That last kid might have been a hooker, but she was only seventeen years old. And Norman Hastings was, as you've laid out thick and clear, an upright citizen. You think his family don't want a result? It's not just old whores. One dead bitch like the one you dug up from your pal Sparks can be put on ice. Hastings can't. A pretty blue-eyed angel called Holly can't. You with me? And she was found on our turf—they'll start sniffing around if we don't watch out.''

Rooney felt the rug being pulled out from under his feet. If they wanted a profiler then he'd get one. If they wanted Clint Eastwood they could have him, too. Anything, so long as they didn't give him the sidestep just before he was due to retire. "I hear you loud and clear, Chief."

"Good—and Bill, any other bright ideas you get, run them by me first. You started the ball rolling, now it's out of control."

Rooney got out fast.

Unfortunately, Bean was in his office sitting in his chair. It was a bad omen and Rooney yelled at him to get off his butt. "Find one of those profilers—and by tonight. And *don't* say one word. Then I want every man on this fiasco in the main incident room in one hour. We want Helen Murphy's fuckin' husband found and brought in."

Bean coughed. "There's another one."

"What?" Rooney's face flushed a deep puce.

"I said there's another one come in, from a Brian Johns, Santa Monica, details on your desk."

Rooney reached over and picked up the fax sheet. Prostitute murdered 1992, found inside the trunk of a Cadillac, face and skull beaten. Mona Skinner, age forty. Possible murder weapon: a blunt instrument, some kind of hammer.

Bean shut the door as Rooney thudded into his chair. It creaked ominously, the springs taking the strain of his 250 pounds. Mona Skinner had been an ugly, square-faced woman with long, frizzy, bleached-blond hair and a mouth turned down in a thin scowl. Her mean, aggressive eyes stared back at Rooney with a "fuck you" expression. She had been charged with soliciting more than fourteen times over a period of fifteen years. She had also served four years for assault and battery, and receiving stolen property.

Rooney leaned back and swiveled around. He was angry with himself for opening the can: the worms were wriggling out all over him. He ran a check to see if there were any links between Mona Skinner and the others. He got lucky: Mona Skinner and Helen Murphy had both served time together at the same women's prison and had once lived in the same motel. Rooney stepped up the order to find Helen Murphy's husband, who had now become his main suspect—for real.

Rosie ate the spaghetti, waded through the garlic bread, and, filled to bursting, heaved herself onto the sofa. Switching on the TV, she paused briefly to watch the news, then flicked the channels to find a game show. Lorraine chewed her vegetables and rice slowly. She was eating for energy now and keeping off fats. "They still haven't found the guy that bumped off that local fella. You know what always amazes me?"

Lorraine continued eating slowly, sipping her water, and when she finally finished, began to clear the table. "No. What?"

"Well, you know when they put all these ads out for people to come forward if they saw anythin'? That murder happened weeks ago. How do they expect anybody to remember? I wouldn't be able to remember if I saw a guy in a metallic blue car this morning, forget a few weeks ago."

"You'd be surprised," Lorraine said, wiping around the sink. "I was working on a case once, and we were up shits creek without a paddle, and then this boy was hypnotized and he gave not only the car's license plate but about four or five others parked in the same street as well. It's amazing what the subconscious mind retains."

Rosie switched channels again. "I wouldn't have that done, you know why? Because it means they always got you in their power."

Lorraine sat down beside her, her mind miles away. She thought again about the wallet, the man who had attacked her. She was vaguely surprised that he hadn't been traced yet. She closed her eyes, conjuring up a mental picture of him, the way he had picked her up at the curb, how he had wanted her to give him a blow job in a public place. She saw him as clearly as if it had been yesterday. She remembered his hands: long, thin tapering fingers. Had he worn a ring? She concentrated hard, no, she was sure he had no ring, but then she saw his cuff, his jacket sleeve, and the cuff links. She leaned forward, frowning in concentration, and then shook her head. It was no concern of hers, she had enough to think about, and besides, the farther removed she was from it the better.

The following morning Lorraine went off to the gallery, pausing on the way to buy a newspaper. The headlines shrieked in big bold letters: POLICE HUNT SERIAL KILLER. Sitting in the gallery, she read the entire article, then folded the paper. It seemed almost comical that Captain Bill Rooney should be heading the investigation. From her own past experience with press releases, they had trouble on their hands. She could tell they were covering up, the old phrases they all used to churn out about "making headway," "confident of an arrest." But the biggest giveaway was the police request for any member of the public having further information to make contact. It meant they had zilch.

The buzzer sounded and a flushed, excited Art rushed in, carrying a small gym bag ready for his workout next door. "I think, my dear, I just made a killing. Last night I had a friend over who knows a big dealer out of New York. He saw the new stuff and went ape-shit! He's back tonight and he's not just interested in one or two but the whole show!"

Lorraine was genuinely pleased, since it also meant more money for her. Art had promised that as soon as business picked up she would get a raise. He danced around, checked the mail, and then said he would be next door if anyone wanted him.

She took another look at the canvases hanging on the walls, still not impressed with the daubs of color and squiggles that Art's new discovery had supplied.

Later, Nula dropped by. She posed in the doorway and did a slow turn on her high-stacked platform shoes. Today's wig was blond and she wore large diamanté sunglasses. "Hi, babe, how you doing?" she put her arms around Lorraine. "You know, I think you're looking even better. As soon as your hair grows a little more, ask Didi to style it—she's an artist. She can color, too—she does all my wigs and styles them, and she does Holly's—" She froze, and covered her mouth. "Oh, God, I forgot."

"There's a big article in the paper this morning, and a photograph."

Nula looked at it and turned away, her deep voice dropping down another octave. "She was much more beautiful than that, a real stunner. You know, the cops have been out every night. Here and Sunset, terrible for business, but they figure this maniac only does whores, so everybody's pretty tense. First time they came around, hardly any of us were out, but you know, business is business. And I doubt if he'd come to our end of the street—we just have our usuals and a few that have been tipped off."

She suddenly gave a deep-throated chuckle. "Besides, trannies can take care of themselves. When I was . . . well, before, you know, I could do a side sweep karate kick that'd knock your teeth out. Don't do it now, well, you can't, not with a tight skirt."

Lorraine smoothed her skirt. "All the same, you two should look out for yourselves. Take down the licenses of the johns you're unsure about—or better yet, don't go with them."

Nula cocked her head to one side. "That's just what the cops told us."

Lorraine smiled. "Well, make sure you do it."

Nula opened her tapestry bag and took out a small package. "Give this to Art for me, would you? It's just some more postcards, and our rent. See you soon."

Lorraine put the package in the desk drawer and was just about to shut it, when she noticed a thick wad of notes secured with only a rubber band. She looked to the door, then back to the open drawer. She took the money out and flicked through it. There was at least two or three thousand dollars. She held it a moment, tapping it in her hand, then replaced it.

About an hour later Art returned, pink from his workout, his bald head gleaming. He dropped his gym bag and fractionally adjusted a canvas.

"You mind if I say something?"

He turned, and smiled. "Oh, my, you sound so stern, why should I?"

"There's a lot of money in the drawer, Art, and it's not locked or anything. Anyone could just walk in and take it."

Art danced over and banged open the drawer. "I meant to deposit it this morning but I forgot and I didn't want to leave it in the health club."

Lorraine watched as he tossed the money into his gym bag.

"Right, I have to go. Will you lock up, leave the keys next door with Hector?" Then, pursing his lips, he delved into his pocket, dragged out his wallet, and started counting out ten-dollar bills. "Whoops . . . I'm a tad short. Can I give you the rest on Monday, darling?"

Lorraine flushed. "I need it all today, Art. I have to go somewhere this weekend." She couldn't help but flick a look at the gym bag.

"That belongs to a friend."

She shrugged. "Monday will have to do."

"Okay." Art smiled. "Is that your paper? Have you finished with it?"

She passed it to him. He glanced at it and then held up Holly's photograph. "I didn't know her but she was a friend of Nula and Didi's. You know the car was found not far from here—did you know that?"

He strode out without waiting for an answer, and the door slammed behind him. Remembering Nula's package, she hurried after him, only to see him driving away in a cab. She felt pissed off: she needed her money to buy a little something for the girls. She put the package away, then opened the drawer again, took it out and looked at it. Nula had said that her rent was in it; maybe she could just take out what she was owed and leave a note.

Lorraine eased open the package, pulling the Scotch tape away, making sure she didn't rip the paper. As well as some postcards wrapped in a sheet of paper, there was a brown manila envelope. She crossed to the card table that held an electric kettle, and turned it on to steam open the flap. Inside was a big pile of bills. She was surprised by the amount—unless they were behind with their rent. She counted out sixty dollars for herself, and was about to replace the rest and reseal the envelope when she wondered if the postcards were meant for the gallery, so she opened the paper.

Lorraine sat down. She felt sick. It wasn't that she hadn't come across pornographic material when she worked Vice, but each of these was especially revolting because they featured Nula and Didi. Maybe if she'd been more together she would have realized when she visited that they used their apartment for photographic work—there were certainly enough props. She sighed, looking intently at each disgusting picture, sad that Nula and Didi could subject themselves to such degrading acts, displaying their genitals, their heavy breasts. They were featured together, just the two of them, on the first few cards, and then they were joined by various animals and masked figures, and on four cards a pretty sweet-faced blond girl appeared, her face childlike but her breasts overlarge and her curved body taut and firm. Her eyes unfocused, she looked, at first, as if she'd been drugged, but then Lorraine recognized her. It was Holly. No wonder Didi and Nula had been so upset. They knew her because both had screwed her. If the cards had been just of Nula and Didi, even with Holly, Lorraine would have been less upset, but the rest showed obviously underage boys committing homosexual acts.

Lorraine lit a cigarette and inhaled deeply. She was no innocent—in fact, it was more than likely she herself had taken part in some perverted session in the past to make a buck. She paced the gallery and kept on returning to the postcards, picking them up and putting them down. She was uncertain what, if anything, to do. Her first thought was to send them to the police, let them deal with it, especially since they featured Holly. She asked herself if the girl's murder could be connected to the pictures. She doubted it—it could just be coincidence. But one thing was for sure: Holly was no innocent and already on the game, so she would have been fully aware of what she was doing. Then Lorraine looked again. *Had* Holly been drugged? If so, had she been forced into the pornographic session against her will, or agreed to do it because she was drugged?

"It's none of my business," she said aloud. She was angry with herself for opening the package. It changed everything. If she sent the contents to the police, they would question Nula and Didi. They might come to the gallery, too. Art was involved, so she would also be questioned—by Bill Rooney. So much for feeling safe and secure. The thought of having Rooney barging into her fragile existence made her feel weak. She was caught, trapped first by stealing the wallet from the man who had attacked her, and then because, as it turned out, it wasn't his wallet after all but Norman Hastings's. She even remembered the dead man's name, could picture his face on his driver's license.

"What a fucking mess!"

Lorraine lit another cigarette, sat at the desk propping her head on her hands. She steadied herself. She knew the wallet was of no great importance to the investigation. More to the point, and this she knew, too, was that her attacker had been in possession of it. It was obvious he had to have taken it from Hastings's body. If the newspaper reports could be relied on, and Hastings's body had been discovered in his own car, then it was surely the same vehicle driven by the man who had attacked her. So that meant that all the time she was in the shopping mall parking lot, the dead man had been in the trunk of the car.

The officers who had come to the apartment had been trying to trace her, but had never returned. Were they still looking for her? She swore, wishing she had kept the newspaper, but she was certain there had been no mention that the police were looking for anyone seen in Hastings's car that afternoon. She had given them a good enough description, they even repeated it in the paper, so they must be taking it seriously. There was nothing else she could do.

"This is all I fucking need!" she said aloud, as she stubbed out her cigarette, immediately lighting another. Her neck felt tense, her whole body was strained. She began taking everything out of the drawer—leaflets, notes, letters—without knowing what she was looking for. There was no appointment diary, and nothing of any particular importance. She flipped through the sales ledgers, noting the prices Art had paid for his canvases. They were all low. According to the sale-or-return memos, most of the paintings she had presumed sold had been returned. She started to replace the papers, and then stared hard at the money and the photographs.

"Shouldn't open people's private property."

Lorraine gasped. She hadn't heard him return—thanks to that damned broken buzzer! Picking up the photographs, Art began to shuffle them, stacking them, clicking them against the desk as he straightened them to stuff back into the envelope. "I've been watching you sifting through my desk. What were you looking for?"

Lorraine blushed. "I don't know."

Art replaced the photographs, folding the envelope into a tight packet. "Well, Lorraine, did they turn you on?"

"No, no they didn't."

"Takes all kinds, dear."

"I suppose it does . . ."

Art unzipped his bag and tucked the photographs inside. "I only came back because I felt bad about not giving you your money. Lucky I did. I'd forgotten Nula was delivering these."

Lorraine moved out from behind the desk, gesturing to the gallery. "This is all a front, isn't it? A sham."

Art glanced around. "Not all sham, dear. Sometimes I sell some, but I've been ripped off so many times, I keep it up as a kind of pastime. Maybe one day when I've made enough dough I'll be able to find some real talent. This stuff is from Venice Beach, I buy it for peanuts.''

Lorraine shook her head. "The porn sells, does it?"

Art looked at her, his eyes so enlarged by his glasses that they seemed like a gargoyle's. "How else do you think I've been able to stay open? I have regular customers, you met most of them. In fact, if I recall, you called them." He picked up the cash and peeled off a fifty-dollar bill. "Here, it's a bonus.''

Lorraine didn't take it. "The pictures of Holly, the girl who was murdered . . .''

"What?"

"There are pictures of Holly."

Art shrugged. "Well, they won't bother her, will they?"

"Maybe the police would be interested, though."

He pursed his lips. "I don't see why, she was obviously enjoying herself and nobody forced her. In fact, I didn't even know the girl.''

"Who takes the photographs?"

He sighed, hands on his hips, then looked back at Lorraine. "None of your fucking business. Now, let's just forget this, shall we?"

She stared at him, forcing herself to keep her voice steady. "Why don't you make it worth my while not to make it my business?"

"What?"

"You heard me. You've got underage kids in those pictures—so pay me. And . . . like you said, it's none of my business.''

Art hesitated. He picked up the money, seemed to weigh it in his hand before he made the decision. He threw it at Lorraine. "You know what my big problem in life is? I trust people. I make friends with people, I give them a break, and they always fuck me over it. Take it, you scrawny, ungrateful bitch!''

She picked up the money and stuffed it into her pocket. As she reached over for her cigarettes and lighter, Art gripped her wrist. "Just one thing, sweetheart. I want you to sign for that cash, just as a safeguard for me. Just in case you want to rap about me and—''

Lorraine yanked her wrist away and rubbed it. He was

strong and he had hurt her. "You'll never see me again, I promise you that."

Art didn't say another word. Lorraine signed for the money, walked to the door, opened it, and the buzzer shrilled. She turned, a half-smile on her face. "You should get this fixed, you know, Art."

As the door closed quietly behind her, he kicked at the desk. He was, and always would be, a shithead when it came to sniffing out people.

Lorraine did some shopping. She was feeling pretty high and kept on touching the thick wad of notes in her pocket. She bought two dolls for her daughters, some cans of paint, brushes, and a small wardrobe. She bought some tights, underwear, a shirt, and, finally, a nightgown for Rosie. Laden with goods she caught a taxi home.

Rosie's jaw dropped as Lorraine staggered in. "Jesus Christ! What did you do? Win a lottery?"

Lorraine laughed. "We sold four paintings and this is my bonus!"

Rosie peered at the cans of paint. "Who's gonna be using all this, then?"

"You and me!"

Rosie snorted, but by now she was busy unwrapping her gift. She took out the white cotton nightgown. "Oh, wow! This is pure cotton, *and* it's new!"

She saw two boxes. "What's this, shoes?" She opened one, and looked at Lorraine. "Wow! I might act like a nine-and-a-half-year-old, but . . ."

Lorraine took back the box, closing the lid. "They're for my daughters."

"Oh, so you made contact?"

Lorraine walked out without answering. She had left more bags piled outside on the steps and yelled for Rosie to lend a hand. Jake arrived, unannounced, and was immediately recruited to carry in the rest of the paint, trays, and rollers. He began to wish he hadn't dropped by, since he was quickly cajoled into shifting furniture to clear the room ready for painting. He promised to return later in the evening to help out some more. Lorraine didn't say goodbye—she was carefully putting the two doll boxes under a cushion in case they got damaged.

She and Rosie had a snack and then, draped in old night-gowns Rosie was now prepared to throw out, set to work. After seeing the way Art, Didi, and Nula had transformed the gallery, Lorraine imagined it would be easy, but she had underestimated the threesome's expertise. By the time Jake reappeared they had covered only one wall.

He and Lorraine finished the main room and by the time they had pushed all the furniture back into place, it was after midnight. Jake promised he'd return in the morning so they could start on the kitchen and maybe get around to the bedroom.

Lorraine showered and combed the flecks of paint out of her hair. It was good to feel so tired—it meant she didn't have to think over what had happened during the day. She felt stiff from painting, and her back ached, but when she flopped onto the sofa she was too tired even to work out what she was going to do the following morning. She had a bus schedule, a street map of Santa Monica; she had even decided what she would wear. The two dolls were packed in a shopping bag: one was blond, the other dark-haired. She didn't think about the future, about having to find a new job. Tomorrow, seeing her daughters, was all that mattered.

SIX

Rosie woke up with a start, and then flopped back onto her pillows. Lorraine was in the bathroom. She squinted at the alarm clock: eight-thirty. She couldn't go back to sleep, so she got up and went into the freshly painted main room. Lorraine's bedding was neatly folded, and a pot of coffee was on the stove. Rosie toasted some muffins, then went out to see if the Sunday paper had arrived.

Lorraine emerged, made up and in her new blouse and the safari suit. She also wore the high-heeled slingbacks and skin-tone tights. She no longer needed to raid Rosie's makeup or jewelry box, since she had bought her own cosmetics and a pair of fake pearl earrings.

Rosie gaped, and then sniffed. "My God, you look good and you smell terrific. Are you working today?"

"Yeah, there's a big art dealer coming, so I've got to open the gallery early. I'm sorry if I woke you."

"No problem. You want a muffin . . . coffee?"

"No thanks, I've had breakfast. Gotta run."

Jake arrived about an hour later. Rosie was still reading the paper. "Morning. It's baking out already. Where's Lorraine?"

"Gone to the gallery. You want some coffee and muffins?"

"Wouldn't say no."

Rosie bustled around getting him a cup and plate, then sat and ate another muffin, washing it down with more coffee.

She divided up the paper and they sat opposite each other, reading.

"They found another body," said Jake. "Prostitute. They think she was killed the same way as the others couple months back, this time in Santa Monica."

Rosie slapped down the paper. She looked at Jake. "She lied. She hasn't gone to that gallery, she's gone to see her kids in Santa Monica. She's so secretive . . . but I know she's traced them 'cos I saw the address on a note by the telephone and I know she's gone because she's taken the dolls she bought. Now why does she have to lie?"

"Maybe that's just the way she is," said Jake, folding his paper. "Why don't we surprise her? Let's get the kitchen started."

Rosie pulled a face. "I was hopin' you'd forget all about it. I hate painting, it gives me a backache and my arms ache. Even Walter's taken off—paint gets to cats, you know." She glared at him. "This is Sunday morning, for chrissakes, a day of rest!"

Jake began to clear the kitchen. It was so small it wouldn't take long, and then maybe they could do the bedroom, really surprise Lorraine.

Rooney was sweating. Ten o'clock and it was way up in the high eighties. It was going to be a roaster, usually was in July. He hated losing his Sunday: there was nothing he liked better than sitting in the yard with the papers. He had them all stuffed under his arm, regardless of the fact that perhaps his wife may have also liked to glance over them, but then Rooney rarely if ever gave a thought to his forever waiting and uncomplaining wife. He plodded flat-footedly along the corridors toward his office. He saw Bean up ahead with a balding man talking animatedly. The man was casually dressed and seemed to be rather stooped, taller than Bean and bent forward as if to listen to or catch every word. Bean looked over to Rooney.

"Morning, Captain."

Rooney glowered and waited for Bean to join him. "That's not him, is it?"

"Yep, he's been working from home, seems a nice guy, real low-key."

Rooney snorted, and together they went into his office. Andrew Fellows was younger than Rooney had first thought and not in any way stooped. If anything he seemed very fit. Prematurely bald, his rather handsome face was marred by a pair of enormous ears that constantly caught the attention—they moved up and down when he talked. The more animated he became, as Rooney was to discover, the more the ears worked overtime—and Professor Fellows was an animated man. He used his hands like a conductor, and his tall, trim body in its pristine white T-shirt and tight jeans seemed incapable of staying still for a second. Rooney took him into the "Hammer Killings" incident room. Photographs of all the victims had been posted up on the walls, above the rows of computers. He looked up expectantly at Fellows, craning his neck to be able to look him in the eye. "So, you come up with anything for us?"

Fellows nodded, his ears waved, and he opened a worn leather briefcase. "I've spent three days studying all the evidence to date, and I've tried to assimilate the most important aspects so we can cut through the dross. Much of the evidence you gave me was of no use, so I concentrated on this detailed description apparently given by an anonymous caller. . . ."

He began to pace up and down. "The caller gave a concise and exceptionally clear picture of the assailant—apart from his actual size . . ." Rooney sighed, looked at Bean, and raised his eyes to the ceiling. Fellows flapped his hands. ". . . leading me to believe she had not met the man before. He was in the car when he picked her up, so she may have been a stranger to him. Let's give him a name rather than have to keep calling him the assailant or killer. Why not, for want of something better, 'the Teacher' . . ." Fellows laughed. "Sorry, it's just that the description fits an old college professor I had." Rooney gave a faint grimace that was supposed to be a smile.

Fellows moved to the row of victims' faces. "Now, we're led to believe that all these women and Norman Hastings were killed by the Teacher—and this woman, Helen Murphy"— Fellows pointed to the wrong picture, and Bean corrected him. "Ah, sorry, the body of Helen Murphy was found in the trunk of a car, so we are to presume the Teacher first attempted to kill her, failed, then tracked her down, or knew where she lived or the area she worked, whatever, and killed her, using the same method, claw hammer blows. Am I right so far?"

Rooney sighed. "Yes, but frankly, you're wasting time.

What we need to know—what *I* need to know—is what sort of man is this bastard?''

"That's obvious. You've been given a remarkably clear description, but don't get me off track. Something's wrong, you see. When I went over the information regarding Helen Murphy, I was confused.''

Rooney coughed. "What we got from that description, Professor, was that he's probably got a good income, a good job, and—''

"Yes, yes, but let me get around to that. What's bothering me, as it doesn't make any logical sense, is, if a woman is badly beaten—as witnessed by, er, that couple, Mr. and Mrs. Summers—and assuming that it was the same woman who subsequently gave you the killer's description—going so far as to report the incident to the police, describing the hammer— would she go with him again? He had to pick her up again, correct? Now, she was found in a car that had been left unattended, a wrecked vehicle, abandoned for possibly two or three days, yes? Not like any of the other vehicles used. All of those were reported stolen shortly before the crime was committed. So that means our Teacher had to pick her up in another vehicle, kill her, and then dump the body. So Helen Murphy's murder does not follow the same pattern as the others.''

Rooney frowned. He'd given this a lot of thought himself and was about to say as much when Fellows continued, pointing at Bean.

"Whoever took the call said the woman was precise, articulate, and spoke fast in an almost clipped tone. She refused to give any details about herself, and they were unable even to ask her name because she continued to talk so quickly, but they jotted down almost the entire conversation, and then she hung up. Right?''

Bean nodded, feeling oddly guilty, as if he'd done something wrong, because Fellows was glaring at him, wafting his hand impatiently.

"You took statements regarding the victim Helen Murphy, correct?''

"Yes,'' Bean said, "but I didn't do them all, a few of the statements were taken by—''

Fellows interrupted, his arms swinging like windmill sails. "Who was Helen Murphy? Previously Helena, Helena Dubjeck, an alcoholic, drug abuser, persistent brawler, and . . . I can't recall all her previous charges. And she had false teeth. Also, according to the pathologist, a possible malformation of her upper lip, which you can even see on her photograph . . ." He paused. Rooney was rising slowly to his feet, when the windmill arms waved again. "One moment. Didn't your anonymous caller say that the assailant, our Mr. Teacher, was possibly around one hundred and eighty pounds? Odd, don't you think? Not 'fat' or 'thin, skinny, well-built'—but she gave you his possible weight? Doesn't that strike you as an odd thing for this kind of woman, Helen Murphy, to say? And you make no allowance for the fact that she might have had a speech impediment, might even have had—and you must ask those who knew her—the trace of a foreign accent. She was not born in America, was she?"

Fellows ran his hand over his head, then pulled at one of his ears. "Do you see what I'm getting at? I would say that whoever made that call describing her attacker was someone familiar with police procedure, familiar with shortcutting a description. Am I right? It was not made by Helen Murphy."

Rooney sat back, transfixed by the information Fellows spouted like bullets.

Fellows faced the wall lined with photos. "These women were all prostitutes, but none of them had been penetrated at the time of death. No sexual intercourse took place. So why did he pick them up? What was he wanting them to do? I doubt he wanted intercourse—perhaps he wanted simulated sex, or to be jerked off. Or I would say he has a sexual problem, probably impotence. They get into his car or stolen vehicle, he drives them to some location. If they are bending over his groin, then it's simple for him to strike the back of the head. Again, go back to Mr. and Mrs. Summers. The woman they saw was bleeding badly, but also bleeding from her mouth. Correct?"

Rooney nodded. "She also said she'd bitten the man in the neck."

"But she also said she'd broken the skin, *his* skin, I presume, so the blood on her mouth could easily have been his blood, not her own. She was facing the Summerses, who saw no wounds to her face apart from the bloody mouth, but the back of her head was bleeding. Nevertheless, she was quite capable of calling a cab, giving an address. Now, would that woman, just a few days later, go with the same man again? And be caught the same way, yet again, with a hammer blow to the back of her head? Unless she knew him or was an accomplice to the other killings, I doubt it. If she was an accomplice and made that call, then she could be arrested. If only some stupid clerk had had the sense to trace the call, her identity might now be known.''

Rooney felt inadequate. This big-eared windmill of a man, after just a few days' thumbing through their files, was throwing out mind-blowing stuff. He half expected Fellows to have another pull at his ear and then name the killer. But Fellows had become silent, and was sitting staring down at his sneakers.

''He is a sick man, a tormented man, deeply disturbed, and I think he has killed regularly. I don't think he's ever been put away or locked up. On the contrary, he's walking around confident, *very* confident, because he's gotten away with it for years. Now, with this press coverage, will it make him stop killing? Possibly. I hope so. But it may make him irrational. You see, he'll want to prove, even more, just how clever he is. You won't catch him unless he makes mistakes. On the other hand, the press coverage could also make him stop, for a while anyhow. But he won't be able to stop completely, because, I would say, these murders are the only way he's able to get sexual gratification.''

Fellows got up again and marched up and down the wall of victims, peering at the faces, turning to retrace his footsteps. ''He must be in full employment, possibly some kind of traveling sales executive. He's moving around a lot of areas. He could even be a car salesman—he certainly knows about cars and how to steal them. I would say he might have a garage, or a storage place where these cars can be hidden. I doubt if he has a family—no wife or children. This man has a hatred of older women, a terrible hatred—''

Rooney interjected to ask about Angela Hollow. Fellows took a deep breath. ''Yes. She was young—and the most recent victim? Prostitute, working the streets the night she was killed?'' He looked at the picture of Holly. ''Find out if, on the night she was killed, any other girl or woman was next to her. Maybe Holly crossed to him when he was really after another girl close by—it's possible. Because I have to admit she makes my theory wobble, as she's not in the same category as the others. This worries me . . .''

He tapped the picture of Norman Hastings. ''There's something odd about him, too, if we talk it through. He leaves his car, I can't recall the exact location, our Teacher steals it, or is even in the process of stealing it, and is caught red-handed. Hastings calls out, may even try and stop Teacher, so, in that case, why the wound to the back of his head like the women? Unless Hastings was actually opening his car, Teacher, ready for the kill, simply walks up and strikes him?''

Rooney wiped the sweat from his upper lip with the back of his hand; he was feeling very inadequate. ''He went to the bank and—''

Fellows wafted his hand. ''That's immaterial—Teacher's not after money, he even left the victims' jewelry on their bodies. No, he's not after something as mundane as that, he's not a robber. He's a sex killer, he wants sexual gratification, nothing more.''

Rooney waited, almost afraid to interrupt. Fellows sighed, and sat down, looking at the picture of Hastings. ''It's possible they knew each other. I could be wrong, and nothing in the reports gives any indication, other than that Hastings was an unfortunate man who was simply in the wrong place at the wrong time. What's not clear is where that place was. Outside his bank? In a parking lot? No one has come forward to say they saw Norman Hastings on the day of his death, so where did it happen? We don't know.''

Fellows fell silent, chewing his lower lip before he returned to the photo wall, to the graphs and memos. He stared at the photographs of the vehicles in which the dead women had been found. A Lincoln Continental, a Chrysler Le Baron, a Saab, a Mercedes, a Cadillac Eldorado—the last the wreck from outside the Paradise Apartments where Helen Murphy had been found. Then he looked over the chart of the locations. Glendale shopping mall, Plaza Mall, Holly—odd that, girl's nickname being the same as the road she was found on . . . never mind! It's of no consequence. Next, West Hollywood, Santa Monica Boulevard, Century City, and lastly the Santa Monica shopping center. He stood staring for at least three minutes, his eyes roaming the photographs, the locations. Santa Monica or Pasadena. There had to be a link between them, a pattern beyond the method of the murder itself. He needed to know as accurately as possible the times when, one, Helen Murphy was killed, two, the attack in the Glendale shopping mall occurred—on the woman they had been presuming was Helen Murphy—and, three, what time Holly was murdered. The three incidents were crucial because Holly's murder was the most recent, and the failed attempt would have been between the last two murders.

"How close are these, time-wise?" Fellows flicked his hand to Helen Murphy and Holly.

Bean crossed to the information section and looked up. "The reported attack on the woman in the Glendale shopping mall was on the same day Hastings was killed, the seventeenth of May. This woman, Helen Murphy, was, as close as the lab can tell us, murdered about three days before we found her."

Fellows nodded. "But they can't be exactly sure, can they? I mean, it could be a day either side. Her body was pretty high, wasn't it? Already decomposing?"

Bean nodded and then checked the information on Holly. Fellows had taken a small black leather diary from his pocket and was flipping through it, licking his fingers as he pushed the small pages over. "And, Lieutenant, Holly was killed on what date?"

Bean looked at Rooney. "June twentieth."

Fellows pursed his lips. "You got dates for all the others? See if it's always around the same time. I know some of them are four to six years old, but I'd like to get a calendar made up. Would you do that for me?"

Bean nodded. Fellows turned to Rooney and gave a glum smile. "I'm sorry, but that's about it for today. It's not much because I need more time; hopefully I'll come up with something else. I expect you've already come to the same conclusions yourselves. Basically, a lot of what I do in the end is simply common sense."

He picked up his briefcase. "You're not going, are you?" Rooney asked anxiously. "I mean, the whole team is coming in today to talk this over—"

Fellows snapped his case shut. "I'm sure you can repeat everything, and I have a golf game waiting. If you just keep me informed of any new developments, I'll get back to you."

"What did you think of him?" asked Bean after he'd shown Fellows out.

"I take back everything I said. How's that for starters?"

Bean grinned. "Odd character, wasn't he?"

"Big ears." Rooney sighed. "We're almost back at the starting gate, aren't we? From what he's said, we're off by a long way with Murphy's husband. Nobody's found the fucker anyway."

He flicked at the blinds on his office window. "You know, way back I was on a case, a missing kid—long time ago—but we'd all given up, we just had nothing. You remember that woman I saw that night when we went to the Kwok restaurant?"

Bean raised an eyebrow. He had good reason to remember it, he'd spent most of that night in the bathroom; so much for raw fish.

"Well, she was on the same case, a little girl missing. She found her body at the school. She was such a cute little kid, and . . ." Rooney sighed, seeing the little girl's face again. "Anyway, Lorraine—that was her name, didn't I tell you about her?"

"Drunk on duty, right?"

"This was before she became a lush, years before, and she was a good cop, dedicated—well, as much as a woman can be. Anyway, she wouldn't let go, she was so sure it was this janitor, but we had nothing on him. He even had a strong alibi for the afternoon the girl disappeared. We'd all scrapped him as a suspect; she was even warned off from visiting the school and his place. Did it on her own time. She just wouldn't back off him. And we had not one shred of evidence, it was just her intuition . . ."

Bean yawned and looked at his watch, he could hear the team members starting to arrive outside, and he wondered where the story was leading. Rooney, too, seemed uncertain, still flicking at the blinds with his fat stubby finger. "She broke him down. I don't know how, none of us did. She brought him back into the station for maybe the tenth time, questioned him over and over, and meanwhile there was the captain going ape-shit, saying we'd be accused of harassment. Then she walked out, and she had this look on her face like some prizefighter. She lifted up her fist, said he'd admitted it, that he'd just broken down and admitted killing the little girl . . ."

Bean wasn't listening, his attention on the doorway as he looked at the men that passed. "Everyone's gathered. You want to go in?"

Rooney hitched up his pants, displaying his socks as his trousers lifted ankle-high. Red socks, Bean noted, and wondered where on earth Rooney bought his crumpled suits. He had never seen him wearing a decent one, and they were always creased like an accordion. "Maybe we try again with Hastings's wife, maybe we've been going too softly, maybe he wasn't such a good, upright, honest citizen. And we start trying to trace that missing witness again. We don't back off, but keep on going—okay?"

Bean sighed. "You know, even if we do find her, maybe all she knows is what she told us and that won't help."

Rooney jabbed at him with his finger. "Wrong. She never said where he picked her up. She probably knows a hell of a lot more than she let on. Now, let's get fucking cracking before the entire day's been pissed away. We got to trace that bitch and all leave is canceled starting now . . ."

The cab drew up outside a narrow, three-story house facing the ocean that didn't look like much but, Lorraine knew, would have to be worth at least three million dollars. Mike Page was certainly doing a lot better for himself nowadays. The cabdriver, who had been watching the clock, now turned to face Lorraine. "You want to drive around some more or are you getting out?"

"Drive around a while longer."

He sighed. "Okay. Anything you want, lady, this is your ride."

They did another tour of Santa Monica, then returned and parked in exactly the same place as before.

"This is it, lady. I got an account customer I need to pick up, so, if you don't mind . . ."

He was lying, she knew, he just wanted her out of his cab, probably because it was Sunday and he wanted to get home. She paid the fare and stepped out. Hardly had the cab door shut behind her before he tore off. She felt marooned, afraid to walk the few yards to Mike's front door, yet unable to turn and walk away. She stood there, frozen.

"Lorraine?" The voice was unmistakable. It was Mike. She turned and shaded her eyes. He was wearing an open-neck shirt, white slacks, and flip-flops. A big dog with long scruffy hair padded beside him. Her heart was thudding and she knew she must be flushed a bright red. Her whole body broke out in a sweat. Mike had a deep suntan and his teeth gleamed; his dark brown eyes had lines at the side, crow's feet, but apart from that he didn't seem much older than when she had last seen him.

"Hi!" He stood about a foot away from her. "I wasn't expecting you until later."

"I got a taxi."

He smiled, reached for her bag, and she let him take it.

"I got something for the girls. I don't want you to think I'm staying over . . ."

He took her elbow, about to lead her toward the house, then he stopped. "They're out swimming but they won't be long, so we can have a chat, catch up."

She followed him toward the front door, but he went down some steps to enter the house through large French windows that opened onto a veranda.

"This is nice," she said lamely.

"Yep—and it's breaking me financially, but the kids love it." He paused. "Oh, maybe you don't know. I've got two sons—they're with the girls and Kathy."

Lorraine nodded, presuming Kathy to be their stepmother. She stepped into the big open room, where toys and newspapers, even breakfast dishes, had been left on a huge round table facing the ocean window.

"Sorry about the mess but Sundays we just let everything hang out. Now sit down and I'll get some coffee going."

Lorraine sat on the wide sofa. She looked slowly around the room, at the paintings, the throw rugs, the grains of sand that sparkled on the floor. "Can I smoke?"

Mike cleared the table, and looked up. "Sure, I'll find you an ashtray."

She lit up, her hand shaking so much that she glanced over to see if he'd noticed, but he was carrying a stack of dishes into the kitchen. The door closed and she inhaled deeply, letting the smoke fill her lungs. She got up and stood by the open window, taking deep breaths to calm herself.

Mike held on to the edge of the sink, shaken. Nothing had prepared him for the way she looked. She had aged so much— she was skin and bone, her face scarred so badly she seemed to squint. He shook his head, wishing he had more time to prepare the girls. Then he heard Sissy calling, and before he had time to warn her not to come down, she was in the drawing room. He listened at the door.

Sissy was wrapped in a cotton kimono. She was deeply tanned and had waist-length, ash-blond hair. She was as tall as Lorraine, but full-breasted, her legs muscular and taut. Her long arms and perfect hands immediately pulled the kimono closer as she had no belt and was naked beneath it. "I'm sorry, I didn't know anyone was here."

Lorraine bowed her head. "I'm, er . . . well, I guess you knew I was coming. I'm Lorraine."

"Oh, yeah, I'm sorry. Where's Mike?"

Lorraine swallowed. "He's making me some coffee."

She wondered who the beauty was, but Sissy seemed totally at ease, striding toward the kitchen. "Darling, you should have said, or yelled up that Lorraine was here. I'll go back up and get dressed, leave you two to have a chat . . . Mike?"

He walked out of the kitchen and slipped his arm around Sissy. "Well, you've met. This is my wife, Sissy."

Lorraine forced a smile as Sissy walked out and up the stairs. "She's very beautiful," she said quietly.

Mike nodded. "The girls adore her, and—well, lemme get the coffee."

Lorraine looked out onto the veranda and lit another cigarette from the stub of the last one. Then she started to cough, one of her awful, chesty, phlegmy coughs that made her feel weak and her eyes run. She gasped, trying to control it as Mike appeared with a glass of water.

"You should give that up!"

She shrugged, still coughing, and took the glass. Mike returned to the kitchen, and Lorraine remained outside on the veranda, sitting on one of the wooden bench seats. She drained the glass and set it carefully on the table. At least her hands were no longer shaking.

Mike carried out the tray of coffee and set it down. He poured a cup, and she smiled. It was the first time she even faintly resembled her old self: Mike noticed that she still had the palest of blue eyes.

"So. It's been a long time, hasn't it? I've often wondered how you were, hoped you'd get in touch."

He waited for her to reply but she stared ahead. He could

see the deep scar down her cheek, and her body shaking slightly. He'd sometimes wondered how he would react to seeing her again. He'd expected to feel anger, or perhaps attraction, rather than this deep sadness. He had worried that she might have some custody query, or have become financially secure enough to want the girls to live with her. But the cheap, old-fashioned safari suit, the run-down shoes, everything about her looked seedy and worn. Worse still was Lorraine herself. She had always been so positive, arrogant even, now all he could see was a pitiful shell of what she had once been. That was what he felt more than anything: pity, and an overwhelming relief she was no longer part of his life.

"I don't drink anymore, Mike." Her voice was smoky from too many cigarettes, deeper than he remembered.

"Good, that's good . . ." he said, hesitantly.

"But I sure as hell could do with one now!"

SEVEN

Lorraine sat on the veranda shading her eyes, waiting for the first glimpse of her daughters. Mike stepped out carrying two photo albums, and came to sit beside her. Momentarily her shoulder rubbed against his.

"These are my boys—Chip, whose real name is Charles, and this is Mike junior." They were both blond, both as beautiful as their mother. She quickly turned the pages back to the beginning, barely interested in Mike's sons. The first photograph was one she remembered: the girls were sitting side by side on a piano stool, Sally with a front tooth missing.

Mike looked up, hearing a shout from the beach. "Here they are . . . that's our nanny, she's wonderful, that's Kathy."

Lorraine stood up and leaned on the rail. Sissy had one boy by each hand, and behind her walked Kathy, a dark-haired teenager—but running up ahead were the girls. Sally and Julia, torn jeans, faded T-shirts, as suntanned as Sissy, they shouted and waved. Lorraine was stunned. They were both so tall, so different . . . she would have passed them in the street and not recognized them. "My God," she murmured.

Mike laughed. "Yeah, they grow up fast, don't they?"

Sally was ten, Julia twelve. Six years was a very long time. Their initial exuberance faltered as they reached the veranda, and they turned to Sissy as if they needed her to be with them, but Mike called for them to come on up. Julia was tall for her age and as slim as Lorraine had been at twelve.

"Hello."

Lorraine smiled. She would have liked to put her arms around her daughter, but she wasn't sure if that was what Julia wanted. Sally wouldn't come close; she hung back as if afraid. Sissy slipped her arm around Julia's shoulder. "Now, why don't you three show Lorraine the photo album, and I'll make some lunch?"

"Okay," said Julia.

Sally sat beside Lorraine, but Mike followed Sissy into the house and pulled the doors half closed behind him. Kathy called out to Mike that she was not staying for lunch and would be back later, then smiled warmly at Lorraine before she walked toward the driveway. Mike watched for a moment before joining his wife in the kitchen.

"Kathy won't be having lunch," he said.

"She never does on Sundays, idiot," Sissy said.

The three were left in uncomfortable silence. Lorraine knew the dolls were a mistake—certainly for Julia, who seemed sophisticated and grown-up. Sally sat with her head bowed.

"I'm sorry not to have kept in touch with you both . . ." Lorraine said haltingly.

Julia gave her a strange, furtive look. "That's okay. This is me winning a swimming prize at school." Lorraine leaned forward to look at the photograph, and the tension eased slightly.

Lunch was served inside because it was cooler, and Julia showed Lorraine where the bathroom was so she could wash her hands. Lorraine crept from room to room, peeking in at each door, until she found her daughters' bedroom. It was full of posters and rugs, old teddy bears and a closet bulging with clothes. Untidy comforters lay on their unmade beds, but it was a room any girl would covet. The last door she opened revealed Mike's study, the walls covered with pictures of the family, and some of himself on fishing trips. There was a large modern desk with stacks of files and papers, and Lorraine was just closing the door when she caught sight of a picture of herself, with the girls. It surprised her that he would have it, and she edged into the room, afraid someone would hear her creeping around.

She leaned across the desk to get a better view of the photograph and then froze as she inadvertently knocked some papers onto the floor. They were business letters, and as she picked them up, one of the letterheads caught her eye. It belonged to a vintage automobile reconditioning firm, specializing in imported cars. The letter confirmed that leather upholstery had been installed in a Mercedes 1966 classic sports car, and the client had refused to accept the costs. It was not, however, the contents of the letter that caught Lorraine's attention, it was the small black and green oval raised letters of the company logo: S & A. She was almost certain she had seen it before . . . and not on a letter. . . . It was on a pair of cuff links.

"Lorraine? *Lorraine*?" Mike was calling her, and she quickly slipped the letter back into the pile and hurried out.

At lunch, the conversation—strained at best—turned to the subject of cars.

"What do you drive now?" Lorraine asked.

Mike grunted and prodded one of the boys. "I have to have a bus for this crowd, it's an old station wagon. But Sissy has an MG—it's an English sports car."

"I do know what an MG is," Lorraine said.

Sissy flicked a look at Mike and then smiled. "That was more for my benefit—it's always in the garage, not because I've done anything to it, but because of the spares."

"Is there a good garage near you?" Lorraine asked innocently.

Mike nodded. "Yeah, there is. It specializes in vintage and foreign cars, big money in it. They've got Rolls-Royces and Bentleys and Mercedes-Benzes—"

Lorraine interrupted, "Is it a big company?"

"Pretty substantial, well, their cars are. I don't really know how big a business it is."

"How many people does it employ?"

Mike looked a little puzzled, but said, "Maybe twenty or thirty, I don't know. Why?"

Lorraine smiled. "I'm sure a friend of mine bought a car from a garage around here—maybe S and A?"

Mike nodded. "Well, that's the company's logo all right—

in fact, I'm doing some business with them. Got your license back, have you?''

Lorraine blushed. ''No, but I can't afford a car anyway.''

''Not from S and A.'' Mike laughed, then gave Sissy a side look, wondering if Lorraine was going to hit him for money and he blushed slightly.

''Does your friend live around here?'' Sissy asked.

''No, I just heard the garage mentioned. And I don't need any money, Mike, I didn't come for that, okay?''

Julia got up, cupping her hands to whisper in Sissy's ear. She frowned and shook her head. ''No, you can't, now sit down.''

Julia pouted and slumped back at the table. The room grew silent. Sissy shrugged her perfect shoulders. ''She wants to go play tennis.''

Julia snapped, ''I always play tennis on Sunday afternoons.''

Mike wagged his finger. ''Not this Sunday. Now, help your mother clear the table and—''

Lorraine stood up. ''No, that's okay—you go play tennis, Julia. I don't mind, I have to go in a few minutes anyway.''

Mike stacked the dishes, anything to cover his embarrassment. ''Well, it's up to you, but since you've come all this way—''

''I can come again—if you don't mind . . .''

''Where's Rufus?'' Sally demanded, and suddenly they were all calling the dog. It seemed they all wanted to find an excuse to leave the room. Lorraine went over to the bag she'd brought, and took out the box with the doll. ''Sally?'' She went out to the veranda. ''I brought you this—maybe it's a bit childish for you, I just thought you'd kind of like it.''

Sally opened the box and looked at the doll. ''Does it talk? My friend Angela's got one that talks and sleeps and cries, and you feed it with a bottle and it wets itself.''

Lorraine looked at the moody-faced child. ''This one drinks and then if you press its stomach, it spits in your face.''

The little girl's mouth trembled.

''Sally, it was just a joke!''

The child ran into the house, past Mike. Lorraine laughed at his worried expression. ''S'okay, Mike, I was never very good with them anyway. I got to go.''

Mike sat on the edge of the bench seat. ''I'm sorry. It'll

take them a while to get used to you—that is, if you're planning to make this a regular—"

"Would you mind?"

"No, well, maybe . . . I don't know, it's kind of taken us all by surprise. I think they're scared you've come to take them away." He stared at her. "You haven't, though, have you?"

Lorraine hugged her arms around herself tightly. "I wouldn't want to do anything that'd upset them. Besides, I kind of don't know them anymore—and you've changed. She's got you domesticated, carrying dishes back and forth."

Sissy came out, overhearing the last remark.

She put down the coffeepot, and went back into the house.

"Can you call me a taxi?"

Lorraine was relieved when the cab arrived. She kept the doll she had bought for Julia, because she didn't want Julia to know that she had still thought of her as a little girl; she noticed that Sally hadn't even taken hers out of its box. Sally wouldn't kiss Lorraine goodbye, but hung on to Sissy. Mike kissed her cheek, and Sissy shook her hand—she had a strong, firm grip. She stared coldly at Lorraine as she said, without any warmth, "Do come again." Seeing them grouped together, waving, Lorraine knew she would never come back.

She asked the cabdriver to take her past the S & A garage. Two large showrooms were filled with vintage cars, but it was closed. Lorraine got out and walked along the showroom window, peering inside, and shaded her eyes to look at the counter. Dinky toy cars and memorabilia were displayed, but she couldn't see any cuff links. By the time she returned to the cab, she was sweating again. It was three o'clock, the sun was blistering, so she asked the driver to stop at the next grocery store so she could buy a can of Coke.

At ten o'clock Rosie called Jake to say that Lorraine still hadn't come home, and she was worried. Maybe she was staying over, he suggested. If she was really worried, why not call? She had the number. Jake was exhausted: they had finished painting the kitchen and the bedroom, and put all the furniture back in place. Rosie waited until eleven before she called Mike Page, and was told that Lorraine had left around three. She called Jake. Already in bed, he was annoyed at being disturbed again. "Rosie, what do you expect me to do? I'm not her keeper. I'm not responsible for what she does or does not do. Now let me get some sleep, okay?"

At midnight, Rosie went to bed. The smell of fresh paint made her feel sick, and she couldn't get to sleep, so she got up, made herself some iced tea, and sat by the window. Then she watched some late-night television and eventually, at two-thirty, went back to bed.

Monday morning and Lorraine had still not returned, so Rosie called Jake again, but he had left for work, and she didn't want to pester him there. She told herself she was overreacting, but when Lorraine had still not appeared at four in the afternoon, she took a bus to the gallery. It was shut so she squinted through the window and saw that all the canvases had been removed. The place looked deserted, so she went home.

For want of something better to do, and to take her mind off Lorraine, Rosie began to clear out her bedroom cupboards and drawers, tossing out junk she had hoarded. A new portable wardrobe had been assembled in a corner of the newly painted bedroom. Rosie pushed it into position and began to fill it with Lorraine's few possessions. Last of all she put in the shoes—and that was when she found the roll of money. She was amazed at the amount, then felt guilty because it would look as if she had been searching through Lorraine's personal belongings. She had, of course, but not with any ulterior motive.

Jake dropped by at seven o'clock that evening. There was still no word from Lorraine. Rosie was upset. Jake took her to a meeting; he had a good idea that Lorraine would eventually come home, and he refused to borrow his friend's car to go on a street-by-street search. If she had started out in Santa Monica, God alone knew where she was by now.

They came back to Rosie's just after ten, and ate some take-out food. Midway through the meal they heard a screaming, hoarse voice. Jake gestured for Rosie to stay at the table and crossed to the window, peered out, and sighed. "She's home. I'd better go and give her a hand."

Rosie could hear the sound of breaking glass, and went to the window.

Lorraine was standing in the middle of the road, swinging a doll by its arm. Her blouse was torn, her skirt hanging off, and she was filthy. She swiped at Jake.

"Fuck off! *Fucking leave me alone, you shit!*"

Jake backed off, arms raised, and Lorraine kicked out at him, swearing. A woman with a shopping cart was passing by and Lorraine caught her stare. "What you fucking looking at, you cunt? *Fuck off—go on!*"

Jake had to coax and cajole her to come to the stairs leading up to Rosie's apartment. It took him fifteen minutes to get her up them. She took two steps up and fell down three. She screeched with laughter, then slowly crawled up, only to insist on going down again to pick up her doll.

At last Jake got her into the apartment. She stood by the door.

"Hi, Rosie. He fucked you yet?"

Rosie went into the kitchen as Jake tried to get Lorraine onto the sofa. Halfway there she yanked off her shirt, stripping it away from her skinny body: she fumbled with Jake's pants. He swiped her hand aside and dragged her to the sofa, she fell, and slithered onto the floor.

"Run the shower, Rosie," Jake said.

Lorraine stank of booze, vomit, and urine. She was dirty, her face looked as if she had been facedown in some dirt track, and her eyes seemed even bluer than usual because they were red-rimmed. She had obviously not slept during the missing day. She refused to release the doll even when they half carried her into the shower, ran the cold water over her, and between them stripped off her clothes, Jake paying no attention to her naked body, apart from glancing at Rosie when he saw the fresh red bruises, and then again when he saw how badly scarred her body was—old scars, deep marks, crude stitches.

Rosie wanted to weep at seeing her friend like this, but instead she determinedly gathered towels and soaped Lorraine clean. Lorraine became subdued and listless, but she would not let go of the doll. Washed, with a clean nightgown on, she lay down on Rosie's bed.

"Best to let her sleep it off," Jake said, and ushered Rosie out of the bedroom. They picked up the filthy clothes and tossed them into the trash can. Lorraine fell into a deep, coma-like sleep. Rosie checked on her throughout the night, in case she vomited and choked to death. Jake left, depressed, though it was hardly unexpected. He'd seen it all before with Rosie— but at least Lorraine had been easier to get up the stairs.

Rosie slept on the sofa. She was woken by Lorraine stumbling out of the bedroom. Her face looked pale green, and there were deep, dark rings beneath her eyes.

''Coffee'' was about the only word she could squeeze out. Her head felt like someone had attached a chunk of concrete to it, with a bolt hammered into her skull to keep it steady. She needed Rosie to help her back to bed, and she moaned in agony as she lay down. Ice packs were prepared, and gently Rosie rested them on her forehead. Lorraine slept for the remainder of the day, waking again in the early evening. By then she was able to move around more easily. ''What day is it?''

''Tuesday evening.''

''Wake me up on Friday.'' Lorraine gave a wan smile and lay down on the sofa.

Rosie shopped, using Lorraine's hidden savings: she would tell her when the time was right, but she couldn't talk to Lorraine the way she was, and the rent was due. So Rosie kept dipping in.

It was Friday before Lorraine's hangover lifted. She was quiet, staring into space, unable to hold a conversation. Every time she attempted to explain herself, her voice trailed off in midsentence.

Rosie stroked her head. ''Honey, you don't have to explain. I've been there. Just get better, then we can talk.''

Lorraine clasped her hand. ''Thanks.''

Rosie smiled, dipped into the savings again, and went out to buy some steak: Lorraine needed her strength built up. She also paid the telephone bill, the electric bill—dip, dip, dip— but she'd admit it when Lorraine was better. It wasn't stealing, she told herself—what was hers was Lorraine's, after all—it was just that, right now, she was short of cash.

On the weekend when Jake came by Lorraine greeted him warmly.

He cocked his head to one side. ''Back in the land of the living now, are we?''

Lorraine blushed. ''Oh. Were you here?''

''Who do you think carried you up the fuckin' stairs? You really went for it, didn't you?''

Lorraine gave him that odd, lopsided, squint-eyed look. ''Christ only knows who I went with. I don't remember anyone's dick making a great impression.''

Jake turned away: he was never sure about her, she had a

filthy mouth one minute, the next she came on like a real lady. "If I was you, I'd get down to a clinic and get checked out. You smelled like a sewer."

She was unable to meet his steady gaze. At least she could still be ashamed, he thought, that was something in her favor. "Rosie's been taking good care of you, so you make sure you say thank you."

"I don't need you to tell me to do that, Jake." Her voice was so husky he had to strain to hear what she said.

"What?"

"I said I'd go and have a checkup, *okay*?"

"Good. I suggest you come to a meeting, and keep on coming for a few days, unless you got to go to work. You still think you got work at the gallery? I passed it two days ago and it looked all shut up."

She walked into the bedroom. "Soon as I feel fit enough I'll be out looking for another job."

Rosie banged open the screen door, her arms bulging with groceries. Jake took the loaded bags from her. "You've been spending a lot lately, haven't you?"

"Let's just say I've had kind of a windfall. Now, will you stay for dinner? I got some steaks and salad and I'll make baked potatoes."

Jake put the bags on the kitchen table. "Sounds good!" He continued, whispering, "She should have herself checked out at a clinic."

"She's only got a hangover, Jake."

"She could also have HIV, venereal disease, and Christ only knows what else, so get her down to a clinic."

Rosie looked toward the bedroom wondering if Lorraine had heard, then started unpacking the groceries.

Lorraine had heard, and rested back on Rosie's bed. She was sober. She had little or no recollection of what she had done or where she had been. She dimly remembered stopping off in the cab, going to buy a can of Coke, and coming out with two liters of vodka. She had a vague impression of having been thrown out of the same taxi, thumbing a lift from a trucker, and then—blank.

She sighed. Maybe it was better this way. She didn't know why she was getting herself straightened out again. Now she knew she didn't have anyone to do it for. She closed her eyes, making a silent decision that as soon as Rosie and Jake left the apartment, she'd pack up what she had, get her stash of money, and go. Go and get so drunk she would never get sober again. Her resolution to blow it all—blow herself—made her feel lighthearted, and she sat up, wrapped her robe around her, and went into the kitchen.

"This smells so good. We having a party?"

Rooney looked around the tastefully furnished room, and at the pictures arrayed on a bookcase. Norman Hastings with his wife, Norman Hastings with his daughters, his dog, his car, Norman Hastings smiling. Norman Hastings the nice, ordinary husband and father. Rooney could smell baking, mixed with furniture polish, or maybe it was some kind of room spray. He could hear Hastings's dog out in the backyard with the kids, barking as the creaking swing swung back and forth. The little girls were calling to the dog, to each other, and the sound of their voices added to the air of normality. The only thing missing was their father.

Mrs. Hastings came in with homemade cookies and a pot of coffee. She was a pretty woman, with nice, honey-colored hair and a sweet-faced smile. She perched rather than sat on the chair opposite Rooney. She had good hands, square-cut nails without any polish.

"I'm sorry not to have any news," Rooney said. She bit her lip, trying not to cry. Rooney hated having to do it, but he couldn't put off what he was there for, and she seemed to sense he wanted something.

"Mrs. Hastings, I'm sorry if this seems like going over old ground, but I just want to ask a few more questions."

She began to nibble a cookie.

"Tell me about a normal, everyday week—where your husband went, who he saw, that kind of thing."

The familiar story unfolded. Norman Hastings got up at the same time every day, even on weekends. He took his kids to school, he went to work, he came home, he had supper with his family. Two nights a week he went bowling or played poker with his friends. Weekends were kept for the family.

"Did he have any other hobbies?"

"Just taking care of the garden, that kind of thing. He did all the decorating and he built the kitchen and the girls' shelves and wardrobes."

"Nothing else?"

She shook her head, then hesitated. "We did join a country and western club two or three years ago. We went four or five times, but he didn't really enjoy it. I did, but he said they weren't his type."

"Did you continue going?"

"No. You need a partner, you see, for the square dances. . . . I'm not being much help, am I?" she asked.

"Was there anyone you didn't like among his friends?"

She shook her head.

"Would you show me around the house?"

She seemed surprised, but stood up and walked to the door. Rooney trailed after her. She was like a tour guide, pointing out what Norman had done—the extensions, the custom-built closets. She was boring him and he began to feel faintly irritated. The last room they went into was Hastings's den. Its walls were painted the identical color as three other rooms, the pictures indistinguishable from those in the living room. Norman with his wife, his kids, his bowling pals, his poker pals. Four men standing, hands in their pockets, staring at the camera. Rooney moved closer, peering at the photographs, half hoping he would see a man with wide lips, glasses, and a bite out of his neck, but they were all potbellied, jovial types with just a faint glimmer of enjoyment on their faces. Rooney sighed and turned away, but as he did he noticed a faint mark on the wall where another picture had hung. "What was there?"

Mrs. Hastings blinked. "I can't remember."

He knew she was lying, the house was too orderly for her not to know every inch. "Was it a photograph?" Rooney asked, relaxed and casual.

"I can't remember. Norman must have taken it down."

"Do you mind looking for it?"

She hesitated, then crossed to the desk. As she opened a drawer, they heard a noise outside, and one of her daughters started to cry loudly. "I won't be a minute—I think she's fallen off the swing."

"Can I look through the desk?"

She paused in the doorway. "I'd prefer if you didn't."

He lifted his hands in apology. Stepping back from the desk he sat down in Hastings's chair. "I'll wait for you."

As soon as she was out of the room Rooney looked over

the contents of the drawers. Tax forms, house insurance, life insurance, dental and medical checks, they were like the rest of the house, orderly. He drummed the desktop with his fingers. On it was yet another photograph of Mrs. Hastings, a daughter on either side. Rooney picked it up and stared at it, then he turned it over. There was a hook, and a stand. He looked to the space on the wall, then back to the photograph. When he placed it against the faint dust outline, it matched.

He crossed to the window. Mrs. Hastings was examining her daughter's leg, so he returned to the desk and picked up the photograph again. He pushed open the small clips at each side and opened the frame. There was nothing underneath. He swore, replaced the clips, and was about to stand it upright on the desk when she walked back in.

"She's all right, just a grazed knee." She stared at Rooney, then at the photograph.

"Pretty photograph—in fact, they're all very nice."

She prodded the frame into exactly the same position as before.

"Yes. They were taken by a professional photographer."

"Ah, just goes to show—you can always tell!" Rooney paused. "Mrs. Hastings, that photograph was the one off the wall, wasn't it? Was someone else's photograph in it? Is that why you took it down?"

She pursed her lips: she didn't seem quite so pretty now—there was a steely quality to her. "Yes, it was, now I come to think about it." She folded her arms. "I'd like you to go, please."

Rooney remained where he was. "Mrs. Hastings, your husband was found brutally murdered. Now, I have no motive, no reason why anybody should have done that."

"Robbery. You never found his wallet. It was robbery. That's what the papers have said and the television news."

"And you can think of no other motive?"

"No. He's buried now anyway. It's all over. I'd like you to leave." She pointedly held the door open and Rooney walked past her.

He stopped as they reached the front door. "The photographer. Do you have his name and address?"

"No, I'm sorry I don't. Norman always arranged the sittings."

Rooney scratched his head. "Was he local?"

She colored. "I can't remember."

"But you had them taken every few years, you told me so yourself. Surely you must remember?"

"I don't."

She had the front door open when he leaned close. "Why are you lying?"

"Please leave me alone."

Rooney shut the door with the flat of his hand. She pushed against him, and then backed down the hallway. "I don't want to talk about it!"

Rooney followed her. "What don't you want to talk about, Mrs. Hastings?"

Her hands were flailing, her face bright pink.

"Why don't we go and sit down?"

"No."

Rooney gazed at the freshly painted ceiling. "Don't make me get a whole bunch of officers checking out every photographer, Mrs. Hastings, don't waste my time...." His voice was low, flat, and expressionless. "Seven women have been killed in the same manner as your husband—a blow to the back of the head with a hammer, and their faces battered beyond recognition. If you have anything—*anything*—that will help me find the killer, you had better tell me!"

She stood with her arms wrapped around herself, her whole body shaking. "I said if I ever caught him doing it again, I would divorce him—I'd tell his parents, his boss, his friends . . ."

"Doing what, Mrs. Hastings?"

She turned around and her face was ashen. "He was dressed in women's clothes."

Rooney didn't show a flicker of distaste or surprise. In fact, he was slightly thrown only because nothing had prepared him for this. He'd just wondered if there was some family friend that might have been a possible suspect, a photograph of someone Mrs. Hastings had hidden, but she had been hiding a lot more.

She had come home from one of the country and western nights—when Norman had said he didn't like it, she'd gone alone. She started to cry. "I was only there a few minutes and I felt stupid all dressed up in cowboy boots, and I just thought he was right, it *was* stupid, so I came home. But he didn't hear me coming in. I knew he was in the bedroom because I saw the light on, and I thought I'd surprise him." She gave a strange, bitter, high-pitched laugh. "I don't know who was more surprised, him or me. He was all made up, with a blond wig, a cheap awful frilled dress, high heels . . . I—I just couldn't believe my eyes."

She broke down and sobbed, and Rooney remained silent, waiting.

"Anyway . . . a long time after, because I ran into the bathroom and wouldn't come out, he was on his knees outside the bathroom sobbing, and I was scared he'd wake the girls, so I came out. He'd taken everything off, but he still had traces—his face . . ."

Norman Hastings, on his knees before his wife, had sworn on the Bible that no one else knew, that he had never done it before. But she knew he had, because of all the clothes. She found more in the garage, more wigs and shoes. She had burned everything.

Rooney asked, still being very nonchalant but beginning to sweat with the excitement of this new lead, "This photographer . . . do you think he might have had the same inclinations?"

"He was homosexual, but after I found Norman, I refused ever to go to him again."

Rooney took out his notebook. "What's his name?"

She wrung her hands. "Dear God, this won't come out, will it? His parents are elderly—all his friends, his daughters—please tell me this will never come out?"

Rooney promised he would do his best to keep it from being disclosed to the press. He was lying. The photographer's name was Craig Lyall; she even supplied his studio and home address.

Rooney walked down the immaculate path from the tidy little house, and crossed to his car. Arden Avenue was a nice quiet neighborhood, though it didn't feel like a warm one where neighbors knew one another well. It was more refined than friendly. The big-eared wonder had been right—now he had a lot more to go on. He suddenly remembered Lorraine Page again, and the Laura Bradley case. He recalled how shocked he had been at the normality of the killer's house, his distraught family. Nothing gave a hint that their only son, the janitor, was a madman; they had even accused the police of harassing him and making their lives a misery. He looked back at the Hastingses' house, and suddenly it wasn't so neat or tidy and homey. He felt deeply sorry for the man, trapped in that perfect little prison. For the first time he also felt an odd compassion for Lorraine Page; she had been a crack officer all those years ago. What a terrible waste.

"Lorraine! *Lorraine!* We're leaving, did you hear? *Lorraine!*" Rosie bellowed.

"Okay, I'll see you later." She was desperate for them both to go, wanting to take her savings and get the hell out. She was so impatient that as soon as the screen door closed she ran to her closet, and wrenched it open, falling to her knees to search for the money. She found the shoes, and then stared in disbelief at the pitiful remains of her hoard. She began hurling things out of the closet, convinced there must be some mistake. Then she sat back on her heels and punched at the door.

"Rosie!" she snarled.

Rosie and Jake were at the bottom of the steps when the screen door flew open. Lorraine hurled herself down the stairs, her hands splayed like claws. She grabbed Rosie by the throat. *"Where is it?"*

Jake tried to haul her off, but she thrust him back so hard that he crashed into the garbage cans. She dived at Rosie again, screeching at her at the top of her voice.

"My money! *You stole my money, you fucking bitch!*"

Lorraine punched her in the face and Rosie reeled back, tripped on the edge of the sidewalk, and fell over backward. Lorraine sprang onto her, pulling at her hair. "You fucking bitch! That was *my money, my money*—you two-faced cunt, you piece of shit . . . *you fucker!*" People were coming out of the grocery store to watch. The Hispanic family gathered on the front porch. One of the men started to applaud, laughing, and the kids picked it up, jeering and shouting. Lorraine was on top of Rosie, hitting and punching her. Jake was trying to drag her off, but nothing he did could stop Lorraine. She swiped and spat like a wildcat, and then rolled off Rosie and collapsed, kicking and pounding the grass with her fists.

Rosie's nose was bleeding, her face was scratched, her dress ripped, and she was shaking with terror. She had never seen anyone so crazy—well, not when they were sober.

Jake had handled crazies and drunks, but Lorraine's immense strength surprised him—she'd almost broken his jaw. He now hauled her to her feet and dragged her over to the steps. He turned on two gawking onlookers: "Show's over, okay? And you bunch of so-called parents, get your kids out of here. Go on, get, go on, kids shouldn't be seein' this kind of thing."

Lorraine didn't resist. She let Jake propel her up the stairs, and a trembling Rosie followed slowly, keeping a good distance.

Jake sat Lorraine on the sofa, then squatted back on his heels in front of her. "What the hell was that all about?"

Lorraine glared at Rosie. "Tell him!" she shrieked.

Rosie started to cry, dabbing at her face, and Lorraine swung back her fist and threatened Rosie with another blow, which started her screaming. Jake pried them apart, pushing Lorraine away. Abruptly she raised her hands. "Okay, okay . . . but if she won't tell you then I will. Every cent I've saved and fuckin' worked my ass off for . . . she has stolen. I've got no more than twenty, thirty bucks left from over a thousand."

Jake frowned. "Where did you get a grand from? Rob a bank, for chrissakes?"

"What is this? An inquisition? It was my dough. She's the one who stole it. Why not interrogate her?"

Jake stood up, ran his hand over his thinning hair. "How much is left?"

Lorraine closed her eyes. "Not enough to drink myself to death, which is what I intended doing."

"So, you want to die. Fuck you—and your attitude. Anyone that can make a thousand bucks in less than a week gotta have somethin' goin' for them—unless you did pull a heist, but somehow I doubt it . . ."

Lorraine gave Jake her odd squint-eyed look. "Okay. You want to know how I made it? Blackmail, I blackmailed a little queer bastard . . ."

Jake grinned. "Can we all get a piece of the action? Or is it just you that's got the information on him?"

"It was Art, at the gallery, he's into porno—not paintings, porno—with kids, satisfied?"

• • •

Rooney walked into his office and beamed at Bean, who was sitting morosely on the edge of the desk, picking his teeth with a matchstick. He was hot and wanted to go home, and he had a toothache. "Guess what? Norman Hastings was a cross-dresser!"

Bean gaped as Rooney displayed the photographs from Craig Lyall's studio. Norman Hastings in a blond wig, dressed up and in full makeup, smiling with thick, glossy red lips into the camera lens.

"Jesus Christ, I don't believe it!" Bean was so flabbergasted, even his toothache disappeared.

Rooney was pleased with his efforts. He told Bean to bring in the pictures of the dead women, as he slowly eased into his desk chair, never taking his eyes off Hastings's photograph. He was unable to stop grinning. He looked up when Bean returned with the pictures of the dead women, then rested his hands behind his head with a smirk.

"I think I just cracked it. What if Teacher picked up Hastings? Maybe thought he was a hooker? I mean, he might have told his wife, sworn on the Bible that he wouldn't get his dresses out, but what if he did and was picked up?"

Bean deflated Rooney by reminding him that Hastings was found in men's clothes, so that theory was out the window.

"Shit, yeah, I forgot. So, maybe he knew him? Maybe they dressed up together?"

They were going down the maybe road again, but at least they now had a road. All Hastings's friends would be requestioned.

"What was the photographer like?" Bean asked.

Rooney sniffed. "Real gay, probably a cross-dresser, too. Better get him in, have a talk with him. I got so excited when he showed the photos I might have missed something. Works out of a studio in the old firehouse building, you know, high ceilings, lots of camera equipment, well, he would have, he's a photographer, right?"

"Fellows was right, wasn't he?" Bean mumbled. They had begun walking toward the exit when he stopped and rubbed his jaw.

"I gotta see a dentist, got some meat stuck between my teeth. I used dental floss and made it worse, then I dug around with a matchstick and now I think I got a splinter in my gum!"

"Lemme have a look."

"What?"

"Open your goddamn mouth!" Rooney sighed and peered into Bean's open mouth. "Nope, nothin'."

Bean rubbed his jaw as they continued on, then stopped and stuck his finger into his mouth. "Ah! Got it." He spat out a sliver of something or other.

"Captain."

Rooney sighed, turning to Bean again.

"Now what? See a dentist, all right?"

"Captain, what if Helen Murphy wasn't the woman who phoned us? Maybe we should have another interview with that woman Laura Bradley, go over everythin' again."

"What did you say?" Rooney snapped.

"I don't need a dentist, it was just something stuck between my back molars."

"Jesus Christ, not the fucking dentist, after—what did you say?"

"The last thing, about requestioning the woman interviewed."

Rooney nodded. "Yeah, what did you say her name was?"

"Laura Bradley?"

Bean patiently explained again about the two uniformed guys who had interviewed a woman at the address where the cabdriver thought he had dropped off the injured woman.

"Laura Bradley? That her name?" Rooney stood in the corridor, blinking. He could picture that little girl, see Rookie Lorraine Page's face when they found her, and she'd said, "Oh, my God, she looks like my little girls."

"Check her out."

Lorraine told Jake and Rosie the entire Art, Nula, and Didi story, and described her visit to Mike. She felt drained—by them, by everything.

Jake gently touched her head, fixing a stray strand of hair. "You gonna come clean about that time you got a crack over the back of the head? You had money that night, too."

"You really are grilling me tonight, Jake, what's with you?"

"I just know it helps to talk things over. You still want to slit your wrists?"

She smiled. "Maybe not quite so much."

''Good. So, how did you get that crack on the back of your head?''

Lorraine yawned. ''Well, you know the grocery store? At the end of the street? Not the liquor store but right on the intersection of Marengo, just at the side of it? There's traffic lights, a pedestrian crossing, right?''

''Yes,'' Rosie and Jake said together.

''That's where I tripped and fell.''

Their faces made Lorraine giggle and suddenly they broke into laughter, too. They were all laughing when they heard the footsteps coming up the wooden staircase. Rosie looked out of the window.

''It's the cops.''

Jake watched Lorraine's expression change. Her face was suddenly drained of all color.

EIGHT

Lorraine didn't panic. She calmly picked up her cigarette pack and headed for the bedroom.

"Jake, if they ask for a Laura Bradley, she's not here. She stayed awhile and then left."

"They coming for you?" Rosie asked.

"Yeah, but I swear I've done nothing wrong. I just got a lot of outstanding violations, and—"

Jake took her by the elbow, pushing her even farther into the safety of the bedroom. "Why Laura Bradley? Who the fuck is she?"

"It was the name I told them, they came here before. That fat cop, the one you recognized, Rooney, must have told them where they could find me. I dunno, please, Jake, get them off my back and I swear I won't kill myself!"

"It's a deal," Jake said as he closed the door.

Rosie hardly said a word, just gave her name. Jake did the rest, smooth-talking, open, and friendly. Sorry he couldn't help them, but Laura Bradley had left. The young uniformed cop smiled, tipped his hat: with his perfect white teeth and suntan he could have come straight out of a movie. He returned to his partner, waiting below in the car, and Rosie watched them pull away.

The patrol car traveled one block up and parked. The cab-driver had said a short balding guy and a fat woman had helped the injured woman, so they radioed in for further instructions.

In some ways Lorraine knew they'd be back—even wished she hadn't played games and had come forward, rather than involving Jake and Rosie. They heard the cops returning, and Lorraine gave a long sigh. "Okay. Remember that night I cracked my head? Just tell them we were all at an AA meeting, agreed? That's what you say and you stick to it."

"Why do we have to lie?" Rosie gasped, the footsteps almost at the screen door.

"So I don't get arrested for nonappearance in court. I got traffic violations. I also blackmailed Art Mathews, and you, Rosie, spent the dough—you need any more reasons?"

There was a knock on the door and Lorraine opened it. She stood there waiting for them, with her jacket, purse, and cigarettes. "Okay, guys, I'm Laura Bradley, and I'm all yours." She smiled at their surprise. "You wanted to talk to Laura Bradley, right? Well, that's me, you gonna take me in?"

Lorraine held out her hands as if for cuffs and nodded toward Jake and Rosie. "They don't know anythin' about it so let's go." As a second squad car drew up outside, sirens blasting, a crowd started gathering around their building. Rosie and Jake were driven off in one squad car, while Lorraine traveled solo with two officers in another. She was chatty, overchatty, on the short drive to the station and then fell silent as they drove her around the new building—or new to her—to the station's main entrance. Both officers were very cordial, taking her gently by the elbow as they steered her into the building. "Wow, been some changes since I was last taken in."

Lorraine continued to be awestruck as she was led through the vast building and up to the second floor. The officers had instructions to take her straight to Josh Bean on her arrival, and they had to ask her to move it along as she kept stopping and staring at the high-tech building. She was truly impressed, but covering up at the same time the fact that she was getting more and more tense at what she knew was ahead of her—meeting Rooney face-to-face for one thing, and for a second trying to explain away why she had used Laura Bradley's name. Stupid.

She was taken straight in to see Josh Bean, and offered a seat. Rooney was not evident and without hesitating Lorraine admitted that she had lied, that she was Lorraine Page. He seemed to accept her excuse that she hadn't wanted to get involved, because, as she presumed he already knew, she was an ex-cop. As they spoke, from the corner of her eye, she could see her details rolling off the fax machine. But she was relieved that Captain Rooney was not around. Just being inside the station had put her in a cold sweat, but she was in control.

Bean elaborated as to why they had asked her to accompany the officers. He told her they were investigating a murder and asked where she was on the night of the seventeenth of May.

Lorraine said she was at an AA meeting and gave the address. Bean was quiet, almost too friendly and apologetic for any inconvenience they had caused. "You see, we're searching for a witness, a woman we believe is a very valuable witness."

Even as he spoke she could see him scrutinizing her, and it was obvious he doubted that she could be the same woman as described—she had all her teeth, for a start. Lorraine remained in control, smiled and joked. He was so young, so spic-and-span—she wondered how he got along with the loudmouthed Rooney.

"Well, we sure get a lot of riffraff in the street. Only the other night there was some drunken woman out there, screaming the place down. Used to be a good area, but maybe before your time. We had to clear it up, drug pushers used to park up and down Marengo."

In a second interview room, Rosie and Jake kept to the AA meeting story. They were being questioned by a fresh-faced officer, even younger than Bean. Rosie told how she had met Lorraine in the hospital, how long she had been staying. When they were asked if they had assisted a woman from a taxi on the night of the seventeenth, a woman with injuries to her head and face, both repeated that they were not at home that evening. But they kept glancing nervously at each other.

"You ever see a blue sedan parked in your street, like this one?" They were shown a photograph of Hastings's car.

"No, not that I can recall." Rosie peered at the picture. "This has been on the TV, hasn't it?"

"Do you know or did you know a Mr. Norman Hastings?" Rosie shook her head.

"He was the guy that was murdered, right?" Jake asked.

"I didn't know him," Rosie said, "but I seen all the papers. What's this got to do with us?"

Rosie and Jake were released, but were told that they should inform the police of any change of address in case they were required for further questioning. Jake asked if Lorraine was also free to go, and was told that she was still being questioned.

''We'll wait.''

Rosie and Jake huddled together to review the officer's questions. They were confused. It seemed a lot more serious than Lorraine had said, but now they were in too deep, and the spacious waiting room made both feel small and conspicuous. It was to be a long wait.

Four hours after Lorraine had entered the station she was told she was being held for a lineup. She remained calm, accepting a tepid cup of coffee and an extra pack of cigarettes. When she heard that her friends were waiting for her, she asked for someone to tell them they should go home. So at two A.M. Rosie and Jake left the station. They had no idea why Lorraine was still being detained. But Jake had been around too many cops, in too many stations not to know that this was something a lot heavier than traffic violations.

Lorraine knew the procedure by heart, and made it clear she was more than willing to cooperate. She waited patiently, knowing what a runaround would be going on behind the scenes. Captain Rooney had still not made an appearance and for that she was grateful. She figured they must be searching around for a bunch of tall blond women to stand with her in the lineup. She breathed a little easier when she was told that Jake and Rosie had left the station.

The lineup corridor annex was like all the others she had dealt with years before, but much larger and with better equipment. The more she looked around the Pasadena station the more impressed she was with the massive building. She wondered how Rooney fitted in, recalling his old squalid office, his grimy-walled, smoke-stained room so different from these white, neon-lit, airy offices with the red NO SMOKING signs on every door.

Lorraine spent an exhausting, nervous night in the station, waiting until morning when the Summerses could be phoned to come in and view the lineup. Unfailingly polite and pleasant, Bean had begun to get on her nerves by the time he finally ushered her toward the viewing room to join the other women. She chose place number seven, for no particular reason except to avoid being dead center or at either end, which were not good positions. The other eleven women carried in their cards and lined up on the small, narrow platform. Some were prisoners; others Lorraine could not imagine where they had been dragged in from. Probably a couple of hookers, housewives, or coffee shop workers, maybe station clerks. Anyone was acceptable if they looked right, and most people, when asked, were always willing to make a few bucks.

When Mr. and Mrs. Summers arrived, Bean told them to take their time, to look at each subject closely. If they recognized the woman they should walk out and give the number. If they wished her to speak they must ask the officer at their side to repeat whatever they wanted the prisoner to say. Mr. Summers stared through the glass at each woman in turn. Then he left the room. Next came his wife. She, too, took her time, but she was confused since she was even more sure than her husband that they had already identified the woman. They also felt slightly guilty. Had they made a mistake earlier? Both had been so certain that the deceased Helen Murphy was the woman they had seen in the parking lot.

"Could they all smile?" Mrs. Summers asked nervously. "I want to see their teeth."

Captain Rooney walked into the viewing room. There was Lorraine, at number seven, taller than any of the others. It was strange to see her, chin up, holding the card in front of her, her face expressionless. He moved closer to the glass and stared at the deep scar running down her cheek. She looked different, meaner, harder; and yet there was still an attractiveness about her. Her clear eyes seemed to stare back at him through the one-way glass, almost as if she knew he was there.

The third person to be led across the lineup was the cabdriver, unshaven, having been ordered out of bed as he was now working night shifts. He was bad-tempered, asking over and over if he was going to get paid for all the time they had used up. He had already identified the woman, hadn't he? In some ways he'd half expected a row of corpses.

Rooney turned to Bean. "Anything?"

"Yeah. The Summerses both said it could be number four— she's from Records! And the cabdriver said it was the skinny woman, number two. She's a hooker, but she was locked up on the seventeenth for breaking into a car.''

"Great.'' Rooney sighed.

Lorraine was asked to wait in reception. She was exhausted from keeping up her calm front during the hours she'd spent at the station, as well as from standing very erect in the lineup—that was another little tip: never slouch, makes you look guilty, always look straight ahead. Never smile, just look. They can't deal with a straight confrontation.

Rooney sat at his desk, swiveling his chair from side to side. In front of him were Rosie's and Jake's statements, and Lorraine's own statement. Why had she used that poor little mite's name? It made him angry. He sighed and then stared at Bean, who was looking over Lorraine's charge sheet. "We can hold her if you want. You have a look at this? Vagrancy, prostitution . . . she's got twenty-five traffic violations, five nonappearances for court hearings . . .''

"Yeah, I know,'' muttered Rooney.

"She said she was at an AA meeting, so did her friends. We can check it if you want.''

Rooney shrugged. Lorraine didn't fit their description, she looked to him to be doing okay for herself—and she was sober. "I can understand why she didn't want to be brought in.'' He held out his hand for the sheets. "I'll talk to her, you can go home. Get some rest while you can.''

"This is gettin' out of control, isn't it, Captain?''

"Not your problem, Bean. Just be in early tomorrow morning.''

As Lorraine was led along the corridor toward him, Rooney leaned against the wall. He gave a noncommittal nod and held the door wider for her to pass into his office. She sat in the chair opposite his and waited. Rooney walked slowly around to his chair, sank into it heavily, then rested his elbows on his desk.

"Laura Bradley.''

She smiled. "Yeah. I don't know why I said it, just came into my head. Maybe the little kid's always there, I don't know . . . I'm sorry I wasted your time.''

He stared at her charge sheets.

"I guess whoever you were looking for must have used my

address—old ploy. You tried the apartments either side? There's a lot of oddballs live around Orange Grove, some right on Marengo, a few real choice ones right in our building, in fact, and then there's the liquor store on the corner—''

Rooney interrupted, "I know the area. How long have you been sober?"

"A year," she lied.

Rooney sighed. He hadn't revealed to Bean why he hadn't been around when they'd brought in Lorraine. He'd been with Chief Michael Berillo and he'd been hauled over the carpet. "I'm being really pushed on this one. Chief implied I'd be off it if I didn't get a result soon."

"What's the case?" Lorraine asked knowing perfectly well what it was.

"Seven hookers cracked over the skull with a claw hammer. One of 'em's only seventeen, rest are real dogs." Rooney smirked. "Maybe some of 'em are your friends. You want to take a look?"

"Cunt."

"Okay, relax. What are you doing now?"

"Work in an art gallery, go see my kids—Mike still pays me alimony, pretty boring but it keeps me. Can I go?"

"No. I need someone to talk to. What do you think of the new station—well, be about five years old now. It wasn't built when you left, was it?"

She lit a cigarette, and was surprised when he slumped forward, clasping his head in his hands. "I'm fucking coming up for retirement, and what happens? I get a case that's . . . I keep going up one blind alley after another. Nothing makes sense."

He suddenly looked up, and then got to his feet. "Come on, take a look, maybe you did know one of these whores."

She glared at him, and he laughed. "Hey! You be nice to me. I could have you locked up. You know how many violations you got outstanding? Twenty-five, sweetheart, so move your butt."

Lorraine followed Rooney into the incident room. The officers in there turned and stared. Rooney announced loudly that she was an ex-cop, and there followed a few strange glances and a whispered exchange between two women cops who knew that she'd been in the lineup. Lorraine gazed around the room and then said aside to Rooney, "Jesus, Rooney, these cops all look like kids to me."

She lit a cigarette from the butt and heard someone say it was a no-smoking zone. She paid no attention and puffed her cigarette alight. She turned to one of the female officers and said quietly, "You want to arrest me?"

Rooney now glared at the watching officers. "None o' you got work to do? Go on, piss off outta my hair, go on."

They shuffled out, one by one turning back for a last look. Ex-cop, somebody had said. She sure as hell didn't look like one—and why had she been brought in for the lineup? She wasn't bad looking, but none liked the cold blue eyes that stared right through them.

Rooney took her over the photographs, pointing out each woman in turn, where they were found, the dates. She looked closely at Hastings. Pinned next to it was one of him in drag.

"How about that for a turnup? Drag artist in his spare time, I found that out," Rooney said, as if he expected her to applaud. She remained with Rooney for two more hours. Back in his office, he talked on and on. She knew he was running everything by her, for no other reason than that he wanted to run it all by himself. She let him ramble on with barely an interruption and wondered if at the end of all this he was going to book her. Then came: "You ever think about that kid? The one you took out?"

She turned away. She didn't think of him, and she suddenly felt guilty. But Rooney continued, "You were good, you know. I wish I had someone here with your dedication. If you hadn't been a drunk, you'd be somewhere now. A lot go the same way—well, not quite as low as you. You hit the skids, didn't you? Worked the streets?"

"Yes. Look, can I go?" She stood up.

"No, you can't. Fucking sit down."

She sat down, and then he blew her away. "I want you to do something for me."

She stared.

"Make you a deal." He picked up the charge sheets between finger and thumb and dangled them. "See what you can come up with for me. Ask around the whorehouses, the—"

"You kidding me?"

He shook his head, his voice suddenly low and unpleasant. "No, I'm not kidding. The deal is I'll clear these," he indicated the long list of charges, "*if* you help me out. Somebody's got to know these hookers, somebody's got to know something, maybe where Murphy's hiding out. We're trying to trace Helen Murphy's husband, but so far no joy—and I doubt if it's him anyway. If you find anything, any link, you got a clean sheet.''

Lorraine laughed. ''I got a job, Bill.''

He leaned closer to her, and she could smell his stale breath. ''This is not a job, sweetheart, this is a deal. You get a clean slate for helping me out or I'll bust you.''

''Then I'll need a car—''

''Fuck off, Lorraine! Look at this. You've been charged on eight counts for driving without a license, without insurance, and under the influence. No way can I get that cleared. The other stuff, yes—the no-show for court appearances, prostitution.''

''What about expenses?''

He laughed, shaking his head. ''You sure try it on.''

''I got to eat, pay rent. I walk out of my job, and—''

He sneered, ''Do what you did before, Lorraine, sell your little ass—''

She leaned over the desk. ''Screw you. Take those charges and shove them up your ass—it's big enough to take the entire filing cabinet.''

He roared with laughter and slapped the desk with his hand. ''Okay. Fifty bucks.''

''A day.''

''A week.''

''Fuck off. I know how much you pay informers, I also know you'll have a nice little stash that you'll divvy out between you and your pals at the end of each month, filling in fake names and places. I know, Billy. Fifty bucks a day. I can go on the streets, into the bars, the clubs. I'll find someone with information. Like you said, I was good.''

Rooney got up and crossed to his window. He stood playing with the blind. ''How long you been sober?''

''I told you, a year. Call my husband, he'll tell you. Call my roommate, she'll tell you. I'm straight, Bill.''

He stared at her, meeting her unflinching eyes, and then he turned away, stuffing his hands into his baggy trouser pockets.

''You'll call in every day?''

''I'll call in on the hour, if that's what you want.''

''Yeah, it is,'' he said quietly, and opened his wallet.

Lorraine couldn't believe it: he was going to pay her there

and then. "Is there any way I can get copies of the statements you got to date?"

Rooney nodded, counting out a hundred bucks. "This is it, Lorraine, and believe me when I say I'll have you brought back in here so fast if you try to fuck with me. I need information."

"I'll also need photographs—everything you got so far."

Rooney looked at her, suddenly uncertain.

"I got to know what's going on, Bill."

"Yeah. I guess you do."

Rooney watched Lorraine walk out of the building. His bladder felt full but he didn't want to take a leak. He was wondering if he was crazy, he could see the folder she was carrying, full of copies of the thick case file. If the Chief found out he'd be in real trouble. He told himself he must be nuts, especially not even getting her to sign for the cash. He had a moment of blind panic: if she was to take it to the press he'd be screwed to the floor. Then he relaxed; he was almost nailed there already. He checked the time and put in a call to Andrew Fellows.

"Ah, Captain, I'm so sorry not to have gotten back to you since you gave me this new stuff on Hastings. Reason is, I haven't had much spare time, I'm on a lecture tour."

"I'd appreciate your input as soon as possible," Rooney rumbled.

"I'll get back to you as soon as I've got a moment to go over the file, but I'm up to my ears right now."

Rooney listened to the drawling voice, half smiling at the "ears" line, waiting for what he suspected was coming. It came.

"I don't suppose there's some way you could finance me, is there? This does take up a considerable amount of my time."

Rooney said he would run it by his chief and dropped the phone back on the hook. The chief would, no doubt, arrange payment—it had been his idea to bring Fellows on board, so let him budget for him. Rooney was stretched and he was not about to pay Fellows out of his own pocket, not like Lorraine.

He remembered finding her on the floor in the old precinct, looking into her face in the patrol car when he held that poor kid's Sony Walkman under her nose. She'd given that half-dazed smile. He thought about that moment now. That kid would've been alive if it wasn't for that bitch. He wanted to be deeply angry, but he couldn't, and it confused him. She had to be pretty tough to have survived, to have gotten herself back together. At least he hoped she was, that she wasn't right that moment walking into a bar with his case file in one hand and his cash in the other. If she was, then he would make sure, no matter what else he did, that she paid a high price. That decision made, he felt free to rush to the men's room, really in need of a leak.

When Lorraine got home she fell onto the sofa and slept for the rest of the day, then spent that evening reading through the case files. Her concentration blanked out Rosie and her television shows. When Rosie went to bed, Lorraine continued working, sifting through every statement, studying each photograph, jotting down notes. It was four in the morning when she stretched and got up. She had sat with her legs tightly crossed, just the way she had when she was working in the old days. She massaged her thighs, easing out the cramp, then sat staring into space. Rooney was right, they had nothing: no witnesses but herself. If only he knew! Lorraine had seen the killer—had almost gone down on him, had almost gotten herself killed. And now she also had a clear memory of the killer's cuff links. She wondered if Norman Hastings had ever bought or owned a reconditioned vintage car. From what she had read so far, she doubted it, but then, everyone had sure been wrong about him being the perfect family man.

Lorraine didn't go to bed until almost five, and by then she was so wired she was unable to fall asleep. The sofa was uncomfortable and too soft, her back ached and her legs still felt as if they were going to cramp up. She was in the half-dream state when suddenly she had a vivid image of the boy. She saw him running, saw the flash of the bright zigzag on his jacket.

"Freeze!"

She sat up, wide awake now. She didn't want to see him, didn't want to see herself, didn't want to see the boy's jerking body as the bullets tore into him. She flipped over the sheet, got up, and drew back the curtains. She forced herself to think about the murderer, remembering exactly where he had picked her up, right at the corner intersection. She could feel the sweat begin to trickle down from her armpits; it was another hot clammy night, but she didn't put the air conditioner on in case it woke Rosie. She got out some ice cubes and ran them around the back of her neck. She saw his face again in her mind, the rimless glasses, the wet lips. She remembered the smell of him, his underwear. She wondered if he lived nearby. On Orange Grove maybe? Or in one of the apartments Nula and Didi lived in? She flicked through the files. She didn't know why, but she doubted the man who'd attacked her was from this area. Maybe he lived in someplace like her old condo, that was certainly upmarket enough for his tasteful clothes and mani-cured hands. She knew he also was familiar with the area, the way he had driven directly to the shopping mall. Was he Helen Murphy's husband as Rooney suspected? She doubted it, no way that man had a wife whoring, no way was he a truck driver, as Murphy's file stated was his employment. Murphy was their only suspect, and Lorraine dismissed him. She closed her eyes, making herself visualize the face again, forcing her-self to try and recall every single detail: the rimless, gold-framed glasses; the close-set blue eyes; the straight nose; and the wide, wet, thick-lipped mouth. She conjured up a picture of his hands, went over exactly what he had said, how he had picked her up, how he had reached into the glove compart-ment. She wasn't scared, she just let the killer move into her mind. And just as she had done with the Laura Bradley mur-der, she repeated to herself, over and over again, her voice a soft whisper: "I'll get you."

NINE

Rosie was so immersed in the horror of the statements and pictures she didn't hear Lorraine walking into the bedroom.

"That was private, Rosie, you shouldn't be reading it."

Rosie, seated on the edge of her bed and surrounded by photographs, looked up and hunched her shoulders apologetically. "It's those morgue shots that get me—really close up, aren't they? I didn't know you looked like that when you were dead. How can they clean them up like that?" She held up Helen Murphy's photograph. "This is her when they found her, and this is her at the morgue and this is her after—I mean, here she looks like she's sleeping."

Lorraine walked into the bathroom. "They had her face fixed up with plaster for an ID. Makeup, that's all. The only suspect they got is her husband, a trucker, but they're way off, he's not the killer."

Rosie shut the file. "I doubt if anyone'll grieve over these women, they look like they're all pretty shot up—in fact, some of them look happier dead, know what I mean? Well, not the little blond girl, she's sort of cute."

Lorraine leaned on the bathroom door. "Yeah. She doesn't fit in, does she? All the others are older, worn out, hard . . ."

"You know what I think?" Rosie licked her lips. "I think he picked *you* up. You were hit on the back of the head but somehow you got away from him. The taxi brought you back

here and . . . I worked out that it *was* the seventeenth of May."
Then she shrugged her heavy shoulders. "It couldn't have
been you, though, could it?"

"Why not?"

"Because that was the day Norman Whatcha-call-it was
done—they found him in his own car, right? So he wouldn't
have been whacking you over the head and killing somebody
else, would he?"

"I fell on the sidewalk, Rosie."

"Yeah, and I'm Julia Roberts's look-alike."

Lorraine walked into the shower and pulled the curtain
closed. Rosie surprised her—not that she had said anything
intelligent, or especially intuitive: Lorraine had been cracked
over the back of the head in exactly the same manner as described not once but eight times in the files. But it was the
simple dismissal of the possibility that the man could have
killed Hastings and then on the same day attempted to kill
again. Lorraine made a mental note to check through the exact
times and dates of each murder.

Lorraine felt tired, but a good sort of tired. She had worked
hard last night just assimilating all the evidence, and although
she didn't like to admit it, she had liked talking it over with
Rosie. That's what had surprised her: that she had, for a few
brief minutes, felt like a player again. "Marking out the jigsaw" was the way she used to describe it to Mike.

Jets of water sprayed down onto her uptilted face. She and
Mike had talked over her cases in the beginning, but gradually
he'd become uninterested, telling her that he didn't want to
hear about the victims or the details of the murders, he had to
study. She had no one to talk it out of her system with: she
had just bottled it all up inside.

She gasped, having turned the taps to cold. She didn't want
him to come back into her life, not now, please, not Lubrinski,
she couldn't deal with him. It had been Lubrinski who'd realized she was bottling up all the horror, anger, disgust. It had
been Lubrinski, after a particularly heavy night—when they
had found two teenagers in a boardinghouse, stiff from death,
stiff from drugs, stiff and stinking, but they were so beautiful,
like frozen angels the pair of them—who had insisted they go
to a bar, insisted they get smashed. Drunk, she had suddenly
broken down and Lubrinski had gripped her tightly, had even
cried with her as he said it was okay to let go, to let the poison

out, rather than have it seething inside her. Lubrinski.

Rosie was eating muffins, a smear of jam across her cheek and also over the file, which Lorraine promptly snatched away from her. "Don't get it sticky with jam!"

Rosie washed her hands in a great display, and then returned to reading the files and statements. "This Andrew Fellows is something else, isn't he? You read what he came up with about Helen thingy? The killer really likes them in bad shape, doesn't he?"

Lorraine couldn't help but be drawn in. "Apart from Holly."

"Oh, yeah. Well, maybe he just got lucky that night."

Lorraine dressed and made up her face. When she came back into the bedroom Rosie was still engrossed in the files.

"Could you borrow that car from Jake's friend?"

"What do you need a car for?"

"I need to go to Santa Monica. Do some investigation work. Maybe you could help me."

Rosie's face lit up. "Do I get paid?"

"Yeah, you'll get paid, Rosie."

They eventually found W-rent W-rent Wreckers, where Lorraine had to put a hundred bucks down in case they made even more dents in the Mustang. The man was not overly interested in the invalid license Rosie waved at him, but the car cost fifty bucks for a week, plus gas, on top of the hundred-buck deposit. Rosie drew a diagram of all the dents to avoid them being conned on their return, and in a cloud of exhaust fumes, bangs, and the engine clacking at an alarming rate, they bombed out of the parking lot.

The roof was down—it could not go up—but it was a bright clear day, and not too hot for the second of August. Lorraine smiled; whereas one time she had been unable to recall the month or year, she now kept a diary. And she would need it for Rooney. She rested back on the torn seat and considered how they—she, she corrected herself—would go about interviewing the men working at the vintage car garage in Santa Monica. All she wanted to know was if they sold cuff links; if so, how many, and how many men they employed. And she needed to know if they had someone fitting the description of the killer. With Rosie at the wheel, Lorraine relaxed for the journey, as much as Rosie's driving style would allow: she was an incurable horn tooter, thrusting an abusive finger up to anyone who cut her off. Yet, and again Lorraine found herself surprised, she was a competent driver, even if she did cut across lanes. But she did it with such assurance that it didn't make Lorraine nervous.

Rosie sighed as they turned into yet another road, Lorraine shaking her head. She simply could not remember where the place was, or which route the cabdriver had taken. She knew they were close, but she didn't want to ask directions. Instead, she told Rosie to drive to Mike's address: maybe she would recognize landmarks, and since Mike's house was along the shore, she was confident she'd be able to direct Rosie from there.

With a screech of tires Rosie made a U-turn and headed for the beach.

"Keep going, we're almost at Mike's house now." They drove on until she spotted it. She hadn't meant for Rosie to stop, especially not so close, but she jammed on the brakes hard. Lorraine felt the confidence draining from her. "That's it, just across the street."

Rosie peered over the road. "Very nice. Worth a few dollars, this area's not called the Gold Coast for nothin'."

"Just drive on, Rosie."

"But you don't know where we're going!"

"Just drive, will you? I don't want him to see me." As they set off, Lorraine tried to concentrate on the road ahead. But all she could think of was Mike and the girls. She closed her eyes, and then jerked forward as Rosie hit the brakes again.

"You're not even looking, for chrissakes! We carry on at this rate and we'll run out of gas."

Lorraine yanked open the door and got out of the car.

Rosie sighed heavily. "We lost again?"

Lorraine didn't answer, but walked over to the railing and stood looking out at the ocean. Rosie sat in the car for a few moments, then joined Lorraine. "You okay?"

"Not too good, Rosie."

Standing side by side they looked like a comedy duo: one so tall and slim, the other so round. A female Laurel and Hardy, but nothing was funny.

"I've lost my girls, Rosie, I know that. It wouldn't be right for me to see them. They're happy, settled, they call her Mom.

They've forgotten me—but then, I wasn't really worth remembering.''

"Don't say that. Everything's worth remembering, the good and the bad, and things *are* gonna get good for you. You never know, maybe next time you see them it won't be so bad.''

"You think so?''

"I know so.''

Lorraine looked down into the plump, concerned face. "You're the eternal optimist, aren't you?''

"Yep. That's why I got myself so together.''

Lorraine slipped her arms around her, gave her a squeeze. "I'm glad I found you, Rosie.''

"Me, too,'' Rosie said.

Lorraine released her and turned to face the road. She remembered the cab took a right at the next intersection. "Okay, let's go. I think I know the way.''

"You sure you want to do this?''

Lorraine threw up her hands in frustration. "Why do you think we came here? Now get in the car, I've been working out exactly what I want to say. I'll draw a picture of a cuff link and you show it to the salesman. You say your husband has lost one, and you want to replace it—are you listening? Left, take a left.'' They drove on for another seven or eight miles and then Lorraine leaned forward.

"Keep going, I think it's on a corner. Not so fast . . .''

They were heading down Santa Monica Boulevard, and near where it crossed Robertson Boulevard they saw the car dealers' garage. They pulled up in front of the building next to the vintage car showroom. Rosie got out carrying the sketch, armed with the questions she had repeated four times to Lorraine.

Lorraine watched her disappear as she passed between the vintage cars on display in the parking lot. When she slid up to sit on the back of her seat, she could see Rosie inside the big glass-fronted showroom, waiting at the long mahogany counter. Then she lost her as Rosie accompanied a man to the far end of the showroom. Lorraine dropped back into her seat, and lit a cigarette, never taking her eyes off the showroom entrance. Had she asked too much of Rosie? She was about to go in after her when she appeared.

"Christ, what have you been doing? Do you know how long you were in there?''

"Sorry, but the guy never stopped talkin'. You want the good news?"

"Yeah, yeah. Come on, tell me."

"Okay. They sell the cuff links, or they used to. They were originally part of a promotional thing, started in 1991. You know, spend a hundred and eighty-five thousand dollars on a vintage car and they'll throw in a set of cuff links."

"Shit!" Lorraine hit the dashboard with her fist. But Rosie wasn't through. She had the number of workers, forty-eight in all, each of whom had been given cuff links with their Christmas bonus. Around two hundred and fifty sets had been made up—that was the bad news. Further good news was that the first batch had been made in cheap silver, which had proved so popular that they had had a second batch made. These had been handed out last Christmas—and only to their executives, the difference being that these were made in nine karat gold. Rosie beamed. "There's a board showing the top salesmen and the directors, listing their offices, so I presumed they'd be the executives, right? Eight in all." She fished around in her purse and dragged out a dog-eared Mickey Mouse notepad and a felt-tip pen. She sucked the end and then scribbled down as many as she could remember. Lorraine watched in astonishment. Rosie chuckled as she underlined the last name: she'd remembered all eight, even their titles.

"I always win every time! Those game shows where they show you a sort of runner thing with articles and you gotta remember each one! Now, were the links you saw gold or silver?"

Lorraine couldn't remember. "You see anyone with blondish hair, rimless glasses, wide wet mouth?"

"Nope. The guy was short and fat and looked like he had a sack of potatoes in the back of his pants . . ."

Lorraine grinned, and then looked over the list of names, wondering about her next move. Forty-eight workers, all with cuff links, eight executives all with gold ones—and a few hundred vintage car owners with God knew how many more.

"He also said that the silver ones were crap and most of them broke after a few outings. He gave me a set for free."

Rosie revealed the box and Lorraine snatched it from her. She opened it and knew at a glance that the man who attacked her had worn gold cuff links. She snapped it closed. "Rosie, you are a fuckin' marvel!"

Eight names, eight men with gold cuff links. Now she would work on eliminating each one. She knew she had to be careful: if she confronted her attacker she could be in danger. At the same time, she had to be sure; if she gave Rooney bum information he could arrest her, charge her, and have her locked up. She wouldn't put it past him, especially because he had brought up the shooting incident. It must still lay heavy on him, maybe he felt the guilt he wanted her to feel. Lorraine knew she couldn't make any mistakes—there was too much at stake.

TEN

The following morning Lorraine could not summon up any energy and had no idea how to snap out of it, so at eight o'clock she took herself off to Fit 'N' Fast.

"I just feel so tired all the time," she complained to Hector.

He shrugged. "Bound to feel that way, you've punished the hell out of your body for years, right? You can't suddenly force it into feeling fit. Nothing happens overnight, it takes time and dedication." He agreed to make out a diet and a tough workout program for every other day, including weights, a strict high-carbo diet, and a high-protein drink. Armed with a boxful of new vitamins, Lorraine went home.

Rosie looked over the array of cans and pills and the charts Lorraine was pinning up. "I'd join you, but I've got a built-in resistance to that kind of stuff."

Lorraine laughed. "Well, you're so full of energy you don't need it. Do you have a camera?"

"It's in the pawnshop—been there about seven months."

"Can I get it out?"

"I dunno where the ticket is, and it'll cost a few dollars. It's a very expensive model." Rosie started sifting through her papers and eventually found the pawn ticket: there was a hundred and fifty dollars to pay. Lorraine wondered if she could buy a cheap camera instead.

"Has it got a zoom lens?"

"I dunno, there's all kinds of attachments for it. I never used it so I dunno what it's got."

"So how come you got such an expensive camera?"

Rosie wrinkled her nose. "Well, to be honest, it wasn't exactly mine. It was my husband's and we'd had a big bust up. I think I was loaded, I wasn't living with him, and, well, to cut a very long story short, I knew he sort of prized it more'n anything, so I—"

"Took it."

"Yeah, I took it. I always thought that if he was nice, I'd give it back. He wasn't, so . . . at least I didn't sell it."

"Okay, go get it, I'll wait here for you. You'd better take this—it's the last of my stash."

Rosie departed, moaning about being used as a gofer, but when Lorraine asked if she had anything better to do, she said, "I guess not, but why do you need it?"

"To take photographs."

Lorraine worked through the telephone directory, matching the names on Rosie's list. She called each one, checked if they worked at the garage, slowly narrowed down all the wrong numbers, and compiled home addresses. She was still busy when Rosie returned two hours later.

The camera was a professional fast-slide action with zoom lens. Rosie watched in fascination as Lorraine quickly checked over all the accessories, testing out the viewfinder, attaching the different lenses and grinning in triumph because it even had a laser night shutter: she could photograph at night.

"How come you know so much about cameras?" she asked.

"Part of my job. On surveillance we used high-tech equipment and I took a couple of courses—"

The phone rang. It was Rooney. "You out on the streets? What you doing?"

"Gimme time, for chrissakes. Like I said, as soon as I have anything, I'll be in touch. One thing, this Fellows guy, can I get in touch with him?"

"Why?"

Lorraine could hear his chesty breathing down the phone. "Just like to talk to him. I won't if you don't want me to."

"Maybe stay away from him, okay?" Rooney said flatly. "Call me. I need anything you can come up with."

Rooney hung up. Why did she want to talk to Fellows? He remembered how intuitive she was. Maybe she'd come across something he'd missed—or was she just ripping him off?

Bean reminded him that the second-shift team was waiting for their daily briefing. Rooney slowly stood up. "Be right with you." Bean joined the men in the incident room. When he saw Chief Michael Berillo pass, he hoped he wasn't going to see Rooney, as that meant keeping everyone waiting, but Rooney appeared right behind the chief.

He snapped out orders to his men to begin spreading their inquiries to drag clubs and transvestite hangouts. "I want everyone, and this is priority, to check out Norman Hastings's contacts. Hastings is our main link to the killer because out of all the murders he's the odd man."

There was a loud guffaw, and when Rooney saw the funny side, he snorted. He also divulged that he now had a reliable informant working on the streets who he hoped would soon bring in some information.

The chief jerked his head for Rooney to follow him to his office, giving a quick pat to his hair as he passed one of the one-way mirrors, never able to resist himself. "Who's your informant?"

"She's a hooker, been arrested a number of times, she owes me a favor. She's asking around the street girls, the pimps— the ones who won't talk to us. She'll be useful."

The chief nodded. "So that's it, is it?"

Rooney attempted to bluff his way out, saying there'd been the breakthrough with Mrs. Hastings. "Not enough, Bill. I can't let this continue, I'm under pressure. I've had the mayor on me, City Hall. I need an arrest, Bill. There's seven fucking women dead."

The desk phone rang. The chief picked it up. He listened and scribbled on a notepad, which he passed to Rooney. "They just got Brendan Murphy, bringing him across state today." He underlined the word "state" three times, his face darkening, and then he repeated the name "Bickerstaff," and put the phone down.

"Good news, they picked up Murphy, your number one suspect. Bad news is it's now FBI business since they've had to get the documents to bring him back to us. He's in Detroit. Looks like you're gonna have to hand over the entire inquiry to a guy called Ed Bickerstaff, you know him?" Rooney swore under his breath. "I don't like it but I've got no option. I've even been asked if you're capable of controlling the case. I've gone out on a limb for you, especially since I know you'll be retiring soon. Bill, if you don't pull the stops out, you'll be taking retirement earlier than you expected."

Back in his office, Rooney opened a fresh bottle of bourbon and poured himself six fingers, downing it in one gulp before he repeated the dose. Not until his third hit did he relax and feel he could think straight. What possibilities had he missed, or glossed over? The FBI would go through everything with a fine-tooth comb. It pissed him off, even more so as he was sure Brendan Murphy was not their man. He rubbed his chin. This was the most complicated case he had ever worked on and he was nowhere. He had so little that he was almost depending on that whore Lorraine Page to come up with something. He reached for the phone to call her again. There was no answer.

Lorraine sat with Rosie in the car outside the address of Suspect One from the S & A garage, a Sydney Field. He was their first choice since he did not live too far from Rosie's. His house was the same vintage as Rosie's but on Summit, and a lot better maintained. He lived in the ground-floor apartment. When he pulled up outside his house, Rosie got out and asked if he was a Mr. Sam Field. He shook his head. She carried a clipboard. "I'm doing some market research, Mr. Field. Do you work in computers?"

"No." He was surly.

"But you are Mr. Sam Field, aren't you?"

"No, Sydney Field. I'm a car salesman, you got the wrong man." Rosie turned to leave and gave an almost imperceptible nod to Lorraine, who took two photographs. They spent the rest of the evening checking five more names listed from the vintage car garage. It had been a long, tedious afternoon and an even longer night. Six down, two more to go, and Lorraine had not yet seen the man who had attacked her.

The cost of the car rental and payment to get the camera out of hock meant she was already out of pocket, so the next morning she called Rooney. "I need some more money, Bill."

"Give me something first," he snapped.

"I'm checking somethin' out. I'll have it by the end of the day."

"Drop by, I'll give you a hundred bucks, but this is out of my pocket and I'll be out of here in forty-eight hours. FBI is taking over."

"I'd prefer if we didn't meet at the station."

He swore and then agreed to see her near his Japanese restaurant on Holly Street.

Lorraine replaced the receiver and turned, knowing Rosie had overheard.

"What's going on?" Rosie asked.

"Just trying to get us some more cash." Lorraine chewed her lips. "I'm doing this work for an old cop friend, that's all."

"That why we're taking photographs?"

Lorraine had underestimated Rosie's dogged persistence. "This cop, he wouldn't be the one you saw outside the gallery? Captain Rooney? Only he's headin' the investigation into these murders, isn't he?"

Lorraine just looked at her for a minute, and then said, "Let's go."

They drove to the outskirts of Beverly Hills and parked outside a neat row of small houses on Ashdown Road, a heavily gay area. The house they were watching was unique only in the blue-and-white-striped awning that shaded its ground-floor windows. Men were already parading up and down or gathering on street corners talking. A blond woman was tap dancing on a small square piece of cardboard, tap-tapping away, her flowered hat filled with coins on the pavement beside her.

A car drew up and Rosie got out with her clipboard. Lorraine watched her approach a red-haired man and suddenly felt the adrenaline pumping. She knew he was not the man, which left only one to go. He had to be the man, if—*if*—she was right.

Rosie returned to the car, smiling. "This is better than licking goddamned envelopes. Where to next?"

The final address was on the other side of town, on Beverly Glen. Out of all the addresses, this one was underlined because it was in one of the most wealthy residential areas of Hollywood. With a screech of tires, Rosie took a sharp right, directly across the traffic.

"Bastards, it's my right-of-way!" Lorraine clung to the side of the car as Rosie swerved across the road, and steered onto Sunset Boulevard. She peered over to Lorraine. "You sure we're on target here? This is movie-star territory."

"Yeah."

They drove past the Bel Air Gates and took a left, ending up by mistake on Stone Canyon Road. The scenery was plusher, a profusion of palm trees and high fences, eighteen-foot-high brick walls hiding some of the houses from view. Many had warning signs, high-tech security signs, signs about dogs patrolling, signs that all said in one way or another, KEEP OUT. They headed up the winding road, passing the signposts to the Bel Air Hotel. Rosie veered from one side of the road to the other as she caught glimpses of the magnificent properties on either side of them. They drove past the entrance of the hotel itself, where they could see a profusion of expensive cars and valet parking attendants jumping to attention.

"Some place, huh?" Rosie said, making another swerve across the road. Eventually they found themselves on Beverly Glen and the correct address. Rosie pulled up outside a secluded, three-story house, surrounded by a high wall, a barred gate that could easily let through two city buses side by side, never mind a car. The large signs on either side of the barred gates warned of guard dogs and electric fences. The bushes and palm trees were thick and high, and shaded the road, the magnolia and jasmine in such profusion they perfumed the air. It was here that Steven Janklow lived, the last name on the list. Rosie got out and crossed the road to look through the gates. A Buick was parked in the driveway, alongside an old Mercedes SL180. She rang the intercom bell at the side of the huge gate. "Hi, I'm doing market research into computer users and we have a query for a Michael Janklow. Could I please speak to him a moment?"

The phone went dead. Rosie rang again and repeated as much of her rehearsed speech as she could before the phone went dead again. A gardener tending what she could see from the gates were well-kept lawns walked toward her. Rosie smiled and waved at him. "Can you gimme a minute?"

His English wasn't very good, so she had to ask two or three times if a Michael Janklow was at home.

"No, no, his name not Michael."

"Does he work in computers?"

"No, he work in big garage, you have wrong man, go away."

Rosie returned to the car. "I think he's the last guy." She repeated what the gardener had said and recited the car's license plate number.

They waited a long time but only saw the gardener drive out in an old truck, the gates closing automatically behind him. Then they saw a German shepherd sniffing and prowling around inside the gates. Expensive cars passed by: two Rolls-Royces, a Porsche and a couple of BMWs, two Jaguars, a Lincoln, and Rosie counted four Mercedes. Lorraine checked her watch and decided to call it quits for the day, so they headed for home. Knowing she was to meet Rooney and not wanting Rosie with her, she told her they would come back the next morning.

"Drop me off at Fit 'N' Fast," she told her, making the excuse that she wanted to work out. After Rosie dropped her off, Lorraine waited until she was out of sight before she headed down the road to wait outside the Japanese place.

Fifteen minutes later Rooney arrived. "What you got for me?" he asked as soon as Lorraine had slid into his car.

She hesitated. "Well, I've been questioning a lot of the hookers. So far nothing much but a couple of them remembered a guy picking them up, real edgy, and I'm trying to find Holly's pimp to see if he can help. You got anything on a vintage car garage, Santa Monica?" She told him about it, about one of the girls seeing the cuff links, and said that she herself had discovered that fifty or so workers might have a pair. "What I'm doing is narrowing it all down, taking shots of the workers, taking them around to the girls. It might be your man, then again it might not. It's costing, though, I had to get a good camera and I gotta pay a friend to drive me around, had to rent a car."

Rooney took out his wallet. Lorraine leaned closer. "I'd like to talk to this profiler guy. Can't you swing it for me?"

"Why do you want to see him?"

Lorraine ran her hands through her hair. "Maybe I just want to talk to him. I was always good at piecing jigsaws together and he sounds like he knows what he's talking about."

Rooney folded a hundred and fifty dollars and passed it to

her. "Take it, but I want those photographs, and in the mean-
time I'll do a quiet check on the men who work at that garage,
see if there's anyone with a record."

"Do it quietly, Bill. If your man works there, you don't
want to tip him off."

He glowered. "You tellin' me how to do my job? You?
Whatcha think I'll do? Go in and ask for a fuckin' claw hammer?"

"I'll call you." She had her hand on the door handle.

Rooney hesitated, and then muttered grudgingly, "I'll give
this guy Fellows a call. You can see him if he agrees. I'm up
against the wall. Anything, Lorraine, anything, for chrissakes
get it to me fast, you know what snot-nosed bastards those FBI
agents are."

She got out of the car and he watched her walking down
the street, long legs, tight ass, short blond hair swinging with
a bounce. All the guys had tried to get into her pants, but she
had never, to Rooney's knowledge, gotten it on with any one
of the old team. It pissed them all off that she refused to have
a scene with any of them and they had made her life as unpleasant as possible. To her credit, she had treated it as a joke,
but then she had always been tough.

"You got any complaints?" Rooney had asked.

"No, no complaints," she had always answered, quietly and
firmly. She never ratted or put any man on the line, even when
she found out they were getting free fucks from the hookers.
She was so tough no one would have believed she would
plummet out of control. Rooney wondered now just how long
she had hidden her drinking. He had liked Lorraine, admired
her tenacity. She had proven her guts, too. As he drove, Rooney remembered how he and his partner had been called out
to a brawl in a known prostitutes' hangout at Fair Oaks and
Orange Grove, where a Mexican waiter had gone crazy. Neither was prepared to confront the young Mexican holding a
waitress by the throat. He'd already knifed two men, everyone
was hysterical, and crowds were gathering on the sidewalk
outside.

Rooney called for backup, which arrived in the shape of
Rookie Page and her beer-gut partner, Brian Dullay. Suddenly
there was a single terrible scream from inside the bar. They
needed a decoy: someone to go in the front, distract the Mexican, so they could disarm him from behind. No fucking way,

Dullay said. Just as Rooney was about to order him inside, Lorraine stepped forward. "I'll do it. We can't leave that girl in there."

While Dullay and Rooney's partner headed for the back entrance, Lorraine opened the door to the bar. The terrified girl was held by the hysterical waiter, a knife already cutting through her neck, blood streaming down her dress. Her legs were buckled, she had pissed in her pants with terror, and her face was stricken, frozen, her mouth open wide.

Lorraine walked in holding her hands above her head. "I'm alone, mister, just let her go and you and me can talk."

The man pushed the girl down to the floor, grinning crazily as he lifted the knife. "It's too late, no talk now, no more talk."

Lorraine stood still, never flinching when he switched the knife from his right to his left hand, then snatched a gun from his belt and pointed it at her. She stood still, without taking her eyes off him. "It's never too late to talk. Why don't you tell me what's been going on?"

"They kick me out my place, they take my kids, they got no right to do that, I work hard, I pay my taxes, they got no right, I—"

Rooney's partner fired first, then Dullay. The bullet blew the back of the Mexican's skull apart, his blood and brains splattering Lorraine, his body falling over the sobbing waitress.

Rooney was talking to Dullay as Lorraine approached him. "There was no need to kill him," she said flatly.

Rooney had glared at her. "He would have used this. You got a complaint?" He had shoved the dead Mexican's gun under her nose.

"No," she said quietly. "No complaint."

Rooney was still thinking about her when he let himself into his house an hour later. He called out to his wife, then remembered she'd gone to see her sister or cousin. He hadn't paid much attention to what she had said, he rarely did. She had left his dinner in a covered dish with a small note to say how long he should leave it in the microwave. He opened a bottle of beer. It was a warm night and he didn't feel hungry. He had two more beers while he sat outside on the porch in his shirtsleeves. He remembered Lubrinski and thought about Lorraine. He was sure there had been something going on between them. They were real close, used to drink together after duty.

Thinking of the dark, handsome officer, Rooney felt sad. He was one of the best he'd ever come across, bit of a loner but a real man's man. When Rooney had partnered Lorraine with him, he had expected fireworks, but instead, she and Lubrinski had formed one of the strongest teams he'd ever had. He wished he had a twosome like them with him now, but they only come once in a blue moon. Page and Lubrinski, chalk and cheese and yet . . . He felt hungry now and went inside to figure out the microwave.

Lorraine kept on walking after seeing Rooney. She walked from Holly Street, passing the empty art gallery, a for-rent sign in the window. She was heading for home but then suddenly decided against it. She took a bus to west of Sunset Boulevard and got off at San Vicente Boulevard, then walked slowly south down Santa Monica Boulevard. She passed a few clubs she knew—Revolver's, Mickey's, Denny's, Mama Colls—getting closer to the stripper and hooker hangouts. She stopped outside a coffee bar with a few tables planted on the dirty street. Bibi's. She looked up and down, trying to remember the known transvestites' pickup joints, then headed to Cahuenga. She was looking for Nula or Didi but couldn't find them and eventually went up to a Hispanic hooker with a sequined top and leather miniskirt. She was stoned and half-heartedly checking the johns passing in their cars. Lorraine smiled and took out her cigarette pack.

"Hi, how ya doin'? I need to see Curtis, I gotta pay him off, you know where he is?"

The hooker took the cigarette, bit off the filter, and with glazed eyes shrugged. When Lorraine lit the cigarette for her, she inhaled and wafted her hand.

"Try the Bar Q farther up the strip, back aways. He don't run this area."

The bar was dark, with music so loud it was deafening. There were only a few customers dotted around, none Lorraine knew, so she sat at the bar and ordered a Coke.

"How you doing?" The black bartender smiled. "Haven't seen you in a long while."

Lorraine grinned. "Is Curtis out back?"

"Yeah, he's got a game going."

Lorraine could see a few men in the small poolroom. She

strolled in and stood sipping the Coke, watching Curtis play with three other dudes in snazzy suits and flash ties. Printed silk was the rage among pimps, reminiscent of Mickey Spillane. She knew better than to interrupt, but Curtis looked up suddenly. "You want me, sugar?"

"When you got a second."

Curtis chalked his cue. As she moved away, he asked one of the players, "Who's that?"

The man couldn't put a name to the face. Curtis continued the game.

Lorraine went back to the bar and ordered another Coke. A few more customers had drifted in and a bleached blonde with heavy breasts was perched on an end stool, talking to a boy in leather. She was at least forty, her tight leather skirt up around her crotch. He was leaning forward as if hanging on her every word, but his eyes were focused on her deep cleavage. Her breasts were pushed up by an underwire bra and burst through the clinging Lycra. Lorraine was almost amused watching the old pro at work. Every move was sexual—she didn't even reach for her drink without the carefully orchestrated swing of her hips, or opening her legs a bit, constantly touching her breasts, and licking her thickly painted lips. The boy moved closer, desperate to touch her, and Lorraine waited, knew Blondie would talk money any second. Sure enough, she saw her whisper, then lean back, resting her elbows on the bar, and the boy was hooked.

He passed some bills and the come-on act dropped. Blondie downed her drink, slid off the stool, and, arm in arm, they walked out. Lorraine guessed she'd have a room in one of the motels close by and that the boy was probably a college kid high on grass and desperate to get his rocks off. Well, he would, but he would probably not have wagered on it being so fast.

Curtis leaned on the bar next to Lorraine. He ordered a beer.

"You know some friends of mine, Didi and Nula. I'm lookin' for them, but they're not on the strip," she said.

"Still early for them. What do you want?"

"I'm a friend of Art's."

"You want some videos?"

"Maybe."

Curtis suddenly moved closer to Lorraine. "So you know Didi and Nula." He stripped her with his eyes, then focused on her crotch. "But you're not one of them. You want to turn a few tricks?" he asked casually, as if offering her a drink.

"No, I want to see them and I don't like going to their place in case I interrupt a session."

Curtis tilted his head back and laughed. "Not party to that, sugar, not with kids, not my scene."

Lorraine smiled back. He was relaxing, trusting her, and even more so when a skinny black hooker, Elsa, breezed in and saw Lorraine.

"Hey, how you doin'?" she screamed across the bar, then wiggled over and slipped her arms around Lorraine. "Long time no see, an' you cleaned yerself up. Baby, you're lookin' great."

Lorraine was entwined in strong skinny arms and the thick black curly wig tickled her face as Elsa kissed her on the lips. Curtis looked on, as Elsa, still clasping Lorraine tightly, told him how many good times the two of them had had together. She traced the scar on Lorraine's face with her thumb, the long, hooked, bright-red nail running along it like a claw. "Oh, Jesus, do I remember that night."

"More than I do," said Lorraine.

The bartender summoned Curtis to take a call and Elsa perched on a stool next to Lorraine. "So, what you been doin', sugar? I thought maybe you were dead."

"No, I'm alive. You want a drink?"

"Sure, Coke an' bourbon, if you're buyin'."

They carried their drinks to a booth, but Elsa's attention flitted constantly to the entrance, waiting for a customer.

"Did you know Holly?"

"Sure, sweet kid, one of Curtis's. He's been cut up bad about it."

Lorraine led the conversation around to which was Holly's corner, but Elsa couldn't remember: she had moved around because some of the girls could get nasty and they decided that pretty, young Holly was hedging in on their territory. Curtis was a small fry: he only had a few girls and was too weak to get heavy with any of the other pimps. He mostly had trannies because nobody else wanted them—trannies and a few young chicks that he screwed more than any john got to. Holly was his girl.

"The night she died, did you see her at all?"

"Nah, I was in the Long Down Motel. I got a room there now."

Lorraine tried to ask as much as she could about Holly without it sounding suspicious, but Elsa would only say that on the night of the murder, it had been real slow for business and any john was picked up fast. "You get good nights and bad nights, you know."

"Yeah," murmured Lorraine, but then Curtis returned and Elsa moved off to a prospective client.

He stood and leaned on the back of the booth. "You still want videos? I can maybe get some in a couple of hours, I got business right now. Come back later." The bartender waved him over to take another call. Curtis did his video and drug trade in the bars, just small stuff. His girls made the drops for him. Lorraine gave him an uneasy feeling. He watched her walking out. He didn't buy the line she'd fed him about wanting a porno video.

"Elsa!" She sauntered across and Curtis covered the phone. "Who was the blonde?"

Elsa looked back to her john, and scratched the front of her wig. "Hooker, used to hang around the pool halls, did a few tricks with her way back. She was something else, man, a real sleaze lady, but boozed out—Lorraine. We called her Lazy Lorraine. She'd never score a john, just waited until she was so smashed she wouldn't have known if she had one or not. She went with some weirdos, didn't give a fuck." She hesitated a moment and then leaned closer. "Maybe don't trust her too much, okay?"

Curtis gripped her wrist. "What you mean?"

Elsa twisted free, pissed off because he'd hurt her. "Word was she used to be a cop, that's all."

Lorraine walked along the strip, stopped at two more bars, and then spotted Nula paying off a cab. She was hard to miss, in her frilled Spanish blouse and Lycra pants, but she was wearing conservative, low-heeled black pumps and a blond wig with a long braid down the back. Lorraine called, Nula turned, was puzzled for a moment, and then recognized her.

"You got time for a drink?" Lorraine smiled.

"No, I just come on, I'm late."

"How's Didi?"

Nula shrugged and they walked down the strip together. "She's still got problems with her foot but she won't see a doctor—hates them."

Lorraine asked again if she had time for a drink. Nula looked at her watch and agreed, but only a quickie. They went to a small coffee bar and sat with two espressos. Nula was edgy, constantly looking out at the strip.

"I wanted to ask you about the night Holly was murdered. A friend of mine was picked up by a real creep. He had wet slobbery lips, rimless glasses, very middle-America, not beat up . . . and she was uneasy about him. She figured she'd seen him the night Holly died—maybe it was him that picked her up. Anyway, she did the business and got the hell out of his car."

Nula stirred her coffee. "Never saw nobody like that the night she got it. I tell you somethin' though. Didi, right, she was duckin' and divin', she sees the guy cruisin' down the road, right, she figures she's scored but little Holly beat her to the punch."

"Wait a minute. Are you telling me Didi saw Holly being picked up?"

"She said it was a guy in a sort of beige-colored car."

"Have you told anybody this?"

"No, why should I?"

"Because he might have been the guy who killed her."

"Yeah, and he might not. It was early, just after I come on, so . . ." Lorraine didn't like to push too hard. She started asking casual questions about how they worked it, the trannies and the straight chicks, but Nula wasn't interested.

"You think the john that picked up Holly might have been wanting Didi?"

"Jesus, I dunno. Why you askin' all these questions?"

Lorraine lit a cigarette. "Just curious. Is Didi workin' tonight, d'you know?"

Nula said she was at a motel with a regular, but she'd be around later. "I gotta go. With Art gone, we're short of cash." Nula rested her hands on the table. "I said I wouldn't talk to you again because of Art. That was a bad thing you did, Art was a decent guy."

"Come on, Nula, he was getting kids screwed. I saw the photographs, even saw Holly in a few of them."

Nula leaned in close. "How come you're so interested in Holly? What's she to you?"

"She's dead. Maybe I feel sorry for her—she was only seventeen."

"So was I once! And besides, she was our friend, not yours. We had cops around—some fucker gave them a tip-off. We haven't done any photographic work for weeks—that's because of you, isn't it? You know, I been trying to place your face, like Didi says, we were at an AA meeting but . . . I don't trust you. Stay away from us."

She walked out and Lorraine took the tab to the counter. As she turned to leave, she saw Curtis outside with Nula, who pointed to the coffee bar. Curtis pushed her, they seemed to be arguing, and then he turned to look in at the window. Lorraine saw the sign to the rest rooms and walked out. Curtis came in, asked for Lorraine, and the waitress pointed.

Lorraine stood on the toilet seat. She heard the door creaking open, then footsteps and the other cubicle door pushed open. Since there were just the two, she knew he would try the next door, and find her, but just as his footsteps stopped outside her door, the waitress walked in and told him to get out. Lorraine waited fifteen minutes before she eased open the door and peered into the coffee bar. Curtis was standing directly outside and there was no back exit, or none she could see, so she decided to front it out.

He turned fast when she came out. Suddenly his arm shot out and he grabbed her elbow. "You askin' questions about Holly an' I wanna know why. What you askin' questions about my little baby for?"

She could see in his face he wasn't going to hurt her. He wasn't scared, just upset.

"What's it to you? I just liked her, okay?"

"She was my girl."

Lorraine pulled her arm free. "Yeah, I know."

"You knew her?"

"Yeah, not well, but I knew her." He made to move off. "Curtis, wait a minute."

He looked at her. "I dunno what you want but stay away from here."

She took a chance. "Maybe I'm askin' for the cops."

He stepped back fast, his face altered, his hands tightened

into fists. Suddenly she knew that if they were alone he would hurt her, really hurt her.

"Not in the way you think, Curtis—come on, chill out, man, I was a hooker. All I'm doin' is feedin' back a little information, they got nothin' on her killer. Don't you want him caught? She was your girl, you just said so, she was beautiful, real beautiful, and—"

"She's dead, right, so fuck off."

Curtis walked away and Lorraine followed. He turned into an alley and stopped. Now she no longer had the safety of other people around her.

"You got a fuckin' nerve, lady. Back off me."

She stood four feet from him, far enough to keep out of range of a swinging fist. She held him in a steady gaze, not afraid, showing him she was on the level, letting him look at her.

"I'm bein' paid under the counter, fifty bucks. I'm not paid to do anythin' else, just see if there was anyone who saw her that night, saw the john that picked her up. I don't want to know anythin' else. Help me. Why don't you help me? Come on, man, she was your girl."

Curtis leaned against the wall and, to her astonishment, started to cry. Lorraine moved closer. "She was picked up last time you saw her near Didi and Nula's piece of street, that right?" He nodded. She asked if he had seen anything, asked why Holly had been working with the transsexuals. He sniffed, wiping his face with the back of his hand. "She'd had a fight further up the strip, that's all I know. She'd had this fight and we'd been talkin', she said she wanted to move further down the strip, I was fixin' it for her. I never got to tell her I really cared . . ."

"Now's your chance to make it up to her, Curtis. If you hear anything, know anybody that saw anything, will you contact me?"

"I don't work for cops."

"I'm not a cop."

She made him write her telephone number on the back of his hand. Then he walked off down the alley.

Lorraine sighed. She was about to walk back the way she came when it hit her.

"Freeze."

The boy ran on, his yellow zigzag stripe lit up in the neon lights.

"Freeze."

He didn't turn because he hadn't even heard her, because it wasn't a gun in his hand but a Sony Walkman.

Sweat broke out all over her body. Her mouth felt dry and rancid. All she could think of was getting a drink. She started to run, back up the alley, along the strip, banging into passersby, her whole body aching, her brain screaming for a drink. *"No, no, I won't, don't do it, don't do it, just keep walking, keep walking."* A lethal, whispering voice repeated over and over, "You killed the poor kid, he wasn't involved, you emptied your gun into a little kid's back. How does that make you feel, you drunken bitch? You killed him."

Lorraine walked until the panic attack subsided. She sat down at the café she'd passed earlier, gasping for breath, waiting for her heart to slow down. She knew what she had done, but refused to face it. She had never faced it.

"You okay?" Didi limped toward her. "You ran right past me like you'd seen a ghost."

"I did. I was just running from a drink. Sit down, let me buy you a coffee."

Didi hesitated. She was looking good. Lorraine would never have known that her hair, shining and loose, wasn't her own. She had her big looped gold earrings in, and was wearing a tight-fitting lacy dress and white boots. She sat down. "Okay. My ankle still hurts like hell. I put these on, you know, gimme some stability, but it was a mistake. I think they're makin' it swell up even more." She stretched out her leg, showing off the boots.

"I need to ask you something, about the night Holly died."

Didi licked her thick glossed lips and then flicked her hair back.

"I don't know nothin', I didn't see nothin', and I don't know why I'm talkin' to you. We had cops asking questions, we can't get a shoot together, we're broke, all thanks to you. You gonna order that coffee?"

Lorraine signaled to a waiter. He looked and continued taking another customer's order.

"Eh, man, two cappuccinos." Didi stuck her tongue out at the waiter. She then turned back to stare at Lorraine.

"Why you wanna know?"

Lorraine faced her out. "I'm not a cop. I was once but so long ago even I can't remember it. I've been hookin' for years and drunk for as many, you know that."

Didi pursed her lips. "Once one, always one."

Lorraine gripped Didi's hand, feeling the heavy ring on her finger. "Please, just tell me about the guy. The one Nula said you saw. He picked her up right on your corner."

"I don't remember nothin', not even that night, they're all the same to me."

"Come on, Didi, it was the night you got beat up. Did you see the john that picked her up, see his car?"

Didi shrugged. "Maybe. Nula's been talkin' to you, has she?"

"Yeah, and Curtis. They both want to help me, so please, just tell me what happened that night."

Didi told Lorraine almost the same story as Nula—how the car had cruised down the road, stopped, driven on; how Holly had run across the road and climbed into the passenger seat.

"You think he really wanted maybe you or Nula?"

"If he did we're lucky then, aren't we?"

The prissy waiter appeared with two pitiful-looking cappuccinos and dumped them on the table. When Lorraine passed him five bucks, he just stared.

"You got a problem?"

"Yeah, it's five bucks a cup."

He waited until she tossed him another five and moved off. "Jesus Christ, five bucks? What's his game?"

Didi sipped her coffee. "They always hit us for that much, they don't like us sittin' out front."

Lorraine leaned across the table.

"Close your eyes and think, Didi. Was he dark, blond, balding? Think about him."

Didi tried but her mind was blank.

"Did he wear glasses, kind of rimless, pinkish-lensed glasses?" Lorraine prompted.

"Yeah, yeah, maybe he did."

"Was his mouth wide, wet? Did he have a crew cut? Short, blondish hair?"

"Yeah, yeah, that's right."

"He never cruised by you before?"

"I remember anyone that's near to a regular, darlin'. I'd never seen this guy. Shit it's hot, these boots are killin' me."

Lorraine cocked her head to one side. "You're not holding anythin' back, are you? You're not just saying, yeah, yeah, because that's what I said?"

"Why would I do that? He kind of fit the description you said but it was a while ago. Listen, I knew Holly, and like everybody else around here, we'd like that piece of shit put away, all right?"

"If you think of anything, will you call me?"

Didi pushed the tepid coffee aside and stood up, looking down the busy street.

"Okay, nice seein' you. And sure I'll call. G'night."

Lorraine watched her limping off, then weave to the curb as a car cruised past. Didi gave the guy a come-on, but seeing her at close range must have freaked him, and he drove off fast. Lorraine finished her coffee and then headed toward some pay phones. Rooney was not at the station so she called his home. She wanted him to know she was out and working. When she got through he sounded hoarser than ever, she could hear his heavy rasping breathing. "You can go see Fellows now, he's expecting you—and I'm expectin' somethin' soon for my dough, understand?"

"Yeah, yeah, I hear you. So it's okay for me to call this guy then, is it?"

"I just said so. Where you callin' from?"

Lorraine held the phone out to the busy traffic passing back and forth on Sunset. "Working, Rooney, I'm workin' . . ."

Rosie, meanwhile, had returned to Janklow's house on Beverly Glen. At night it was easier to park and remain somewhat hidden. She pulled out the camera, double-checked the instruction manual, and then took a few practice shots. She heard a car come up the hill behind her and stop in front of the barred gates. It was the Mercedes. Crouching, Rosie inched up over the front seat. "Come on, you bastard, get out of the car, lemme get a good shot." Rosie aimed the camera rather than line up the shot. She clicked two or three times and by the fourth click hoped the car, if not the driver, was in frame.

The driver opened the gates by remote control, never looking in Rosie's direction. She could see the glint of his glasses but nothing more—the top of his head was hidden by the roof of the car. She clicked a couple more times before the gates closed behind him as he drove up to the house. Rosie got out and, still carrying the camera and keeping close to the hedges, made her way cautiously toward the gates, hoping to get another shot as he got out of the car to go into the house. She fiddled and muttered, the zoom lens was loose, and by the time she had it tightened the man was inside.

Rosie returned to the car. She had tried, she told herself. As she turned on the ignition, the engine coughed and died. She tried again, it coughed, spluttered, and then died again with a low, whirring sound. "Oh, fuck it!" She tried another three times to start it but the ominous whirring sound grew fainter and she was miles away from the main road. She got out and started to walk. The road was badly lit—a number of houses had kitsch lamp lights outside or framing their gateways, but the streetlights were well spaced and subtle. Not many residents of this area ever walked, so she kept to the center of the dark road as much as possible. Two cars passed her going down the Glen and, even though she stuck out her thumb, they didn't stop. Her feet were aching and she was working up quite a sweat. She wished she'd locked the camera in the trunk; it was heavy and the strap cut into her shoulder.

When Rosie reached the main road, she was past caring about Janklow or anything else. She was hungry, she was dying of thirst, and she was not sure where she was. She stopped and stared at the cardboard sign: HOLLYWOOD STARS' HOMES MAPS HERE. She saw a woman walking a small white poodle and waved to her. The woman turned and stared.

"You know where the nearest bus stop is?"

"Where are you going?"

Rosie got closer. The woman was elderly with a maid's uniform under her light coat. Rosie explained she wanted to get back to Pasadena and they walked together for a while, the tiny poodle sniffing at every square inch.

"You'd best head for Sunset, get a bus from there."

Rosie saw she'd have to wait fifteen minutes for a bus on Sunset and, worrying that Lorraine would be wondering where she was, used the pay phone at a McDonald's. The place was jumping, kids on motorbikes, kids in cars their parents could obviously afford. When there was no answer, Rosie checked her wallet, wondering if she had enough cash for a taxi back to Marengo plus a Big Mac with fries. She also had to arrange with the rental company to pick up the car. She hesitated and was about to go for the burger when she saw the ice-cream parlor and the decision was made: she'd have a chocolate chip and vanilla cone, and then call about the rental. She had just paid for her ice cream, just parked her butt on a bench, when she saw the Janklow Mercedes passing. It stopped as there was a lot of traffic. The blond woman driving was alone, wearing a draped silk scarf half hiding her face, hunched over the steering wheel and wearing black gloves. She reminded Rosie of an old movie star, or maybe someone else, but she couldn't put her finger on it. Rosie balanced her ice-cream cone between her knees and picked up the camera. She took three shots but the Mercedes was already moving away. She picked up her melting ice cream, wiped her knees with napkins, and then licked her hands. Everything was sticky with ice cream.

Rosie was good at remembering faces. She could match those puzzles, the jigsaw faces of stars, faster than a bat of the eye. Julie Andrews's lips, Goldie Hawn's eyes, Jane Fonda's nose. She concentrated and then remembered. She was sure she'd seen the blond woman at the art gallery, the one Lorraine had worked at. Confident she was right, Rosie finished her ice-cream cone and went off to call about the car. When she got through they said they could not send anyone that evening but suggested she call first thing in the morning.

Rosie caught the bus back to Orange Grove. She was sweating, sticky, and thirsty, and her feet and ankles were swollen. She hated the heat, August was always boiling hot, even at night. Passing her local drugstore, she saw the sign PHOTO QUICK and a while-you-wait booth just beside the store. She went inside—might as well show Lorraine how professional she was; while she waited for the film to be developed she had a snack at the small deli on the other side of the store.

By the time Rosie heaved herself up the stairs to her apartment it was after ten and there were no lights on. She let herself in and fed the cat before she sat down to look over her photographs. On the whole they were disappointing, especially the ones she had taken up in Beverly Glen. There was only a half-blurred shot of the man driving the Mercedes, a very good one of the top of the electronically controlled gates, another of the hedges, and one that was just the hedge itself. But there was one clear shot of the blond woman who'd driven past in the Mercedes when she had been on Sunset. She turned the clear one of the woman around, held it up, studied it from every angle, and then it hit her. It was not a woman at all, but a man. When she squinted at the photograph of the man who had first driven in through those gates in the Mercedes, even though it revealed only half his face, Rosie was sure that the blond woman and the man they presumed to be Steven Janklow were one and the same. She laid them side by side on the kitchen table, positive she was right; she couldn't wait to show them to Lorraine.

ELEVEN

Lorraine had called Andrew Fellows's home number as it was almost nine-fifteen in the evening. The answering machine gave a few blasts of classical music before suggesting the caller try his mobile number. She liked the sound of his voice, even more so as he repeated the long mobile phone number slowly and she was able to jot it down on the back of her hand. She was of two minds whether to leave it until the following day but decided it might be a good idea if she made an appointment, so she rang the mobile. Fellows had been equally pleasant-sounding when he suggested Lorraine meet him after his game of squash. He'd be in the John Wooden Recreational and Sports Center and if she drove to Murphy Hall near the east entrance of the campus, there would be someone there to direct her. She didn't mention she would be coming there by taxi.

UCLA, according to its catalog, is cradled in the rolling hills of California's Pacific slope and is one of the most beautiful campuses in the nation. Lorraine and her cabdriver, arguing as they drove, got completely lost in it. They drove in circles for half an hour until Lorraine jabbed the driver in the back as she saw a sign pointing the way to the Recreational Center. She paid off the disgruntled man and checked her watch. It was after ten by now and she was worried she might have missed Fellows. She was about to turn back to the taxi and ask him to wait but he had already taken off in a haze of backfiring exhaust fumes.

Lorraine entered the vast complex. It was a bright modern building, very aerodynamic with a lot of glass and very high ceilings in the main entrance hall. There was a large semicircular reception desk, where a woman wearing round, gold-rimmed glasses was using a computer.

"Excuse me, I'm looking for Mr. Fellows."

The woman peered up without acknowledging Lorraine as she checked down a list for the courts in use.

"Is he expecting you?"

"Yes."

She seemed irritated and looked over her glasses. "He should really sign in his guests. He's on court four, playing with a Mr. Brad Thorburn. If you go up the stairs to the second floor and ask someone up there . . . but it's almost closing time."

"Thank you," Lorraine said tartly and headed for the wide blue-railed staircase. There were signs to gymnasiums, weight lifting, dance aerobics, and martial arts, but she didn't see any sign for the squash courts. She eventually headed down a wide polished wooden-floored corridor following signs to Lounges, Meeting Room, and Offices for Student Activities. She felt out of place, wishing she would meet someone, but the place seemed empty.

At last Lorraine saw a young man carrying a tennis racket, wearing a track suit with a towel strung around his neck. He told her she was on the wrong floor. She turned back to the staircase and went up another flight. No one paid her any attention as she approached the main squash court entrance. A group of students wearing tennis whites passed her, laughing and talking loudly; young tanned limbs, healthy fresh-faced kids, gleaming teeth, shiny hair. They made her feel old, unclean, and uneasy.

Lorraine passed the first of three enclosed empty squash courts. She could see via small windows and eventually approached the large glass walls for spectators to sit outside and watch the game. She was, apart from the two players, the only other person there. Lorraine slipped into a seat at the end of a row overlooking the court. As neither player looked up to acknowledge her, she was able to watch both men and wonder which was Fellows. She leaned forward, her concentration on the man she thought must be him, red-faced and sweating profusely as he lunged and hurtled around the court. She was sure Red-face was Fellows, hoped he was, because his partner attracted her. She had not been attracted to any man for so long that it threw her slightly, but it was not until she had thoroughly sized up Fellows that she slowly turned her attention to Thorburn. He didn't yell but gave small grunts of satisfaction, like a man fucking somebody well, those short hard grunts. He snapped out, "Yes, yes, yes," every time he made a particularly good shot and gave a smile of recognition when he missed one. It was his smile, a half parting of his lips, that attracted her. He was even taller than Fellows, she guessed about six two, maybe more. His body was perfectly proportioned with long, muscular legs, dark-tanned with not too much hair, though she knew he would have a thick thatch around his genitals—a man with black hair always did. Because he was sweating, his hair clung to his head, thick, short hair, and she knew he would have a chest to match—she could see it, just, through his cream-colored Ralph Lauren T-shirt. This man was very different from Fellows. He kept hitching up his shorts as he swung his racket back and forth, bending forward as Fellows lined up a shot, and dragging his wristband across his forehead. His hands were strong and big. Lorraine inched farther forward to get a better view of his face. His dark eyebrows were fine and his eyes . . . He turned and looked up. They were dark greenish-blue. Fellows looked up, too, and waved, and then said loudly, "Are you Lorraine Page?" She nodded. "Won't be long."

The game continued for another ten minutes and then she presumed Fellows won as he yelled his head off and flung his arm around his partner, who picked up a pristine white towel and wiped his face, arms, and neck before draping it around his shoulders. He didn't acknowledge Lorraine as he walked out of the court. Fellows, however, gave a wide grin and shouted that he would meet her in reception in five minutes.

She sat for a few moments. She pressed her crotch. It shocked her just how attractive she had found Brad Thorburn. She hadn't wanted a man since she could remember and this one had sneaked up like the hard black ball they had been thrashing around the court. She felt as if it had hit her in the groin: she ached, she was wet, and she was scared to walk out and face him. Not until she felt the old Lieutenant Page sur-

face, the one that didn't give a shit what any man said or made
her feel, did she leave her seat.

Lorraine stood waiting in the now-empty reception area. An
even pinker-faced Fellows finally emerged with his gym bag,
wearing clean, pressed, closely fitting jeans and a striped blue
shirt with a sweater tied around his neck. "Sorry to keep you
waiting but I didn't want to break up the game."

"That's okay." She looked past him, half hoping his partner
would come out, half hoping he wouldn't. He didn't.

"Did you find the parking lot?"

"No, I came by taxi."

Fellows took her by the elbow and walked her down to the
basement and the underground parking garage. He continued
to chatter in an open, friendly manner, hoping she didn't mind
having their discussion at his home, as the main laboratories
and his office were closed for the evening. Still with a light
gentlemanly touch to her elbow, he guided Lorraine to the
marked-out area that said STAFF ONLY. An English MG sports
car, like Mike's wife's, Lorraine remembered, headed toward
them from the opposite side of the garage and to the exit ramp.
Fellows waved and Lorraine purposely didn't look as she knew
it would be Brad Thorburn. Instead she kept her attention on
Fellows, saying how kind it was of him to see her. When she
was seated in the passenger seat of Fellows's odd little Japanese car, she clenched her buttocks, angry because she was
still sexually aroused. She had wanted to look at Thorburn,
wanted to see a man that had made her feel like a woman
again.

"It was a very interesting game," she said rather lamely.

"Yes, first time I've beaten him this year. He's an old
friend—we were at Harvard together."

"Does he teach here, too?"

"Good God, no. He's rich as Croesus. He's a writer, but he
runs a big vintage car garage out in Santa Monica. He imports
the cars, has them refurbished, and then sells them at immense
profit. It's just a pastime really, because he's got a garage full
of his own. He started up to keep them in good condition and
now it's a flourishing business. Anything that man touches
flourishes. He's got the Midas touch, but you'd never know it.
He's a charming, unassuming man. I'm sorry I didn't have

time to introduce you, but you didn't come to meet my old
college buddy, did you, Ms. Page?''

As they headed out of the campus Fellows chatted on about
real estate and how his property had lost its value. Nothing he
said was of any importance, but he was trying to work out
what had suddenly made her so tense and distracted. He wondered if she was uncomfortable being driven to a stranger's
home, though she seemed the type who could take care of
herself, especially after what Rooney had told him about her.
As if she had read his mind, she suddenly asked what Rooney
had said to him.

"That you used to be a lieutenant, and a good one."

She laughed and he found it attractive, a low, soft gurgle
more than a laugh.

"Was that all?"

He paused at traffic lights. "Yes, well, he implied that you
made a mess but he didn't embroider."

"So what did he tell you?"

Fellows drove on, turning into Marmont Avenue. "Something about a drinking problem."

Before they could continue, he turned into a driveway. The
house was as neat as Fellows himself, a swimming pool and
trim hedges taking up most of the backyard. Lorraine calculated the property would be worth around one and a quarter
million dollars, perhaps more. Again Fellows seemed to read
her mind; he smiled.

"Too good for just a lowly professor, Ms. Page? You'd be
surprised how much some of us earn, but it looks more splen-
did than it really is."

Fellows opened Lorraine's door for her and waited for her
to get out. The front door opened and a pleasant, rather plump
woman waved from the porch. "Dilly, this is Lorraine Page.
She's working on the case I told you about. Sorry I'm late,
darling, but we had a hell of a game."

Lorraine wasn't sure she'd caught Fellows's wife's name
correctly.

"Dilly?"

"Yes, short for Dylisandra, but to be honest I can't recall
ever being called that. Stupid name, God knows where my
mother got it from. Please come in. If you haven't eaten, I'll
cook up something. Andrew is always hungry so I always have
enough for a small army . . . so, you hungry?"

Lorraine nodded and felt an immediate warmth toward Dilly, who welcomed her into the house, the interior of which mirrored her generous personality—open plan, comfortable, not ostentatious. The living room was filled with deep, inviting sofas and thick Moroccan-style coffee tables, big lamps, spotlights focusing on large, bright canvases. The one that hung over a stone fireplace was of a man reclining, stark naked. The painting was impressive: no matter where you sat in the room you couldn't help but be drawn to the figure, or, more specifically, to his large penis and balls, which were overprominent.

Dilly worked in the kitchen, opening wine, talking nonstop as she listed who had called and left messages. Fellows, after excusing himself, disappeared for a few minutes to go to his study and his answering machine.

The meal was simple—tossed salad, steak—but served beautifully. Lorraine was relaxing and enjoying their company, when Dilly brought the conversation around to Brad Thorburn. "Now there's a man I could go for," she said to Lorraine. "That's his portrait over the fireplace, by the way. I know it doesn't look like him—that's because he refused to sit still long enough for me to get his head right, but I think I got everything else okay. Well, Andy says I've been a little optimistic about the genital area but I'm not. I just painted what I saw and, to be perfectly honest, at times it was very difficult to hold my brushes straight." She laughed loudly, tossing her head back.

Fellows smiled adoringly at his wife, without a hint of jealousy. "I've tried to introduce him to more girlfriends than you could imagine. They all fall for him, but he's a real choosy guy."

He suddenly stood up, ruffling his wife's hair. "We haven't come here to talk about Brad Thorburn. Can you bring coffee into the den?"

"Sure. How do you take it, Lorraine?"

"Black, with honey if you've got it."

Fellows said, "I thought you'd take it that way. It fits with how clean-cut you are, direct."

Dilly snorted. "Don't pay attention to him, he's always saying things like that! It used to be his big come-on trick, now he just does it for effect!" Lorraine smiled, but she had seen Fellows check the time on his wristwatch. She did the same, noting it was almost midnight.

Fellows's study was lined with books and photographs, many of them featuring Thorburn. Lorraine walked around the room, with its leather armchairs and wide mahogany desk. She looked at a photograph of Fellows and Thorburn together on a fishing trip. Fellows stood behind her.

"Where does he live?"

"Up in the Canyon. It's the family home, he's got them littered all over the world but that's his sort of base. He had quite a strange upbringing. His father left his mother when he was just a toddler and remarried God knows how many times."

"Is he an only child, then?"

"No, I think there was an older brother, but Brad was left the money."

Dilly appeared with the coffee and said her good nights. Lorraine liked her and Fellows, too. He was a man she felt she could talk to, a man she *wanted* to talk to, but not about the murder. She felt he would be dependable, honest, a man with no ulterior motive, a rare creature. Fellows briefly outlined his interest in the murder. She listened intently, knowing much of what he was saying because she had read the files, but she liked the reassuring sound of his voice.

"I hear there's been a development with Norman Hastings— a cross-dresser. Well, I said Rooney would probably find something. Interesting, huh?"

He had thrown the ball neatly into her court.

"Yes, it is."

"You asked to see me. For what reason?"

"To see if you knew more."

"You think I do?"

"I don't know."

"I think *you* do."

She met his steady gaze. Lorraine was the one to break the look. "Why do you think he kills?"

Fellows leaned back. "Lorraine, nobody knows what makes a man kill, if not in the armed forces or under pressure or supreme emotional strain. I don't believe any man simply kills. There is always a reason."

"What reason is behind our killer?"

"I don't know because there is no cohesive pattern. They are not all hard-faced prostitutes. One was a cross-dresser, one a seventeen-year-old."

"What if the seventeen-year-old was a mistake?"

"What do you mean?"

Lorraine repeated what she had discussed with Nula and Didi, and Fellows leaned forward, frowning. "So you're saying our killer was after one of your friends. Is she a blond?"

"Sometimes—she wears a lot of wigs. She said the driver stopped and Holly ran across the road to him and got into the car. I think Hastings knew the killer," Lorraine continued, "and that the killer is a cross-dresser or a transvestite."

"Why?" Fellows asked.

"Because he seems to hate women, maybe women his own age. I think he hates the woman he becomes, the woman he attempts to be when he's dressed up."

Fellows closed his eyes. "Where does Hastings fit in?"

"Hastings may have known him and been suspicious. Maybe he was about to expose him to the police . . ."

Fellows tugged at his ears. "There is one person who must be found, the woman he attacked, the one in the parking lot. I don't think the police realize the importance of this witness. She saw him, his face, she even bit him, for God's sake, he attacked her and, according to the witnesses, she was covered in blood. Both they and the cabdriver have described her— tough, hard-faced, tooth missing, scrawny, lank-haired . . ."

Lorraine's heart was thudding.

"I don't think she was a whore, though, or at least not like the other women. I think this one was different. She was educated, knew enough to . . ." He looked directly at Lorraine. "Did you read the transcripts of that phone call she made? Clear, concise description. I told Rooney it was almost like a professional description, as if she had been attached to the police in some capacity."

Lorraine coughed. He was damned good; did he know? She flicked him a glance, saw him check his watch again and could feel he was becoming impatient . . . for her to go? Or was there another reason? Fellows impressed her, she liked his intelligence, but she was also on uneasy ground and she didn't want him to know it.

"I agree, but I don't think they'll find her."

He shrugged. "Then they're not looking, are they? Because she's still in this area."

"Why?" She blushed and she knew it.

"Because she wouldn't give her name. She wants to remain anonymous."

"That doesn't mean she didn't pick up a trucker and ride out of town. Just because she didn't give her name doesn't mean anything."

"She wanted him caught! If she was moving on, why bother calling the police? I think she's still around."

He checked his watch again and began to pull at his ears. He was tired, it had been a long day and a very hard game. His foot tapped but he seemed to be waiting for Lorraine to respond to his last statement. But she didn't, she changed the subject, moving it away from herself. Although Fellows, she was sure, had not connected her as the valuable missing witness, she knew he could detect her uneasiness.

"Will he kill again?"

"Of course, when the mood takes him. He must be feeling good—he has to know that the police have nothing. Even the press has died down." He paused, then went on, "This is his sex life, his action, and it's connected to his own sexuality. He will get no pleasure from masturbation, he's probably impotent, so his masculinity is warped. He is both male and female, and he is killing as a man. We know this because the anonymous caller gave a good description of what he was wearing. So we're not looking for a man who dresses as a woman and then kills. We're looking for a man who consistently wants to kill. Just as you said, I, too, think he wants to kill the woman inside him."

Fellows suddenly crossed from his desk to another chair and sat on the arm of it, swinging one leg. He cocked his head to one side and stared at her. "You killed a boy, Rooney told me. He said you were drunk on duty."

Lorraine felt as if she'd been punched.

"Do you remember what it felt like?"

He had to strain to hear what she said. "I had to kill a number of people in the line of duty and you never forget a single one of them."

"But, Lorraine, you're not answering the question. I asked if you recalled what it felt like to kill that boy."

"Yes," she said quietly, "of course I remember."

He stared at her intently, knew she was lying, but he was astonished at the way she held his gaze and didn't flinch away.

"But you were intoxicated."

"Yes."

"But you remember."

She broke his gaze and he knew she was in trouble. Lorraine stood up, pulling her skirt straight. "It's not something I'm likely to forget."

"Why?"

"Because it must be fucking obvious why. The boy was innocent and I was drunk."

"Even though you were intoxicated, you remember. As you said, you never forget. What exactly don't you forget?"

Lorraine remained standing, edgy, hating herself for showing it. She sighed and lit a cigarette. "I don't see the point of this." She inhaled deeply, let the smoke drift, was about to take another drag when she paused and, without any emotion, described the boy's jacket, the yellow zigzag stripe, the way he fell, as if in slow motion, the way his body folded, the way his head rested against his outstretched arm, the way his soft hair fanned out, the way his body jerked a few times before he became still. Once she had begun she couldn't stop, remembering Rooney pushing past, ordering her into the patrol car, displaying in his filthy handkerchief the boy's Walkman, the tape still in the deck. That there had been no gun, that she had fired six times. She fell silent. Fellows had expected her to break down and weep, fascinated by her stillness throughout her long explanation of the killing. And he didn't feel tired anymore, this woman interested him.

"Sit down, Lorraine."

She hesitated, looked pointedly at her watch before she sat down.

"What about afterward?" he asked softly. She really intrigued him now.

Lorraine stubbed out her cigarette, becoming annoyed that he had swung their meeting over to her life rather than the killer's.

"I felt fucking angry, desperate, disgusted, and all I wanted was to forget it."

"How did you do that?"

"With booze, of course."

"And did it block it out?"

She shook her head. "Yes. I suppose you want me to say no, that it was always there, that it always will be. Well, I'm sorry to disappoint you, I don't think about it."

Fellows was on the prowl again. Returning to his desk, he picked up a paperweight. "But you were drinking before this boy. What made you dependent on alcohol?"

"I was just addicted to it, like my mother. It's supposed to be inherited, isn't it? Look, Mr. Fellows, before I go . . ."

"Why did you drink, Lorraine?"

"I guess I liked the way it made me feel, the confidence it gave me—not having to think or feel. Now, can we get back to the reason I asked to see you?"

"What main thing did you not feel?" He looked into her eyes, with an expression of concern, almost apologetic. "I'm sorry, I don't mean to pry."

She laughed. "Oh, no? You have a funny way of showing it."

He liked the way she laughed, he liked this woman, and he crossed to her side, smiled, and gently touched her cheek. "You're a clever woman, a strong woman—possibly the strongest I've ever met. I'm sorry to delve into your private life but I'm trying to get you to think like him, understand him. Like you felt the compulsion to have another drink, he will feel this compulsion to kill. He will be in a kind of torment because maybe something happened to him that twisted him, hurt him, and the only way he is able to live in society and carry on in a state of apparent normality is like this. When this consuming pain takes hold of him like a rage, he will control it, contain it, and release it when he hammers a victim to death. Only then does the rage subside and calm or normality return."

Fellows paced up and down in front of his shelves of books, all of which were histories of serial killers, and slapped each in turn. "I have pinpointed the rage syndrome in so many of these cases. It manifests itself in an overpowering need to wound, to destroy, to hurt, to inflict pain. Time and again it is sexual: stalking, peeping, watching, and knowing what they were about to commit will be exquisite, relished—and enjoyed. Many collect the newspaper clippings to gloat over. The fact they are clever enough not to be detected adds to the overall feeling of enjoyment. And when it's over they integrate back into their homes, their work. Their secret is like a lover, precious, nurtured, controlled until the pain starts again. It's a horrific vicious circle that cannot be broken until the killer is caught."

Lorraine put her cigarettes and lighter into her purse. "I really must go. Would you call me a cab?"

Fellows reached for the phone, and started to punch the buttons. Seemingly intent on his task, he didn't even look at her.

"Why? If you want to assist the inquiry, Lorraine, why don't you at least admit to me that I'm right."

"Right about what?"

He spoke into the phone and asked for a taxi to come right away, then covered the receiver asking Lorraine where she wanted to be taken. She gave him Rosie's address and he repeated it to the cab company before he slowly replaced the receiver. Now he turned to her.

"I think I am correct that you are the woman, the witness. It was you the killer attacked, am I right?"

"No, Professor Fellows, you are wrong, I am not the woman. I'm sorry to disappoint you."

He stuffed his hands into his trouser pockets and continued pacing. "I know you were a prostitute, I know the address you've just given to me for the cab tonight was also close to the area where the witness was dropped off by a cabdriver. Marengo Street, yes? Not far from Orange Grove. You see I have a very good memory, and you are an ex-cop. That to me is the main clue, why I think it is you, because if you called the station, if you gave the description, you would, as the anonymous caller did, use similar terminology. What I just don't understand is why you're lying."

"I'm not." She stared at him and didn't flicker. It was a long eye-to-eye confrontation and she didn't back off in any way.

"He said you were one of the best he'd ever worked with."

Lorraine snapped, "Rooney has a big mouth, but he knows nothing about my life since I left the force."

Fellows also started getting edgy, opening a file and pushing it across the desk. "I'd say this is pretty informative."

She pursed her lips as she saw the copy of her record. "The bastard," she said, and then she deflated, slumping into the big leather chair. "Does he know? Rooney?"

"No, in fact *I* wasn't sure, until I met you, talked with you. You're in a very precarious position, my dear."

"How did you work it out?"

"I just took one almighty guess." He snickered. "I threw in a wild card."

She laughed, tilting her head back, a deep, warm laugh that made him again feel an odd warmth toward her, or a protectiveness that slightly fazed him. He turned away, blushing slightly.

"The description in the files fits—tall, thin, blond—except the missing tooth."

"I had it capped."

Fellows now sat on the arm of her chair. "I can't see any need to tell Rooney, unless you're holding anything else back?"

Lorraine took hold of his hand, gave it a squeeze, and then looked up into his face. "I'm not holding anything back, Professor. Just wish I had something else to get me fifty bucks a day when Rooney's off the case. I doubt if anyone else would trust me."

"They're fools. Does that mean the FBI will take over?"

"Yes, within the next forty-eight hours. What about dates? Is there anything in the dates the killings took place?"

Fellows frowned. "I doubt it. He just kills when he feels the urge, no specific date code." He sighed. "I'm sorry I couldn't be of more help, but if I sift through the files again, find something, can I call you?"

She nodded.

"Good, and will you call me if you find anything? It's interesting to me or I wouldn't have spent so much time on it already."

The doorbell rang. He walked her to the cab. "It's paid for, so don't worry. And if you need me, call."

She smiled her thanks and he remained watching her until the cab turned out of the driveway.

Back in the den, he picked up the dirty ashtray piled high with cigarette stubs—fifteen. He tipped it into the wastebasket, then straightened the leather cushions, and went upstairs to the bedroom.

Dilly was sleeping, her arms entwined around a pillow. She hardly stirred when he slipped into bed and turned off his bedside lamp. He rested his head on his arms and thought about Lorraine. There was an arrogance about her that attracted him and a directness he admired. There was also, he detected, a deep, hidden pain which, in his professional opinion, was about to erupt. Maybe that was why he had felt so protective of her. Thing was, could he keep his promise?

TWELVE

The taxi Fellows had called was much more upmarket than the usual dented and rusted yellow ones. It was more like a mini-limousine and very comfortable. As she leaned back on the plush seat, she saw the portable telephone. She coughed, hesitated a moment before she asked if she could make a call, only now thinking that Rosie might be worried.

"Hi, it's me."

Without pausing for breath, Rosie launched in and gave her a real tongue-lashing—how worried she was, and that she was just about to call Jake and get a search party for her.

"I'm sorry, I got caught up. I'm on my way home now."

Rosie started to tell Lorraine about returning to Janklow's house and how the rental had broken down.

"What? You left the car outside the goddamned house?"

"No, not right outside, well, not too close . . . I think it was the battery. Anyway, they said they'd pick it up first thing in the morning and give us a replacement, so I left the keys under the front seat."

Lorraine was furious. She asked Rosie if there was anything inside the car to connect her to it; just when she was trying to act professional, all she needed was Rooney to get something on her, even more so after Fellows had guessed just how connected she was to the case.

"Well, I'm sorry, but what was I supposed to do, push it

back home? Maybe there are the rental papers, I dunno. Did you leave anythin' in the glove compartment? I mean, I didn't, I even took the camera and . . .''

Lorraine cut the call off, angry, and asked the driver to take her to Beverly Glen. If there was any extra fare she'd pay it in cash.

Rosie glared at the telephone. She hadn't even had the time to tell Lorraine about the photographs, there wasn't even a thank-you. Typical. It wasn't her fault the battery had died on her.

By the time they parked a short distance outside Janklow's house, Lorraine was even more annoyed with herself for not making Rosie aware of how important it was to do what she told her to do, and not go off on harebrained schemes by herself. She got out of the cab and checked the rental, removed the documents from inside the glove compartment. There were even her notes on all the suspects from the S & A garage, which she stuffed into her purse, even more angry with Rosie. Lorraine was just about to get back into the car when she noticed there were lights on in Janklow's driveway. She told the driver to wait just a moment and then she crossed to the big double-barred gates. The dog was still loose, sleeping about ten feet inside. He woke and growled, his tawny eyes daring her to lay so much as a hand on the gate. Although the driveway was lit by small decorative lanterns, the house was in darkness, curtains drawn on the lower-floor windows, and there was no car out front. It seemed ominously quiet and yet there was nothing creepy about the property, quite the opposite. Lorraine stepped closer and her body set off the automatic security lights. The gardens, the lower story of the house, the gates, even the road she was standing in were suddenly bathed in brilliant light.

She started back to the taxi when she heard someone calling. She paused and looked back.

"Bruno must have set the security lights off again. *Bruno!*"

Brad Thorburn, wearing shorts and flip-flops, appeared at the front door. The dog ran to him, standing on its hind legs to lick his face. Brad ruffled its fur and scanned the garden for an intruder, but his voice was mocking when he clapped his hands and said to the dog, "See them off, go on, good boy."

Lorraine whipped around as the cabdriver tooted his horn.

"You want to stay here much longer, lady? I got another pickup radioed to me . . ."

She was very flustered—and not just because she was now standing in virtual daylight; she had recognized Thorburn and it had thrown her sideways. What the hell was he doing at Janklow's house? She actually had her hand on the cab's door handle when the gates opened. Thorburn looked across the road toward the cab and was about to close the gates, when he looked again. "Hey! Weren't you at the university earlier?"

"Sorry," Lorraine said innocently. "Are you talking to me?"

He nodded. "I was playing with Andrew Fellows."

Lorraine smiled. "What a coincidence." It was more of one than she could actually piece together and she knew she must be red with embarrassment at being caught there.

"You got a problem?" Thorburn asked.

Lorraine walked over to join him. "No, not really. I was supposed to drop in to pick up something for a friend of mine. I thought it was number three eight hundred but I must have been mistaken."

"Do you need to make a call? You can use my phone."

This was too much of an opportunity, to actually be invited into the house, but so much was crisscrossing her mind: what if the man who attacked her was in there and recognized her? Or had she and Rosie made one hell of a blunder?

"I won't be a second," she called to the driver, who gave a surly nod. She grinned at Thorburn. "My driver's fed up since we've been all up and down the Glen. I didn't like to start ringing doorbells, it being so late and with so much security around here."

Thorburn pressed the gates closed and released the dog, which immediately launched itself at Lorraine, wagging its tail and slobbering. "He's not quite gotten it together yet, he's only a puppy. This way . . ."

Lorraine followed Brad up the pathway. The house could have been Scarlett O'Hara's Tara. It had two massive white pillars, three stories high, and four marbled entrance steps up to a white marble porch. It was certainly some property. The hallway alone took her breath away. It was an antique mixture of Baroque furniture, massive chandeliers, and gilt mirrors, but it was not oppressive because the pieces were not crowded together. The hallway was of such a grand scale, it could easily have accommodated several cars parked side by side.

"Phone's on the table just through that arch. I'm Brad Thorburn."

"Lorraine Page."

He walked off and Lorraine went toward the wide archway. The room was sunken, with deep white sofas and a single glass-topped coffee table with a basket of flowers the likes of which Lorraine had only seen in magazines. The paintings were all huge, and it struck Lorraine as she picked up the receiver that the white telephone was the smallest object in the room. She called Rosie.

"Hi, it's me again. Look, can you double-check something for me."

"What?" Rosie asked, half asleep.

"Check that last address, where the car broke down—you with me, Rosie?"

"What are you talking about? You mean Janklow's?"

"Yes, you sure it belongs to who you just said and not someone else?"

"Yes, we both checked out the address. Why?" Lorraine could hear the sound of the flip-flops across the white marble hallway.

"I won't bother tonight, I've got a taxi waiting. Good night." She replaced the receiver before Rosie could utter another word.

"Can I get you a drink?" He had put on a loose white caftan over his shorts.

"Ah, no, I'd better go, but thanks for the offer and the use of your phone." She could feel herself blushing, so she dipped her head.

"Did you go over to Andrew's?"

"Yes, we had a relaxed dinner, just Dilly and Andrew."

He smiled. "I've offered her money to take that painting down. I know you've seen it because you won't look at me."

She hadn't even thought of the painting, it was him she couldn't look at. They walked toward the front door, which was still ajar. As they stepped onto the porch, her taxi drove off.

"Since your transport has departed, will you change your mind?"

"No, thanks all the same, but if you could call me another cab . . .''

"Don't you drive?"

"Yes, I do, but I also used to drink. The two didn't go together. Now I don't drink or drive."

He gestured for her to follow him. "Come and sit down. Let me fix you a soft drink, or tea or coffee, if you'd prefer?"

Brad took her into the kitchen. It was like a movie set—more appliances and high-tech equipment than she'd seen in any restaurant. He poured her a glass of ice water, then crossed to a wall phone as he asked her what she did for a living. She told him she worked part-time at an art gallery. He turned to look at her. "Anyone I'd know of?"

"I doubt it, it's not very successful." She knew she had to concentrate on using this situation and told herself to stop acting like a tongue-tied teenager. This was too good an opportunity to pass up. Maybe she was attracted to him, but she had to ignore it. It was unlikely he'd have any interest in her—Dilly had said that all his women were young, perfect beauties. But she was sure, unless she was kidding herself, that—wasn't he putting out signals? She noticed the bottle of wine open on the table, and a bottle of Scotch, had he been drinking? Was he maybe a little drunk? He did seem very relaxed and she could smell liquor on his breath; maybe he'd had a few too many. She gave him a hooded glance as he picked up the receiver, but he turned and caught her looking at him. He didn't smile but met her eyes and then his attention was drawn to the phone.

"The cab will be here in about fifteen minutes."

"Thanks." She decided to start doing the job she was there for.

"You have a wonderful home, do you live here alone?"

"No, my brother's here as well. You want me to show you around?" He downed a glass of wine and then smiled, gesturing with a half bow for the tour to begin. Politely, he led her through one vast ornate room after another. He was obviously uninterested, so they viewed each quickly and Lorraine hardly said a word. It was not until they went upstairs that his closeness made her feel uncomfortable. He touched her elbow as he showed off the master bedroom, with floor-to-ceiling white silk curtains that Barbara Stanwyck might have draped herself in. It lacked the freshness of the other rooms.

"This room's different," Lorraine said, and walked farther inside, her feet sinking into thick-piled, soft, rose-colored carpeting.

"My mother's room. She likes it kept this way."

She saw photographs in heavy silver frames, at least fifteen of them, clustered on the dressing table. The main one was of an astonishingly beautiful woman, pale blond hair, elegant, a classic beauty.

"My mother."

"She's stunning, very beautiful."

"Yes, she is—or was. She's now made herself into a plaster cast, hardly recognizable as the same person. I don't think she has a single feature she hasn't attempted to freeze in time. She's refused to age gracefully. And that was my father. I think the only reason it's here is because she looks so wonderful in the same photograph. He died a long time ago."

Lorraine picked up a smaller picture frame. "That's my brother, well, half-brother. I think I was four, he'd be about twelve, different fathers."

They heard the sound of a car heading up the driveway. He replaced the picture and, crossing to the window, drew back the drape.

"Is that my cab?"

"No, they'll call from outside. It's just the staff returning." He walked briskly to the door, impatient for her to follow, yet he remained the gentleman, holding the door open until she passed him, about to head down the stairs. He had changed, she could feel it, he was very edgy now.

"No, come into my office." He gripped her elbow and they walked quickly along the landing and through another archway. "Go in and sit down, I'll be right with you."

He crossed to the banisters and looked down as the front door slammed. "Don't put the alarms on, I'm waiting for a cab."

"Are you going out?"

Lorraine was just about to go into the office. She paused. Although she had heard a man's voice, she had also heard the click-click of high heels.

"I've got somebody here—they're just going, so stay down there."

The click-click faded and a door below closed. Brad beckoned her into his so-called office, which was mostly windows with a vast array of books lining what walls there were. A modern desk was covered with a word processor and stacks of manuscripts.

"What kind of books do you write?"

He closed the door. "You mean attempt to write! I haven't done it yet."

He frowned as footsteps could be heard on the polished wooden stairs, but they continued on up to the floor above them. Then he seemed to relax, pointing to a photograph of a vintage car. "I have a collection."

"Do you keep them all here?" Lorraine asked.

"No, I have a garage. I bought it to house my own vehicles, then I hired a mechanic to keep them in condition, and every other day somebody with a comparable car would appear and ask if my mechanic could help them repair it or where they could get a part, so I opened up a garage, dealing only in vintage imported or American cars."

Lorraine could feel herself sweating. It was the mention of the garage, the vintage cars, and she recalled what Fellows had said about Brad. They had, she thought, the right house after all.

He looked up as the footsteps passed over the ceiling from the room above. "Excuse me."

He walked out and closed the door. As soon as it shut, Lorraine was at his desk, opening drawers, checking. She found stacks of notepaper with the S & A logo, envelopes, drawers full of magazines and more manuscripts. She looked over the bookcase—novels, theology, medicine, dictionaries, biography, autobiography—then opened a door into another room and saw the professionally equipped gym. She suddenly looked up as she heard low voices arguing. It was frustrating because she couldn't hear a word they were saying. A door slammed and then there were running footsteps. Lorraine hurried to sit down as Brad returned.

"Maybe you should call me another cab."

He walked to the bookcase and removed a book. The entire wall fell back to reveal a large bedroom.

Brad extended an arm. "There's even a private staircase leading out and down to the garden. If the cab hasn't arrived by the time we get there, I'll run you home."

Lorraine passed him to walk into the bedroom. The king-size bed had several mirrors above it yet it didn't feel overtly sexual. The room was too orderly, everything pale oatmeal, even the polished wooden floors. The walls were covered with photographs, mostly of blond women.

"My harem, as Dilly calls them." Lorraine moved to look more closely and he followed and stood directly behind her.

"She says they were interchangeable. What do you think?"

She could feel the heat of him but she calmly looked from one girl to the next. "I think they're lovely."

He touched her shoulder, a light feather touch, and then slowly traced down her arm. He reached for her hand and drew it back slightly to feel his erection.

"I want to fuck you." His voice was hardly audible.

She did not withdraw her hand but allowed him to press it against his erect cock. Her whole body seemed to catch fire, and then she laughed. "Dilly's painting doesn't exaggerate, does it?"

She moved her hand, without his assistance, slowly over his erection and he moaned. She closed her eyes, she didn't want it to happen. He pressed closer and his right hand began slowly to unbutton her blouse, pushed beneath her bra to feel her nipples. They were hard and he knew she was aroused. He bent his head to kiss her neck. His tongue licked as he pulled her blouse open more, while her legs began to spread as if out of her control.

"No," she whispered. "Please don't do this to me. I don't want this, I have to go."

She wanted to scream, wanted him to go on. She could feel herself start to pant as he massaged her nipples. She knew that if he reached down, put his hand between her legs, she wouldn't be able to resist—but she had to make it stop, walk away from him. She pushed his hands off but he turned her roughly to face him and kissed her lips. It was a sweet, gentle kiss and she craved more and pressed against him. She felt her arms lifting to hold him.

"How did you get this?" He traced the scar on her cheek. "It drives me crazy, you know that? It's so sexy, the way you tilt your head. You have beautiful eyes. I want to make love to you, Lorraine."

She was embarrassed about her body, her scars, and hearing his husky voice saying things she had never expected to hear from any man, let alone one as handsome as he was, made her want to weep.

"I have to go."

"No, not yet."

"Yes. Just get away from me."

He stepped back as she buttoned her blouse, pulled down her skirt. She had to keep talking because if he laid so much as a finger on her again she'd be unable to say no. "I don't know what you think I am but you've got a fucking nerve. Now just stay the hell away from me—go fuck one of your classy blond college kids but don't come on to me because I'd make you pay, sweetheart. You picked the wrong lady."

He stepped away from her, his face like a boy's in his confusion.

She ran her hands through her hair and looked up to the mirrors. "They may get turned on by this crap with the mirrors but please don't play out your fantasies with somebody you don't know, and will never know. Now, did you really call me a cab or was that all part of your come-on game?"

"How much do you charge?" His face was taut with anger.

"*I* choose my clients. Now how do I get out of here?"

He grabbed her wrist and she did a quick twist, released her hand, and brought it up as if to slap his face. "Stay off me, rich boy."

"I said, how much?"

She could feel her stomach lurch, wanting him to hold her, wanting him to stop her tough talk, wanting him to kiss her just like he had a moment ago.

"Name your price!"

She looked for the door to get out. Shocking him hadn't worked. He was humiliated, angry, and even more attractive.

"I said name your price."

She glared at him. "You don't have it."

"Want to bet? Five hundred? You want more? Seven fifty? You don't look like a thousand-dollar whore to me, but if that's your price . . ."

He crossed to a wardrobe, opened one of the drawers, and took out a wad of notes. Just as he was about to proffer them, the telephone rang. He tossed the money at her as he picked up the receiver. He listened and then let it drop. "It's your cab. Why don't you leave me your number? Maybe we'll make it another night."

She laughed as he opened the hidden door leading to the staircase into the garden. She didn't wait for him to direct her but headed straight down. He didn't follow, but stood, watching her.

"I meant what I said, Lorraine."

She paused and looked up at him. "I'm not a whore, Brad. I don't want you or your money. Good night."

He waited until the door below closed, then relocked it automatically, stood to see her stride down the pathway, and pause to give the dog a few words. Then he used the remote switch on the main gates, saw her hesitate as they swung open, but she didn't look back. Maybe she didn't know he could see her.

He lay down on his bed, looking up at himself in the mirror, confused and still smarting from her rejection. He was not used to it, nor was he used to meeting a woman who excited him so much. The phone rang. He sighed with irritation and snatched it up.

"What do you want?"

"Did you switch the security lock for the gates back on?"

"Yes."

Steven Janklow replaced the phone and walked into his bathroom, closing the door silently. Locked inside the house he felt safe and secure. He let his silk dressing gown fall away from his body, gazing at himself admiringly as he stepped into the perfumed water. As he slid slowly beneath the soft warm bubbles, he sighed with satisfaction.

Lorraine traveled home in style. The car was a stretch Mercedes, the driver wearing a uniform. Yet another step up from Andrew Fellows's company. The driver did not say a word the entire journey. She was glad, she didn't feel like talking. Rosie, however, was still up and ready to launch in as soon as Lorraine opened the front door, her ludicrous slippers on, and her cotton nightgown leaving little or nothing to one's imagination.

"You cut me off before I could tell you."

"Rosie, I'm real tired. Can't this wait until morning?"

"No. I got the photographs developed, that's what I got for going back to the Janklow house."

"You did *what*?" Lorraine snapped. She threw her purse down. "Listen to me, Rosie. This is not a game. You never—do you understand me?—never do anything unless you run it by me first. This is *my* job, not yours."

Rosie stuck out her lower lip like a child. "I was only trying to help and then the car broke down. I walked from the Janklow house all the way down to Sunset, are you listening to me?"

"Yes," she responded, "but I'm tired out—it's almost three o'clock in the morning."

"I saw the Mercedes and I got a good picture of the driver." Lorraine was hooked. "Janklow?"

"Yeah, well, I think so. You tell me."

Lorraine stared at the photographs, lingering longest on the blond woman driver.

"Is that a man or a woman? You tell me." Rosie made an elaborate show of matching the two sets of photographs, the ones with Steven Janklow driving, and the ones with the blond woman.

"It would be hard to tell if it wasn't for the mouth."

It was a wide mouth, a mouth Lorraine was sure belonged to the man who had attacked her. But she was concerned about Rosie, that she was becoming too involved and might do something that would get her into trouble or, even worse, get her hurt. "We'll see if we can get them enlarged. Now, if it's okay with you, I'm going to bed."

Lorraine slipped into her bed on the couch and drew the covers close up around her chin. She gripped the sheet tight, twisting it around her knuckles. She had wanted to be loved tonight, she had wanted to be held, kissed, but she had been so afraid because, after all this time, after so much loss, she didn't think she had any feelings left. Lubrinski's death had been the worst moment of her life. He was the only person who had given her the love she had craved from her husband, who had loved her for what she was and asked nothing in return.

It began with a single, dry sob, wrenching upward from the pit of her stomach. Afraid Rosie would hear, she bit the sheet, held it between her teeth as the second sob shook her body. She told herself to get control. "Fucking take control of yourself, Page. People depend on you to be a rock. You start howling and you'll make us a laughingstock. There's a mother out there needing to know if her little girl is alive or dead—you show any emotion and she won't be able to take it. You want to weep, do it at home, never on duty. You hearing me, Page?"

"Mrs. Bradley, I'm sorry but we've found Laura, and I'm sorry to tell you . . . Laura's dead, Mrs. Bradley."

Rosie sat up. Something had woken her and she was afraid

for a moment. Then she heard the strangled, awful sounds. She threw back the blanket and went in to Lorraine. She was rigid, the sheet clenched between her teeth, her knuckles white from the strain of gripping her fingers so tightly. The sound was like a wounded animal, a low mewing sound, as she tried to suppress the desire to scream. Rosie reached over and picked her up in her arms, holding her and rocking her. "Let it go, Lorraine, let it free. It's only me, it's only big fat Rosie. You have a cry, let's hear you cry . . ."

The dam broke and the mewing sound erupted into gasping sobs as the tears flowed. Lorraine held on to Rosie as if she was drowning, as if she was terrified to let her go. She sobbed for almost two hours. She wept for everything she had lost, for her children, her husband, her dead mother, her brother, her father. She cried for the boy she had shot, she cried for Lubrinski and called out that she was sorry, sorry, and at long last she wept for herself, for what she had done to herself, for what she had forced herself to become.

At last the crying stopped. She was drained, so exhausted she couldn't speak. Her body still shook, and she made soft, hiccuping sounds as Rosie gently dried her face and together they walked into the bedroom. Rosie helped her into the bed, rinsed a washcloth so she could pat her face cool, and then got in beside her. Lorraine rested her head against Rosie, whose big fat arms cradled her friend as she said softly over and over, "It's all over now, everything's going to be better now, honey. It's gonna be easy now."

The ring of the telephone by the bed made Rooney's heart thud so loudly he thought he was having a heart attack. It was Bean. They had just gotten a report in. The body of a white woman, aged somewhere between thirty and forty, had been discovered in the trunk of a stolen vehicle. Judging by the look of the corpse, the killer had struck the victim from behind with a hammer, and she also had horrific facial injuries. Rooney flopped back, cradling the phone against his chest. His wife peered up at him, her face masked with night cream. She then squinted at the bedside clock, it was five-thirty in the morning.

"Jesus Christ, we've got another one. He's done another."

THIRTEEN

Rooney and his lieutenant waited in the anteroom of the City Morgue. Having dragged himself out of bed, he had joined Bean, who had been contacted even earlier regarding the corpse. It was now after nine and they were still waiting for results. They could do little until they had further information from the pathologist. The stolen vehicle, a Lincoln Continental, had been towed to the police lot and was being checked over by forensic experts. The owner of the vehicle had been traced, having reported his car stolen the previous day from outside his house in Ashcroft Avenue, in West Hollywood. Rooney was morose, knowing that the press would be on to the killing and had, more than likely, given it front-page coverage as he had declined to say anything to the photographers and reporters waiting outside the morgue. He slurped his cup of disgusting machine-made coffee and looked at Bean, irritated that even though called out at some ungodly hour, he was looking as neat and pristine as always.

"How's your toothache?" Rooney asked him through clenched teeth.

"S'okay, hasn't come back. I think I might need some dental work, but I use floss every morning and night now."

"Maybe you shouldn't bother. I'd like to know how the fucking press get on to everythin' so fast, pisses me off.

Chief'll be havin' heart failure at his gym by now, he been told?''

Bean nodded, then chewed his lips. "You know where it was found, don't you? The car?"

Rooney took another gulp of the disgusting coffee and lit up a cigarette directly under the NO SMOKING sign.

"Yep, another fucking shopping mall."

Bean nodded, "Yep, the ultimate mall this time—the Beverly Center. Maybe he uses them because the parking is free."

"That a joke, is it?" Rooney asked bad-temperedly, and then turned as a detective from the L.A. police squad looked through the large double doors.

"Hi, you Captain Rooney?"

"Almost," Rooney grunted.

The sandy-haired officer, wearing a neat gray suit and white shirt, walked in and joined them.

"I'm Detective Maynard from Parker Center, Homicide Squad."

Rooney nodded as the pushy detective sat down and opened his file. "I've just been talking this over with my chief. Situation is that your crowd takes the case and, as we've been informed, the FBI might be brought in, you're welcome to it."

"Thanks a bunch," Rooney said.

"You got use of our facilities if you need them, so this is what I've got for you."

The Lincoln had been left in the third story of a garage where it could have remained for days, along with all the other cars on long-term contracts. The only reason it had been investigated was that the alarm had been triggered when another car accidentally touched the rear fender. According to the night security guard, he'd heard the ringing, so he had gone to take a look. No long-term parking ticket was displayed on the window or on the dashboard, and he was about to return to his booth to double-check his records when he saw something dripping from beneath the trunk. At first he presumed it was oil, but on closer inspection realized it was blood and called the police.

Rooney sighed. "He give a description of the driver?"

Bean shook his head. "He said he wasn't on duty until late and the car was already parked. We've got a number for the daytime security officer, all there for you, but we haven't spoken to him yet."

Rooney checked his watch. "Get on to that right now."

Bean looked. "Me?"

"No, the invisible man, who the hell you think I'm talking to?"

"I'm on my way." Bean bristled.

Maynard passed over the statements and details his team had acquired and then, rather smugly, Rooney thought, made to leave, clearly pleased he wasn't on this case. As he reached the door he turned back to Rooney.

"How many does this make to date?"

"Too many," Rooney muttered, not looking up as he flicked through the folder. Rooney waited another two hours before the doors opened and the masked and gowned attendant gestured for him to follow. Draped in green sheeting, the body dominated the white-tiled room whose strip lighting gave a surreal white brightness to the rows of instruments and enamel sinks.

"Morning, Bill," said Nick Arnold, the pathologist, as he washed his hands at a large sink. He was a squat, gray-haired man in his late fifties with half-moon glasses perched on the end of his puglike nose. "You're pretty impatient for this one, aren't you? I hear you've been hovering outside—you should have come in."

Rooney hated being anywhere near an autopsy. He'd never gotten used to the way corpses were sliced open, never been able to stand hearing the hiss of stinking gases or looking at the blood pumping out; the open, sightless eyes of the victim as the body was systematically inspected.

Arnold knew Rooney of old and understood he wouldn't want to take a close look. He appeared distinctly greenish already. "Come and have some coffee," he said pleasantly. "It'll be a while before we get the photographs and tests completed." He yawned. "Got called out of bed for this one."

"So did I," muttered Rooney as he slumped into a low chair, its cushioned seat puffing loudly as his bulk made contact. "So what you got for me?"

"Death occurred late evening—can't be more specific. Until I get my reports back, I can't pinpoint the time, but it was evening and the last meal was banana bread."

"That's a big help." Rooney slurped his coffee, then licked his lips and looked up at Arnold. "Doesn't anyone brew coffee anymore like in the old days? This is like drinkin' . . ."

"It's the machine age, Bill. You can have chicken noodle soup if you'd prefer it."

"I think I got it, minus the noodles," Rooney said, squinting into his plastic cup.

"Victim's age was late thirties, may even be forty, but fit—good muscle tone."

"Was she blond?" Rooney asked.

"That's right, but who said she was female?"

"What?"

Arnold grinned. "He was almost a she, and at first glance I'd have said definitely female, heavy breasts, but he was also well endowed in the nether regions. Transsexual, Bill, one who'd been on a lot of hormone replacement treatments; Adam's apple had also been removed at some time." He stood up and pointed to drawings. "Hammer blow here to the base of the skull, which would have almost certainly rendered her unconscious. Her face was beaten to a pulp—nose, cheekbones, and frontal lobe shattered—very heavy blows, one eye forced back into this region and the other socket split open by the force of the hammer. Not a pretty sight now, but I would say she or he had at one time been quite attractive. Hair is bleached blond, well-cut, a good wig. Own hair is wispy blond, as you can see. We've also got nothing from under her fingernails, so the first blow was unexpected. She put up no resistance."

Rooney went into the forensic laboratory to see the victim's clothes. They were reasonably expensive, some with well-known labels. A female assistant, with a pair of plastic gloves on, was carefully sorting each garment. She held up a pair of high-heeled platform sandals.

"The clothes are bought from most malls and stores but these might be useful. As you can see they're a very large size and there's a label. They're specials and the store is a well-known one catering to transsexuals and transvestites."

Rooney nodded, jotting down the information, watching as the girl placed each shoe in a plastic bag. Then his beeper went off, and he asked to use a phone.

It was Josh Bean. He'd spoken to the day security officer, who had no recollection of even seeing the Lincoln. Rooney told him to make a few inquiries at the transsexual shoe shop, giving the size and style of the shoe from the corpse. He said he would meet up with him back at the station, but if he got an ID on the body he was to buzz him directly. Bean agreed and after a beat, knowing the effect it would have on Rooney, he said quietly, "I think the suits have arrived. FBI, Bill."

Rooney replaced the phone, swore under his breath, and then gave a weak smile to the still busy attendant. "Thanks for your help."

Rooney radioed to his team from his patrol car to check out the owner of the Lincoln, exactly when he had reported his vehicle stolen. By the time he got to his office they had already discovered the car's owner had been away for a week and only knew the car was missing when he returned home. So neither the security guards at the mall nor the owner could be certain of when the Lincoln had been stolen or the exact time it had been dumped in the mall.

By midday, forensic reports from inside the Lincoln yielded no bloodstains, no fingerprints in the interior or the glove compartment, and the steering wheel had been wiped clean. They did, however, find long strands of blond hair, which were sent to be tested and matched to the victim's wig. All this took considerable time—time Rooney did not have. At lunchtime, Chief Michael Berillo summoned him.

Rooney listened to him glumly. He was still to lead the officers in the inquiry but only until the FBI officers had familiarized themselves with the evidence. Then they would take over and, as Berillo had so kindly phrased it, "You can start mowing the lawn, Bill." He'd sounded gloating, even if unintentionally. Mowing the lawn was not something that Rooney pictured himself doing even if he'd retired of his own free will. Now this enforced "release from duty" was just what he had been dreading and he gave a long low sigh. "You shouldn't feel you've been ousted due to any unprofessional conduct or lack of ability. It's just that—"

Rooney leaned on the chief's desk. "You gotta have a scapegoat, someone to blame for not making an arrest. Sure, I understand. I just didn't expect to go out this way. I've given the best years of my life to the force, but it don't matter. Somebody's got to pay for not finding this crazy bastard, so why not make me the sucker?"

"I'm sorry you feel that way, Bill."

"At least I should have a chance to talk to this guy they brought in with them."

The chief coughed. "They're with him now, but I'm sure they'll let you talk to him later."

Rooney knew they'd all been aware of the possibility he'd be replaced, but his men seemed taken aback that it was happening so quickly. For all his bad-tempered ways, he was well liked. Bean, too, felt sorry for him; he hadn't been the easiest captain to work for but he liked him. If Rooney was being moved, it meant that everyone on the case would be scrutinized. He repeated Rooney's request to the team that until the FBI formally took over, they must all work double time.

No one attached to the case had yet had access to Brendan Murphy or had seen him brought in. Bean gave a rueful half smile.

"Be just our luck if they walk in with a suspect and pin the whole string on him. They'll get all the glory and we'll be made to look like assholes."

"No, son, there'll just be one of us with egg on his face and you're looking at him, so before it congeals let's get moving. We just have to find the suspect first. How did you make out at the shoe store?"

"It was closed, sign said it'd be open later in the day. Seems they stay open half the night. No phone number of the people that run it, so we'll go back."

Rooney jerked his head at the pictures of the last victim, already being pinned up, and plodded out of the incident room. He had decided to have one more crack at Mrs. Hastings. The link between her husband, victim and cross-dresser, and the latest victim was too much of a coincidence.

"Captain, should I take what we've got over to Andrew Fellows?" Bean called after Rooney. "See if he can help us out at all?"

"Sure. I'll be interested to hear what Big Ears has to say, and get on to the shoes, or get someone on to 'em, get anyone on to something, for fuck's sake!"

While Bean went off in search of Fellows, the rest of the team split up to make inquiries with known transsexuals, shoe and clothing stores that might recall the victim. Rooney sat in his office, resting his head in his hands. He knew they'd all be talking about him being retired earlier than anticipated and it gnawed at him. He downed a good belt of bourbon, replacing the bottle in his drawer before he forced himself to get up and moving as he had instructed Bean. He barked out and assigned two men to run checks on the employees at the S & A vintage car garage in Santa Monica, then crooked his finger for them to come close, telling them to keep it low-key. They could smell the booze on his breath but went off as instructed to the garage without comment.

Rooney stepped into the elevator and went down to the basement. He could see his reflection in the highly polished chrome cab of the elevator; he looked as beat as he felt. He proceeded along the brightly lit corridor toward the holding cells, or the famous ''pods'' as they were nicknamed. He had to pass through innumerable security doors and left his weapon in the locker outside the last main security section before he took the key. He was aware of the cameras monitoring his every move, knowing up in the control room they would be following his journey, corridor by corridor, section by section, and more than likely, as they had to know the FBI was here questioning a suspect, they were all gassing about his demise.

Rooney eventually joined the duty sergeant at his computerized board, which not only indicated every corridor but every occupied cell on a maze of small red and green lights. Microphones could if desired be upped so conversations taking place between officers and suspects or simply between prisoners held in the cells could be overheard.

''Where they got the suspect?''

The sergeant indicated cell fourteen's monitor.

''Any way I can hear what's going on?'' he muttered, knowing the answer.

The sergeant gave him a sidelong look and flicked a switch. ''FBI been with him for hours.''

Rooney crossed to the bank of screens and gazed at the one showing the occupant of cell fourteen. Brendan Murphy was sitting on the bunk bed, his hands held loosely in front of him. He was wearing a denim jacket and a stained T-shirt. His shoes had been removed. His beer gut, even larger than Rooney's, hung over his baggy ancient jeans. Rooney could not see who was in the cell with him but he heard the soft voice asking him to start from the beginning again and to take his time. Murphy seemed to stare directly into the camera and then ran his thick stubby hand over his unshaven jaw.

''Jesus Christ, I'm gettin' confused, I'm hungry, I want

some cigarettes. I dunno how many more times I can tell you I ain't seen my wife for almost ten months. I didn't meet the other woman more'n once or twice and that was fucking years ago. You got the wrong man.''

Rooney dragged on his cigarette. Murphy did not resemble the only description they had of the killer—no one could be more different. He was thickset, overweight, looked over six feet, and by the look of him, had never worn a jacket in his life. Murphy listed plaintively where he had been on the night of the murder and then stood up, angrily swinging his fist. ''I wasn't even in Los Angeles, for chrissakes. I told you all this in Detroit. You're gonna make me lose my job. Shit, I dunno what date it is today, how am I supposed to remember where I was in May?''

The soft voice told Murphy it was the fifth of August and could he be more explicit. He would not be released until they knew his exact whereabouts on the dates in question, starting with the seventeenth of May.

Rooney had seen enough. He did not believe for a minute that Murphy was their man, so *let* the FBI question him. The longer they were out of his hair the better.

Rosie was woken by Lorraine presenting her with a cup of tea. She was dressed for a workout. ''I'll be back for some brunch,'' she said brightly. Rosie yawned and squinted at the bedside clock, she couldn't believe the time.

''Yeah, we overslept, it's after eleven.'' She hesitated a moment before she bent forward and kissed Rosie's cheek. ''Thanks for last night.''

She pushed herself at the gym and Hector monitored her weights. She also did a full step-aerobic class. Then she had a sauna and an ice-cold shower and felt fit and sharp. She even ran from the bus back to the apartment—long, slow, steady strides, not pushing herself but working up a sweat, it was in the mid-nineties, another blistering August day.

Rosie had laid out all her vitamins, the protein drink, cereal, fruit and yogurt, frying up eggs and bacon for herself. Lorraine ate hungrily. After all her exertion she didn't feel tired, it was good to have had a long sleep for a change. She was feeling like the old Lorraine Page used to feel before she hit the bottle.

''I met this guy called Brad Thorburn last night,'' she said to Rosie. "He knew the professor I went to see at UCLA, Andrew Fellows. They were playing squash and . . ." Lorraine stared into space, seeing him again, his handsome face, his athletic body. "He lives at that house in Beverly Glen. He owns it. And that vintage car garage."

Rosie pulled out a chair and sat down as Lorraine sifted through her photographs. She looked closely at the Mercedes, then at the man they presumed was Steven Janklow. All they had in focus was his chin and part of his nose. She drew the clearer photograph of the blond woman beside it. "I think you're right—this is the same person."

Lorraine flipped through the files, looking for paperwork on Norman Hastings. "I want to go and talk to Hastings's wife. I'll have another shower, change, and go over to Arden Avenue. While I'm doing that, I want you to rent another car and pick me up there in a couple of hours. But first see if you can get a section of this picture of the woman blown up so we get to see more of his or her face." Lorraine counted out some cash. It was running low again.

"Any chance you can get that friend of yours to pay us some more?"

"I'll try, but I doubt it." Lorraine handed out sixty dollars, plus Mrs. Hastings's address.

"You going to tell him about those photos?" Rosie asked.

"Not yet. We need more, I don't want to foul this up." Rosie picked up the newspaper from the steps outside and tossed it to Lorraine. "See you later."

As the screen door slammed after Rosie, Lorraine opened the paper. She couldn't miss the blazing headline: HAMMER KILLER STRIKES AGAIN. She laid the paper out flat on the table: no name for the victim, just that she was white, aged between late thirties and early forties, and found in the trunk of a stolen vehicle. The murder had taken place the previous evening, the license plate number of the vehicle was given and the location where it had been found, along with a request to the public for any information that would assist the police inquiry. A suspect was being held.

Lorraine called Rooney but was told that he was not at the station. She checked her watch. It was too late to change her plans because Rosie had already left.

•   •   •

Rooney drove to Mrs. Hastings's house on Arden Avenue. It was as it had been before when he questioned her—neat, orderly, not even dog crap on the sidewalk or the manicured green lawns. Rooney had stopped on the way to buy some bourbon and a pack of mints. He pulled over and put the car in park but left the engine running. He took three heavy slugs from the bottle but it didn't give him the energy to get up out of the cool, air-conditioned car, so he had another drink. He'd hold off on the mints for a while. He sat back, closing his eyes, trying to face the prospect of being shafted out to pasture, and knowing there would be no bonus or golden handshake.

He sighed, unwrapped a peppermint to hide the smell of booze, and eased his bulk out of the cool car into a wall of heat. With his weight he felt every degree of the mid-nineties afternoon.

Fifteen minutes later Rooney was still waiting outside Mrs. Hastings's house. She was not in but, according to a neighbor, was probably taking her daughters back to school as they came home each day for lunch, so she would not be long. He took another few swigs of bourbon, screwed on the cap tightly, then unwrapped another peppermint. He settled back, reached for one of the newspapers he had bought, and broke wind loudly as he glared at the front page. A few cars passed by him but there was little or no traffic as this area was also a no-parking day- and nighttime zone unless resident, and all the neater than neat, well-kept orderly houses had their own garages inside the white-painted picket fences or neat, low-clipped hedges. Mrs. Hastings finally returned. She parked her car in the driveway and carried a bag of groceries inside. Rooney figured he'd wait a while longer before paying his visit. He glanced into his side mirror and saw Lorraine walking up the sidewalk. She paused as if checking she had the correct address. As she walked past his car, Rooney lowered the window. "Afternoon," he said loudly.

When she saw it was Rooney, Lorraine said without a pause, "Hi, I was going to talk to Mrs. Hastings."

"I'll come in with you."

Rooney saw her hesitate, then say, "Fine, but maybe I can get more out of her without you."

"You seen this late edition of the local paper? It's not public yet but it wasn't a she, it was a he—or an it, according to the pathologist. That's why I came here, thought I'd give Mrs. Hastings another shot.''

Lorraine didn't react to the information. This was the moment she should have discussed Janklow but she didn't.

"Says they got a suspect in custody."

"Brendan Murphy, husband of one of the victims. The suits have arrived. They brought him in from Detroit. I haven't even had access to him yet, but . . ."

"But?"

"It's not him, I know it. Let's talk to Mrs. Hastings."

"Let me try before you, Bill. You been checking out that vintage car garage?"

"I got two guys on it this morning."

She could smell liquor on his breath. "You okay?"

He shook his head. "Nah, they gave me the fucking kiss-off this morning. Well, until the FBI is ready to roll. They want me for a briefing later today."

Lorraine straightened. "You mind if I say something, Bill? It's just that I can smell the booze—that and peppermints. If I were you, I'd grab a cup of coffee. Mrs. Hastings sounds like the type of woman who'd report you and you don't want to give the FBI any excuse to ditch you . . ."

Rooney swore and cupped his hands around his mouth, blowing into them. His jowled face wobbled childishly. "Okay, I'll be back in fifteen. I'll grab a bite to eat. If you're through wait for me on the sidewalk. You know a place around here?"

Lorraine frowned and then told Rooney there wasn't a place that close, but if he went a few miles down, crossing the main intersection on Colorado, there was a grocery store with a deli attached. He nodded. "Yeah, I know it, just thought maybe there'd be a place closer. Never mind, you wait for me."

Rooney parked the car and went into the deli. As he waited for his order he thought how incongruous it was for Lorraine to be telling him to sober up. He'd always been a heavy drinker but now he was drinking more during working hours than he ever had. He wondered if that was the way Lorraine had started. She'd had marital problems, but then so did all the men. He dreaded the thought of being retired and at home with his wife. It gave him nightmares while she chattered away excitedly about them getting a trailer and traveling around the country. He could think of nothing worse. He couldn't recall the last time he had taken his wife out to dinner, or, for that matter, when he had taken her anywhere. He became more and more despondent as he plowed through his lunch. Everything he did revolved around his station, his men, and now it was going to end.

Hoping to push these morose thoughts from his mind, he tried to concentrate on the case. He wondered why Lorraine had wanted him to check out the vintage car garage. Did she have something for him, something she'd held back? She hadn't made it sound important, but in the old days Lorraine always kept her cards close to her chest. He'd reprimanded her about it, reminding her that she was not a one-woman agent but part of a team. He remembered her snapping back at him, saying when the men treated her as part of the team, she would work with them. She had put him down hard and fast because at that time she held a higher rank. It had always needled him, needled a lot of men, that she had gained her stripes before them.

"You got a problem with the men?" He could see himself leaning against his old wooden desk as she stood straight-backed in front of him. "You want to make a complaint?"

"No complaints, but if one of them sends me out on any more fucking wild-goose chases with that Merton, who wants to open fire on any kid he sees within ten yards of him, then I will. He's a lousy backup. He's in need of treatment and everyone on this unit knows it."

Rooney had promised to look into it but he never did. Even after the shootout when she was almost killed he had not given her anyone decent. Just suggested she take a refresher course at the pistol range.

"I'm a crack shot, Bill. I wouldn't be here if I wasn't and neither would my partner. It's him that needs the refresher course."

Lorraine had taken two weeks off for further training anyway, and her ex-partner died in a shootout the next time he was called out. Maybe she'd been right, but no one ever bothered to make an official inquiry. Officer Reginald Merton was given a posthumous medal for bravery and Lorraine a new partner. Lubrinski had actually filed a complaint a year or so back when he'd been partnered by a female on a stakeout, saying he had enough problems on the job without having to look out for a dumb broad, but when told Lorraine Page would be his new partner he'd said nothing. He didn't tell Rooney he'd already met Lorraine at the pistol range and had liked what he saw. Rooney figured it was Lubrinski that had started Lorraine on her drinking sessions. He had a reputation as a hard drinker, and before long it was rumored that she was matching him. It was Lubrinski who nicknamed her Hollow Leg.

They were partners for three years. When he was injured in some cross fire, she used her tights as a tourniquet for his leg. He'd taken three bullets: one in his thigh, one in his shoulder, and one in his stomach. It was the last one that had killed him. She had returned to duty the next week and never spoke about Lubrinski until the internal investigation. He, too, received a posthumous award and she gained a commendation, which many of the men opposed, insinuating that, had Lubrinski had one of them as backup instead of a woman, he would still be alive. She had never complained or asked for an easier assignment or taken up the offer of a few weeks' compassionate leave. She had gone straight back to work and remained on the same beat for another year. Rooney wondered if perhaps she had begun drinking alone. Then, at her own request, she was moved from Vice to the Drug Squad. Six months later she shot the kid. No one ever knew what she had felt on that night or why she had been drinking.

Rooney pushed his half-eaten ham and eggs across the table. For the first time he felt guilty that he, like everyone else, had given Lorraine the cold shoulder. He decided that, even though it was too late, he would talk it through with her. Maybe because he himself felt as if he could finish his bottle of bourbon and not care that he was on duty. He was past caring and he wondered if she had felt that way all those years ago. Angry. In some ways they were similar because he had never complained; he was the man who had always drummed into his officers, get on with the job no matter how tough, never complain, complaints are for losers. It didn't matter if they were male or female, nobody deserved any favors. If they couldn't take it, then they weren't tough enough to gain respect. Nobody respected him now, he concluded, and nobody had respected Lorraine Page.

•   •   •

"My name is Lorraine Page," she said to a nervous Mrs. Hastings.

"I wonder if I could come in and talk to you for a few moments, to iron out a few things about the inquiry into your husband's murder. It won't take long."

Sitting in the living room, Lorraine was relaxed and complimentary about the neat house, calming Mrs. Hastings's nerves.

"I've told that Detective Rooney everything. I just can't understand what more there is to discuss. This only makes it worse, these constant questions."

Lorraine opened her file and smiled. "Well, let's get this over with as fast as possible, shall we?"

She asked if Norman Hastings had ever owned a vintage car, or used a garage in Santa Monica that specialized in imported vehicles. She went through the different makes of car to see if Mrs. Hastings reacted, but the woman shook her head and said that her husband could never have afforded anything so expensive. Lorraine asked if he had owned a car before they were married.

"Yes, of course, but I've no idea what kind it was." Lorraine said nothing, seemingly more interested in her file. "I've got a photograph of it, I think," Mrs. Hastings added.

Lorraine looked up and smiled encouragingly. "Can I see it?"

Mrs. Hastings left the room and Lorraine took out the photographs she and Rosie had taken. Mrs. Hastings returned with a photograph album and began to flip through the pages until she found what she was looking for. "I think that's it. I have no idea what make it was, but I'm sure it wasn't one of the cars you mentioned."

Lorraine looked at the snapshot taken in 1979, the date neatly printed below the photograph. Norman Hastings, in shirtsleeves, stood beside the car. It was a low sports car, a British-made Morgan—and, by the look of it, quite an old model.

"Do you have any idea where he bought it?"

Mrs. Hastings shook her head again. She had never seen it.

"Your husband was a few years older than you," Lorraine observed, about to turn the album page, but Mrs. Hastings took it back.

"Yes, fifteen, but we were happy." She hesitated. "I suppose you know about Norman's little problem. I told that man Rooney.''

''I don't think we need to discuss it. You were brave to tell Captain Rooney about it—it must have been very distressing.'' Lorraine opened her purse and took out the small square box, opening it as she passed it to Mrs. Hastings. ''Did your husband ever own a set of cuff links like these, Mrs. Hastings? They could be gold but with that distinct S and A logo in the center.''

Mrs. Hastings looked down at them. ''They're silver, but the chain's broken.''

''Do you still have them?''

She left the room again and Lorraine leaned back in the sofa. Next she wanted Mrs. Hastings to look at the photographs. It was going well but the woman was tricky, nervous and jumpy. Lorraine wanted her nice and calm. The cuff links were still in their little cardboard box and one was broken. Lorraine examined the links, then looked at the box. No date, just the same logo and the Santa Monica address.

''What do you want to see these for?'' Mrs. Hastings asked.

Lorraine replaced the cuff links, shut the box. ''We may have a possible link to the killer. We think he was wearing something similar. Thank you.''

Mrs. Hastings was beginning to pluck at her dress in agitation. ''Will it all come out? About Norman?''

Lorraine put her box into her purse. ''I doubt it. I always think personal details that have no connection to the case should not be released to the press, especially if the family have requested them not to be.''

Mrs. Hastings clasped Lorraine's wrist. ''Oh, thank you. I've been so worried—the children—then there's Norman's parents and his friends at work.''

''He was an engineer, wasn't he?''

''Yes, yes, he was, for refrigerators and domestic appliances.''

''Did he work on his car engines?''

''He could repair anything from a toaster to a car. The neighbors were always asking him to fix things and he was such a kind man, he'd never say no.'' She leaned forward and lowered her voice. ''Some people around here complain, you know, about anything and everything. They complained about Norman working on other people's cars, said they cluttered up the driveway. Unless it was *their* car, of course."

Lorraine used the opening and showed the photograph of Janklow.

"Did he ever help this man out?"

"I can't tell, there's not all his face there, but I don't think so."

Lorraine now showed the photo of the white Mercedes driven by Janklow in blond wig and makeup. Mrs. Hastings glanced at it. "I don't know her."

"Have you ever seen the car?"

Mrs. Hastings took the photograph and stared at it. "I don't know, a lot of people came to see him. As I said, he was always helping people out."

"It's a vintage Mercedes sports car, a real beauty. It would also have a hard top. Maybe you saw it with that on?"

Mrs. Hastings frowned. "I don't know. There's something familiar about it, it's difficult to say. What color is the hard-top roof?"

Lorraine took a chance, figuring if the body was white maybe the roof was, too.

"Well, no, I remember a similar car out in the driveway once, but it had a black top, sort of dipped."

Lorraine began to put away the photographs, still relaxed. "Did you see who was driving it? Who it belonged to?"

"No, they were in the garage out in the yard. Norman used to keep odd spare parts out there—and that was another reason why he had so many people coming around. He'd charge them—just expenses, it was his hobby but I hated it. It made his hands all dirty, and left oil on everything, and then with the complaints . . .''

Lorraine stood up and smiled. "Thank you very much. You've been very helpful, and I really appreciate it. Would you mind if I come back if I get a better photograph of the man in the Mercedes?"

"No, I don't mind. In fact, I haven't minded talking to you at all."

Rooney was just pulling up when he saw Lorraine walk out. She waved to Mrs. Hastings and he saw her glance toward his car. He opened the passenger door as Mrs. Hastings shut her front door and Lorraine got in beside him. "I'd stay clear of her—she's nervous, more worried about her husband's 'little problem,' as she calls it, getting out to the press than she is about the murder.''

Rooney sniffed. ''You got anything for me?''

''I might have a suspect, but until I'm sure I'd rather do some more digging around—maybe in a few days.''

''I need anything you've got now. I don't have a few days.''

She pursed her lips. ''Give me until the end of the day. I also need anything you've got on the latest victim.''

''I told you all I've got. Until they've finished the tests, that's it. She was a man and her last meal was banana bread.'' She had her hand on the door ready to leave when he said, ''You and Lubrinski, were you an item?''

''Why do you want to know?''

''I'm just trying to figure you out.''

''Little late for that, isn't it?''

''Yeah, I know. I was just mulling things over, and I started to think about him, he was a great guy.''

She nodded but made no reply. He reached down for his bourbon and unscrewed the cap. He drank from the bottle and she turned to look at him. ''It's the bourbon that reminds you of him. Because he always had a bottle under his seat. Why are you drinking, anyway?''

He gritted his teeth as the bourbon hit his stomach. He took another swig. ''I need it. Did you drink with him?''

''You know I did.''

''On duty?''

''Sometimes, but mostly we waited until we were off.''

''Did he get you started on the booze?''

She laughed. ''I didn't need Lubrinski to start me drinking, Bill, I managed it all by myself.''

''Why?''

She suddenly became touchy. ''How about I was just screwed-up, tense, and scared I'd foul up. And there's nobody else to blame but myself.''

''Your husband? The kids, was that it?''

''For chrissakes, back off. Why do you want to start on this?''

He took another swig and screwed on the cap. ''Because I'd like to know, and maybe I feel guilty. Maybe this is a conversation I should have had with you years ago.''

She got out of the car and leaned in. ''You're too late, Bill, there's nothing you can do now. What happened happened. It's over.''

"I'm sorry." He said it gruffly, not looking at her, and she straightened up, about to slam the car door, when she bent down to look at him again.

"About Lubrinski, Bill, he was the best friend I ever had. I trusted him with my life but he was a crazy fool, he took risks, got into a lot of things that I tried to stop, but he wouldn't listen to me, he never listened to anyone and, in answer to your question, we were not an item, we were just partners.''

Then she shut the door and walked off just as Rosie drove up on the opposite side of the road. Rooney pulled away in a cloud of exhaust fumes.

"How'd it go?" Rosie asked cheerfully.

Lorraine told her to drive to the S & A garage in Santa Monica. Then she closed her eyes and leaned back. She could see Lubrinski's face as clear as if it were yesterday. They had gotten drunk together on so many evenings, they'd talked about everything under the sun, always carefully skirting around themselves. But eventually it had happened. She'd been drinking heavily and he'd insisted she sober up at his place before Mike saw her. He was always joking about Mike, snide one-liners about her house-proud husband, but she wouldn't let him run Mike down. She snapped back that he should try and clean up his own act, no wonder his wife had kicked him out of their house. They had squabbled like teenagers and eventually called a truce, agreeing that neither of them would discuss their partners.

"Does this make you a single woman now?"

She had tried to slap him but he ducked so she hit the window of the patrol car. Her knuckles hurt and she sucked her fist. He reached over and caught her hand, drawing it to his lips.

That night they were totally smashed, even though he seemed never to show it. Not until she watched him attempting to brew the coffee did she know he was as drunk as she was. "You're plastered, Lubrinski, talk about the blind leading the blind. Here, lemme do it.''

He lay back on his unmade bed in his new one-room bachelor apartment with dirty clothes strewn all around. Lorraine offered to help him clean it up. He said he liked it this way, he knew where everything was, but after they'd finished the coffee he couldn't find the patrol car keys. He started throwing things around, swearing. Then he suddenly stopped, smiled at her, and laughed his wonderful, deep bellow. "I'm lying, they're in my pocket." He pulled them out and dangled them. "I just wanted to keep you here a while longer, but now that I'm sober I don't have the guts."

"For what?" She was still laughing at him.

"To hold you. You ever think how much I want to hold you, Lorraine Page?"

She stopped laughing, got up off the bed, walked over to him, and gently slipped her arms around him. He held her close, he didn't kiss her, he didn't fondle her, he did exactly what he had said he wanted to do: he held her in his arms. She rested her head against his chest, could feel his heart beat, could feel him tremble. She had smiled up at him and then released herself. "I got to get back to the kids."

"You love him, don't you?" he asked.

She was confused. She didn't really know. The fights and bitter arguments had been wearing her out. Mike hated Lubrinski, constantly implied that he was more than just a working partner. He also hated the way she had started drinking so much. He blamed that on Lubrinski as well. Mike blamed everything on anything and anyone but himself.

"Yes, I love Mike. Now I got to go home. We both got enough problems without starting up any new ones."

She had never seen Lubrinski ill at ease but he was that night, pulling at his thick black curly hair. "It's kind of different for me, Lorraine." He shook his head, looking at her. "You don't know, do you? You got no idea. Jesus Christ, Lorraine, I love you. Some days I don't know what to do with myself I love you so much, and sometimes I get scared for you and I know that's not a good thing but I can't stop it, can't stop loving you, wanting you. And sitting so close to you, day in day out, is driving me crazy. I'm gonna ask for a transfer. It's nothing to do with you being a good or bad partner, it's just that I want you and . . . well, now you know."

Two nights later he was shot on a stakeout. When she tore off her tights to wrap them around his thigh as he was bleeding to death, Lubrinski had joked that at long last he was getting her pants down—he knew he would in time. If he'd known

she'd do it when he was shot, he'd have stood up months
before . . .

She held him in the ambulance. His breathing became labored, his eyes unfocused. She kept telling him to hold on, to
keep talking. The last thing he said was that he loved her and
the last thing he heard before he died was Lorraine saying that
he was a stupid, dumb bastard because she loved him, too, and
if he didn't hold on and pull through she'd strangle him with
her tights. She saw the light go from his eyes in disbelief.
She'd seen so much death, been so close to it, but this was
like losing her own soul, as if he was taking it with him.

Lorraine went back to her apartment, needing Mike more
than ever, but he wasn't there. She drank herself into a stupor
and collapsed on the bed. Mike came back about two hours
later. As soon as he saw her he shouted that Lubrinski had
gotten her drunk again and she had said quietly that this time
Lubrinski had nothing to do with it.

"I don't believe you. I'm gonna see him, report him."

"Try the City Morgue, Mike, but I doubt if he'll talk back
to you, he's dead."

Mike was stunned, had tried to hold her, but she couldn't
stand him near her, couldn't bear anyone to touch her. All she
wanted was to drink herself into oblivion. Poor Mike had tried
to understand, to persuade her to take leave when it was offered, but she refused; she couldn't stand not to be busy, not
to be working. She began to believe that Lubrinski had taken
a part of her with him when he died. Nothing she did made
any sense, neither did anything Mike said. She was irritable
with the girls, she was bad-tempered and uncooperative at
work, but somehow she carried on until she finally lost control
and killed an innocent boy.

"We're almost there," said Rosie.

Lorraine opened her eyes. She wanted a drink. That was all
she could think about. She didn't care about anything else. "I
want a drink."

Rosie stopped outside a grocery store and hurried inside.
She returned with a six-pack of Coke. "Here, you wanted a
drink!" Lorraine opened a can and gulped it down. Rosie
opened one for herself and then proffered a piece of homemade banana bread.

Lorraine sat bolt upright. What had Rooney said? The latest
victim, all they had on her or him was that his last meal was

banana bread. She felt her body break out in a cold sweat.
Was it Didi or Nula that was always making banana bread?
Could it possibly be one of them? Shit—they were the right
age. He had said it was a transsexual—but it couldn't be, it
was impossible.

"I got to make a call, Rosie."

Rosie looked at her. "Oh, yeah, like you just got to go in
there and make a phone call. You think I'm dumb. I know
what you'll be making, a bottle of vodka. No way."

Lorraine had her hand on the car door. "Fuck you, if you
feel I can't be trusted then come in with me."

Lorraine had Rosie right at her elbow as she placed the call
to Nula and Didi's apartment. Nula answered, her voice grav-
elly drowsy. "It's Lorraine, who's this?"

"It's Nula, sweetheart, how you doin'?"

"I'm great, Nula. Is Didi there?"

"Nope, she hasn't come in, been out all night, the dirty cow.
She'll be back soon though 'cause she's got a girl comin' to
have her hair cut. You want me to get her to call you?"

"Do you know where she is?" Lorraine asked, trying to
keep her voice laid back.

Just then the doorbell rang at Nula's end. "That's Didi coming home now," she said; if Lorraine wanted to hang on and
wait she'd bring her to the phone.

"No, I got to go, I'll call later."

Rosie waited, head on one side. "What was that all about?"

Lorraine shrugged. "I thought maybe something had happened to Didi, but she'd just gotten home."

They left the grocery store and headed for the S & A garage.
This time Lorraine was going to go in. She needed to speak
to the man Mrs. Hastings had recognized. She also knew that
Steven Janklow might be there and if he was, she was going
to have to come up with a good reason for her presence.

Nula grabbed her purse and dark shades. It hadn't been Didi
at the door. The two officers didn't say why they wanted her
to accompany them to the station, but she knew it had something to do with Didi because they had asked for photographs
of her. If she had just been arrested for prostitution, Nula knew
they wouldn't want photographs. All they had asked was if
she knew David Burrows. Nobody ever called Didi David,

only the cops. Half an hour later Nula identified Didi's body. She was in such a state of shock she was unable to speak coherently. All she could do was whisper Didi's name over and over. The face didn't resemble that of her beloved friend. Only the red nails and the big topaz ring made Nula sure it was Didi. Two uniformed officers drove her back home in a patrol car. They helped her inside the apartment, and then asked when she had last seen Didi.

The FBI checked into the complex list of dates and pickups that Brendan Murphy could remember. They contacted the trucking agencies he worked for and released him. He had not lied: Brendan Murphy was not in Los Angeles when his wife, Helen, had been killed, and neither had he been near any of the other locations where victims had been found. Deprived of a suspect, they began to study the case history. Having been brought in to trace Murphy, they were now assigned to the "Hammer" murder investigation.

FOURTEEN

Lorraine sat with Rosie in the parking lot adjacent to S & A Vintage Cars. It was a Mexican tile import company, to the trade only, and there were just two vehicles parked in front of their showroom. "Right, here I go. You wait here and if I'm not out—"

"I'll shoot myself." Rosie laughed.

Lorraine got out of the car, gave her jacket a quick tug to straighten the back, and walked briskly toward the main reception area. No one was around and the vast stretch of the polished mahogany counter held leaflets sprayed out like fans. Dull soft music, songs from the twenties, was in the air. A number of Oscar-like statues, racing cups, and awards stood in glass cabinets, and everywhere there were pictures of vintage cars.

Five gleaming automobiles were lined up in front of the showroom windows: a Rolls-Royce Silver Cloud, a Rolls Corniche, a 1950s Bentley, a Bristol, and a two-door Mercedes convertible. The leather interiors were as immaculate as the gleaming chrome, wooden dashboards, and large steering wheels, which by today's standards were almost fragile-looking. Lorraine could see her distorted image reflected in the hubcaps. She looked squat.

"Hi, how can I help you?"

She turned to the equally polished salesman. His hair

gleamed, as did his teeth, his deep tan, his eyes. He had the S & A logo on the pocket of his navy blazer and on his maroon tie. He smiled expectantly, one hand shifting his immaculate starched cuff closer to his wrist; he was all logoed out. She wondered why he hadn't had S & A stamped on his forehead.

"Do you have an office? I'd like to discuss something with you."

The teeth gleamed as his lips drew slightly apart in another fake smile. "Would you like to tell me what it's about?"

"Sure, if you have an office. I am Mrs. Page, and you are?"

He stepped behind the counter. "Alan Hunter. I am the sales manager. How can I help you, Mrs. Page?"

He gave her a cool, studied appraisal. Even though his eyes didn't seem to leave hers, she felt as if he were scrutinizing her from her worn shoes to her secondhand suit. "May I ask what you're selling?"

She would have liked to hit him in the face. She used to love times like this, times when, confronted by a real smart-ass prick, you pulled out your badge and said in a low voice, "You want to check my ID, sonny?"

"I'm not selling and I'm not buying. I need to talk to you in private. What did you say your name was?"

Something in her voice unnerved him. He hesitated and repeated his name.

"Right, Mr. Hunter. I don't want to waste any more time and I don't want to discuss anything in this swimming pool of a lobby." He touched the knot of his tie and gestured toward a glass-windowed door.

Lorraine walked across the reception area and paused when she saw a picture of Brad Thorburn. He was sitting on the wing of a racing car wearing a white racing-driver's suit. One hand clasped a helmet, the other lifted a glass of champagne. To the right and left were more pictures of him posing at racetracks.

Hunter opened his office door, motioning her to enter ahead of him. "Are you with the police?"

She placed her purse on his empty polished mahogany desk and took out her cigarettes. "Do you mind if I smoke?"

Hunter did not demur and Lorraine surveyed the room. "You don't appear to be very busy."

"We are, I assure you. Most of our customers wait for us to deliver, few come to the building. We have hangars and workshops out at the rear of the showroom. Can I ask what you wanted to talk to me about? Is it traffic violations?''

Lorraine sat in the perfectly positioned chair, not too far away from the desk. "No. It's not about traffic violations."

"Is it connected with . . ." Hunter opened his desk drawer and withdrew a card. "A Lieutenant Josh Bean?"

"No, it isn't."

"He was here earlier, some kind of check on stolen vehicles."

"That's not my department. I'm investigating an insurance claim." She took out Rosie's pictures. "Do you recognize any of these men?"

Hunter leaned forward, sifting methodically through the photographs. He put seven aside. She watched as he glanced at the one of Steven Janklow. He frowned, hesitated a moment, and then looked up. "These seven men work here in various capacities."

She tapped Steven Janklow's picture. "How about him?"

Hunter picked up the photograph. "This could be Mr. Janklow. He's one of the partners but it's not a very good picture. I recognize the car more than the face. It's one of ours—it's actually owned by Brad Thorburn. Is it something to do with Mr. Thorburn?"

Lorraine nodded, looking around for an ashtray. As Hunter passed her a silver one with the S & A logo stamped into the center, she noticed his gold cuff links, which also carried the insignia. She tapped the ash from her cigarette and eased out the picture of the woman driving the Mercedes. "Do you know her?"

He stuck out his bottom lip, shaking his head. "No. It could be Mrs. Thorburn, Mr. Thorburn's mother, but I'm only guessing since I've never met her. But the car is the same. It belongs, as I said, to Mr. Thorburn. Has it been in an accident?"

"No." Lorraine packed away the pictures. "Do you have a schedule of who was on or off duty over a period of time?"

He nodded, tapping his foot. She then pulled out Norman Hastings's picture. "Do you recognize this man?"

Hunter sighed irritably. "His name was Norman Hastings. Is it his insurance? He was murdered, is that what this is about?"

Lorraine assented.

"Well, I'm sorry, but I never dealt with him. All I know is

he was a pain in the butt. He bought a car from us, long time ago before I joined the company.'' He leaned back, splaying out his hands affectedly. ''If you buy one of our vehicles at the prices we ask, we have first-class mechanics and maintenance engineers at your service. We attempt to make sure no vehicle ever leaves here without its engine having been re-checked, rebuilt if necessary. Many purchasers have the cars customized to their own specifications. Every modification is made to ensure a trouble-free vehicle, but, that said, we're not dealing in new cars. Some of these are twenty, even thirty years old, and sometimes there will be problems. But we give a six-month guarantee to every vehicle, and for the first six months we will pick up and redeliver should any mechanical fault occur.''

He laughed like an actor, his speech, even his own humor rehearsed. ''We had someone here not long ago, I think he had a Bentley, and he called us out simply because he was unsure where he should put the gas!''

''Norman Hastings?'' Lorraine said quietly.

''His car was a Morgan. He was on the phone almost every day wanting it picked up and tested. And then we discovered that the faults were self-inflicted because he was constantly taking the engine apart and rebuilding it—or that's what Mr. Janklow said.''

''Is Mr. Janklow here today?''

''Yes.''

Lorraine asked if it was possible to find out who was on or off work at the time of Hastings's murder and that included Mr. Janklow.

Hunter plucked at his lip. ''Why would you want that for an insurance claim? Anyway, Mr. Janklow doesn't work on any schedule system. He comes and goes when he likes.''

Lorraine asked if Janklow was around on the evening of June 20, the evening Holly was murdered, but Hunter shrugged his shoulders. He stared at a wall calendar. ''I simply couldn't tell you. All I know is he arrives and leaves when he feels like it.''

''Is there a place for parking workers' cars?''

''Out back. It's like an old aircraft hangar. There are always cars there—our own, some waiting for work to be done, others that have just been shipped in.''

Lorraine opened her notebook and reeled off details about

the car each body had been found in but to little effect. Hunter could not recall any of them. He was becoming puzzled by the dates and lists of cars, and she knew she was running out of time. She played a wild card. "Not even, say, Norman Hastings's blue sedan?"

"Ah, yes, he left that here on a number of occasions."

Lorraine felt her heart jump, like a kick of pleasure at her own cleverness. "Would you just check the last time you saw it here."

Hunter looked at his watch. He picked up the phone. "Sheena, can you please check the last time Norman Hastings came in and left his vehicle? Thank you." He hung up. "The police asked this, and they've already gone over the hangars."

Lorraine lit another cigarette and tossed the match into the ashtray. "Hastings sold his car, didn't he? Quite a few years ago. Do you know if he purchased any other vintage car? Did he sell it via S and A?"

"Not to my knowledge, but I didn't have anything to do with him."

"Did Mr. Thorburn also know Hastings?"

"I believe so."

The phone rang and Hunter answered it. He drew a notepad toward him, said "yes" a few times, thanked the caller, and ripped off the page. "Hastings apparently had some arrangement to leave his car here—my secretary isn't sure who he made it with or the last time he came."

"So he parked his own car here and yet he hadn't owned one of your vehicles recently?"

"Seems so."

"Do you think the arrangement would have been made with Mr. Janklow?"

"I have no idea. My direct boss is Mr. Thorburn, not Mr. Janklow."

"What do you think of him?" she asked nonchalantly.

"Brad? He's great to work for. He's firm, you know where you are with him, but he's also fun, loves a good laugh."

"I meant Steven Janklow."

Hunter pursed his lips in distaste. "I have little to do with him so I can't say what he's like."

"You could try."

"I don't see eye to eye with him, that's all. He's volatile.

One day he's friendly, the next he'll cut you dead. He's witty but it's that put-down humor, that's all.''

"Is he married?"

"No."

"Is he homosexual?"

Hunter was surprised by the question. "I don't know."

"Do you think he could be? Or could he be something else?"

"Like normal?"

Lorraine stood up. "Fine, so you think he's a nice, normal guy. I'm sorry, but my firm insists on me completing these amazing questionnaires. Insurance companies are gettin' to be tougher than the police."

"But I told you, he's not that nice."

Hunter gave her a hooded look and she smiled broadly. "How about not that normal either?" she said. She was beginning to like the Ivy League car salesman. She decided he was being honest with her and was green enough to have taken her at face value as an insurance claim officer. She looked through the white blinds to the parking lot.

"Is he suspected of something?" Hunter asked. "The police asked a lot of questions to some of the other staff, but they weren't very interested in me. I wasn't here the week of the Hastings murder." He sounded disappointed.

Lorraine got out the photographs again. "What about taking another look at that photo of the blond woman? Can you tell me if it could be Janklow?"

Hunter looked at her, blushing, then picked up the photograph. He studied it and his voice went quiet. "I honestly don't know, Mrs. Page, and I would hate to embarrass Mr. Thorburn. He's a good friend."

"Norman Hastings's family cannot sell his car or claim any monies on his insurance until I have completed my questionnaire."

"Is Mr. Janklow under suspicion?"

Lorraine ran her fingers through her hair. It was difficult to ask what she wanted to know without getting into trouble.

"There are rumors," he said suddenly. She waited as Hunter determined whether or not to continue. "I don't know if I should repeat them as they are just rumors." He came to a decision. "He has some odd mannerisms and he can be affected. Nobody here knows much about his private life, just that a few years ago there was an inquiry. He was interviewed by the Vice Squad, arrested. Nothing came of it."

There was a light tap on the door and a pretty girl peered in.

"I'm sorry to interrupt, Mr. Hunter, but you have a customer waiting."

Hunter introduced his secretary, Sheena. Lorraine asked if she and Sheena could have a quick chat and look at the hangar where the cars were kept. He said he had better ask his superior.

"I'll wait here with Sheena then," Lorraine said.

Sheena looked at Lorraine. "You wanna know about Norman Hastings? He used to come here quite a lot. He used to park his car out back—loved to look over the new arrivals. I had to check back this morning for the police. As far as I can tell from our records these were the dates when his car was left here. I gave the officers a copy, too." She passed over a neatly typed list. "I was so shocked when I read about his murder. He was such a quiet, unassuming man, sort of like my dad."

Sheena was young, with soft blond hair swept up with two pink combs, one of those "apple pie" types that were becoming extinct. Lorraine looked over the dates and then smiled warmly at her. "If I were to give you a list of other cars, could you see if they were parked out in the hangar at any time?"

Sheena bit her lip, patted one of her combs that didn't need readjusting. "I've already got one list from the police but I told them it's not a garage, we just let the workers park there and a few friends. Sometimes there's no free space."

"Could we take a look at the hangar?"

Sheena hesitated, looking from Lorraine to the showroom via the blinds.

"Only take a minute."

Sheena nodded and opened the door, ushering Lorraine ahead of her, taking the left corridor away from the salesroom. She opened a door facing onto the back lot. There were two steps down and the heat hit them like a blast in the face.

Lorraine followed Sheena across a wide yard and her apple pie image dimmed slightly as she called out to various men working or passing in dirty overalls. Lorraine also noticed that the young girl had solid legs, showing rather a lot of just how solid as her skirt was very short. There were a number of outbuildings and Lorraine could see cars on ramps and mechanics working. The business seemed to be thriving. The aircraft-type hangar was boiling hot, and packed with rows of cars, parked fender to fender. Some had tarpaulins over them and seemed to have been left for a considerable time. Dust covered others waiting to be reconditioned and then came a large section of what looked like the workers' cars. Sheena hurried through the sweltering hangar, heading toward a door marked OFFICES PRIVATE.

"Mr. Thorburn likes the employees' vehicles out of sight, says it's not a good advertisement. We park here and this is where Mr. Hastings's car usually was, just for a few hours at a time, but he always left the keys. We have to leave the keys in case they need to be moved if a delivery arrives."

They reached the back of the hangar and looked over three racing cars, all draped in protective silver covers. Sheena's face was now shiny with sweat in the unrelenting heat. "These are Mr. Thorburn's specials. He used to race a lot, but not so much nowadays. One of his wives created a stink about it . . .'' Sheena opened a door at the back of the hangar into a corridor. It was air-conditioned, freezing cold compared with the hangar. They passed large offices with modern white blinds on the windows. One was Brad Thorburn's, his name on a wood plaque cut into the door. They arrived at Sheena's, where she took out a large log book to check the list of cars Lorraine had given her. "It's the same list the police gave me. I told them there was just the one. Mr. Hastings's."

Sheena was not quite so forthcoming in the office section, constantly looking toward the door. The phone rang. She answered it, listened, and then said, "I'd better go. I've got to take the sales invoices to Mr. Hunter. Every week the top salesman gets a bonus."

"Can I wait?"

"I'm not sure, er, well, I'll tell Mr. Hunter you're in here." Sheena gathered up a file and walked out. She left the door ajar. As soon as she was halfway down the corridor, Lorraine closed the door, picked up the log book, and began to search through it. She was getting close, she knew it. She felt herself getting excited. She was sure Steven Janklow was connected to the case.

●   ●   ●

Rosie got out of the car, her dress sticking to her in the heat. A number of people had already taken a good look at her from the window of the tile showroom, noticing that she was parked in their lot but quite obviously not a customer. She walked around the car, fanning herself with her hand, and stood in the shade a moment. She was thirsty and Lorraine had been gone over an hour. Just as she thought she would go into S & A, a workman walked out of the building and headed toward her. "This is a private driveway, you want something?"

"No. My friend's inside." She pointed to the S & A building.

"Why don't you wait over there? We're expecting a delivery any minute. Go on, move."

Rosie returned to the car. The seat scorched her backside and when she started up the engine it gave off even more hot air. W-rent W-rent Wreckers didn't come with air-conditioning. She backed out and parked for a while in the street. Then she circled the block. She was heading past S & A when a white Mercedes passed her and drove into the front lot. Rosie watched Steven Janklow head around to the rear of the building and disappear before she could get her camera out. She dabbed her sweating face with a tissue. "Come on, for God's sake, Lorraine, what are you doing in there?" she muttered. From where she was parked, she could see a sharply dressed salesman talking to two Japanese men. All three disappeared inside. Still no Lorraine.

Lorraine heard running footsteps, then the door opened and Sheena came back in. She was even shinier and more flushed. "Sorry, but I got held up. I haven't been able to speak to Mr. Hunter yet—he's still with a couple of clients and I think they want a test drive. I think you had better go and wait to speak to him because . . ." A voice from one of the other offices called out brightly, "Good morning, Mr. Janklow."

Sheena pulled a face. "He's here. You'd better leave or I'll get into trouble, I'm sorry."

Lorraine picked up her purse. "It's okay. Thank you for your time."

"I hope I was of some help. It was just so terrible, poor Mr. Hastings."

"Did you see him when he was here the last time?"

"No, but when he came to see Mr. Janklow, he'd always stop in and leave me his car keys. I think he banked up the street, but his office isn't far away. He was always worried about parking tickets. Funny, really, worrying about something as small as that and then . . . he gets killed."

"But Mr. Janklow was here *then*?"

"Yes. Do you want to speak to him? He's here but he doesn't like seeing anyone without an appointment." Sheena looked back down the corridor and then to Lorraine. "He can get moody sometimes, you know . . ."

"Then I'll just go see Mr. Hunter. Thanks for everything."

Lorraine walked out into the corridor. Her heart jumped as she passed Janklow's office but he was not inside; through the blinds, she could see a secretary placing papers on the desk. She continued along the corridor, came into the boiling hangar, and walked quickly out into the hot sunshine. She stood for a moment to get her bearings and then took off toward the path winding around the building, intending to go back to Rosie, but without passing through the building itself. Then she saw the Mercedes parked by a car-wash area. She hugged the wall when she saw a man talking to one of the attendants. He was gesturing to the car's wheels. Then he leaned into it and pointed to the interior. She saw the attendant nod, then heard him tell two black kids to wash and vacuum Mr. Janklow's car, and polish up the chrome on the hubcaps and fenders.

Lorraine waited, half wanting Janklow to turn around so that she could see his face but not wanting him to catch sight of her. He was wearing a pale blue linen jacket, white slacks, and loafers. Slim, immaculate, his hair cut short and tight to his head—blondish-brown hair—just as she remembered. Steven Janklow was the man who had attacked her, she was almost sure of it. If only she could get a good look at his face.

Hunter appeared at the showroom doors. "We've got a customer who wants a test drive, Mr. Janklow. It's the Silver Cloud but we've already got someone that asked if we'd contact them if it looked like we'd get a sale."

Janklow walked slowly toward him and Lorraine pressed closer to the wall. They were about to enter the building, Hunter stepping aside to allow Janklow to go in ahead. As soon as they disappeared, Lorraine hurried along the driveway, past the Mercedes, to the street, missing the fact that Hunter had caught sight of her.

As Janklow was walking toward the Japanese customers, Hunter mentioned that the police had been in to speak to him that morning about Norman Hastings. He added, "There's also an insurance broker, or something to do with Hastings's car, here. She was in my office but I just saw her outside. She wanted to know about Hastings parking his car in the hangar."

Hunter was used to Janklow's mood changes but he was stunned when he turned abruptly, pushed past him, and walked back out the way they had come in.

"What about the Silver Cloud, Mr. Janklow?"

Lorraine hurried to join Rosie and jumped into the passenger seat. She let out a yell as it was red hot. "Let's go, I think we just got Rooney a suspect."

"Oh yeah? Well, I nearly got sunstroke out here, thanks, thanks a lot. Well? You gonna tell me? Did you see the guy? Is it him?"

Janklow's fists were clenched as he strode along the corridor to Sheena's office and opened the door. She gave a nervous smile at the sight of him. "Where is this woman from the insurance company?" he demanded.

"She just left, Mr. Janklow."

"What did she want?"

Sheena swallowed. "Same as the two officers. She was making inquiries about vehicles we allowed to be parked in the hangar."

Janklow picked up the log book. "Did you get her name?"

"I presumed Mr. Hunter must have. She was interviewing him earlier today."

"What do you mean, 'interviewing'?"

"Well, just talking to him. I don't know what he said or anything. I was only doing what I was told, Mr. Janklow."

He walked out and into his own office, banging down the heavy book in a fury. He then rang through to the showroom.

Hunter was turning the engine over, the Japanese looking on with interest, when the phone rang. Hunter excused himself and went to answer it. Janklow seemed hysterical, screaming for him to get into his office immediately. He didn't care if they had customers, he wanted to speak to Hunter this second. If he valued his job he would get himself over there. Before Hunter could reply the phone was slammed down.

Rooney was sweating in spite of the chill of his air-conditioned office. He expected the FBI any minute; it was ominous they hadn't even asked to see him because he knew they'd been going over the case history, no doubt the murder inquiries, and his lack of progress. He'd finished the bottle of bourbon, his nose was redder than ever, his eyes were bloodshot, and he hadn't as yet glanced over Josh Bean's reports of the day. Bean walked in and plunked a large mug of black coffee and a roll of peppermint Life Savers down in front of him. Rooney gave him a hound dog look and sniffed the coffee.

"It's real, they got a percolator in one of the clerical offices and the peppermints you left in your car. Guessed you might be in need of one."

Rooney wagged a fat finger. "Don't you get cocky with me, you son of a bitch. Is there sugar?"

Bean nodded, watching Rooney down his coffee. He noticed that Rooney had seemed less than interested in the new victim; he hadn't even glanced at the reports and photographs. "So, Mister Know-it-all, what was she? Man, woman, or what?" Rooney muttered.

Bean indicated his report. "A transsexual prostitute. It's in the report, happened last night around ten-thirty."

The only thing different about this one was that she had been hammered to the side of the head first, and had no rear scalp wound but multiple facial injuries. It had not yet been ascertained if the weapon was the same as that used in the previous murders.

"Any witnesses?" Rooney asked.

"Nope. She or he was seen on the streets, then said she was going to have a break because she had something wrong with her right foot."

"That it?"

Bean nodded.

"Well, let these smart alecks figure it out. Any sign of them yet?"

"Due any time. They went out for something to eat. Oh,

you wanted a low-key inquiry done at the S and A garage
about the workers. One of the guys you put on it mentioned
it to me so I did it.''

Rooney nodded, now flicking over the report. Bean made
no mention that the officers had said the captain was stinking
of booze. He waited as Rooney still shuffled the papers, turning over one page, then back to another.

"You were right, Captain. Hastings's car was parked there
in a hangar but he removed it the day before he was killed.
He used it as a free parking lot—he knew the management.
Place belongs to the Thorburns.'' Bean rubbed his thumb and
finger together when he said the name. "You want to take it
further?''

"If his fuckin' car wasn't parked there on the day he died
then it's not much use to us, is it?''

The phone rang and Rooney motioned for Bean to leave.
Out of the corner of his eye, Bean saw Rooney swivel around
to face the wall behind him, the report of the interviews at S
& A left open on his desk. He hoped Rooney would get his
act together before the FBI grilled him. He looked shot and
still stank of liquor. Lorraine was calling from a phone booth.

"You got something for me?'' Rooney snapped.

"Yeah, but I don't want to discuss it over the phone.''

"Dunno if I can get away. There's been another one.'' He
told her Didi's real name, David Burrows, and that she was a
transsexual prostitute. "She was in the car like the others,
similar head wounds. Car was reported stolen a few hours after
we found it.''

"When did it happen?'' she asked bluntly.

"Last night, around ten. Nicknamed Didi. You ever hear
the name?''

They agreed to meet in an hour and a half at Rooney's
Japanese place. Just as he picked up the reports, the phone
rang again. He was required in the chief's office. The FBI was
waiting.

Lorraine joined Rosie in the car. "Where to now, partner?''
Rosie asked.

"Didi's dead—one of the transsexuals you met at the gallery.''

Rosie started the car and Lorraine told her to step on it: she was meeting Rooney but wanted to talk to Nula first.

"You going to tell him everything?" Rosie yelled over the noise of the car engine. "Only you could maybe get some more dough out of him if you got a suspect. Maybe then we could upgrade this rent-a-wreck."

Rooney slipped the knot of his tie closer to his sweat-stained collar. The chief cracked his knuckles, waiting impatiently for an answer. "I don't need this, Bill. Who the fuck did you send there?"

Rooney shifted his weight. "Lieutenant Bean and another officer."

"The complaint was about a woman."

"She used to be a cop and she's been doing some work for me on the streets."

"This isn't on the street, Bill; this is somebody impersonating a police officer." Rooney pulled at his tie again. He had no idea what Lorraine had been doing at S & A, or why his chief was getting so uptight. "It's not in any report, Bill. What was she fucking doing there? That family has big connections and they're screaming about this. I want you to go there personally and iron it out. We've got enough bad press as it is and I don't intend to lose my job over this."

Rooney gave a half-smile. "Yes, sir. They that powerful? This garage a big deal, huh?"

The chief glared. "It's the Thorburn family, old money, big money. Fucking back off them. Go on, get out."

"What about the suits? I thought I was having a briefing with them."

"Sort this out first."

Rooney knew who the Thorburns were, not that you heard much about them nowadays, but their donations to police charities were legendary. Lorraine Page had better have something for him.

Nula was distraught. Her face, devoid of makeup, looked haggard, her eyes without their false eyelashes were puffy and red from weeping. She wasn't wearing a wig and her kimono was torn and half open. As soon as she saw Lorraine she broke down again. In the raw light of day the apartment was claustrophobic with its drapes and stuffed animals. Rosie hovered, finding it difficult not to stare at the overtly sexual pictures that hung on all the available wall space. Lorraine poured a glass of water and sat by Nula, holding her hand.

"Tell me what happened."

Nula wiped her face with a sodden Kleenex. "She used to have a number of regulars—she often stayed out all night. When she didn't come back I thought she'd scored. It wasn't her at the door when you phoned—it was the cops to tell me."

"Do you have a list of her regulars?" Lorraine asked.

"No, of course I don't. Nothing was ever arranged, they'd just turn up on the street and sometimes she used that motel Roselee, but the rooms there were getting expensive. Sometimes she brought them back here, why would I know their names? I've got my own clients and she's got . . . Oh, God—I don't know what I'm going to do without her."

"Can you describe any of her johns? Did you see any last night?"

"*No!* She was with me one minute and then she just walked off."

Lorraine opened the envelope. "Will you look at these photographs and tell me if there's anyone you recognize?" Nula looked at each one, sniffing and blowing her nose. Lorraine saved the blonde in the Mercedes until last. "What about this woman?"

Nula took the photograph. It was the only one she showed any interest in, but she shook her head.

"Are you sure? Keep looking at it, Nula, look at the car— it's an old Mercedes sports car. Look at the woman . . . is it a woman?"

Nula turned away. "I don't know, I don't *know*. I want to be left alone, *please* just leave me alone."

Rosie leaned forward. "That car was driving along Sunset last night. Did you see Didi speak to the driver—maybe get into the car?"

Lorraine gave Rosie a discreet wink. Rosie remained silent, eyes swinging from Lorraine to Nula; she was impressed with her friend, she was hot shit.

Nula scrutinized the picture of the blonde. "Does this woman have something to do with Didi?" Nula asked. "Do you think she had something to do with her murder?"

"She might, but do you recognize her?"

"No, I just said so, didn't I?" Nula passed the picture back.

Lorraine stood up and packed away the photographs. Nula began to sob again, burying her face in her hands.

"We'll let ourselves out, Nula, and I'm so sorry, really sorry."

Nula hugged her kimono tighter around herself, the Kleenex in shreds now as she plucked at it with her long, painted fingernails. "She was the nicest person I've ever known. I'm all on my own now, I don't have anybody, she was my best friend. I don't know what I'll do. I can't afford this place— I've got no money."

"What about Art? Have you called him?"

"He's left town. We haven't heard from him since the gallery closed. I'm not sure where he is."

Nula waited until she heard their car driving away before she went into the bedroom and opened a drawer in the bedside table. She took out a black diary and thumbed through the pages. Just seeing Didi's childish, scrawled writing made her want to weep again, but she gulped back her tears, flicking over the pages until she found what she was looking for. She went back to the hallway and picked up the phone. She methodically pressed each digit and waited.

"Hi, this is Art. I'm not in, but please leave me your name and number, and I'll get back to you, okay? And wait for the tone before you leave your message."

"Art, it's Nula. Will you call me? It's very urgent. We have to talk."

She replaced the receiver and went into the bathroom. She'd have a long perfumed soak, that would make her feel better, and she *was* going to feel better. But before she turned on the faucets, she went into the bedroom and knelt down by the bedside table. Lifting the curtain, she opened the bottom drawer and withdrew a large, square manila envelope. She pulled out a number of photographs, then sat back on her heels. The one she wanted was black and white, of a woman sitting on a bed, wearing a long fifties evening gown with padded shoulders, like Barbara Stanwyck, of that era. She was elegant, exceptionally beautiful. He had wanted to look like her, had brought the photograph for Didi to match, and she had worked for hours on him. The wig had been on a stand for days as she had teased and set it, ready for him. He had paid a lot of money for the session and Art had taken the photographs, draping the room to his specifications, down to the flower arrangements. The blond woman featured in the photograph set up by Art was the same as the one in the picture Lorraine had shown her. The woman driving the Mercedes. Nula didn't panic. She slowly got to her feet and began to search through all the stacks of photographic files.

Rosie dropped Lorraine outside the Japanese restaurant and drove off. Rooney was already sitting at a table with a glass of beer. "This had better be good and you'd better have a fucking good reason for barging into that S and A place. What the fuck were you doing there?"

Lorraine picked up the menu, calmly asked if he'd ordered, but he snapped back that he wasn't hungry.

"You run a check on the S and A employees like I asked?" she said, her eyes running down the long menu.

Rooney swigged his beer, then banged the glass hard onto the table.

Lorraine ignored it. "There was a vice charge against Steven Janklow. You got a record of it? Be a few years back. Picked up for soliciting, I think. He part-owns the garage. His brother is Brad Thorburn."

"What's your interest in him?"

Lorraine laid her hands flat on the table. "I think he's your killer."

Rooney burped, gulped another mouthful of beer, and wiped his mouth with the back of his hand. "What evidence have you got?"

She noticed he wouldn't meet her eyes. "I don't, but I do know that Hastings's car was left in their hangar."

Rooney lit a cigarette, inhaling hard and deep to make sure the smoke hit low down in his lungs. A killer draw. "Page, you got any idea who Janklow's family is?"

She shrugged. "I guess they must be important if they've got you running. Can you check if there was a vice charge? If there was, you can bring him in for questioning, see if he can account for himself over Hastings. It's him, Bill, I'm sure."

"Why?"

Lorraine took her time, and then stared at him directly.

"Because I got a good look at the bastard before I took a chunk out of his neck."

It didn't sink in for a moment. Then he looked into the ashtray, stubbing out his partially smoked cigarette.

"You wanna say that again?"

"I think he was the man who attacked me. I'm your witness, Bill. I made the call to the station, me. It was me that gave you his description in the first place."

He leaned back, partly in disbelief, then got out his cigarettes again and stuck one in his mouth. He stared fixedly around the restaurant, feeling as if the floor was opening up. "You stupid bitch."

"I'm sorry, I was scared to come forward. I picked him up—"

"Sweet Jesus." Rooney shook his head.

"He attacked me with a claw hammer. I'm sure it was Steven Janklow. You gonna light that cigarette or suck on it like a pacifier?"

Rooney slapped the table hard with the flat of his hand.

"You seen him face-to-face? Or, more to the point, has he seen you?"

"No, I've held off facing him, I don't want to tip him off."

Lorraine's order was placed in front of her. Rooney waited until the waiter had moved off before he leaned toward her. "Say it is him—say he's the guy that attacked you. You can identify him . . ."

She had picked up her fork but put it down again. "I identify him, he denies it, he walks. It's just the word of an ex-hooker, ex-drunkard against a fine, upstanding citizen, right? All he's got to say is he wasn't anywhere near the street where I was picked up and I got to admit I was picking him up for a few bucks. It wasn't his car, it was Hastings's car and Hastings's body was in the trunk. Now, who's gonna believe who?"

Rooney drained his beer and beckoned the waiter to bring another.

Lorraine played around with the food on her plate, then pushed it away. "I think he's a transvestite."

Rooney ran his hands through his hair. "*What?*"

"I think Janklow's a transvestite."

"*Think?* I need more than you fucking thinking, I need evidence, I need *facts*. Jesus Christ, Lorraine, you know how crazy this all sounds?'' He put his head in his hands. The more she told him, the worse it all sounded. ''You think the guy that hit on you was Steven Janklow, right? You also think Steven Janklow is a transvestite. Is there anything else you might have just glossed over—like maybe he has two heads?''

''Back off me. All the dead women have a similar look, similar age.''

''What about Holly?''

''I think she's the mistake. Because of the last one, Didi.''

Lorraine explained that she thought the killer was trying to pick up Nula or Didi on the night Holly was murdered. She told him how they had both seen a car, had both seen Holly run across the road to a john. Her pimp Curtis saw her—but maybe the john was trying to pick up Didi or Nula. Once he ended up with Holly he had to get rid of her. Maybe he panicked.

Rooney argued that it didn't make sense. Why didn't he just kick her out, if he'd gotten the wrong one? His head throbbed and he still couldn't believe how she'd held out on him like this. Lorraine banged the table. ''Wait a minute! The wrong one. What if they were all the wrong ones? What if he was looking specifically for Didi all along? They're all the same age, all dyed or bleached blondes, but he can't find the one he's looking for, the main one. She had a blond wig on, right? Yes? Did you say she was found wearing a blond wig?''

Rooney blinked, Lorraine drummed her fingers. ''Shit, shit, Bill. I might be right. You see, sometimes she didn't wear a blond wig, she's got every color under the sun . . .''

''Are you trying to tell me that this guy clubs seven women to death because he's looking for one, and we forget Norman Hastings? Did he think he was one as well? I mean he wasn't wearing a fucking blond wig, he was wearing a goddamned suit! This is dumb, Lorraine. You lost your touch, sweetheart. We're looking at someone who's bumped off these women over five years, and he's doing it because of mistaken identity? Nuts!''

Lorraine twiddled with her fork. ''Okay, let's try something else. Let's go through every victim, including Hastings. He was a drag artist, right? He parked his car at S and A years after he was doing any business with them, but he knew Janklow. Maybe he found out something?''

Rooney put his head in his hands, kept it there for a while, and then slowly looked through his thick fingers. It was coming down on all sides, his head ached, his whole body felt leaden. He slowly delved in his pocket for his wallet. "Maybe I'm wasting my time. I got to go take a leak."

"But listen to me, there's every type of tool and hammer at the S and A. Can't someone check there? Match them? What if the hammers came from there?"

Rooney jabbed the air with his finger. "Stay away from that place, is that understood? From now on you don't go anywhere near it. I'll have the place looked over again—in fact, I'll do it personally—but you stay well away." He squinted at the bill and looked up at her. "I'll check out what I think fit."

"The Vice Squad, can you check that for me? See what Janklow was picked up for?"

"For *you*? Who in chrissakes do you think is runnin' this show? I'll take it from here. If you wanna press charges for assault—"

She leaned back. "You know I won't do that, but if you get more evidence, then I can be used as a lever. We let him confront me, let him know I'm alive and can identify him, and then see what he does. Use me to catch him. I'm willing."

Rooney hauled his bulk out of the booth. "Lemme think on it."

She followed him as he headed for the rest room. "Bill, he used a hammer on me. It's him."

He whipped around. "I could have you for withholding evidence. I only paid you to get out on the streets to talk to the hookers, so back off. I'll contact you when I need you."

"I need a few dollars, I'm flat broke."

"Not my problem," he said as he pushed open the rest room door, and let it close behind him.

When he came out of the restaurant she was waiting by his car. She gave that strange, lopsided smile and he relaxed slightly. Although he was loath to admit it, she had pushed the investigation further—had even supplied him with a suspect.

"Lemme see what I come up with—but you do nothing until you hear from me, okay? Here's a few bucks, go home, wait for me to call. If it's Janklow, leave him to me."

She took the money and watched him drive off. As she walked to the bus stop heading home, she was thinking over everything she had said to Rooney. She had been clutching at straws, but what if she was right? What if there was a connection between Didi and Janklow? She suddenly decided against going home. She could walk to Nula's from Holly Street and it was a little cooler now. She could walk and think over everything at the same time. If she had been correct and Janklow was in actual fact trying to trace one particular whore or transvestite, maybe Nula could provide her with the clue.

FIFTEEN

Nula wasn't at home, so Lorraine waited around for a while and then went home, picking up a bus on the corner of Holly Street. Rosie was waiting and wondered what they should do next; she hadn't enjoyed herself so much for years. But Lorraine knew that without Rooney making contact, it could be dangerous to try to see Janklow again. It was after eight by now, but there was still no word from Rooney. She grabbed a light sweater, tying it around her neck in case it got cooler.

"Where are you going?" Rosie asked nervously.

"You stay put so I can call Rooney back if he makes contact."

"Don't you need me with you?"

"I'd prefer it if you stayed here in case he calls. I've got to keep him sweet, 'cos if I don't the old bastard may well have me arrested."

Rosie sat moodily in front of the TV. She didn't even say goodbye as Lorraine let herself out. So much for partnership—all she'd been doing all day was sitting waiting for Lorraine in the apartment. When she heard the rental car starting up Rosie shot to the window as fast as her bulk allowed her. She pushed up the window and was about to yell after Lorraine but it was too late, she was already at the corner.

* * *

It had been so long since Lorraine had driven that her knees were shaking, but she talked to herself steadily, telling herself to calm down. She just hoped she wouldn't get pulled over.

Lorraine headed back to Orange Grove and then passed Holly Street until she saw the massive old Moorish-styled building. The lights were on in Nula's apartment. Lorraine sighed with relief, locked the car, and headed into the apartment block. She rang the bell and waited. Nula's voice asked who it was but Lorraine rang again, afraid that if she said her name Nula wouldn't let her in. She kept her hand on the bell, and eventually Nula peered out the window above the entryway.

"Fuck off."

"Let me in, Nula, otherwise I'll stay out here and ring your bell all night if I have to."

Nula buzzed her into the main entry door below and Lorraine hurried up the old wide mosaic stone-floored staircase. She then rapped on Nula's front door, which Nula eventually opened. Lorraine looked around. Suitcases had been dragged down from the wardrobes. Nula was on the move—she had her red wig on and a trouser suit, and full makeup.

"What happened?"

"I'm going away."

"Why do you have to go?"

Nula hurled a cushion at her. "Stop asking me questions, just leave me *alone*."

Lorraine took out the picture of Steven Janklow in drag. "Will you have another look at this, Nula?"

Nula picked up the cushion and hugged it to her chest. Lorraine dangled the photograph between finger and thumb. "It won't hurt you to have a look at it. Is it Steven Janklow?"

"If you fucking know who it is, why are you asking me?"

"Because I need to be sure."

"I said I don't know, didn't I?"

Lorraine was deflated. She didn't know what her next move should be. She flopped back on the sofa.

"You gonna leave now?"

Lorraine slipped the photograph back into the envelope and stood up, facing the big four-sectioned screen behind which the models changed for a session. It was plastered with photographs of males and females, males and males, part females. Nula looked at her, then her eyes darted to the screen. Lorraine started to walk toward the door, then stopped and glanced back to Nula, who hid her face in the cushion. She turned back toward the screen. At first she wasn't sure that she was right, so she moved closer, then she bent down and peered. She straightened up. "You don't know him? Then why is his photograph up on the screen?"

"Because it fit the hole."

"Who took the photograph?"

"Why?"

"Because if you don't know who it is, then whoever took the photograph might. Who took the picture, Nula?"

"Art." Nula sighed, hurling the pillow aside. "Art, I guess he took it, I don't know."

Lorraine could feel the adrenaline pumping; it was all as crazy as Rooney had said. "What's Art's scene apart from the porno?"

"Use your head, clever bitch. Where do you think he gets all his dough from?"

"Why don't you tell me?"

Nula headed toward the bedroom. Keeping her back to Lorraine, she leaned on one outstretched arm in the archway of the door.

"Blackmail. Some fucking detective you are. Art blackmails everybody, he's a bleeder—you should know, you copped a few grand from one of his little leech jobs."

She turned to face Lorraine, her deep voice husky with controlled anger. "I don't know that blonde in that photo on the screen and I don't know whoever it is in your precious picture. That's not my screen, it's Art's. Now would you get out and leave me alone? And have some fucking decency, my best friend just got killed so why don't you fuck off out of here, you bitch."

"Where's Art?"

Nula swore under her breath as she walked into her bedroom and said loudly, "I don't know."

Lorraine followed Nula into the bedroom. "Was he blackmailing Steven Janklow?"

Nula kicked at the open bedroom door and screamed, "*I don't know, leave me alone.*" She began to pull clothes out of her wardrobe.

"He was blackmailing him, wasn't he?"

Nula was hurling dresses onto the bed.

"The night Didi died—"

"Yes, what about the night Didi died?"

Lorraine kept her distance. Nula was becoming increasingly hysterical, dragging things off their hangers, dropping them, kicking them. She suddenly turned to Lorraine in a fury. "He used us. If we had a john, he'd be sniffing around. He never let us have any peace, but then we couldn't have any because he'd give a few dollars here, a few dollars there, he let us have this apartment, okay? He said we never had to pay rent, okay? Well, if you believe that you're dumb. Art used me, used Didi; he made us both pay. Now if you don't get out of here and leave me alone I swear to God I'll scream this place down and have you arrested."

Lorraine didn't budge. "Was Art blackmailing Norman Hastings?"

Nula picked up a vase and hurled it at Lorraine. She backed away, her hands up. "I'm going, okay, I'm going . . ."

Lorraine passed by the screen with all the laminated photographs. She was frantically glancing from one blonde to another in a vague hope that one or another of the dead women as well as Hastings would have been photographed. "When did Art make this screen?"

She knew Nula had come out of the bedroom and was behind her, but she kept looking over the screen. She heard Nula sigh, then blow her nose.

"Years ago. He brought it here with him when he left Santa Monica—he had a place there on the beach." Nula was tearful now and she wiped her eyes. "I'm sorry I shouted, sorry, but . . . honestly, I don't know who anyone is on that screen and I'm all upset, and . . ."

"Did he, Art, ever own a vintage car?"

Nula rolled her eyes and sniffed loudly. "What do you mean?"

"A custom-made car or an old sports car."

"Nah, he had a Bentley once for about six months, then he went broke again and sold it."

"The blonde in the photograph, the one I showed you on the screen, did you meet him?"

"No," Nula sighed, distracted. She stepped into the bedroom a few paces, Lorraine followed but kept her distance; she didn't want another vase hurled at her or smashed over her head.

"What about Didi? Did she meet him?"

Nula was holding a long chiffon dress. "This was her favorite. It never fit her but she wouldn't throw it out."

"Nula, please, did Didi know the blonde?"

"She may have, she used to do wigs, she was always good with hair. Art used her sometimes for photo sessions, so she may have. I don't know who she knew, we weren't joined at the hip, you know, we weren't always together...."

"Did Didi know Art before you?"

Nula was sniffing the chiffon dress, brushing her cheek with it. "Yes, I met him through her. She paid a lot for this, but she was always a little on the plump side, and she never wore it, not once."

Lorraine watched Nula carefully place the chiffon dress into her open suitcase, then continue packing, ignoring Lorraine's presence.

"Have you ever heard of Craig Lyall, a photographer?" Lorraine asked tentatively.

Nula clicked the suitcase shut. "Professional, is he?"

"Yeah, takes family shots, portraits. Lives around here, in that old fire station."

Nula shrugged. "Name isn't familiar, but then I'm never good with names."

"What about Didi? Do you have her address book? Maybe she has his phone number."

Nula took a small key and locked the case. "No, she never kept one, and now, if you'll excuse me, I am going to take a bath. Unless you want to watch me soaping my tits I suggest you leave."

"You need a lift? I've got a car."

"I'll get a cab."

"Can I ask where you're going?"

"You can, but I don't see why I should tell you."

"Just in case I need to get in touch with you."

Nula carried her suitcases to the door, dumped them, and went back to pick up two more bags.

"Curtis knows how to contact me."

Lorraine reached out to shake Nula's hand but she turned away. "Goodbye, and thanks."

Nula stood in the center of the room, arms folded. As soon as she heard the front door slam behind Lorraine, she clutched the sides of her head and started to scream. She had been holding on to her rage, waiting, waiting until she was sure the bitch was out of earshot. Then she screamed and screamed, and kicked out again at the sofa before she got herself back in control. Then she crossed to the telephone and started to dial.

Lorraine drove to Craig Lyall's studio, literally within a few blocks of Nula's and situated in the oldest part of Pasadena. She parked and headed toward the main entrance of the converted firehouse. She checked down the residents' numbers and pressed Lyall's bell. She waited, but getting no response she pressed again, and again, and was about to walk away when a fuzzy distorted voice screeched. *"Yes? Yes, who is it?"*

Lorraine licked her lips and moved close to the speaker. "Friend of Art Mathews's."

"Oh, shit, wait . . . just wait."

Rosie heard the footsteps thudding up the steps and opened the door. Two uniformed police officers stood outside. Rosie wasn't unduly worried, partly because she was expecting Rooney to call. She even asked if they were there because of him because she knew Lorraine wanted to speak to him.

"Will you pass that on to Captain Rooney?"

They did not answer her questions but asked if there were any other ways into the apartment, then stomped back down the steps and surveyed the building from all sides. Rosie had begun to get uneasy. Now she was edgy, because they'd remained outside in their patrol car and didn't look as if they had any intention of driving away.

Lorraine moved up the old stone staircase to the first floor. The big square building had been Pasadena's main fire station, but had been sectioned off into apartments many years ago. They were mostly occupied by artists because of the size of the windows and height of the ceilings. Outside Lyall's apartment and studio there was a small plaque with his name and beneath it PHOTOGRAPHER. She could also hear opera being played at full volume. She pressed the bell and waited. Lyall unbolted the door. Small and dapper, he was a good six inches shorter than Lorraine.

"What do you want? You're not a cop? What do you want?"

"Like I said, I'm a friend of Art's."

Lorraine followed Lyall into the studio. Pine floored, it was dominated by a photographic equipment setup, with an area sectioned off as a living room. The stereo thudded out an aria from some opera. He picked up his remote control switch and turned it off.

"I was working in the darkroom. You were lucky, I only stepped out to change the disc. Can't hear a thing, dear. So, let me finish up these negs, then I'll be right with you. Make yourself at home."

Lorraine put down her purse and remained standing, looking at all the framed photographs lining the walls. She then crossed the room to check out two bulky albums, filled with portraits of kids and families. She turned over the heavy pages, awful smiling brats in too-colorful dresses, all much the same, similar to the pictures she had seen in Mrs. Hastings's home.

Lyall returned and offered her a drink. He seemed jumpy.

"Art's told me a lot about you. I worked for him in his gallery, you know, the one on Holly Street. In fact, weren't you one of the guests at the opening night party?" Lorraine perched on the edge of the sofa and opened her purse, keeping up a constant chatter, trying to relax Lyall, trying to make him trust her. She indicated her cigarettes. "Do you mind if I smoke?"

"No, go ahead."

"In fact, I was the one that did all the calls, his guest list, maybe we met there? Do you remember me?"

Lyall twitched his shoulders, looking her up and down. She looked sort of scruffy, not Art's type of weirdo in any way, but he was not so edgy. She lit her cigarette, offering the pack.

"Art. He's in trouble, you know that?"

"He's always been in trouble, ever since I've known him."

"Yeah, well, this time he's involved in murder."

Lyall pursed his lips. "Jesus Christ, it's not this fucking Hastings thing again. I've had them here, you know, asking me all kinds of questions. All I did was take some photographs—poor bastard liked to drag up, right? What's wrong with that?"

Lorraine shifted her seat on the edge of the sofa as he placed down a glass ashtray on the coffee table. "Can I see them? Just out of interest. I'm trying to help Art. I wasn't all that honest with you—I'm a private investigator and I need to get as much—"

Lyall jumped about a foot in the air. "I've got nothing to do with him! I know him, that's all, I just know him, and a few times I've taken the odd photo for him, or if he's sent somebody to me. I'm discreet, okay? That's all there is to it. If he's trying to con me for some cash, I don't have any."

Lyall was even more nervous now, walking up and down.

"Did you ever use a transsexual called Didi?"

"What do you mean, use?"

"Did you ever take photographs of her? Pornographic ones."

"No way. I wasn't into that kind of thing. I just do straight portraits."

"But sometimes you photographed transsexuals, or transvestites?"

"Yeah, they just wanted a photo of themselves, nothing wrong with that, is there?" He fidgeted, repeating that it wasn't against the law and that he'd answered all the questions about Hastings; the police had been to question him, he'd given them his photos.

"Did you know Didi well?"

"Yes and no. She was useful sometimes. She did their makeup and hair, that's all."

"Did she do Norman Hastings's wigs?"

Lyall chewed his lips. She could almost see his brain cells working as he started to say something, stopped and fidgeted with his collar, plucking at it.

"There's no big deal, I mean, if she did do his wigs, I'd just like to know. Did she?" Lorraine pressed.

"Yeah, I think so."

"Could you check for me? I mean, do you have any photos that I could see?"

Lyall pulled at his shirt again, sighing. "I didn't get asked about this by the cops, why do you want to know? What has Art been saying about me?"

Lorraine shrugged. "I'm interested, and you're good, I can see by the pictures on the wall, very professional. Some of the kids look kind of posed . . . just, I might be able to put some work your way.''

''*Posed!* Don't I know it, dear, I loathe the little bastards. But you got to do bread-and-butter work. I don't honestly know if I've got any around that Didi worked on, I mean, it wasn't regular, just on the odd occasion, you know.''

Lorraine watched as he bent down to a filing cabinet and took out some envelopes. He sifted through them, then searched in another drawer. ''She was good, knew her stuff, could make even Hastings look reasonable.'' He showed her two or three photographs of Hastings. Lorraine complimented each photo, and Lyall preened himself, started to take out more. She asked nonchalantly if he'd ever photographed a man called Steven Janklow.

Lyall was still looking through his work admiringly and didn't hear, so she repeated the name and he straightened. ''Look, I don't always ask who my clients are. This is a private thing between me and them. I have to make them feel at ease—they get pretty excited, and then when Didi has finished with them, they're almost orgasmic. It's a big turn-on for them and after the session they take away their photos and that's it.''

Lorraine nodded. She didn't immediately mention Janklow's name again but took her time, letting Lyall relax.

''Did Art help out on any sessions?''

''Not for years. He did once—I didn't have a darkroom of my own and he had a big place over in Santa Monica, so I used to use his stuff. If I'm honest, he taught me a lot. Many of them have a slight problem—you know, the skin. Art taught me how to airbrush all that out—hair, lines. I can make them look beautiful.''

She tried again. ''Did you photograph this Janklow?''

Lyall paused. ''I really don't know. Some of them use assumed names, or call themselves by their female name. Is it important?''

''He's Art's alibi.''

''Why don't you ask Janklow?''

''I can't trace him and Art thinks he wouldn't want to come forward—doesn't want his family to know about his private life.''

Lyall repacked his photographs in their envelopes.

''Do you know the S and A vintage car garage?''

"Yes, it's in Santa Monica. I'm going back years now. Art used to cruise around in an outrageous Bentley. He bought it from them but he's useless mechanically. It was always breaking down. Art just about knew where to put the gas in." Lyall gave a high-pitched giggle and smiled waspishly. "Art's not much taller than me, and behind the wheel of that old thing he looked ridiculous. But he used it for cruising, said it was a come-on, but I wasn't ever into his scene. That's when we sort of parted, I just didn't want to get involved. That said, he was a good friend, so if there is anything I can do to help . . . I mean, I didn't even know he'd been arrested or anything."

Lorraine took out the photo of the blond woman and gave it to Lyall. "Have you ever taken that person's photograph?" she asked.

"I can't say. You've seen how many I've done and they're just the recent ones."

Lorraine took it back, and asked if the clients got to keep their negatives. That was part of the deal, Lyall said, suddenly becoming evasive again. "Look, I know what you're implying. My clients always have the negatives. Some even wait until I've done them. I've never been in trouble with the police and I would never— Look, we all know about Art and I've always said that's his business. No way do I get involved. He's been done before, he won't stop."

"You mean his pornography?"

"No. Blackmail."

Lorraine nodded. "Yes, I've warned him about it and I think that's why this witness won't come forward. I figure Art was blackmailing him."

Lorraine was very good at teasing out the information from Lyall, her voice low and conversational, but inside her stomach was churning because she was getting closer, she knew it, could feel it. She was finding those jigsaw pieces and some of them were fitting into a strange connecting picture.

Lyall groaned. "Art's been in prison and that didn't stop him. He's always after making the quick buck, but it disgusts me. These poor bastards, they come here and they're like kids, you know, shaking with excitement, and they're so harmless. I mean, who does it hurt if a man likes to pretty himself up? It's no crime, but society makes them hide."

Lorraine agreed. "I feel sorry for the guys Art's been tapping. Poor Norman Hastings, a decent married man, scared it would come out—''

Lyall looked anxious. ''I never told that to the police—I couldn't, it would incriminate me. Then I'd have to tell them about Art.''

Lorraine stubbed out her cigarette.

''How did Art get hold of Hastings's pictures if, as you said, they always take the negatives away?''

Lyall blushed, plucked at his shirt collar again. ''I don't know.''

''You didn't give them to him, did you?''

''No, of course not, but . . . maybe his friend did. I photographed Hastings's family—I knew them and I wouldn't want to hurt them. They're not even wealthy, but that was Art, he'd even settle for fifty dollars a month—awful, I hated it.''

''By his friend, do you mean Didi?''

''Yes, I suspected it was her. She was here, she made Norman up—did a really good job, too.''

''She's dead.''

Lyall gaped. ''But you were just talking about her. When? Why didn't Nula call me? Or Art? I don't believe it.''

''Last night.''

Lyall seemed genuinely shocked, so she said, ''Will you take another look at the photo I brought, just in case you might remember. I think it's a cross-dresser, don't you?''

Lyall took the photograph again and held it near the lamp. He viewed the picture through an eyeglass for at least thirty seconds before he nodded. ''Yes, but it's a very good wig and makeup . . . It's the jawline, I can always tell.''

''You don't recognize him then?''

''No, I don't think so, but I do so many . . .''

''He never came here with Hastings?''

''Norman was always alone, unless he was with his family.''

A buzzer sounded from the darkroom and Lyall checked his watch. ''I've got to get these ready for tomorrow. It's a twenty-first portrait.''

Lorraine was heading for the door, when Lyall exclaimed, ''Of course! Let me see that picture again.''

Lorraine watched him, almost willing him to say that he *had* taken pictures of Janklow. Instead he shook his head. ''There was a famous society hostess, very wealthy—now, what was her name? She came for a sitting, very crippled, arthritic, in a wheelchair. She had two sessions, I think, but turned the pictures down. Well, honestly, if I'd airbrushed any more of her she wouldn't have had any face left. They paid just the sitting fee. That's why I remember it, because I was out of pocket, and I'm going back a few years.'' He traced his thin lips with his tongue as he tried to remember, and then he beamed. ''Thorburn, that was the name, Della Thorburn, and it must have been at least eight, maybe nine years ago. She could even be dead by now. Isn't it strange? Really weird.'' Lorraine waited for him to continue. ''It's odd that I can remember her so well and from that photograph, it's just that . . . Let me have another look at it.'' He used his eyeglass again. ''It isn't her— she couldn't drive, she was very crippled. But the way the scarf is draped reminds me of her. She always wore these chiffon scarves to hide her neck, and the blond hair, that old-fashioned style, a simple Grace Kelly roll at the back.''

''Did Didi do her makeup and hair?''

''Good God, no. She was Society. She wouldn't want somebody like Didi around. I'm talking old money.''

Lorraine wasn't sure where this new development was leading. She asked if Mrs. Thorburn had been accompanied by anyone. ''Yes, of course, she was in a wheelchair. Her son, if I can recall, he brought her.''

''Did you hear his name?''

''Well, I presumed it was Thorburn.''

''Can you describe him?''

Lyall screwed up his eyes. ''God, I'm going back years, and I'm sorry I can't. But Art maybe could, he has a mind-blowing memory—he can even remember phone numbers.''

''Art was here?''

''Oh, no, it was in Santa Monica, I told you, we worked together, had our own clients. But then I left and came here.''

''Was Art doing similar photo sessions, with transvestites or transsexuals?''

''Oh, yes—in fact he started me off, sent me clients. I told you before.''

His darkroom buzzer rang loudly again. ''I've really got to go, I can't leave them soaking any longer.''

Lyall opened the front door. Lorraine thanked him but the buzzer from his darkroom was going again and he was eager for her to leave.

"I hope you can help Art. He's not all bad, most of him but not all!"

Lorraine smiled as the door closed behind her and the bolt rammed into place. As she headed down the stairs, she heard the operatic aria start up again. She felt like singing herself and couldn't wait to talk to Rooney.

Lyall closed the darkroom door and set to work. He didn't hear the telephone ringing, and he hadn't heard it earlier either.

Lorraine returned to the car. She was buzzing inside like Lyall's timer, and since it was cooler now, she decided to sit and think everything through before she contacted Rooney. She rolled down the window and lit a cigarette. She now had a link between Hastings and Janklow. She even had a tentative link between Didi and both men, and Art was linked to them all. Art was blackmailing Norman Hastings, she concluded, and Hastings might have discussed this with Janklow. But what if Art was blackmailing Janklow as well?

Lorraine started up the engine and then turned it off again. What if she was wrong about Janklow and Art was the killer? But she knew that couldn't be right. Her attacker hadn't been Art Mathews. What was the link between each of the dead women who, apart from Holly, all resembled each other in age? But then she thought again about Holly's murder; according to Didi, the killer had gestured to her, had wanted her. She had even said to Lorraine that she was lucky because if Holly hadn't been picked up then it could have been her. What if it was Didi the killer had wanted? Just as she had said to Rooney, the women were or could possibly have all been mistaken for Didi. She, Lorraine, was tall, about the same height as Didi, and blond. Was the killer looking for one woman in particular, a woman he knew worked the streets, a woman he knew was a transsexual?

By now the buzz had died down, Lorraine's head throbbed with all the jagged sections of information. Her attempts at trying to make them all fit exhausted her. She closed her eyes. She had left Art Mathews in the gallery the night Holly had died. What had he done after she left and where did he go? Were he, Didi, Nula even, all connected to the murders? She was too tired to get it together, tired and hungry. She started the car again and headed to the grocery store on Marengo to

buy some supper, since she'd been too keyed up to eat the
dinner Rooney had bought her. She parked the car and was
heading into the store when she decided to call him.

"Where are you?" he barked.

"Oh, just doing some shopping, then I'm on my way
home."

"Where are you shopping, Lorraine?"

"What's it to you? I'm at our local grocery, all right? Is
that all right with you?"

"You were supposed to call in, you said you were stayin'
at the apartment."

"Yeah, I was, but it was you who was gonna call. What's
with you, Rooney? You got a development?"

"I got fuck all," he snapped.

"Well, Bill, I got something I want you to check out. Photographer, guy called Art Mathews. I think he's involved,
blackmailer, porno stuff. He knows Janklow . . . Bill? You
there?"

"Yep. You going home, are you?"

"Yeah, I just said. Are you okay?"

Rooney hesitated and then lied, told her he was fine and
he'd check into the Art Mathews guy. Lorraine replaced the
receiver. Not a thank-you, he didn't even cross-question her.
It was strange; something was wrong.

Rooney stared at his phone, his hand still resting on top of
the receiver, then he pushed his chair back and began wandering around his office, hitching up his pants. Through the
venetian blinds he could see the suits working with the computer officers, sifting through the investigations. He let the
blinds fall back into place. He was, in some way, hiding out—
he'd skirted around them all afternoon and evening. He had
nobody to take out or vent his anger on as he had virtually
marooned himself in the office. Bean breezed in and Rooney
jumped. "Fuckin' knock, for chrissakes, you almost gave me
a heart attack. You ever hear of a porno photographer, Art
Mathews?"

"No, Captain."

"Run a trace on him then. And then bring him in. I want
to have a talk with him, me, understand? I don't want you
gabbin' to the suits about this one, not until I've talked to him,
so make it a priority. I just got a tip about him."

"Okay, will do. You wanted to know if Vice had anything

on a Steven Janklow? There's no record, nothing . . . but the Thorburn family funded an entire section of the LAPD forensics lab and—''

"Thank you," grunted Rooney.

"You're welcome, and maybe have a word with your informant."

Rooney glowered, Bean eased the door shut. "The crew-cut one in the shiny gray suit, Bickerstaff, he sent two officers to Lorraine Page's apartment, wanted her brought in for questioning."

"What?"

Bean shrugged. "They're checking out everythin', Captain, and since we brought her in for that lineup . . ."

"So they're bringin' her in? You serious?"

"No, I'm making it up. I'm just telling you what I was told. They want to requestion Lorraine Page so they sent a squad car for her. I don't know how long ago."

Rooney banged his desk. "Pull it off her, get it off her, I don't want her questioned by those bastards. We need that Art Mathews brought in, right? So make it—"

"Priority. Right, I hear you." Bean walked out.

Rooney glowered after him. He was getting on very well with the suits but then he would. He kept on watching Bean as he joined the FBI officers, saying something, and then passed into the main incident section. Rooney shut his door and called Lorraine.

Rosie answered the phone. She hardly had time to say hello before Rooney barked out that he wanted to speak to Lorraine. Rosie told him she hadn't returned home and he paused.

"Go see if there's a squad car outside your place, will you?" Rosie said that one had been there most of the evening, but she still crossed to the window and checked. It was just pulling out. She returned to the phone.

"It's just leaving. Is this Captain Rooney?"

"Yeah, it's Captain Rooney but not for much longer."

Rosie was fazed by the barking voice. "I know Lorraine wanted to speak with you."

"She just did, g'night."

Rosie stared at the receiver and then replaced it. She crossed back to the window, the street was empty and dark. She switched on the air-conditioning. It was going to be a hot clammy night.

Lorraine returned twenty minutes later, arms laden with groceries. Rosie opened the screen door. "Well, thank you. You know, I been stuck in this place *all* day and that cop pal of yours just called, rude bastard."

Lorraine passed Rosie, heading for the kitchen. "I just spoke to him, what did he want?"

Rosie started to help take out the groceries from the brown paper bags. "First he asks if there's a squad car outside, I says that there was one and it'd been out there most of the day."

"What? You tellin' me the cops have been here?"

Rosie banged down a yogurt. "Read my lips, the-cops-came, the-cops-went."

Lorraine opened the fridge. "What did they want?"

Rosie waited for Lorraine to straighten before she said quietly, "I think they wanted you."

She saw Lorraine stiffen, her lips tighten, but she continued unpacking the groceries. She was freaking out; would Rooney have told them she was the witness? It was a while before she spoke again and her voice gave no hint of her worries. "Did Rooney say anything else?"

Rosie took out a frying pan, banging open the cupboard doors, unaware of Lorraine's fears. "No, but when I said the squad car was leaving, he hung up."

Lorraine washed the lettuce, trying to figure it all out. Maybe Rooney had kept his word, but one way or another she'd find out; she just hoped he hadn't given her away. Rosie and Lorraine worked together, preparing their late supper side by side, tossing the salad, making the dressing.

"You know what I've been thinking about? May sound dumb, but I was wondering . . ."

"What?" asked Rosie, cutting up some bread.

"Don't laugh, but you know I still get a real buzz from putting all the pieces together—you know, interviewing possible suspects and—"

"They'd never have you back, would they?" Rosie asked as she carried the cutlery to the table.

"No way, not with my history. But what if I opened up an investigation agency of my own, what do you think?"

Rosie put the cutlery out on the table and then cocked her head to one side. "I'm not laughing. I think you could do anythin' you want. You certainly got nothin' else on offer, unless of course . . ."

Lorraine carried the salad bowl to the table. "Unless what?"

"You get arrested. Be tough being a private dick from inside a prison."

Rosie saw Lorraine's expression change. For a second she seemed afraid, so she went over to her and put her arms around her.

"Joke, I was just joking."

At eleven o'clock Art Mathews had been brought in for questioning. He had attempted to run from the police, who had been about to tell him that he was not being arrested, that they just wanted his assistance with their investigation. But as they entered his new studio he had dived past them, which aroused their suspicions, and of course they went after him. He gave himself up after an abortive run between oncoming cars, zigzagging across the road, nearly getting himself killed. A routine search of his studio yielded a vast selection of pornography stills.

Rooney had begun to question Mathews as soon as he was brought in. He was expansive and overtalkative, as if high on drugs. He had not as yet asked for a lawyer. He admitted to mild pornography, but it was not until one of the officers entered the room with a black and white photograph of Holly that the interview took an upward spiral. Art admitted knowing her; he had even taken photographs of her. Agitated and sweating, the little man tried to recall where he was on the night of her murder.

At almost every turn he incriminated himself. When he admitted that he also knew the most recently murdered transsexual, Didi, Rooney could feel the hair lift on the back of his neck. He knew they had to get legal representation for Art and fast, and suggested as much to him. If he so wished, they would be prepared to wait. Rooney had also asked for a doctor to examine him: if he was drugged up they needed to know; they would have to wait until he came down from whatever he was on.

Suddenly Art jumped up, spittle forming at the sides of his mouth. "This is crazy! You think I killed Holly? Why would I do a thing like that? This is all a misunderstanding."

At no time had Rooney suggested there was any suspicion that Art was involved in the murder. He had him on selling pornographic material by his own admission. Now it seemed he was about to talk himself into being accused of murder.

As the interview swung up a notch, the tension in the room grew tighter. Rooney began to ask him about each of the victims.

"What? Why?" Art began to screech, his voice getting higher and higher in his agitation. "Why are you asking me about these women? This is insanity. You think I had something to do with those murders? This is crazy. I've admitted I knew Holly, okay, I knew Didi—"

Rooney probed into Art's business, his background, his previous criminal record. Only then did he detect the fear. Art now demanded legal representation: he would not answer any more questions. Rooney knew that most of what he had admitted might not hold up in court, especially as he had still not been checked out for drugs. He was so wired when they brought him in, he could have confessed to any number of crimes. But Rooney was pushing, he was excited, he felt that old rush of adrenaline. Art Mathews was like a scared rabbit almost caught in a trap and Rooney was eager to snap the door shut on him. So much was riding on his getting results, on grabbing them right under the FBI's nose.

"The suits," as Rooney had always thought of them, were not even in the station, so he had Art all to himself. When Art eventually quieted down, Rooney took it as a sign of guilt. It was obvious to everyone in the interrogation room that he had only become uncooperative when the murders were mentioned. While they waited for the lawyer to arrive, Art continued to declare his innocence. He kept rubbing his shining bald head, looking from one man to the next. "Just because I knew Didi and Holly doesn't mean I'd kill them. This is some kind of frame-up. Did somebody tip you off about me? Is that what this is all about? Did some piece of shit put me in it?"

He demanded to know what time Didi had been killed, as he had been with friends the entire evening, but when Rooney told him and asked where he was between nine and ten-thirty he suddenly refused to say where he was or who he was with until he had a lawyer present. A doctor examined him and gave him the all-clear, but suggested they give him plenty to drink as he was sweating so much from nerves.

His lawyer arrived and he was allowed a private discussion. Once that had been completed, he was faced yet again with all the questions that had been asked earlier. One of the reasons he had refused to state where he was on the night Didi died was that he had been filming a session. Having already served time for selling pornographic videos and working with underage kids, he was scared that he'd be charged with a similar offense. He was also becoming increasingly alarmed that details of his blackmail activities might leak out. The more he was questioned the more nervous he became. When the list of the dead women started unfolding he became hysterical, screaming that they were setting him up, and some of the murders had happened so long ago he couldn't remember where he had been living. He might even have been serving a sentence. Meanwhile, his new studio was being ransacked by the police, and more pornography discovered.

He was taken down to the cells. It was almost three in the morning and both Rooney and Bean were still working. Rooney's head ached but he was back in form, and he was sure now that Art was not their killer. He had learned that Art had been in jail when two of the earlier murders had been committed.

When he returned to his office, Bean was waiting, equally worn out, and it pleased Rooney to note his shirt was stained with sweat and coffee—and was creased!

Rooney eased his bulk into his chair and sighed. "I think we've been wasting our time, Bean. That little bastard should be locked up but not for murder. He's just into his porno and probably the blackmail rackets again."

Bean coughed, waited a moment. All night they'd been at it with Art Mathews. They had called more than twenty officers out and some were still bringing caseloads of pornographic tapes and photographs from his studio, and just like that Rooney dismisses him. He coughed again, worried. It was him after all who had instructed the squad to move on from outside Lorraine Page's apartment and help on the Art Mathews arrest, so he wasn't exactly sure where it left him; possibly in the shit. "Does that mean Lorraine Page is into all that, too?"

Rooney sighed. "I don't know. Maybe you should get this information ready for the suits. Lay it out on the chief's desk, let him see we've worked our butts off tonight."

Bean took Mathews's prison record to the FBI agents' office and Rooney glanced at his watch. It was too late or too early in the morning to call Lorraine, but he knew he wouldn't get any sleep. He'd give it a couple more hours and call her after he'd showered and shaved.

He was running his small battery-operated shaver over his beefy chin when Bean peered into the washroom. Rooney gave him a worn-out smile and clicked off the shaver. "I don't suppose we just got lucky and Art Mathews admitted killing eight women and Norman Hastings?" he asked him.

Bean was even more crumpled than he had been earlier, and even had a faint stubble on his chin and upper lip. It was bad news. He ran the cold water into the basin, worried that when Rooney heard the latest development he'd be more than worried. "No, we didn't get lucky. Our prime suspect is sobbing his heart out down there in the cells. Meanwhile, his lawyer doesn't want us to press criminal charges if he admits to what he was doing on the night of the last murder. He has already remembered where he was when Holly was murdered and this you're not gonna believe."

"Try me," Rooney said heavily.

"Art Mathews was working in that gallery right next to your Japanese place. He worked there until late, all night, and Lorraine Page is one of his alibis."

Rooney stared at his reflection. Bean dried his hands under the blow dryer, shouting over its roar. "Any money the FBI'll release him on bail, he'll get locked up for a few years for his porno trade, if we're lucky. Been a long night for nothing and I won't take any shit for pulling that squad car off Page, and just to make your day, there's press outside. Somebody tipped them off we got a suspect."

Rooney swiped at the washbasin with his towel. "Shit! That stupid bitch! I'm going to call that two-faced bitch right now."

Bean followed Rooney down the corridor. "You know they got Andrew Fellows coming in to talk to the FBI later this morning? Maybe you should hang around—what do I tell them if they ask me about why I pulled officers off her?"

Rooney snapped. "You tell 'em we needed every man we had on night duty to bring in fuckin' Art Mathews and that's the reason." Rooney checked the time, it was coming up to five. He didn't give a shit if he woke her up or not. As he drove out of the station parking lot, he watched two new patrol cars pulling in with the FBI men all bright-eyed and bushy-tailed even if they had been hauled out of their beds at this ungodly hour. He drove away, his anger mounting. Art Mathews had been another of Lorraine's theories. She had been partly right: he *had* known Holly and Didi, but he had no connection with Steven Janklow. And Janklow, yet another of Lorraine's suspects, turned out to have no vice record. He felt he had really gotten himself into deep shit, acting on her information. Rooney might even force her to give him back his dough. Maybe he'd have her hauled in, spill it about her being the witness they'd been searching for. He'd like to grab her by her scrawny throat and strangle her. He was through, period. The more he drove, the angrier he became. As he headed toward Lorraine's apartment, he was ready to explode. He really needed to sound off at somebody so it might as well be her! The two-faced, lying whore.

Rosie shot out of bed when the doorbell rang. She grabbed a robe and noisily scuttled to the door. Lorraine was sitting up on the sofa yawning. "What time is it?"

"Five-thirty in the morning! Who the hell is ringing the bell at this hour?"

Rosie opened the door and stepped back. Rooney was leaning against the doorframe. He looked past Rosie to Lorraine. "I'm gonna arrest you."

Lorraine got up quickly and pulled a cardigan around her nightgown. "Arrest me? Why, for chrissakes?"

He sauntered in. "Art Mathews, sweetheart. You were with him the night the . . ." He couldn't remember Holly's name. "You were with him the night she was murdered, you're his fucking alibi. *You!*"

Lorraine filled a glass at the kitchen sink and drank it straight down. "Is that why you sent cops here? Did you do that to me?"

Rooney tossed his hat aside. "They were courtesy of the FBI, sweetheart, time's up."

She faced him in a fury. "Did you tell them about me? Bill, did you tell them I was attacked?"

"You know I didn't, but I sure as hell intend to because you are full of bullshit and you've lied to me right from the start. When I tried to help you out, all you did was lie."

Lorraine clenched her fist, she could have thrown a hell of a punch at him she was so angry. "They still holding Mathews?"

"Far as I know. Maybe you were mistaken about this Janklow and maybe it was Mathews who attacked you in the gallery when you were working together, hanging up pictures, the night Holly died."

She sighed. "That's stupid. He's right-handed."

"What?"

"Art Mathews is right-handed. The guy who attacked me and all the others was left-handed, according to all the forensic and pathology reports and even the reports from Andrew Fellows. The killer is left-handed, opens the glove compartment with his left, holds their heads down with his right . . ."

Rooney looked at her, then turned away. "Get dressed. We're out of here."

She pushed him onto the sofa "No. You sit right where you are."

He pouted and then tugged a bottle of bourbon out of his pocket. He slowly unscrewed the cap and took a heavy pull. He dangled the bottle toward Lorraine.

Rosie eyed it and then eyed Lorraine. She was walking toward it.

Rooney also watched Lorraine. "Want a drink?"

Lorraine snatched the bottle and marched to the sink, about to pour it down the drain, when the smell suddenly hit her. She wanted a drink, everything started to crystallize, all she could think of was raising the open bottle to her mouth and drinking. She didn't care about Art Mathews or Steven Janklow, she wanted a drink. She slowly lifted the bottle to her lips, closing her eyes in anticipation.

"Don't do it, Lorraine." It was Rooney. "Pour it out, don't do it. I'm sorry. Here, Lorraine, give it to me."

Rooney had to pry her hands away from the bottle. It shocked him, made him feel sick. He leaned on the sink pouring the booze away, as Lorraine struggled to wrest the bottle from him. He turned on both faucets so the water splashed out of the sink and over him. "Shit. I'm soaking wet."

"Aren't we all?" snapped Lorraine. "Old washed-up soaks," she said as she took down coffee cups. "I suppose it's black coffee all around?"

There was a sudden hard pounding at the front door. Rosie

went to open it but Rooney stopped her. He peered out of the window and told Lorraine to get into the bedroom. She obeyed immediately, closing the door behind her as the front door was pounded hard again.

"Don't say anything," Rooney said quietly to Rosie. "Just leave this to me."

The two officers framed in the doorway asked for Lorraine Page. Rosie held the door wider to reveal Rooney standing in the center of the room with a cup of coffee in his hand. They were taken aback by his presence and made no move to enter the room.

"Captain Rooney."

"You come to pick her up?"

They nodded, and one passed him a warrant for Lorraine's arrest.

"I'll hang on to this. I'm staying put until she shows. Go back to the station. Soon as I got her I'll call in."

Rooney pocketed the warrant, carried his coffee toward the sofa, and sat down heavily. "Unless you want to hang around here."

"We'll leave it to you, Captain."

A few moments later Lorraine came out of the bedroom. She leaned across to him, hugging his big square shoulders. "Why did you do that, Bill?"

"Christ only knows, I must be nuts."

She sat in the easy chair opposite him while Rosie hovered, uncomfortable and ill at ease with them.

"I'm sorry for bringing the booze in," Rooney said.

"That's okay." Rosie finally wandered into her bedroom, feeling in the way.

"She seems like a nice woman," Rooney said.

"Rosie's great." Lorraine smiled at him. "You want to hear my developments? What I came up with last night?"

He wanted to say no but didn't. Instead he let her talk without interruption, listening intently as she pieced together her talk with Nula, then her meeting with Craig Lyall.

Lorraine's face was expressionless as she explained clearly, without emotion, what had happened when she had been attacked. She described walking up to the car, how he had driven her to the parking space, how she had fought him, bitten hard into his neck, hung on for her life as he tried to push her away from him. He was strong, she said. The grip on her hair had been like a vise, and it had taken all her strength to lever up her body to turn and bite. She was sure that if they hadn't been disturbed by the Summerses, she would be dead. She then told Rooney that she had also taken Norman Hastings's wallet.

Rooney closed his eyes and kept them closed, she was making him feel sick to his stomach, because every disclosure dragged him in deeper and deeper.

"There's something else. At first I didn't think about it. It was his cuff links. They had a logo. I didn't think it was important until I saw the same logo on a letterhead. At my husband's place—Mike, you remember Mike? He has nothing to do with this, don't worry, but it gave me the first clue to the killer.''

Rooney opened his eyes. She was staring at him as he coughed, finding it hard to speak. He felt as if he'd been punched.

"Anything else you've just not mentioned to me?"

She nodded and began describing how she and Rosie had gone to the S & A garage, how she had narrowed the list of cuff links owners down and taken photographs of suspects. None resembled the man who had attacked her. She took the photographs out and passed them to Rooney. As he examined the one of the blond woman, she leaned close to him, saw his hands were shaking.

"I think this is Steven Janklow. I think he's a transvestite, and that he had a photographic session with either Mathews or Lyall. It could have been as far back as eight to nine years ago, maybe when he was just daring to come out. I think Mathews subsequently discovered who he was and started blackmailing him, realizing he'd found the golden goose. I think Art and Didi may have worked as a team. She was used or hired to do wigs and makeup. She made up Norman Hastings, fixed his hair for the photo session. Maybe she even tipped off Art, Lyall said his clients always took the negatives. You interviewed Lyall, too, didn't you?"

Rooney nodded. They hadn't come up with anything as concrete as Lorraine had. He sighed like a man bereaved. She was good, always had been good, but this new evidence was like a time bomb.

"Lorraine, this is . . ." his voice sounded leaden. She put up her hand, gestured for him not to interrupt. Now she began pacing up and down. There was something about the way she moved, tensing, relaxing her hands, and she rubbed her body, almost sexually, her face becoming more and more alive. She was exciting to watch, as she became increasingly animated.

"I've got Hastings linked to Janklow—maybe they discussed the blackmail. Who knows what they discussed? Possible theory is, when Hastings went to the bank that morning, was he going to pay off Mathews? Pay off somebody? The strange thing is that all his bank statements have been checked and the major transactions are accounted for." She suddenly stopped and clicked her fingers. "Unless Hastings was also tapping Janklow for money. It seems strange that he was allowed to park his car in the hangar. Nobody seems to know why he should have been when he no longer owned one of their cars. Did you know that at one time he owned a vintage car? Maybe that was where he could have found out that he and Janklow were the same kind of men. Whatever, we know they're linked, and linked to Mathews through Didi. She's very important. She may not have collected from Mathews's blackmailing activities, but I'm beginning to think she may have been the go-between or, and this is a wild guess, maybe she was the person Janklow believed was blackmailing him. So that brings me to the last piece of guesswork."

Lorraine took out the victims' photographs and laid them along the sofa for Rooney to look at. "They have one thing in common apart from prostitution. Look at the makeup, the type of clothes they wore. Now, look at the morgue shots of Didi. . . . Put her beside each one. You didn't believe me earlier, but what if Janklow was only after her, was only interested in tracking her down and killing her? He's a Thorburn, right? His mother was a big Society hostess, his brother is holding all the purse strings. What if Janklow has been paying out blackmail money because he's scared his family will find out and it might be made public? Just like Hastings hid his private life from everyone who knew him."

Lorraine tapped Rooney's shoulder in her excitement. He edged away, annoyed by her but more angry with himself. She had run rings around him and his department, and it infuriated him. But the only legitimate complaint against her that he could think of was that she had withheld vital evidence.

"Bill, you have got to break Art Mathews—get him to admit this blackmail. If you do, then you have a clean motive and you've got Janklow, or at least enough to bring him in for questioning.''

Rooney's head was spinning, and as he tried to assimilate everything she had told him he felt dizzy. Tapping his shoulder again, she added, ''And the guy has got to have some mark from where I bit him. Maybe the skin's healed, even the bruising, but I held on for everything I was worth.''

Rooney was unnerved by her toughness. ''You faced him yet?''

''I told you I hadn't, I'm not stupid.''

''You are one hell of a witness, you know that, don't you?'' he said wearily, slowly rising from the sofa.

''Yeah.'' She stepped back, suddenly wary of him. He was a big man and when he stood up straight instead of his usual slouch it was surprising how much it added to his size. She knew what he was going to say, knew it, but she faced him out, made him look at her directly.

''You'll have to come in with me. I'm sorry, Lorraine, there's no way out of it now.''

She turned away. He saw her deflate, wrap her arms around herself, and her voice was hardly audible, almost pleading.

''Come on, Bill, don't make me have to go to court, not now, not when I'm getting myself back together. I go to court, they can start throwing old charges at me, make me admit to what I was and they'll dish the dirt on me, even bring up the shooting. Don't do it to me, Bill.''

He was frustrated because he knew what she said was true, but he also had no option. He sounded more angry than he felt.

''You were fucking attacked! That's what you'd be in court for, nothing else.''

She leaned against the wall, and her eyes brimmed with tears.

''I know what he did but I won't go to court. Don't make them call me out, Bill.''

''Ah, come on, Lorraine, look at it from my side, you've withheld evidence, and you even had Norman Hastings's goddamned wallet! You never even told me about the cuff links, so what do you expect me to do? You are the only witness. You gave me days of fucking waste of time. If you'd been upfront with me I'd have cracked this, I'd have been—''

She suddenly yelled back at him, ''Patted on the back and

given a commendation before you retired, that's what you're pissed off about right now! Instead of moving on what I've just been spewing out for the past hour, you're going to needle me instead. You want me to face Steven Janklow, then I'll do it right now, I'll go over to his place in Beverly Glen with you, with anyone you want, but I won't go to court. Bill, I'm not standing up as ex-cop, ex-alcoholic, ex-hooker so you can get a slap on the back. I won't do it. I'll pack up and walk out right now and you'll never lay eyes on me again.''

He waved the warrant. ''I can take you in, Lorraine.''

''Try it, *just try it*.'' Hands on hips she glared at him. ''Go get Art Mathews to talk, Bill, that's what you should be doing. You know it, so stop bullshitting and get on with it. I won't be taken in, and I warn you, if they drag me into court, then I won't pour the next bottle down the drain.''

He pointed at her with his index finger. ''You don't leave this apartment, you hear me? If you want I can make sure. I can have a squad car out front in two minutes. I can have you watched day and night, around the clock, have guys on your doorstep.''

She sat down. ''I won't leave, Bill, I give you my word. Maybe just to the corner for groceries but I'll stay put.''

His upright position abruptly relaxed and he resumed his habitual slouch. ''I'll call you, see what I can do, lie about you, I suppose. But don't let me down, Lorraine, I couldn't take it.''

She stepped forward and hugged him tightly. He smelled of cigarettes and booze and he grunted at her to get away from him. He walked out of the door without a word and slammed it behind him.

Lorraine slumped onto the sofa. She was hot, angry, frustrated, and a little scared. She should have kept her mouth shut about Hastings's wallet. There was no need for her to have mentioned it—that had been a big mistake. She wondered if Rooney would have the balls to keep her identity secret and not make her go to court. The thought of having all her past made public, having her daughters and Mike read about her, turned her anger to humiliation. For the first time she faced her shame in the light of day. She was disgusted with herself. The tears she'd held back now spilled down her cheeks, but she made no sound. Had she really been stupid enough to think that she could start a new career? Who would want to hire her if her past was splashed across every tabloid? She knew they'd love it, that she'd be hounded, and she knew they'd rake up why she'd been forced to quit the police. She saw him again, the yellow zigzag stripe down his jacket, his young face as he fell, his hair flopping.

Lorraine heard the bedroom door open and the heavy, plodding feet crossing the room. She waited, praying for Rosie to leave her in peace. She bit harder into her hand as she felt her friend's weight subsiding on the edge of the sofa. Rosie stroked her hair. "I listened at the door just in case you needed me."

Lorraine sighed. She never had any privacy. She almost forgot that this was Rosie's place.

"You remember last night, what you said about going into the investigation business? For real?" Rosie asked quietly.

"No, I'd never get a license. I was just kidding myself."

"You shouldn't. I was real proud of the way you just talked to Rooney, the way you were piecing it together. You're good, you know, good and clever."

Lorraine gazed up at the big plump face. "Did you hear it all?"

"Yep, and that's another thing you're good at. He was right, you sure as hell can lie better than anyone I know."

Lorraine laughed softly. "Yeah, I guess you just get used to it, it's part of a cop's life, you know. 'No cause for alarm,' when a whole building's about to collapse."

Rosie rubbed Lorraine's back, like a mother would her child's. "Maybe if you had to go to court it wouldn't be such a bad thing. Maybe your kids *should* know, maybe they'd be proud that you're fighting back, proving yourself—proving your worth."

Lorraine grinned. "Rosie, you're such an optimist."

"Yeah, but I'm looking out for me, too. I think I could get used to this kind of work—being a private investigator's more interesting than sealing envelopes, computers, even!"

Lorraine moved away from the soothing warmth of Rosie's reassuring hand. "You don't know it all, Rosie. It's not just the drinking, the whoring, it's not just that . . ." and she told her about the fourteen-year-old boy. Rosie didn't say anything, but she felt even more warmth toward Lorraine, and especially when, after the telling of the story, she tilted her face slightly and gave her a sweet, sad smile. "Thanks for listening, Rosie. I'm going to take a shower now."

The telephone rang and Rosie answered it. It was Rooney and she knew something was wrong right away.

"She's just taking a shower, Captain Rooney, you want me to get her?"

Rooney coughed. "Rosie, I've got some bad news. Art Mathews committed suicide."

Rosie gasped. "My God, but how . . . how did he do—"

Rooney interrupted, "I'm sorry, but you'd better warn Lorraine. There's not a hope in hell of me keeping her out of this now, you understand?"

"How long does she have before they get here?"

"They're already on their way."

Rosie looked at the closed bedroom door, her heart sinking. "She'll be ready."

SIXTEEN

Jake listened without interrupting. When Rosie had called him before he'd even had breakfast, his first thought was it was she who needed him "urgently." He was relieved to find her waiting for him at her front door stone-cold sober. As she let him into the apartment, she put her finger to her lips, indicating the bedroom. She didn't want Lorraine to hear what she was saying, but she knew she had to make it fast. "They arrest her, Jake, and everything she's accomplished so far will be over. She'll go back on the booze—she as good as said it."

It was hard for him to take in everything Rosie said. Just the pertinent facts were enough to make him break out in a sweat. Lorraine had been attacked by the so-called hammer killer; she was the witness the police were searching for; she was also investigating or assisting the police in their inquiries. It was hard to believe, and even more so when Rosie slipped in that Lorraine's "partner" was also helping the investigation.

They couldn't carry on the conversation as Lorraine walked in. She was surprised to see Jake.

"You come for breakfast?"

"Nope. I was wondering if you wanted to come to a meeting."

"What? Are you nuts? It's not even nine o'clock. Besides, I can't. I've got to stay in the apartment."

"I'm gonna get dressed," Rosie said, eyeing Jake and jerking her head toward Lorraine, who watched her go out and then started to wash the cups.

She ran water into the sink. "So, what has she told you?"

Jake fiddled with a spoon on the counter.

"Is it about me admitting I wanted a drink?"

Jake shrugged. "You may not know it, Lorraine, but you just broke through, and you'll make it even if it doesn't look or feel like it right now. But I want you to come to a meeting with me this morning. According to Rosie you might need a morale boost."

Lorraine put her head on one side. "She tell you I might be arrested?"

"Is it true?"

She put down the dishcloth. "It's true, and I think I'm going to need a lot more than just a morale boost."

"Then you'll come to the early-morning meeting?"

Bean edged into Rooney's office. He'd gotten his wife to send in a clean shirt, he had shaved, but his suit was still wrinkled and he looked less like his usual pristine self. He shut the door and gave a glum look to Rooney. "Ambulance's just taken his body away."

Rooney was even more crumpled, but unlike Bean he had not gotten his wife to send in a fresh shirt; he hadn't even bothered calling her. "How the hell did he do it?"

"Broke his glasses and slit his wrists."

"FBI must be shitting themselves." Rooney snorted with a half-derisive laugh and sneer.

"Yep, all in there blaming each other and patting each other on the back at the same time."

Rooney gaped. "What you mean?"

"Well, it's obvious, isn't it? I mean, why kill yourself if you're innocent? Now they're thinking he must be the one."

Rooney snorted again. "That's bullshit. We know he couldn't have done two of them because he was inside. They got the report of his criminal record, didn't they?"

Bean said that they might have found some discrepancies in the dates. Whatever, they weren't digging too deep since the chief was putting out a press release that the suspect in custody had admitted his guilt.

"*Had* he?" Rooney asked, astonished, because when he'd last seen Mathews he hadn't—far from it.

"They're saying so, but they still want to question his accomplice."

"His what?"

"Lorraine Page. I was told you were bringing her in. They've been waiting for you."

Rooney could feel the warrant in his pocket. He took it out and passed it to Bean, his heart pounding. He felt sick, needed time to plan what he was going to do with the information Lorraine had passed him. He had already decided not to mention the theft of Norman Hastings's wallet, and would maybe tell her to leave out the cuff links. He was even toying with trying to keep the attack on her out of his statements; now it looked as if it was out of his hands. He asked himself why he'd go out on a limb for her like this, but all he came up with was that he liked her. If it got out that he'd used her, paid her, and that she'd been privy to the information, he'd not only be out in the cold but his hoped-for bonus would be history.

The squad car pulled up outside Rosie's apartment just moments after they'd left for the AA meeting. Five minutes later, all vehicles were instructed to be on the lookout for the prostitute Lorraine Page, described as five feet nine, short blond hair, last seen wearing a cream skirted suit and silk shirt. She was to be arrested on sight.

Lorraine was still uncertain as to why she had let Jake and Rosie talk her into coming to the meeting. Maybe, if the truth was to be admitted, it was because she was at a loss and she was also scared.

The woman was neatly dressed in printed cotton, her hair well cut, parted in the center, and constantly falling forward to hide her face. She spoke quietly, nervously. "My name is Carol. Nine months ago I was living on the street, I felt there was no hope for me. I felt no shame, I felt nothing. I had lost my husband, my children, my home, and my job. I had turned to prostitution to feed my drinking. I was a prostitute and a thief. I owned only what I stood up in, I had nothing, and no respect for anyone, least of all myself.'' Carol continued to talk and Lorraine held tightly to Rosie's hand, understanding for the first time what she felt, what she had been through, and that she was not alone. Everyone at the meeting, she now began to realize, had felt shame and rejection, knew loss and humiliation.

When they stood and warmly applauded Carol, when they embraced her and congratulated her, Lorraine was one of the first to leave her seat. She was shy, at first just extending her hand, but then she put her arms around her. "I've been there, too. I know how you feel," she said simply.

Carol hugged Lorraine back. "We've all been there, that's why we're here."

"What was the hardest thing for you?" Lorraine asked.

"Facing myself, not being angry or ashamed. It wasn't me but the drinking. I hid behind it, I know that now, and I'm determined to stay sober. I got a job yesterday. I was scared but I told them I'm an alcoholic and now that I know that's what I am, I feel free. For the first time in years I'm not hiding."

"You said you hid behind drinking. What did you mean?"

"I was afraid of failing. I'm a nurse and I had a patient, a child, who died. I gave the wrong medication and I was never able to face the guilt or come to terms with it. I have now. It will always be with me, but I can deal with it, I'm taking responsibility for myself and I want to stay sober. I *have* to stay sober or I'll go down again."

Jake was watching Lorraine. He winked at Rosie. "It was good we came. You were right, Rosie, it was important for her."

"And for me, too. If Lorraine had started drinking I'd have probably joined her," Rosie replied, and Jake smiled.

Lorraine came up to them. "Thanks for bringing me. Now we should get back in case Rooney needs me."

Rooney watched the FBI agents talking to his chief. He sat in a hard-backed chair at the rear of the room; when anyone looked to him for an opinion he made no comment. The press had been given statements and the suits felt that, with the arrest of Art Mathews, they had been able at least to gain time. Even if they couldn't provide evidence that Mathews had murdered all the victims, they were satisfied that by his own admission and subsequent suicide he had been guilty of at least three.

Andrew Fellows had come in and they had been in deep discussion with him for two hours. He had disagreed with their conclusion that Mathews was the killer. Not until they seemed to have grown tired of the sound of their own voices did Rooney ease his bulk from the chair. "You mind if I put my two cents in?"

They had forgotten he was even in the room. The chief looked pointedly at his watch. "Is it about the Lorraine Page woman?"

Andrew Fellows frowned. "Lorraine Page?"

"We're still looking for her but it shouldn't be long."

Rooney squeezed between a row of chairs.

"Lorraine Page?" Fellows asked again, but no one answered him and she was forgotten as Rooney prodded the photograph of Didi, the last victim.

"What if our killer—and I'm excluding Mathews just for a moment—was looking for this particular woman or man—the transsexual? Looking for her because she and Mathews were blackmailing him." There was a low murmur and Rooney held up his hand. "Let me finish. Take a look at them. Tough, hard-faced women, all bleached blondes, all prostitutes, as was this victim." Again he tapped Didi's picture. "It's a possible motive because I think Hastings was also being blackmailed and possibly by Mathews . . ." The men listened, giving each other sidelong looks. The chief loosened his tie. Mathews had admitted at no time to blackmailing anyone. Rooney continued to repeat almost verbatim what Lorraine had said to him. He did not mention her part in piecing it together, or that she was the witness who had been attacked by the killer. Just before he gave the name of her suspect, he felt a hot flush spread through his body. The Thorburn family was powerful and all Rooney had was Lorraine's theory. They did not have enough evidence: her own admission that Janklow had been her attacker would, as she rightly surmised, be tough to prove. As she had said, it would be her word against his. And as yet no incriminating evidence linked him to the murders. His thoughts racing as he spoke, Rooney abruptly decided that until he had more on Janklow, he would keep his identity to himself.

The room was silent. The chief stared at Rooney—they all did—and Andrew Fellows's face wore a half-smile. It was

hard to determine whether it was through disbelief or because
he was impressed.

Rooney decided he might as well go for the big prize. He
nodded to Hastings's picture. "He used a garage to park his
car, the S and A garage. I haven't gone into this in any depth,
but a number of the company's employees were checked out
against the description we had from the anonymous witness.
The S and A garage is owned by a Brad Thorburn." Fellows
gasped at this but no one paid any attention. Rooney continued, "I'm not suggesting anything without further evidence.
Obviously, considering the family's connections, I have not,
until tonight, even voiced my suspicions."

"Just what are you implying?" Fellows asked, his face pink
with agitation. Rooney looked at him then, and at the chief,
who became aware that Fellows should not have been privy
to this statement and suggested that he might wish to leave.

Fellows had not disclosed that he knew Brad Thorburn. He
was unsure as to why not but, then, he hadn't been asked. He
intended to drive straight to UCLA but changed his mind and
headed for Thorburn's house.

Jake saw the patrol car even before he turned onto their street.
Lorraine was in the backseat.

"You want me to drive past the cops?" Jake asked.

"Yeah, but not for the reason you think. I'll go in but in
my own time. There's somebody I want to talk to first. I misjudged Rooney. He must have told them about me."

She ducked out of sight as Jake passed the police car, turning left at the end of the street before he stopped.

"Where we going?" Rosie asked.

"I need to talk to Andrew Fellows. I won't do anything
crazy, believe me. I just want to run a few things past him."

"I'll drive you," said Rosie.

Lorraine hesitated before she agreed. Jake got out and Rosie
moved into the driver's seat. He watched them pulling away
from the curb but not until they were almost out of sight did
he turn away and walk home.

The car backfired. Jake whipped around. It had sounded like
a gunshot. It made him uneasy and he wished he'd stayed with
the two women. He also wished he'd asked a lot more questions, but as he walked on he realized that he had been part

of Lorraine's cover-up story about the attack. He shook his head. He had known as soon as he saw the injury that it hadn't been caused by a fall, as she'd said. With all her lies, Lorraine had not only used Rosie but himself. The more he thought about it, the angrier he became, and now he started to wonder where Lorraine had gotten all that money from. He remembered the way she clutched it when they'd had her wound stitched up. She was one hell of a liar, he told himself. Maybe there was more to the cops hanging around than either he or Rosie knew.

Rooney told the agents about Craig Lyall, again making use of Lorraine's evidence. When the chief got back, Rooney was in the hot seat. Berillo wanted to know why he had been withholding so much evidence, and neither discussed it with him nor provided the agents with the information on Mathews's blackmailing activities.

"I only pieced it together this morning. Like I said, it's just supposition. I've been up all night on this. I hadn't finished interviewing Mathews when the FBI took over. You tell *me* how such an important suspect with all this high-tech surveillance on his cell was able to slit his wrists. Don't lay that on me, I wasn't even in the station. It's down to the FBI."

The agents took his gibes and accusations without expression. One of them, the one with the blond crew cut and square jaw to match, was making copious notes as Rooney spoke. At one point he held up his silver pen for Rooney to wait a moment, continued to write, and then tapped his notebook and looked up, a frozen smile on his pale face. "Go on, Captain Rooney."

Rooney gave a slightly raised eyebrow. "Thank you very much, Mr. Bicketsall."

Without looking up, the agent underlined something and his voice was icy. "It's Bickerstaff, S-T-A-F-F, Captain."

Chief Berillo could feel the tension about to blow, so he burst it open to get the air cleared. "You're seriously saying that Brad Thorburn is a suspect?"

The atmosphere in the room was really uneasy now. Bean remained silent throughout: he was wondering why Rooney had never mentioned any of his findings to him.

"I never said Thorburn was a suspect. I believe it's his brother, Steven Janklow."

Bickerstaff yet again held up his silver pen to indicate his desire to interrupt. "Excuse me, Captain, does Mr. Janklow fit the description of the killer given to your department after Hastings's body had been found?"

Rooney shifted uneasily. Since he had never seen Janklow or interviewed him, he was hesitant.

"I haven't interviewed him. All I know is he knew Hastings and—"

"And?" snapped the chief. Rooney felt as if they were all against him, closing in on him. He pulled at his bulbous nose, half wishing he'd kept his big mouth shut. He took a flier, lying through his teeth. "I held back giving you this information until I'd checked in the files for a possible vice charge against Janklow in the past. So far I haven't been able to trace it and it was just mentioned to me by one of the workers at the garage. I didn't want to act on hearsay—well, not until I'd run it past you. I could be wrong on all counts."

The chief glanced at his watch and then said, "You go through those vice records, Bill, immediately—but until you have more evidence we make no contact with the Thorburn family. If our man is Janklow, we need hard facts to arrest him; the Thorburn family is High Society and powerful." The chief said the last sentence directly to Bickerstaff, who snapped his notebook closed.

"In other words, Chief Berillo, we back off the Thorburns until you say so. So we'll wait for any further information from Captain Rooney before we open up the investigation." Bickerstaff looked at his team, his eyes were expressionless. "Right, gentlemen, shall we discuss this new development?" Hemmed in by his men, Bickerstaff headed toward his allocated office.

Everyone else passed hooded looks to each other as they filed out of the room. Berillo turned on Rooney in a fury, demanding to know what the fuck he thought he was doing.

"Just trying to do my job."

"Come on, Bill, who are you kiddin'? You're just pissed off because the FBI has been brought in. If you'd even had half of what you blurted out tonight we could have held them off. What else are you holding back? You'd better come clean with me." He stared hard at Rooney and then asked about Lorraine Page.

Rooney covered effortlessly. "She's my informant, but I didn't know until tonight that she knew Mathews or that she was with him the night Holly was murdered."

"I want her brought in and I want to talk to her. I want to know just what the hell Mathews was up to."

"It's in his file. He's been in for blackmail and extortion, along with his porno rap, and Page is apparently on her way in."

"Is that it?"

"That's it. Like I said, let me dig into Janklow's past some more and then I'll come right back to you."

The chief agreed, but told Rooney to call him, no matter what time it was, if he discovered anything else.

Rooney returned to his office where Bean was waiting with a nervous look on his face. "Everything all right with the chief?"

Rooney closed his office door. "Yeah, we're like this." He crossed his fingers.

"You blew everyone sideways in there. That Ed Bickerstaff's nose was sure out of joint. I heard him say to his guys as they left, you know what he said?"

"Bunch of assholes."

"Yeah, I guess you heard him, too . . ."

Rooney started rummaging through his desk drawers. "So what about Lorraine Page?" Bean asked. He just didn't get what was going on between the captain and this strange ex-cop, but it worried him—for himself. "According to Officers Hully and Arthur you were at her place. They said you were bringing her in."

"I left when she didn't show—that all right with you? And for chrissakes, if you are gettin' into a hot sweat over releasing that squad car from outside her place, forget it. I'd say right now the FBI action man has got problems of his own—Art Mathews's suicide for starters."

Bean's face showed his relief. "Yeah, yeah, you're right." He sat down, watching Rooney banging open one drawer after another. He leaned forward, his elbow resting on the edge of the desk. "You did a hell of a lot of legwork since you left here last night, and you didn't mention any of this to me— Janklow, the Thorburn family. If you'd seen those agents' faces, talk about jaws dropping open. I was impressed. They were really pissed. They were patting each other on the back ten minutes earlier about Art Mathews. They really upped the pressure on him, you know, he was crying his eyes out.''

Rooney didn't even appear to be listening as he searched through yet another drawer. Bean picked up a rubber band and began flicking it, eventually got around to asking what had been on his mind from the start.

"So, um, did she tip you off about Art Mathews?''

Rooney raised his eyebrow in mock surprise. "God no, that was supreme detective work on my part, Lieutenant.'' Then he scowled. "If Mathews said he killed them, I figure he'd have said he'd shot his mother just to get those suits off him. He was scared—must have been scared shitless about being sent up for blackmail again. He'd have done eighteen years this time and the little prick knew it. They just wanted to make an arrest, period. I think they were lucky he did kill himself, because if I'd have gotten my hands on him, I might have ended up with a different result, like negative.''

Bean still flicked the rubber band. "So why did he kill himself, then?''

"Because maybe he knew he was in very deep and we'd have dug up something. Christ almighty, I gave them his fucking file, he was serving time when two of the victims were done. I don't care what any of that FBI crowd want to say about copycat killings, those victims were all done by the same man.''

Bean sucked in his breath. "Or woman. That's what Fellows threw in this morning.''

"Bullshit, and stop flickin' that thing, you're gettin' on my nerves.''

"Sorry. He said that all the crap that's written about male or female strength is hyped up out of all proportion. If a woman wanted to kill, she could have done it. He even said that was why the victims took a blow to the back of the head first—incapacitated them.''

"Well, Fellows is looking up his own tight-assed butt. We got that witness, the one that gave us the description, right?'' He almost disclosed who she was but stopped himself. Instead, he leaned over the desk. "She described her attacker as a man, right?''

Bean looked at Rooney. "Lorraine Page. So where does she

figure in all this? What if they were doing it together? She was with Mathews the night Holly was murdered, he said so.''

"I know, I know . . .'' He felt his stomach turn over. What if Bean was right? Could she be that much involved?

Bean now crossed to the internal window blinds looking in on the main office floor. "Well, however you came up with it, it sounded like hot shit to me.'' Rooney looked puzzled. "It was nice to watch you in action, Captain.''

Rooney smiled. "I always was one of the best. Now, why don't you go get some sandwiches and coffee?''

Bean crossed to the door. "Anythin' you say. I can tell it's gonna be a very long day, an' since we were up all night, it'll feel even longer.''

As the door closed behind him Rooney slumped in his chair. He wasn't one of the best, he doubted if he ever had been, but she was. It was Lorraine who was hot shit, and she'd proved it. He just hoped to God she was right, and that she hadn't run off. Did he want to crack this so badly he was going to let her risk her neck? He knew he still had the trump card that she was the witness. If he was forced into a corner he'd bring it out. He wondered how long it would be before they brought her in, then suddenly felt cold. What if Bean was right? What if she had been giving him the runaround all along? What if she'd never been a witness but a killer, and the description was just to put them all off the scent? He picked up the phone and punched out her number. No answer. Where the hell was she? If she wasn't brought in within the hour, he'd go out looking for her personally. She wasn't the killer—that was dumb, that was *crazy*—but he felt a horrible nagging in his gut. She was connected to Didi and Mathews; he'd told the FBI that she had been with him the night Holly was murdered. He should have brought her in with him, he shouldn't have trusted her. She might even now be in some bar drinking herself into a stupor—she'd threatened as much . . .

Bean came back in. He'd called for some takeout rather than schlepp out for it himself.

"What else did Fellows say about it maybe being a woman?''

"None of the victims had been sexually abused, there'd been no trace of semen, not even on Holly. Victims all struck from behind, just their faces mangled. You find what you were looking for?''

Rooney didn't seem to hear but stared blankly ahead. Bean waited a moment before asking sarcastically, "Maybe changing your theory, are you, Captain?"

Rooney frowned; Bean was really getting under his skin now.

"She's an ex-cop, right? She's capable of taking care of herself, she's tough, I've heard you say it, and she's been out hooking. She's got a record. Maybe, just maybe, she's also got a lot of venom in her, a hatred of women that look like her."

Rooney hit the desk hard. "No. No way. Piss off out of here, go on. And, Josh, get a bottle of bourbon for me."

Bean knew now what Rooney had been banging around looking for. He pursed his lips; he didn't like being treated like a messenger boy, first for lunch, then for booze . . .

"You got a problem?"

"No, Captain, but you might be gettin' one."

Rooney watched Bean walk away down the corridor. Any other time he'd have flattened him down with some scathing remark, but he didn't have the energy. He couldn't have lost his touch to that extent. He shut his eyes and recalled Lorraine's face, the way her pale eyes bored into him, the scar making her face switch between vulnerable and street tough. He read through her file again: the arrests, the charges, the no-shows at court, the attacks on arresting officers, even that she had been held in a straitjacket. Drunk and disorderly was recorded time and again. Drunk in charge of a vehicle, drunk when arrested for breaking into a liquor store—she had fought the arresting officer, bitten him, kicked him, and punched him in the face. It had taken four of them to get her into the wagon. She'd been held in the cells for three days, charged with assault, and spent two months in the L.A. women's county jail. If he hadn't known her, he would have described her without hesitation as dangerous. Could she be capable of murder? His feet ached as he walked up and down, swearing alternately at Fellows for throwing this "woman killer" angle into the investigation, at Lorraine, and finally at himself.

When Bean returned with the food, Rooney seemed even more distracted. Bean placed on the desk a ham and cheese on rye, two coffees with their plastic lids on, and then removed from his pocket a brown paper bag with a pint of bourbon. Rooney didn't even say thank you. He took the top off his coffee, gulped a few mouthfuls, and topped it up with bourbon. Just as Bean had his own sandwich raised to his mouth, Rooney barked out, "Check that vice charge, the Janklow thing, get on that first." Bean didn't say he was already working on it, he just left Rooney alone, taking his lunch with him. He'd seen these dark moods often and didn't want to be on the receiving end of one today.

Rooney closed Lorraine's file. She had sunk lower than he could ever have imagined and he felt a certain remorse. The question uppermost in his mind was, had she sunk so low then forced herself back up just to take revenge? Should he warn all officers that she might be dangerous? He knew if he gave that out, and she resisted arrest, she might be shot.

Rooney opened the lowest drawer in his desk, took out his gun, and searched for his holster. He rarely wore it, even though he knew he should. Now he strapped it on, checked the weapon, and slipped it into place. He shrugged back into his jacket and was just about to walk out when Bean returned, still eating his sandwich, his mouth bulging. "We got no record in any Vice section regarding Steven Janklow. This is the second time I've checked, so now I've asked them to go back in Records to 1986, the year of the first murder. There's nothing on him or the Thorburns. Nothing. Even if there had been a possible charge, we'd at least have a record or it would have been in the system—that includes if charges were dropped for any reason, like string-pulling."

Rooney passed Bean, reeking of bourbon. "You got your peppermints handy?" he asked him, guessing what he was thinking from the expression on his face.

"You going home?" Bean asked.

"Nope, I'll call in. I need some fresh air."

"Okay. Want me to do anything about your friend? She still hasn't been brought in, they got a couple of squad cars out looking for her."

"I'll bring her in. Just hang out here until I find her."

"Don't you want me to drive?"

Rooney turned on him. "No, I fucking don't. Just stay put— I'll call in soon as I find her!"

He slammed the door so hard the blinds rattled.

•   •   •

Lorraine asked Rosie to wait. As she walked up the driveway to Andrew Fellows's home, it was almost one o'clock and another bright, cloudless day, but at least there was a slight breeze. In the daylight the house appeared smaller, with virtually the entire yard taken up by the swimming pool, leaving no space for a lawn, just potted plants. She rang the bell a couple of times before Dilly answered. She was wearing a nightgown with a shawl wrapped around her shoulders.

"I'm sorry, are you sick?"

"No, didn't feel like getting up today, I was just watching TV. Come on in, I'll get us some tea. Andrew is at work, I suppose, but sometimes he comes home for lunch. Is he expecting you?"

Lorraine sat down within sight of Brad's portrait. Dilly joined her on the sofa, curling her feet up beneath her. "He went to meet the FBI agents at the station. He gets talking and then he forgets the time."

Lorraine smiled. She had hoped he would be here because she had called his office and he was not there.

"Dilly, tell me about Brad."

She giggled. "Oh, another conquest, is it? Well, just let me warn you, he's some hunk but don't get too interested. He's got a terrible reputation—screws them, sometimes marries them, but then he gets icy, and ditches them. He's ditched more than I can count."

The kettle boiled and she went to make the tea. The kitchen was sectioned off from the room, all pine cupboards and white-tiled floor, a bar counter dividing the kitchen from the room with stools on the kitchen side. Dilly looked over and saw Lorraine studying the painting.

"He had it all, you see, given to him on a plate. Loaded and handsome, always a fatal combination." Dilly brought out cups and saucers, then opened a biscuit tin. "He's so glamorous, motor racing—God, he looks so sexy in those white jumpsuits. Now he's writing thrillers, or whatever he calls them, but he'll never finish a book, I know him . . . Do you like sugar or honey?"

"What about his family?" Lorraine asked.

"Oh, you *are* hooked—or are you seeing cash registers?"

"Just interested."

"I bet. His family is mega-rich. I'll tell you something weird. His brother—he's got an older brother, did I tell you?"

"No, go on . . ."

Dilly carried around the tea tray and placed it down on the table in front of the sofa. She poured them each a cup, passing one to Lorraine, and then snuggled back down next to her, curling her feet up. She loved to gossip. "Well, I only met him once. They're such opposites. He's quite small whereas Brad is tall and well built, dark. Steven's blondish, wears glasses, sort of prissy. I only saw him for a few minutes when I was up at their house. They have God knows how many homes—well, Brad does, he was left everything. They had different fathers—obvious, I suppose, they've got different names, right? Janklow was her first husband, well-off, I think, but it was Thorburn who had the big bucks. She was a great socialite, beautiful, pampered, and I think she was in the movies at one time, very early on. She's ancient."

"And she's still alive?" Lorraine spooned in the honey, and stirred her tea.

"Oh, yeah, in some expensive home. I've never met her but I think Andrew has. But he's useless, I ask him all these questions about his patients and he won't gossip, but I love it."

"She was a patient?"

"Oh, no—well, I don't think so. I just knew he met her once and she sometimes stays with Brad. She has this bedroom, very Greta Garbo-style, different from Brad's taste. His part of the house is all macho wood and the bare essentials."

Lorraine was getting impatient.

"How long will Andrew be, do you think?"

Dilly shrugged. "You're asking me? I'm not his secretary, he just comes and goes when he pleases, but most days he comes home for lunch. What time is it now?"

Lorraine looked at her watch, it was one-thirty. Dilly sipped her tea, watching her like a cat. "Do you want another cup of tea? Look, if it's important, I can call his office."

Lorraine smiled. "No, no, I'll wait a while longer if it's no trouble to you."

"It's no trouble to me. Have another cup of tea."

Brad offered Fellows a glass of wine, which he refused. They walked into the living room.

"What did you want to talk to me about?"

Fellows sat down, unsure how to begin. "Is Steven home?"

Brad looked perplexed. "He may be. He keeps to his part of the house. Why do you want to know?"

Fellows fiddled with the fringe on the sofa. "Just something I overheard today. I was at the station—FBI agents, they've been brought in to oversee these murders. Have you read about them?"

Brad sipped his wine. "Be hard not to. Are you working on them?"

Fellows tugged frantically at his ear. "They brought up this guy Norman Hastings, one of the victims. Did we talk about him?"

Brad leaned back. "I don't remember."

"Well, I suggested they dig deep—maybe they'd missed something. As it turned out, I was right." He smiled. "He was a cross-dresser, you know, a transvestite."

"And?" Brad said softly.

Fellows looked away. "I don't think I was supposed to hear it, about this Hastings guy. Did you know he parked his car at your garage?"

Brad frowned. "Somebody mentioned it to me, but I have no idea who parks there half the time. It's supposed to be just for the employees."

"Have you been questioned?"

"No, but the police have been talking to all the employees—in fact, I was meaning to talk to you about it . . . because I'm trying to write something, and given the work you do with the Homicide Squad, I thought maybe you could help me."

Fellows stood up. "Maybe I'll have that glass of wine, after all."

"Sure," Brad said easily. He uncoiled his perfect body, picked up his glass, and walked out toward the kitchen. Fellows followed. As he passed the stairs he looked upward, instinctively, as if he knew someone was looking down at him, but there was no one in sight. "Is Steven home?" Fellows asked again. Brad poured two glasses of Chablis and offered one to him. "Just thought I saw someone on the landing."

"You asked that already, Andrew! You tired or something? You never did say why you came. Are you canceling our squash game?"

"Oh, no, that's fine, it was—"

Brad walked ahead of him. "Remember the last time we played? That woman was waiting to see you—Lorraine Page?

Maybe I should have told you, she came here.'' Brad was sprawled on the sofa again. "She was looking for someone who lives in the neighborhood."

Fellows sipped his wine, wondering if he should tell his friend what he had come to say. He couldn't make up his mind.

Brad balanced his glass on the sofa arm, twisting the stem between his fingers. "Actually, she's rather attractive, has an odd way of looking at you, sort of sly but not . . ."

Fellows drained his glass and stood up. "Stay away from her, she's bad news. She's not what she seems."

"What's that supposed to mean? I thought she was a friend of yours. She was at your place for dinner, wasn't she?"

Fellows decided he'd tell Brad, whether it was ethical or not. "She's a hooker and a police informer. She's also wanted in connection with these murders. But there's something else. . . . The cops were discussing your garage and the fact that Hastings parked his car there."

"They don't suspect anyone at the garage, do they?"

"They were discussing your brother. Apparently he knew Hastings. He was found dead in his own car so maybe someone at your place had access to it. Look, I'm just repeating what I overheard. Maybe you can tip Steven off, talk to him about it."

Brad walked Fellows to the front door. "He hasn't mentioned any of this to me, and we're not exactly best friends, but thanks, I'll have a word with him."

Fellows stood on the porch. "This is advice, Brad. I'd stay clear of Lorraine Page if she should make contact. The lady may be desirable but her past life isn't."

Brad watched Fellows drive away. He stood there wishing his friend had given him the full story, but then he saw Steven standing on the second-floor balcony. Brad banged the gate with his fist and walked back into the house. He ran up the stairs two and three at a time until he reached his brother's quarters. He tried the door; it was locked. "Steven, open the door—I know you're in there so open the fucking door. I want to talk to you." He waited, hit the door again, but there was silence. "Steven, open the door or I'll get the master keys. *Steven?*"

He pressed his ear to the door. He could hear water running. He ran and got the spare keys. He returned to his brother's bedroom and slipped in the key. He walked inside, barefoot, leaving the door wide open behind him.

As Brad looked around the immaculate room, he could still hear the sound of the bath water running. He'd wait, Steven would have to come out sometime. The room was different from his own, but similar to his mother's—floral drapes at the windows, a canopied bed with swathes of silk caught in a coronet and tied with large satin bows. The carpet was oyster pink, as were the silk-covered walls. The stereo equipment was built into banks of mirrors; the television section was mirror-fronted to match the rows of built-in closets. Steven's tapes and videos were neatly stacked and listed in alphabetical order, hundreds of CDs, old records, and tapes. Brad caught his own reflection over and over again. There was no corner of the room in which you couldn't see yourself. It was all elegant, expensive, even tasteful, if you liked that kind of décor. Brad hated it.

He looked over the dressing table—more fitting for a woman than a man, with jars of creams and perfumes in neat symmetrical rows, silver-backed mirrors and hairbrushes, and rows of silver-framed photographs. Brad had entered this room only two or three times and now he looked around slowly, taking everything in. He opened one closet door after another to reveal rows of linen jackets and a vast array of shirts, each one covered in plastic. The shoes were packed in boxes with color coordinations labeled. There were racks of ties, silk handkerchiefs, even straw hats, a few he recognized as having belonged to his father.

He could hear the bath water draining away. He knocked, waited a moment, then knocked again. The softly playing classical music was turned off.

"Come on, Steven, I have to talk to you. It's important." He punched the bathroom door. "Okay, fucking stay in there. You can come to me, I'm not waiting any longer. But you'd better come and see me, you hear? That was Andrew Fellows, my friend who's the UCLA professor. He's working with the police. He had something to tell me about you, about that Norman Hastings friend of yours. If you want to know what he told me, then . . . screw you, Steven!" Brad waited another few minutes, then spotted the briefcase, placed neatly at the side of the dressing table. He picked it up and tried to open it, but it was locked. He looked over the table and found a thin letter opener. He pried open the lock, removed a file of papers, and then replaced the briefcase. His brother had still not made a sound, so he left.

Two minutes later the bathroom door opened and Janklow walked out draped in a silk dressing gown, naked beneath it. He bolted the bedroom door, to ensure his privacy, then walked casually toward the dressing table and sat on the small frilled stool. He opened a bottle of lotion and began carefully to cream his hands. Every move was studied, each finger massaged, each perfectly manicured nail scrutinized. He used Q-tips to wipe around the cuticles and then looked along his row of clear polishes, choosing one and carefully painting each nail. His hands were steady; he was calm. He slipped off the robe and stood naked, surveying himself in the mirrors. His slim body was still pinkish from the bath, a pale, white-skinned body, but muscular. He never went in the sun, unlike Brad—he never did any of the things Brad did, not as a child or as a man.

He began to do his yoga exercises, studying every posture in his mirrors. His testicles were small, like marbles, and his penis flaccid. He knelt forward, squeezing his thighs together, pushing his penis out of sight and then watched his reflection as he knelt upward, seemingly devoid of any sex organ. His nipples were erect, pink, and he slowly massaged his breasts, breathing deeply. The only blemish on his hairless skin was the mark at the side of his neck. He had used oil of arnica, even makeup to disguise the toothmarks of the bitch who had bitten him. He had been desperate to find her again. She could hurt him much more than the bite had. He breathed deeply, not wanting to become agitated.

It was almost over, he was almost free. It had been a terrible long nightmare. He had even thought of suffocating his mother just so she would never find out; he had done it all for her, because he loved her with an all-consuming passion. But they were not like mother and son, they were one. That was why he couldn't kill her. He couldn't bear the thought of losing her, just as he could not tolerate her knowing about him.

Brad stood in his mother's room. He wasn't sure why he had come here, possibly because it reminded him of Steven's. He stood at her dressing table looking at the photographs and then slipped his finger into the small drawer in the center. Everything here had a place and not one perfume bottle was out of line. He sniffed a cut-glass stopper and recognized the same smell from his brother's room. As he was about to replace the stopper, he accidentally knocked over the bottle, which tipped into the open drawer, perfume splashing over the leather jewel boxes. He swore, snatched a tissue from the white-embroidered box, and dabbed at the leather, then took out the large, fan-styled box to make sure it was not stained. He clicked it open. The velvet-lined case that had once contained four fabulous ropes of perfectly matched pearls was empty. He closed it and then opened the other boxes. All were empty.

He whistled softly as he shut the drawers. He checked that the perfume bottle was once more in line with the others and walked out.

Just as Brad left his mother's room, he heard the front door close. "Steven? *Steven?*" He ran down the stairs just in time to see his brother drive out in the Mercedes.

Lorraine hadn't seen it coming. She was totally taken aback when Dilly Fellows, midway through talking about Brad Thorburn, burst into tears. She sobbed loudly, hands over her face. "This is so stupid, but just talking about him hurts so much because I love him. I don't know what to do about it sometimes. I can usually control it but sometimes it just bursts out of me."

Lorraine stood up. "Look, I'd better go. My friend's waiting outside."

Dilly sniffed. "You should have brought her in. I don't know what's happened to Andrew and I'm so sorry about this, I don't know what you must think of me. Andrew doesn't know. Oh, God, you won't tell him, will you?" Lorraine shook her head. "He's got no idea. He knows I had a passion for Brad—well, it was obvious to begin with—but he doesn't know just how much I care. I think about him all the time, I make up excuses to call him. I'm like a teenager, but I like it. I like this feeling. It's like a pain, it's almost sexual it gets so intense, and then when he comes here with Andrew, I have an orgasm just looking at him. I do, I honestly do, and it's an incredible feeling. I put it back into my work when he's been around, I can paint for hours. Did he touch you?"

Lorraine felt more and more uneasy. Dilly was overbright, overexcited; her voice was verging on hysterical. "Why did you ask me all those questions about him? Did you fuck him?"

Lorraine picked up her purse. "No, I didn't, and I have to go. Thank you for the tea." She couldn't wait to get back to the car.

"Jesus, you took your time, I was just about to come in and get you. A few minutes, you said," Rosie growled. She was hungry and it was way past lunchtime.

Lorraine apologized. "That woman is freaky. I really liked her at first—she seemed so warm and friendly, so totally normal."

Rosie started the car. "Where to next, we can't go home and I've been thinking, I could be arrested for wheeling you around, couldn't I?"

Lorraine hesitated. "You're right, maybe you should get on a bus."

"Oh come on, I was joking, I want to stay with you."

Lorraine shook her head. "No, Rosie, you go home. Stop at the next bus stop, I mean it."

"Great, some fucking partner I am, I'm not in on anything. I don't know what you're talking about half the time."

Lorraine jerked her thumb back at the house. "That was the wife of the guy the cops brought in to help solve the case. He's a professor of psychology, working for Rooney. If you ask me, he should do some work on his wife. She just blurted out she was infatuated with Brad Thorburn, I couldn't believe it."

Lorraine knew she would go and see him, as soon as she got rid of Rosie, and it was strange, she had a dull, low ache in the pit of her stomach. She wanted to see him, but it wasn't just about the case. She wouldn't admit that to herself, or that she was feeling sexually aroused. She refused even to contemplate that.

Rosie was still pissed off about being dumped at a bus stop, and still complaining bitterly about being left out of everything as Lorraine drove off.

•   •   •

Andrew Fellows let himself in and called his wife. She didn't answer. In the kitchen, he noticed the two cups and saucers left on the draining board. He found her in the bedroom, huddled beneath the duvet, the TV on. "You had a visitor?" She looked at him, eyes red-rimmed. "You okay?"

"I'm fine. It's a sad movie."

"Who was here?"

Dilly sat up. "Your friend Lorraine Page. She wanted to speak to you—waited ages." She swallowed and her eyes filled with tears. "She asked me questions about Brad and then she left. She had a friend waiting, she said."

Fellows sat on the edge of the bed. "Just tell me exactly what she said, what questions she asked."

Dilly reached for the remote and switched off the TV. She repeated everything Lorraine had said but deleted any reference to her own outburst. Fellows went into his den. He called the police station.

Brad sifted through the file he had taken from Steven's room, examining bank statements and other private papers. He knew it had been going on for a considerable time—it was obvious from the receipts. Steven, meticulous as ever, had carefully recorded each sale of every item he had removed from his mother's jewelry drawer. The four strands of pearls had been sold for five thousand dollars, although they were insured for three times that amount. The diamond rings, necklaces, the ruby and sapphire bracelets, the topaz ring—all had been listed but with a dash alongside each item. Brad calculated that his brother had accrued over a hundred and fifty thousand dollars, yet he had not paid it into his own bank accounts—unless he had another one somewhere.

Brad was aware that on his mother's death she would leave the jewels to Steven. But that was no reason for him to have been selling them off without her permission—unless she knew about it. It was just after three. He decided against calling the nursing home: better to face Steven first when he came home. He replaced the papers in the briefcase, then went back into his mother's room. One of the closet doors was slightly ajar and he opened it to close it properly. He looked at the rows of her wigs. He found them distasteful, as he found everything about her obsessive drive to retain her youth. The closet was crammed with flimsy gowns and negligees, not fitting for a woman in her seventies. Brad was sweating from the overheated room and the cloying smell of her perfume. He felt slightly nauseous, also guilty. She had always hated anyone touching her things. She herself had never liked to be touched. How often as a child he had run to embrace her, but she had always held up her perfectly manicured hands as if she was scared to be held by her own child. It had been different with Steven. If anything, she had favored him because he was so much older than Brad. She pointedly preferred his company. Brad remembered his father in one of his rages shouting up the stairs, as she stood quivering in pale lime chiffon, that if she didn't want him, he would find other women who did. "Other women?" She had leered down at his father, her perfect red lips drawn back in a snarling smile. "No decent woman would come within a mile of you. Whores! You can only get a whore and that's because you pay her!"

"You'd know all about that, wouldn't you? Janklow picked you out of the chorus line. You were a ten-cent stripper—you think I don't know? Movie star? The closest you ever got to a real movie was paying at the ticket window."

She would throw things, she would rant and rage at him whenever he referred to her first husband, or her chorus line days, and he would roar with laughter, enjoying her fury, her humiliation, encouraging Brad to listen, warning him never to marry someone else's used goods. She would become so hysterical that she would smash mirrors and china, and lock herself into her room for days on end. The only person who was ever able to calm her was Steven.

Back in his own room, Brad lay down, looking up at his mirrored ceiling. The mirror remained, a legacy from Tom Thorburn. Brad wondered if the other legacy was his predilection for young blondes. He had certainly married enough of them. But of late, like his father, he chose to go with whores rather than get involved in yet another relationship. It was rare for women to say no to him: on the polo field, at the racetrack, they were always available, like clutches of twittering starlings.

That was why he had liked Lorraine Page. She had said no but she had almost said yes. Just thinking about her gave him an erection. He was no longer worrying about his brother or

what Andrew Fellows had hinted at. He was even able to put
aside the Norman Hastings query, simply because he felt sure
that the reason Steven had been so secretive was because of
his systematic siphoning off of their mother's jewelry. He
wished he had just come out and asked Andrew for Lorraine's
phone number.

But even his relationship with Andrew was a mess because
his wife was always wanting Brad to screw her, and she wasn't
the first—a lot of his friends' wives wanted him. Some he had
obliged but it always ended badly.

His erection subsided as he looked over his life. He had
wasted it, he knew that. Even his attempt at writing a novel
was futile. He had millions at his disposal, his vast charitable
donations taken care of by trustees, but there never seemed
any point. He hated what he had become: a dilettante—worse,
a clone of his father.

Rosie was back in Pasadena, just crossing from Orange Grove
onto Marengo at the intersection, when Rooney screeched to
a halt alongside her.

"Where's Lorraine? This is important, Rosie, there's a warrant out for her arrest. If you know where she is you'll be
doing her a favor because they got every available officer out
looking for her and if she resists arrest, she could get hurt."
Rosie said nothing and Rooney got out of the car. "Come on,
sweetheart, where is she? If you care anything about her you'll
tell me."

Rosie looked down the street. "She's gone off in the car."

Rooney asked her for the license plate number. Rosie was
in a quandary but then she said truthfully she couldn't remember it as it was only a rental. She'd said enough now and
continued down the sidewalk. Rooney walked beside her.

"Where you going?"

"I got to go home, feed my cat."

Rooney told her to stay in the apartment. If Lorraine came
back she was to call him immediately. "You sure you don't
know where she is or where she was heading? When did you
last see her?"

Rosie shouted that she'd told him all she knew and she
hadn't seen Lorraine since early morning.

"So what's the name of the rental firm?"

Rosie sighed. He asked whose name the car was rented in and she admitted it was in her name, and came from W-rent W-rent Wreckers. She hurried to her apartment and quickly climbed the stairs, let herself in, and crossed over to watch him from the window. Rooney parked opposite the house, watching her. She opened the window and yelled out to him, "I don't know where she is!"

Rooney looked up to the window, dialing on his portable. He'd get the car's license plate number soon enough—put Bean on it.

Bean listened as Fellows reported that Lorraine Page had been at his home and had talked to his wife. He was very agitated and angry. Bean said he would send someone right over.

"She's not here now, she's left."

When Rooney was put through to Bean at the station, he told him about the call. Lorraine had been with Fellows's wife, and he seemed very distressed about it. Rooney took the address; he was on his way. He told Bean to trace the license number of the rental car and get it circulated. It would only be a matter of time before they brought her in.

Lorraine was parked a few houses up from the Thorburn mansion. She sat in the car, half hidden from the street, pondering whether or not to go in. She wished Rosie was with her. She'd feel safer having someone waiting so if anything did happen Rosie could help, maybe even call Rooney. Just thinking about Rooney made her nervous—he probably had the state police out looking for her by now. She opened her purse and checked her face, licked her lips, then combed her hair. . . . Abruptly she snapped her purse closed, told herself she was being stupid, that he might not even be home.

Lorraine got out of the car, locked it, and looked up and down the empty road with its palms and bushes and sweet perfumed trees. She hadn't seen a single car while she'd been parked there. She walked slowly toward the big double-barred gates. The house could only partly be seen, and what she could see looked peacefully silent; the faint sound of a lawn mower buzzed from somewhere on the grounds. She pressed the intercom at the side of the gates. She rang again as the dog appeared. He barked and then stood looking at her through the gates. Brad answered.

"Who is it?"

"Lorraine Page." She was fazed when he laughed. He didn't say anything else, but the gates clicked open. It took a few more moments walking up the pathway before she saw the house and Brad Thorburn. He stepped out onto the porch and leaned against one of the thick white posts, a glass of wine in his hand. He was smiling, watching her as she walked slowly toward him. She was so tall and slim, and the sun made her hair seem more white than blond. She wore high-heeled slingback shoes, a straight skirt with a slit to one side, revealing a fraction of her thigh. The jacket was loose, a little too large, and beneath it she wore a white shirt, open at the neck. She wore no jewelry and it didn't look as if she had on any makeup. She carried only a clutch purse, in her right hand. As she reached the first white stone step of the porch, she tilted her head to one side. The sun was bright, almost blinding her, but Brad could see very clearly, even from this distance, the scar on her cheek, and her eyes like glittering blue stones.

"I was just thinking about you," he said quietly. She wasn't expecting him to be so gentle, just as she didn't expect him to hold out his hand to her. It felt strong, gripping hers tightly.

"Do you know the police are looking for you?" he said, not taking his eyes from hers, trying to see what she wanted from him.

"Yes, but I have to talk to you."

He guided her toward the hallway, his hand now at her elbow, with a firm but not threatening hold. They walked into the drawing room. He remained at the door, finishing his wine, watching her.

"Is your brother home?"

"No."

"Are there any servants here?"

"Just the housekeeper, she'll be leaving at four." He ran his hand over his neck to the back of his hairline. The polo shirt opened a little and she could see part of his shoulder.

Silent, she stared hard at him and his eyes slid away, as if embarrassed by her clear, direct gaze. She opened her purse and took out her cigarettes, flicked open the pack, and placed one between her lips. "Do you have a light?"

He came in and put down his empty glass. She thought he

was going to pick up a table lighter but instead he came close, took the cigarette out of her mouth, and tossed it aside. He then slipped his hand to the small of her back and pressed her to him. In her high heels she was almost as tall as he was. He kissed her and let his hand fall to her buttocks, pulling her even closer to him. He kissed her again and she responded, her tongue traced his mouth and she moved back just a fraction, taking his free hand to place on her heart. She was trembling. He scooped her up into his arms—she was so incredibly light—and carried her with ease out of the drawing room and up the stairs. One of her shoes fell off, then the other, as she rested against him. She was crying, her head buried in his shoulder. He had never known such sweetness, and by the time he laid her down on his bed, she was sobbing. He just held her, rocking her, soothing her, kissing her hair, kissing the tears that poured down her cheeks. He looked up and saw himself cradling her as if she were a child. He was scared of his own tenderness toward this woman, who both excited him sexually and aroused emotions he had not thought himself still capable of having. His arms tightened around her, until the weeping subsided and she lifted her lips to him. This time his kiss was not gentle but passionate, hard and crushing, and she responded.

Steven Janklow walked into the house. He looked into the spotless kitchen. The housekeeper had already left. He picked up his brother's empty wineglass, took it into the kitchen, and put it carefully in the dishwasher. He lifted the lids of two covered dishes left out for dinner. He was hungry, but he didn't know what he felt like eating; his appetite had never been good, he'd never liked rich foods and disliked eating in front of people; that had grown worse over the past few years. If he felt people were watching him he'd become very agitated, especially when he was dining out, which was rare, very rare these days. He'd always mistrusted restaurants, hotels even—full of the unwashed humanity, his mama used to say.

He started up the stairs and stopped. He saw the shoes, first one then the other. They offended him. He held them in disgust, cheap shoes, and carried them up the stairs, turning toward his brother's quarters. He was just about to put them outside his door—he'd done it before, not just with shoes, but brassieres, skirts, and, more often than not, panties—when, as he drew closer, he could hear a high-pitched moan, like a mewing. It made him cringe. They all sounded alike, all his brother's whores—even his wives. Janklow had intended simply to leave the shoes but the door was ajar. He put out his hand to close it, averting his eyes in case he got so much as a glimpse of their writhing naked bodies. The woman moaned again, and even though he didn't want to look, he couldn't help himself.

Her face was tilted toward him, eyes closed, mouth half open. She was astride his brother, her body like a young boy's rather than a woman's—that, perhaps, was what had made him stare. As she moved, thrusting forward, Janklow gasped, quickly covering his mouth with his hand. He didn't shut the door; he didn't dare make a sound as he backed away silently. Not until he was safely along the corridor did he turn and run. He clung to the toilet rim as he vomited, retching with terror, his whole body breaking out in an icy sweat. He couldn't be mistaken, it wasn't possible. There couldn't be two women with that face, that scar. It was *her*—the woman he had picked up, the woman who had bitten his neck until he bled like a pig.

He ran cold water over his face to try to calm himself, but his hands trembled violently. His mind screamed out questions. Why was she here? How could she have traced him here? He tried to control his breathing, stop himself panting. Brad often dragged back whores and cheap bitches, but he would never have believed his brother would have sunk this low, not with *that* woman—she was disgusting. He flopped on his bed, saying to himself it was just a coincidence, it was that and nothing more, just a terrible coincidence. He rolled over, clenching his fists, trying not to break down and weep with fear. It was then that he saw his briefcase, knew at a glance that it had been moved, and worse, that it had been opened.

A thought struck him. He got up and went to his mother's room, where he checked her jewelry drawer. He knew that the boxes had been taken out—they were all in the wrong order. Someone had been in here and into his own room, checking him out. Was it Brad? Or was it that woman? He returned to his bedroom and bolted the door. He had to get rid of her. If she was a call girl, if Brad had done his usual, brought her back to the house, he would just have to wait. They never stayed all night. When he saw her leave, he would follow. It was simple. He would kill her as he had almost done before, only this time he would make sure. He looked at his bedside clock, it was almost five. If she was like the others, she would probably be leaving after an hour or so to start work at night. Walking the streets as she had been doing when she had picked him up. He remembered how she had rested her hand on the car door, asked if he needed her help.

Janklow crept around the house until he found Lorraine's purse; he opened and searched it. She had little money, no cards or checkbook. All she had in her purse was a pack of cigarettes, an old lipstick, a comb, matches, and, he smiled to himself, car keys. The key ring had the name of the rental company on a cheap plastic tag. He pursed his lips; he hadn't seen a car in the driveway and wondered if she'd left it outside on the street.

He left the house, skirting the driveway. He saw Bruno look up and wag his tail, and hoped he wouldn't start barking. He stood, frozen to the spot, until the dog lowered his head. The gardener was on the other side of the tennis courts, using some kind of spray, intent on his work. Janklow cracked opened the gate and walked out, sure that no one had seen him. There was no one on the street and no cars passed him.

He saw a parked car a short distance from the house. He walked casually toward it, turned back the way he had come, and then looked the other way as he tried the driver's door with the key he had found in the slut's purse. It was her car. He was feeling better now, more in control, already working out in his mind how he would kill her, because she had to die.

Rooney rang Andrew Fellows's doorbell, keeping his finger on the button. Fellows opened up and sighed when he saw who it was. "I said everything on the phone to Lieutenant Bean. I didn't think it was necessary for anyone to come out, especially not now. She was here before lunch."

Rooney smiled. "Sorry about this. I just wanted to go over a few things, and I'd like to speak to Mrs. Fellows."

They went into the kitchen where Dilly was sitting. She looked upset, tear-stained. She repeated everything to Rooney, again without any mention of her outburst to Lorraine about Brad Thorburn.

"Can I speak to you alone, Professor?" Rooney asked.

"Of course. Dilly, this won't take long."

Fellows took Rooney into his den. He looked a little sheepish.

"You know the Thorburns?" Rooney asked.

"Yes."

"You didn't mention it this morning."

"No one asked me if I did or didn't know them."

"When you left the station, did you come straight back home?"

Fellows flushed a deep red. "No, I did not. I . . . I went to the Thorburn house."

Rooney stared hard in disbelief as Fellows told him what he had said to Brad. He was obviously ashamed and knew he had behaved unethically. Rooney listened silently, then asked for Thorburn's address and phone number. He left shortly after, not reprimanding Fellows, not saying much at all.

Fellows found his wife in the bedroom. She was crying again. He stared at her for a moment and then walked out. Not only humiliated but furious now, he dragged Brad's portrait off the wall, smashed it against the open fireplace until the canvas ripped apart and the frame snapped. He stamped on it, then lit the log fire and watched it blaze. He had never felt so angry in his life—angry and bitter, but above all foolish. He hated that most of all. He had just jeopardized his work with the police and doubted he would ever be called upon again.

As the flames slowly destroyed the painting, his anger subsided. Now he felt nothing but humiliation. Brad Thorburn's nakedness had dominated his home and he had allowed it, joked about it, encouraged Brad to visit Dilly. What made it worse was that Brad had known of her instability, which made his affair with her even more of a betrayal. Fellows vowed never to speak to or see him again. He couldn't even stay in this room, even though the painting was no longer hanging on the wall. The vast space where the life-size portrait had hung added insult to injury. He picked up a cup of cold coffee and headed into the den. As he shut the door, he could hear his wife still crying, but he had no intention of discussing Brad with her again. Fellows didn't care if he had screwed her once or twice, it was immaterial. The fact that he had fucked her at all was what mattered.

Fellows found little solace in his den. There were photographs of him and Brad together all over the walls, the two of them fishing, playing baseball, waterskiing in Miami, at squash tournaments, on tennis courts. Brad Thorburn and Andrew Fellows had known each other for many years, had always been competitive with each other as sportsmen. In the women stakes, Fellows had never moved in Brad's social sphere, had never wanted to, could never have been any competition there. No man could, not with Brad's looks and wealth.

Fellows sat at his desk. He drew the file on the murder investigation closer and began to go over every detail once again. He had been so sure that Brad Thorburn could have no connection with the killings, but what if he had been wrong? What if he had missed something? If he had, he was determined to find it. It made him feel better. He wanted to hurt Brad Thorburn—better still, destroy him.

Rooney reached his car and picked up the radio to tell Bean he was now on his way to the Thorburns.

"You going to interview Janklow?" Bean asked.

"Nope, I think Lorraine Page is trying to though, so get a squad car out there."

"You going to arrest her?"

"You bet I'm gonna arrest that two-faced bitch."

SEVENTEEN

They lay naked side by side, the sheet loosely covering their bodies. She was on her stomach, her eyes closed. Brad drew the sheet back and ran his hand gently over her body. "How did you get these marks?" He leaned up on his elbow to trace the scar on her face. "And this?"

She pulled away from him, and suddenly stood up, swishing the entire sheet from the bed, wrapping it around herself. "I'd better get dressed."

He remained naked on the bed as she crossed the room. Trailing the sheet, she started to pick up her clothes. Skirt in one hand, she looked around. "Where are my shoes?"

Brad got up and opened a closet. He took out a white caftan and dragged it on over his head. "They must be downstairs. I'll get them." He stood behind her and wrapped his arms around her, kissing the nape of her neck. Then he frowned and brushed the short hair at the nape of her neck upward. "Jesus Christ, how did you get this one?"

The scar, still pink and raised, zigzagged across her hairline.

She tried to move away but he gripped her tightly. "Why don't you answer me? Who did this to you?"

She tried to release herself but he held her tighter. "I need to get dressed."

He let go of her shoulders. "I'll be downstairs."

"Don't go, not yet, we have to talk, the reason I came here."

Brad sighed. "You want to talk but if I ask you a question you refuse to answer. So you go ahead, you talk." His face was tight with anger. He had thought she had come to see him, be with him. She continued to gather her clothes as he sat waiting.

"Look, if it makes it any easier I know you're a whore, you told me that yourself. Is it money you want?"

She moved so fast and it was so unexpected that he did nothing to defend himself. The slap was hard and it hurt. He rubbed his cheek and laughed.

"I didn't come here for what we just did." She stepped back, her fists clenched. He reached out his hand to her but she wouldn't take it. She began to pace up and down, the sheet trailing on the floor. She stopped, head bowed, and slowly, almost as if he were watching her in slow motion, she lifted her chin and tilted her head to one side, as her tongue slowly passed over her lips. She murmured something. He didn't catch what it was she said, she seemed to be trying to set something free. He saw her breathe in deeply; one moment she was frailty itself and astonishingly beautiful, and the next, as she tossed her head back, she became boyish, as if she were angry with herself, tightening the sheet around her slender body. Her shoulders lifted slightly when at last she spoke. "The scars I got from times when I was on the streets. I used to get drunk, I don't know what I did, who I went with. I'm not proud of the hideous things or the cigarette burns, but I never felt them. I didn't care enough about myself to care."

"And now?" he asked.

"Now I just want you to listen—don't interrupt me, just listen."

"Fine." He sat down on the bed and leaned back against the pillows. He was not disgusted by anything she had said—in some ways he didn't really believe it.

"The scar on my cheek was a barroom fight over a bottle of vodka, that's about as much as I can remember, nothing dramatic, nothing romantic. I got it, I live with it, and I was, so I was told, lucky not to lose the sight in my eye. I was a hooker but who I was with and when I don't know. I don't have AIDS, or any venereal disease, just in case you're freaking out. I had myself checked. There's a lot of my life I don't remember. But I do know about this scar, this one at the back of my head, because this is one of the reasons I'm here."

She was very still, standing like a statue in front of him. She wasn't frail or boyish now, but audacious. Her piercing blue eyes were watching him for a reaction, some kind of revulsion that would help her continue, but he gave none. Instead he patted the bed, indicating for her to lie beside him, but she shook her head.

"I used to be a police officer. I was a lieutenant with the Pasadena Homicide Unit."

He half smiled and she glared at him. He lifted his hands in an apologetic gesture. She continued: she was now acting as a paid street informer for Captain Rooney. He had hired her because she knew the girls on the streets and he needed information about the hammer killer. She looked directly at him as he sat up, no longer smiling, but staring at her. Without any emotion she told him about the night she had been attacked, half turning to reveal the scar again. She then told him how she had made an anonymous call to the police describing the man who had attacked her. As she gave Brad the description, she didn't take her eyes off him. If she had described his brother, he showed not the slightest sign of recognition. She explained how she had taken Hastings's wallet. She watched him continuously as she told him about Art Mathews, Didi, and Nula. He listened in silence. He only became tense when she described the cuff links with the S & A logo, the cuff links worn by the man who had attacked her. Brad got off the bed and crossed to a dresser. He opened the top drawer and took out a small leather case. He threw it onto the bed. "Like those?"

Lorraine opened the box and took out the cuff links. She looked at them and nodded. He stood with his hands on his hips and after a moment he asked her to go on. She told him how she had gone to his garage, checked out the workers, checked out the cars in the hangar and had discovered that Norman Hastings had parked his car there the day before he was murdered. That no one could recall what time he had removed it or if he had driven it away himself. Maybe it had been taken by someone working at the company.

Brad returned to the bed. Seeing a muscle working at the side of his neck, she knew he was on edge. His eyes also betrayed him, but he never mentioned his brother, just indi-

cated for her to continue. The more she talked, the more he
realized that, just as she had said, Lorraine Page had not come
to his home for any sexual or romantic reason, but for information. He had misjudged her, misjudged his own prowess,
he didn't know this woman at all; he was becoming more and
more wary of her.

Lorraine detected his anxiety but continued, keeping her
eyes on him constantly. She noticed that it was almost five-
thirty on the bedside clock, and she started to hurry, telling
Brad how she and her friend had photographed each of the
workers and had eliminated them one by one. The reason she'd
come to his house last time had been to continue the elimination process. "You mean me?" he asked.

"Yes, we even took some photographs of your brother, but
none were of much use, so I returned to the Hastings murder,
to his wife, and to the man who had taken photographs of
Hastings. His name is Craig Lyall." She waited a beat but he
didn't react so she continued.

"Norman Hastings was a transvestite."

Brad's eyebrows lifted slightly. It was an open reaction
without guilt. "I think the killer was being blackmailed," Lorraine went on, "and probably for some considerable time. I
think Hastings was, too, but he was only able to pay small
sums that wouldn't alert his wife and family. He was very
protective of them, terrified his private life would be disclosed.
I believe the blackmailers were Art Mathews and Didi, one of
the victims, transsexual. She made up the men for photographs
taken by Lyall. She was then able to tip off Mathews and he,
I think, instigated the blackmail."

She had seen it, just a flicker in his eyes, on the word
"blackmail" but he covered it well, nodding as if he wanted
her to continue. She was combing her hair, watching him in
the mirror. "I wouldn't mind a cup of coffee," she said, and
smiled, then remembered the housekeeper would have left.

He stood up immediately. "I'll make it."

"And I still can't find my shoes."

Brad opened the bedroom door. The shoes were neatly
placed outside. He picked them up, held them by the straps,
and tossed them to her. Lorraine slipped her feet into them
before she remembered they had fallen off as he carried her
up the stairs. Who had placed them outside the door? The
housekeeper? Or someone else? Down in the kitchen, Brad

felt himself start to sweat. Had Steven come home? By now the housekeeper and the gardener would have both left. He looked out of the window and couldn't see the Mercedes. He was sure he hadn't heard Steven return. Maybe he was still out. But if he was, who had put Lorraine's shoes outside the bedroom door? Brad jumped when he heard her footsteps along the marble hall, and then approaching the kitchen.

"Did you say the housekeeper left at four?" she asked nonchalantly, as he ground the coffee beans. She was trying to remember what time they had gone up to the bedroom. "I wondered who left my shoes outside your door."

"Probably Maria, she's obsessively tidy. Am I one of your suspects?" he asked, smiling.

"No, of course not."

He sat on the stool next to her. "Do you need me to call you a cab?"

"No, thank you, I have a car." She sighed, and turned to face him. "Now, can we stop playing games?"

"I'm sorry?"

"Tell me about Steven."

"What about him? Oh, you wanted to see him. Well, he's out, but if you leave me your number I can get him to call you tomorrow."

"Don't protect him, Brad. You'd better be honest with me. That's what I meant about stop playing games. I want to talk about him, I want to see him to eliminate him. It was your brother I came to see—see him face-to-face."

Brad pointed at her. "Why don't *you* stop? You eliminate him? *You?* There's a warrant out for your arrest, as we both know." Brad smiled as he poured the coffee. "You know, I've been fascinated by this monologue you've just delivered. The rogue cop, is that how you see yourself? Maybe the booze did something to your head, Lorraine. I know why you're here."

She was off the stool, heading toward him. "Who told *you* about the warrant out for me? Was it Rooney? Did he speak to your brother?" Brad put his cup down. She had changed suddenly. He thought she was just scared but she said, steadily, "You'd better tell me, Brad. This man has killed nine times. He knows I'm alive and he's looking for me. I'll be next. Who was here and what did he tell you? Was it Captain Rooney?"

"No, it wasn't him, whoever he is."

She glared at him. How he could ever have imagined her as frail? She looked vicious right now. "Who was it? Did he speak to Steven? *For God's sake, stop playing around and tell me who was here.*"

Brad gripped her wrist. "It doesn't matter. What matters to me is you have to stop this right now—whatever you've dug up on Steven, whatever filth you want to make up about him, about this family."

She jerked free. "What are you talking about?"

"How much do you fucking want? You're very clever at what you do, Lorraine. I've had it before, I just didn't think I could be so wrong about someone. So how much and what have you got on Steven? Is that why you took such pains to explain the blackmail by those two whatever-their-names-were?"

"You think I want to blackmail you?"

"Isn't that what you came here for? This family has always been an easy mark, so name your price."

"Nothing you could pay, Brad Thorburn. You just think what you want, I didn't come here for any other reason than to—"

"What?" he interrupted. He was angry but controlled.

"I think your brother is a killer. You won't be able to protect him or buy him out of this. You know why? Because I'll prove it."

Brad sneered. "You expect me to believe a word you've told me? I've had threats from a lot better than you, sweetheart."

"What about your brother? Has he had threats?"

"My brother is no concern of yours. Now get the hell out of my house! Now! Get out!"

He wanted to slap her as she said calmly, "You mind if I get my purse, Mr. Thorburn?"

She didn't hurry out. He could hear her walking across the marble hallway, then, after a moment, the front door slamming behind her. He pressed for the electronic gate to open, waited a moment before he called his lawyer, asking him to contact a Mr. Kophch, tell him it was urgent and that he was to come to the house immediately.

She was almost at the gates, heard them clicking open, when she saw a reflected blue light and knew a patrol car was nearby. She pushed the gate closed and ran to the shrubbery.

She only just made it out of sight as Rooney appeared.

No one responded as he rang and rang the gate's buzzer. Brad at first thought Lorraine had returned. Finally he pressed the intercom.

"Yes?"

"Captain Rooney, police, could I speak to a Mr. Thorburn, please?"

Brad pressed for the gate to reopen, confused. Was Lorraine with him? He went out onto the porch, as Rooney walked up the path and stopped on the bottom step. "Is Steven Janklow home?"

Brad shook his head and introduced himself. Rooney showed his ID and badge and repeated his name as they entered the house, Brad ushering him ahead. As he closed the door, Lorraine watched the interaction from the shrubbery. She felt safer now that Rooney was here. She wanted to get back inside and remembered the door at the back of the house opening onto the small corridor leading up to Brad's bedroom. She crossed her fingers that it would be open and that the alarms had not been turned on.

Rooney looked around the impressive drawing room. Brad offered him a drink but he refused. "Do you know where your brother is, Mr. Thorburn?"

"No, I'm sorry, I don't. What is this about?"

"I think you know. Andrew Fellows stopped by earlier, didn't he? So let's cut the bullshit. Is Lorraine Page here?"

"She was but she left."

"Do you know where she went?"

"No, I don't. I'm surprised you didn't see her, she was here about ten minutes ago."

Rooney's portable phone bleeped. He looked at Thorburn and took it out of his pocket. "Excuse me . . ."

Rooney moved aside, listening to the caller. He turned to face Brad, still listening, then turned his back to him. "I'm inside the house, just have a look around, she was here ten minutes ago."

Rooney slapped his phone off. "Sorry. Okay, Mr. Thorburn, I won't keep you, I'd just like a recent picture of your brother, Steven Janklow."

Rooney wandered over to a grand piano and looked at the

silver-framed photographs. He picked one up and held it out. "This him?"

Brad said no, it was his father. He suggested that the following morning, when he had had time to speak to his brother, he would ask him to let Rooney have a photograph.

"I'd like to take a look at one now," Rooney said stubbornly.

"Is it really necessary?"

"Yes, sir. This is a murder investigation."

Brad disappeared and Rooney stood with his feet planted apart. The call had been to say a second squad car was at the gates. He was on dangerous ground, he knew, standing in the Thorburn household demanding a photograph without any warrant or supporting evidence except Lorraine's theory. He took out his portable again and punched out Lorraine's number. Rosie answered. "It's Rooney. She call in at all?"

"No."

"If she does, get her to contact me. I mean it. This is urgent, Rosie." He put in another call to Bean. Still no sign of Lorraine from any of the street patrols, so he mentioned that Thorburn had said she had left his home only ten minutes before his arrival, that he already had a squad car out checking Beverly Glen. Suddenly, Rooney heard a car on the gravel driveway. He cut off the call, wondering if it was Janklow. His heart sank as he heard voices, Brad saying something about a police officer, a long, whispered conversation. Then Brad walked into the drawing room, with a small, pinstripe-suited, white-haired man wearing rimless glasses and carrying a briefcase.

"This is Alfred Kophch, Captain Rooney."

Rooney shook the pallid little man's hand. It was a very firm grip, which surprised him, and he remained standing. He didn't need to be told who he was, he knew him by reputation: Kophch was one of the most high-powered criminal lawyers in L.A. Kophch sat down and opened his case. "You want a photograph of my client Steven Janklow, is that correct? Do you have a warrant to be on the premises?"

Rooney huffed and said that at this stage of his inquiries he did not require a warrant. It was an informal visit and Brad Thorburn had invited him in.

"Why do you want a photograph of my client?"

Rooney went a deep red. "Elimination purposes."

"I would like to know why no one has contacted Mr. Janklow before, and why you have made an informal house call at
six-thirty P.M."

Rooney sat on the edge of the plush sofa. He was beginning
to sweat, not with nerves but with contained agitation. This
grilling made him feel as if he were the guilty party. He
reached into his pocket and took out a dog-eared envelope with
scrawled dates on the back.

"I would also like to ask—informally—Steven Janklow to
tell me where he was on these dates. As he is not here, you
can bring him with you in the morning, with a photograph."

"Why do you need this photograph if Mr. Janklow is prepared to come in to see you in person?"

"An attack took place in the parking lot of the Glendale
shopping mall. We believe the man that attacked the woman,
our witness, is involved in a series of murders."

Kophch sighed. "So now you're saying that Mr. Janklow is
a suspect for this attack?"

"Possibly."

"And the name of the witness?"

Brad leaned forward. "It's a prostitute called Lorraine Page.
There's a warrant out for her arrest and she's involved in a
blackmail case."

"Is this correct?" snapped Kophch.

Rooney shuffled uneasily. "I am not prepared to disclose
the identity of the witness."

Kophch gave Rooney a warning look. "Blackmail? This is
all getting out of hand, isn't it? I suggest that when you have
charges you wish to relate to my client, you contact my office.
Until then you should leave these premises immediately and I
will forward a complaint to your superiors."

Rooney stood up slowly. "Fine. All I'm trying to do is track
down a killer."

Kophch faced Rooney. "And I am protecting my client. As
you must be aware, the Thorburns are an influential family
and have in the past been subjected to various blackmail
threats and—"

Rooney interrupted, taking a flier, "Then there was the vice
charge against Mr. Janklow that was dismissed. I am aware of
certain activities in the past concerning this family, which is
why I chose to make this an informal visit." Suddenly, he was
on a roll. He could see the hooded looks passing between the

lawyer and Brad, and pushed it further. "However, this is not just a homosexual cruising or pickup, but a murder and one that has been the focus of huge media attention."

Kophch was good. He didn't back off as Rooney had expected but came straight back at him. "And in the late edition of the papers today there was an announcement that a man arrested for these murders had subsequently committed suicide. Are you now saying this man was not the perpetrator of these crimes?"

Rooney sniffed and pulled at his nose. "Possibly not."

His face tight with contained anger, Brad snapped, "It appears that everything and everyone concerned in this investigation is only 'possibly' attached. I suggest that Mr. Kophch should contact your superior and discuss it with him. Now I'd like you to leave my house."

Rooney was shown the door. The gates opened and he stepped through them, hearing them clang shut behind him. As he crossed to his car, he instinctively looked down the street, walked a few yards, and then squinted in the early evening light at the license plate of the parked vehicle. It was Lorraine's. Two uniformed officers were already peering inside. They turned toward him.

"We drove up and down the entire road, we didn't see her, but we ran this through, it's the rental . . ."

Rooney wafted his hand for the officer to shut up. He called his office again to check if Lorraine had been traced. When he heard she hadn't, his heart sank. He walked back to the Thorburn house as the alarm floodlights went out. The house seemed ominously dark and quiet apart from the ground floor, where Thorburn and Kophch must still be talking. The officers asked what he wanted done about Lorraine's car. "Open it up and search it," he snarled. In truth, he wasn't sure about his next move. He felt a dull panic. Where the hell was she?

Lorraine had found the hidden door open and, in darkness, had made her way back up the narrow staircase into Brad's bedroom. The sheet she had worn was on the floor where she'd dropped it, the pillows on the bed where she and Brad had made love were still dented from their bodies.

Lorraine crept along the landing. She had seen Rooney enter, and shortly after the arrival of another man. She didn't know who he was, but was glad of the diversion as she moved silently toward the bedrooms, trying to determine which was Janklow's. Below she could hear Brad talking and the low tones of another male voice, and again, knowing that Rooney was below made her feel safer. She had not seen him leave.

She tried two or three rooms before she entered what she thought must be Janklow's and quietly closed the door. She looked around, checked the bathroom and closets, half hoping to find female clothes or wigs, but there was nothing. She was disappointed. All she wanted was a photograph, something she could take with her, but while there were many of his mother, and of him and Brad as boys, there were none of Janklow as a man. She was about to leave the room when she saw the briefcase.

She picked it up and froze when the locks clicked open loudly, but all she could hear was the low murmur from downstairs. She sifted through the papers as Brad had done, searching for a diary, anything that would give her an insight into Janklow. She found the receipts, all the recorded sales of jewelry, but replaced them and then studied Janklow's bank statements. Again, like Brad, she noted that none of the sums paid to him for the jewels had been put into his accounts. And there was the neat methodical list of jewelry items—maybe these were to be sold? She replaced the briefcase and carefully walked out of the room.

Then she came to the mother's bedroom. She went over to the dressing table and glanced at one silver-framed picture after another. Still none of Janklow as an adult. Lorraine picked up a photo of the glamorous Mrs. Thorburn—so like the woman driving the Mercedes as photographed by Rosie. It looked posed, well lit, and touched up. She turned the frame over, was about to replace it, when she decided to see if the photographer was identified on the back of the picture.

As she opened the frame she almost dropped the glass but caught it in time. A second photograph had been placed inside. At first glance it looked like another photograph of Mrs. Thorburn, but on closer inspection it obviously wasn't. The blond wig was identical, even the diamond necklace, the way the gloved hand rested beneath the sitter's chin. But this sitter was not Mrs. Thorburn. It was someone attempting to look like her, but no amount of airbrushing and touching up could disguise the fact that the sitter was a man.

Lorraine took the photograph and replaced the frame. She checked three more before she found another hidden photograph of the same man. She could not be sure it was Janklow, or even the man who had attacked her, only that it was some man impersonating Mrs. Thorburn. She then heard an ominous creaking sound from above: footsteps pacing up and down.

Quickly, she peered at the back of the photograph and made out a pale imprint of the photographer's name and contact number. It was so blurred that she needed more light, but she suspected it would be either Art Mathews or Craig Lyall. As she eased open the door, she jumped back as she heard voices, louder now. She hurried to the landing to look down to the hall. Should she confront Brad and Rooney together? Or get out, drive herself to the station, and show them the photographs? She crept farther along the landing; they were still talking. Then she heard the same pacing coming from above. Was it Janklow? She hesitated a moment and then moved silently down one stair at a time. She was within yards of the drawing room and she could hear clearly now.

"How serious is this?" she heard Brad ask.

"I have no idea but I will tomorrow, I'll go there personally. It's best not to worry about it. Just leave it to me."

Lorraine was at the foot of the stairs, her heart pounding. She could easily have walked in, admitted being there, but why couldn't she hear Rooney's voice? She turned suddenly, certain someone was watching her. She pressed against the wall, trying to look up the stairs.

"You don't think there's any possibility of there being any truth in all this, do you?" Brad sounded tired. The clipped tone of the other man replied that he doubted there was anything to be worried about, he was fully aware of Steven's sexual preference, and he would make sure it was never disclosed. But he would like to talk to him at the first opportunity. Where was he? Brad had no idea, but knew that he had been home earlier.

Why couldn't she hear Rooney's voice? Wasn't he there? She looked toward the open kitchen doorway, then back to the drawing room, and stepped out of her shoes. She made it to the kitchen entrance and then stopped. She looked up again to the first landing, again sure she had seen someone.

"I'll show you out." It was Brad, and they were walking toward the hall. She dodged into the kitchen, seconds before the two men emerged from the drawing room. Lorraine could see them through a narrow chink between the door and its frame, but she still couldn't see Rooney. He must have already left.

"One thing's bothering me, Alfred. Do you know if Mother instructed Steven to sell off her jewelry?"

"I don't deal with Mrs. Thorburn's private accounts, of course, but I'll get it checked out."

"I'm sure there'll be a reasonable explanation. I know the jewelry will be left to Steven on Mother's death—it's just that I find it strange that neither Mother nor Steven has mentioned it to me."

Lorraine was terrified to move: they were so close. She was hoping and praying that if the front door was going to open, she could get out through the back kitchen door as the security system would still be off. She was headed for it when something Brad said made her freeze.

"This last business, I thought there was no possible way it could get out. You told me there would never be any repercussions and yet that Rooney brought it up as if it was still in the police files."

Kophch again said that he would look into it. Although he had made certain there was no documented evidence left in any police file, he could not guarantee the silence of any officer who had been involved.

"Then pay them off, if necessary, whatever the cost."

Lorraine flattened her body against the wall and inched toward the back door.

"You know, Brad, there's only so much I can do. I cannot in any way jeopardize myself. Do you have any reason to believe that Steven could be involved in this? Because if you do, you must be honest with me. For example, this witness, do you know any more about her?"

Lorraine heard Brad discussing her visit, that he was sure she had only been trying to get money out of him. He sounded angry, his voice rising. "Well, I can have her taken care of if she contacts me again."

He was interrupted. "No, you listen to me. If this woman shows up, you do nothing. Nothing. As I said, I was able to take care of things last time but this is bigger—this is murder—and if the press gets wind that either you or your brother have any involvement, you'll be hounded. Do you understand?

You do not do anything without first discussing it with me!''

Brad walked out onto the porch with his lawyer. They shook hands and Brad watched Kophch get into his car. Then he walked back to the house, pressing the buzzer to open the gates.

Lorraine edged to the kitchen door. She tried the handle: it was open. She said a silent prayer, only to find she was in the garage rather than outdoors as she had expected. She let the door close behind her, just as Brad shut the front door and switched on the alarm circuit.

She looked around the vast dark garage, which had room for at least six cars. At the side of the sliding doors was a row of numbered buttons to open them and above the buttons was an ominous unblinking red dot. She tried to go back the way she had come, but the door was now locked. She was trapped inside the garage.

Rooney was sitting in his car as the lawyer drove past. Kophch stared at him but did not stop. Lorraine's car remained parked along the road; the two officers had found nothing inside. Rooney sat, hoping to see her and becoming more and more worried as the minutes ticked by. He wondered if she was in the house. He even wondered if he should go back in and demand to search the place, but he had no warrant.

The two officers hovered, waiting for instructions. Rooney rubbed his chin; his stubble itched. He was dog tired. ''I think she's maybe up at the house. Williams, go buzz the gate again. Ask if you can look around the grounds. I doubt if he'll let you in but it's worth a try. If that doesn't work, take her car back to the station.''

Lorraine looked around her. A Rolls-Royce Silver Shadow, plus Brad's sports car, two Harley-Davidson motorcycles, a Porsche, and, hidden from her sight at first, the Mercedes. She was sure the garage would be alarmed, like everything else in the house. She looked at the multiple doors, could see wires threaded everywhere. It was like a fortress. No way would she be able to get out that way; she'd have to return to the house. Then she heard the ringing of a distant doorbell. The garage doors began to slide open. She ducked behind a car as they began to whir and grind, pulling back. She peered up and could see Brad standing right outside the garage with a uniformed police officer.

"Take a look around in here and then wherever else you like but not in the house."

She could see Brad's bare feet beneath the cars, and the dark trouser legs of the police officer above his black rubber-soled shoes.

"I'll show you around the back way," Brad said. He hadn't expected to see Steven's car there and it had freaked him. He was sure his brother wasn't in, but he covered his initial re-action by quickly offering to show the officer the gardens.

Lorraine waited until they were out of sight before she dashed out of the garage toward the front lawn and ran flat out until she reached the open gates.

Rooney and an officer were standing by her car, Rooney leaning forward for his cigarette to be lit. She headed to his car. It was open and she threw herself inside, onto the back-seat. Rooney inhaled and let the smoke drift out of his nostrils. He checked the time again; it was almost seven o'clock. His stomach grumbling for food, he plodded back to the gates as Officer Williams appeared, a young, fresh-faced boy, who worked out. His muscles rippled beneath his pristine cop shirt and badge and he edged his nightstick away from his leg.

"There's no one on the grounds, Captain, and Mr. Thorburn wants to lock up for the night. What do you want me to do? This place is alarmed all over, he's standing with his hand on the buzzer, says we can't go into the house."

Rooney waddled toward him. "You didn't see anything?"

"Been around the back, summerhouse, tennis courts, swim-ming pool—checked all over. She's not on the grounds."

Rooney went back to his car but he couldn't just walk away. As the two officers stood in the road waiting to know what he wanted them to do, he reached in for his radio.

"Don't let them take me in, Bill," Lorraine said quietly from the backseat. "Please don't."

Rooney turned back to the officers, but they hadn't heard her. "One of you take her car into the holding bays, the other follow. I'll see you back at the station."

Rooney got into his car and watched the two men split up, one going for Lorraine's car, the other getting a set of pliers out of the patrol car. Rooney started his engine and pulled away, leaving them as they decided who should drive Lorraine's car. Williams laughed as they reached down to fix the wires to start the engine. He said it had been a long time since he'd been caught doin' this.

"You go first, Rambo, I'll follow."

Rooney didn't even head up Mulholland but pulled over about a mile short of it. She'd have felt better if he'd slammed on the brakes and yelled at her, but instead he braked gently and switched off the engine, then slowly swiveled around to face her.

"What the *fuck* do you think you're doing?" He hit the seat with the flat of his hand.

She unfolded the photographs. "These were behind pictures of Mrs. Thorburn. Look at the back. Can you see who took them?"

Rooney snatched the pictures and reached into his glove compartment for a flashlight. He shone it onto the back of the creased photograph.

"Can you make it out?"

"Can you?" He passed the light across to her and she shone it on the faded photographer's stamp. "Professional Photo Studio," she said slowly, disappointed it did not say Art Mathews—yet it could have been his studio, or even Craig Lyall's.

"So you got photographs of a woman," Rooney said flatly.

"They're not of a woman, Bill, it's a man dressed up. And it's not just any woman he's dressed up to look like, but Mrs. Thorburn. I think it's Janklow."

"Jesus Christ, now what you tellin' me? That he's a homo or a transvestite, or what? Is he or isn't he the man who fucking attacked you, Lorraine?"

"I don't know."

"You don't know. Well, that is fucking great."

"I didn't see him, Bill—that's why I went there."

"I told you to stay in the apartment. You promised me. You've done nothing but jerk me around, Lorraine."

She sighed, watching her car being driven past followed by the patrol car. They tooted and waved at Rooney. As Lorraine's car drove away, the patrol car slowed.

"Everything okay, Captain?" The officer stared at Lorraine in the backseat.

Rooney jerked his thumb at Lorraine. "Yeah, it's all fine. I found her. Go on, I'll see you back there."

They watched the patrol car move off and Rooney turned back to her. "I got to take you in. You got no option, I got no option."

"I went to an AA meeting, I was going to go straight back and wait for you but . . ."

He fished in his pocket for his cigarettes, lighting one from the butt and tossing it out of his window. "But you didn't. I've been running all over Pasadena, all over L.A. looking for you. They got half the cops on duty out looking for you. What the hell have you been doing?"

"Getting laid," she said flippantly.

"Very funny, Lorraine, you always had a sense of humor. Well, this time the laugh is on me. Why didn't you tell me you were with Art Mathews the night of Holly's murder, with him all night? You were his friggin' alibi."

She sighed, leaning forward to rest her arms along the front seat. "I wasn't with him all night. I left quite late . . . Rosie'll remember, maybe after twelve."

He passed her a cigarette without her asking for one. "I'm out of matches."

She delved into her purse. "What time was Holly murdered, or as near as they can give it?" He took the matches, struck one, then held the flame out to her. "Thanks." She exhaled, waiting for him to answer her question.

Rooney flicked the flame of the match out. There had been so many murders, he couldn't remember offhand what time they had verified that Holly had died.

Lorraine tapped his arm. "About eleven, wasn't it? She was just starting work so it'd be around ten-thirty or eleven. I was with him so he couldn't have done it."

Rooney lowered his window. "Doesn't matter to him, he's dead, but it matters to *you* because the FBI got your name from him. I can't not take you in." He started the engine.

"Where are we going?" she asked.

"Back to the fucking station, where do you think? I just told you: I'm handing you over. I want you out of my hair, out of my life. You and your theory will land me in a strait-jacket, never mind retiring me. You've been feeding me a line of bullshit from day one."

"Bill, I swear to you I haven't."

He looked at her in the rearview mirror, his eyes watering from tiredness and smoke. "Holly was murdered after twelve. Lorraine, I was just testing you."

She punched his shoulder. He stopped the car. Suddenly he was really angry, his jowled face set rigid. "What the fuck were you doing at Thorburn's house? And from what I gathered, you weren't there for any interview with his brother. Trying to make a few bucks for yourself? Is that what you were up to? I wouldn't put anything past you. Well, now I'm through with you."

"Was he in there?" she asked.

"You tell me. We won't get a foot in there without more evidence than that load of shit you got. I'm gonna get it in the neck about this."

He gunned the motor and the car shot forward. They headed up Mulholland, the road becoming steeper. His car coughed, protesting, but they picked up speed as they moved downhill. Suddenly Rooney stamped on his brakes as they came to the traffic lights at a dangerous intersection. The patrol car was there plus two more cars, and rammed between them, the entire driver's side smashed to smithereens, was Lorraine's car. Officer Williams was still inside, his blood spattering the broken windshield and soaking his muscular dead body.

Rooney barked at Lorraine to stay out of sight. As he got out and crossed to the wreckage, she raised her head and peered out of the window. An ambulance and police van arrived and they began to release the driver.

When Rooney came back, he didn't turn to speak to her but stared straight ahead. "He's dead. He was just a kid."

"Was it an accident?" she asked.

"What would you say? There's one, two, three other vehicles involved. He jumped the lights, this junction's known to be a death trap. He drove straight into it." He faced her. "This is *your* fault. It's due to you, you hear me?"

"Why?" she snapped back. "I wasn't driving the goddamned car, was I?"

Rooney walked back to the scene of the crash. A few people were gathering around to gape, more police, and now they had the dead man free. Lorraine saw Rooney and another officer prize open the car's buckled hood. As they peered inside with a flashlight, another man crawled beneath the car. Rooney was there for almost fifteen minutes. When he got back he sat half in and half out of his car, his feet still on the roadside. "Brake hose is smothered in grease, sliced almost in two, and the emergency cable's cut. Did anyone have access to the car keys?"

"They were in my purse."

"They still there?"

Lorraine fumbled nervously and took them out.

"Did you leave it unattended while you were there?"

"Yeah. For quite a while when I was talking to Brad Thorburn. We were in the bedroom. I left my purse downstairs." She flushed.

He looked at her and shook his head. "Christ, I thought you were joking before. Did you screw him?"

"I wanted information, Bill."

"I bet you did."

"Why don't we go back up there, Bill, just you and me? If Janklow's there, it's him you should be taking in, forget me! If I'd been in that car, it would have been me who was dead."

Rooney swung his legs in, slammed the car door, and started the engine. "No way. Not until I've discussed this with the chief. I'm sorry, but that's the way it's got to be."

Lorraine had been hoping against all hope that this would never happen, but now there was no alternative. She would become a witness for the prosecution and all it entailed. Any idea she had had of starting up as a private investigator would be ruined: when the press got to hear about her part in the murder investigation, she and her past would make the headlines. She stared out the window as they drove toward the precinct. She wanted a drink, could feel it sweeping over her. She wanted a drink rather than face it all.

She hardly said a word as Rooney led her into the station. The duty sergeant noted down all her particulars, she was photographed, and her prints taken. Then she was led away to Rooney's office. He had spoken to the chief, then shaved, but still wore the same shirt, even more stained and crumpled, and by now he was smelling pretty strong. He was drinking coffee and talking to Bean when Lorraine was brought into the room. Before leaving the office, Rooney introduced Bean, who shook her hand and pulled out a chair for her. "When we're ready, we'll take your statement. We'll also tape it and film you, okay?"

Lorraine asked if someone would be selling the movie rights

but no one laughed. Bean found her some water and cigarettes and, as he seemed so helpful, she asked him if she could call her friend Rosie to let her know she was okay.

Lorraine waited in Rooney's office for some time. She was told they'd be held up until the FBI agents arrived; neither Rooney nor the chief could deny them access to her. When she was eventually taken into the large room where everyone was gathered, it was nearly midnight. She remained closeted there for a further four hours. In that time she gave a clear statement of everything that had happened since the day she had first been attacked in the parking lot. When asked why she had not come forward, she said it was because she had removed Norman Hastings's wallet. She didn't lie, she could see no point. She answered all their questions directly and truthfully. No one appeared impressed by her subsequent investigation or her attempts at piecing together the evidence she had accumulated.

"Why are you so anxious to continue this investigation, even placing yourself at risk?" one of the agents asked. She didn't like the look of this one: his square jaw, which worked overtime, his clean-cut face, his blond crew cut and neat gray suit. He looked like a Nazi.

"I'm sorry, what did you ask me?"

Bickerstaff stared at her, and then flicked the tip of his silver pen up and down, click, click. "I asked, Ms. Page, why you placed yourself at risk?"

She looked over at Rooney, who nodded quickly. "I needed the money, I was being paid to do it by Captain Rooney."

Although they knew about her record since leaving the police force, they seemed unwilling to believe that that was the only reason she had taken such risks. Surely she had another motive?

"I suppose I did. I hoped that if I succeeded in assisting the department, then it would stand me in good stead for the future if I ever wanted to start up as a private investigator. But if I have to be a prosecution witness, then it'll destroy that chance. I know this case'll get a load of publicity and like me, well, they'll go for the jugular—that's a joke. The ex-cop ex-hooker'll make good copy, might even get a headline 'Madame Dracula.' I doubt I'll be able to live it down. I might be able to move away, but I've got contacts here and you need contacts in the investigation business, right?"

They made no answer, but she saw them glancing at each other before they all left the room, leaving her with a stone-faced policewoman. They returned an hour later. It was almost dawn. But Lorraine detected another undercurrent.

The chief gave a grimace—she supposed it was some kind of smile, but because he was so tense his lips just curled over his top teeth. "Mrs. Page, would you be willing to continue assisting this inquiry?" Rooney wouldn't meet her eyes and the chief continued, "There could be certain risks involved."

Lorraine looked at the chief, then Rooney. "You want to make a deal with me, don't you? Well, I guess it would depend—"

"On what?" the chief asked.

"On what exactly you want me to do. If I work with you, you'll have a tough time bringing me into court as a prosecution witness, won't you? I have no doubt that anything connected to the Thorburns you'll have to tread on lightly. What is it you want me to do? Is Janklow going in a lineup?"

"The situation is this. If you pick Steven Janklow out of a lineup, it will be his word against yours. You are a chronic alcoholic, ex-prostitute—"

She snapped, "I am also an ex-cop."

The FBI agent retorted, "We know that, and we'd be out of our minds to let that out. With your record, it would make you sound like an even sleazier witness than a hooker."

"What's your name?" She glared at the blond crew cut and he didn't flinch.

"Edward Bickerstaff, Ms. Page. I think we've got Janklow to agree to come into the station. He'll be accompanied by his lawyer. What we don't want is a lineup at this stage. But you came face-to-face with him, you were attacked, so what I want from you is just a good look. We'll set him up in an interview room with a one-way viewing section so you can watch him at your leisure. Because you have to be one hundred percent sure that the man you say attacked you was Steven Janklow."

Rooney took over. "You're the only witness we have, but, that said, we'll need a lot more. If he did attack you, then he will be charged with assault. If you're sure it's him, we can even press charges, but you and I both know, because of who you are and who he is, he'll walk."

"What about the couple that saw me?"

"At no time were they able to describe the man in the car

with you, so they can't be brought on as witnesses—well, not yet.'' So far Lorraine couldn't see any risk, but then she again intercepted the looks between the men. Rooney moved closer, his B.O. now overpowering. Here it comes, she thought.

''You know Brad Thorburn, you've had sexual intercourse with him. He inferred that you may have been attempting to blackmail him. We don't know yet if he has played any part in the murders, but he is Janklow's brother, and you've told us he even has a pair of cuff links, so—''

''You want me to blackmail Brad Thorburn?'' she asked, smiling.

''No,'' Bickerstaff cut in, ''we want you—and only if you're sure that Steven Janklow is the man who attacked you . . .'' Lorraine noticed that the Nazi was gradually taking over and she began to try to assess him and to fathom what they really wanted her to do. He was steely, assured. Eventually she gathered that he was trying to make her an offer to assist them without them saying it for themselves; whatever it was must be either illegal or, as they had implied, risky. They were all watching her, waiting for her to take the bait . . .

''I think I get what you're after. If I do recognize him and I'm a hundred percent sure that the man who attacked me was Steven Janklow, then you've still only got him on assault. You want to use me to do . . . what? Put pressure on him and see what it throws up, and at the same time find out if Brad Thorburn is also involved?''

They all straightened and she knew she had not only bitten their bait but was offering to reel herself in. She looked over at Rooney and smiled. ''I'll do it, but there are certain conditions. If I can get Janklow to admit his part in the murders, maybe by confronting him at his home, if I can get him to admit it and I'm wired up, you won't need to call me as a prosecution witness. You'll already have enough evidence for a conviction. That what you're after?''

They didn't say a word.

''I'll have a try, but I want your word you won't release my part in any of this to the press.''

''We can't guarantee that,'' snapped the chief.

''Then bring him in and charge him. Just do what you have to do.''

There was a low murmur and she looked to the only other woman present and asked if she could go to the bathroom. She took her time: she was exhausted, her eyes dry and her throat parched from too many cigarettes. Checking her clothes, she saw she was almost as crumpled as Rooney. She thanked God that at least she didn't smell as bad. She sat on the toilet, thinking about everything they had discussed. When she was led back from the bathroom, she was taken into Rooney's office. Only Rooney and Chief Berillo were there. Everyone else had gone.

The chief motioned her to a chair. She had never seen such a dark five o'clock shadow on a man before, it looked as if it had been painted on with a thick brush, but compared to Rooney, Chief Berillo at least seemed to have retained some energy. Poor Rooney was out of it, his eyes half closed and his shoulders slumped forward.

"We cannot agree to any deal, Lorraine, you know that, but what we will do is not press charges against you for withholding evidence, and we will endeavor to keep your name out of the proceedings. That's the best we can offer."

She looked at Rooney and gave a half smile. "Okay, I'll do it. Though it's sure a one-sided deal. Now, I'll need some new clothes and I need to get some rest. I also need a car so I'll want a clean license—just so I don't get picked up."

Rooney winked at her as a warning not to press too hard for anything more.

"When is Janklow coming in?" she asked the chief.

"Not sure, but we don't want to make it seem too urgent, so you'll have time to change and rest up."

"Can Bill be my backup?" she asked, and smiled at Rooney, who looked at the ceiling. "He was always a good backup man, one of the best."

"No, I'm afraid not. Bill's been seen in your company and by the look of him if he doesn't get some sleep, he'll fall down. You'll have his lieutenant, Josh Bean. He's a good man, and he's waiting to drive you home right now."

Lorraine was confident, almost arrogant, as she said, "He gonna take me shopping? I want to look good."

The chief replied that they'd wait and see about the new clothes. First she had to view Janklow, then they'd see about the other things she'd asked for. She walked out of the room before the chief had finished talking, saying over her shoulder, "I guess you'll call me when you need me."

"Can we trust her?" the chief asked Rooney. His head jerked up. He'd actually nodded off.

"Huh?"

"I asked if we can trust her."

"Much as any woman, and she hasn't had a drink for nine months. She wants to go straight. You mind if I have a drink?"

Berillo shook his head. "I'll join you."

Rooney poured two good shots of bourbon into the only glass in his office, and drank straight from the bottle.

"Did she tip you off to this Art Mathews? To the transsexual links? And all this possible blackmail scenario?" the chief asked quietly, and Rooney grunted. He knew that by bringing her in it'd come out in the open. He took another swig of bourbon and nodded. "She ran rings around most officers and, so help me God, I'll never know why she blew it those years ago."

"Just hope she doesn't blow it with us. If she puts a foot out of line, Bill, I'll haul her in so fast, I'll have her charged and put away for a long time. You should make sure she's aware of just how serious this is. We've got to get this case wrapped up. And if she fucks up, it's not just us, it'll be the FBI who'll make sure she never works again, not here or in any other state. Let her know that. Make sure she knows we can't have any mistakes—there's been too many as it is."

The chief drained his glass and placed it carefully on the desk.

"I'll make sure she understands."

Berillo walked to the door and opened it. "Good, and another thing, for chrissakes get yourself some deodorant."

Rooney slowly screwed the cap of the bourbon back into place. He would have liked to ram the bottle right up Berillo's ass: forty-eight hours on duty and the fucker has to complain about his B.O.

EIGHTEEN

Rooney had shaved, and was wearing a clean shirt and a fresh suit. He'd had six hours' sleep and a good lunch before he drove into the station. His wife seemed only mildly annoyed that he hadn't let her know where he had been for the past forty-eight hours. Not that she worried for her husband's safety, she'd needed him to change the lightbulb on their porch. Wearing a new roll-on deodorant with a pine forest aroma, he barged into his office. The chief came by almost immediately to inform him that Janklow was being brought in by his lawyer at four-thirty, and to check up on Lorraine. Berillo, word went out, appeared to be in a growing state of panic.

"Bean with her?" he shouted at Rooney.

"Yeah. Don't worry, Chief, he's good and steady. He'll have her here in time."

"I am not panicking, Rooney, but I will, we all will, if she doesn't show." Rooney winced as he slammed the door behind him.

Bean was sweating as he hit a traffic jam. Two P.M. in the heat of the day, and it was always hotter than hell in August. Lorraine sat beside him. If she was nervous she didn't show it, but Josh grew increasingly agitated. He kept on tapping the dashboard clock, then flipping his wrist to check his watch.

He'd had two calls from Berillo's secretary and one from Rooney, all making sure he had Lorraine with him and would be at the station with her before four. His hair was damp at the nape of his neck and he leaned out of the window to look at the lines of traffic up ahead. The trip from Lorraine's to the station should have taken no more than fifteen or twenty minutes. He knew if she wasn't at the station in plenty of time he'd have his ass whipped. He wiped his face with his handkerchief. Lorraine decided it was time to say something. "Get your light on or we'll never make it. Shut it off before we get to the precinct."

Subtle it wasn't, but in the end Bean switched on his siren and his blinking roof light and began to edge his way down the center of Orange Grove. Even less subtly, he yelled through his car speaker at drivers who were slow to get out of his way. Rooney was pacing the corridor as they walked toward his office.

"Is he here yet?" Lorraine asked calmly. Rooney shook his head as he and Bean hurried her along toward the viewing room. It was just an anteroom, with a table and two hard-backed chairs facing a square-curtained window that adjoined the main interview room. There were microphones at ceiling level, the controls at the side of the room. Lorraine was ushered in. She noticed that, like Bean, Rooney was sweating, but there was a pungent aroma of pine and it made her smile; maybe someone had told him about the awful B.O. he'd swamped everyone with the previous night. She knew a lot was riding for Rooney on her identification of Janklow.

"You just make notes and watch, look, and listen. You'll be able to hear every word they say."

"Come on, Bill, I know the setup. Who's taking the interview?"

"Ed Bickerstaff, one of the suits. He's the blond crew-cut guy, a real tight-ass—the one you asked who he was."

It was four twenty-five, five minutes to go. Rooney left the room. Lorraine lit up. Her hands were shaking. She picked up her pen and began to doodle on the notepad, then said to Bean, "What if there's something I think Janklow should be asked?" Bean hesitated. "Give it to me and I'll see if I can go into the interview room, but only if it's—"

"Important?" she said smiling.

"Yeah."

"He's gonna know he's being viewed—any two-bit criminal knows about the window—so why all the secrecy?"

"Protection."

"His?"

"Yours. You're a valuable witness, Ms. Page."

Janklow and Kophch's arrival in a chauffeur-driven Cadillac sent whispers through almost every department. Even though secrecy had surrounded the request to bring in Janklow, rumor spread fast; any suspect being brought in for questioning about the hammer murders would have attracted interest, but a member of Society, like one of the Thorburn family . . .

Rooney stood in the corridor as they filed past him. He was surprised at how confident Janklow appeared, not paying attention to anyone but staring ahead, his face partly hidden by dark glasses. As they passed, Rooney sniffed. He could smell expensive cologne like delicate flowers, wondering if it was Janklow's deodorant. It smelled better than the one he'd plastered over himself. He also noticed the way Kophch stayed close to Janklow, his steely eyes taking in everyone and everything.

Bean replaced the intercom phone and looked at Lorraine. "They're coming in now." He drew back the curtain to expose the dark square windowpane and returned to his seat.

The microphones picked up the sounds of the adjacent room. Bickerstaff was sitting to one side, his back to the window. The table was stacked with files and photographs. As the door opened, he rose to his feet. Lorraine leaned forward: she couldn't see Janklow as the men were introduced. Kophch turned and stared at the one-way glass, aware of what it was, but said nothing and pulled out a chair for Janklow.

Lorraine watched closely as Janklow sat down facing her directly, his chair positioned toward the viewing window and opposite Bickerstaff. Kophch sat on his left, and clicked open his briefcase. Janklow was wearing a fawn-colored jacket and a white shirt with a tie. He had mouse-blond hair combed back from his face, which was angular and more handsome than she had expected. His nose was thin, again not as she had remembered, and she doubted immediately that this was the man who had attacked her. She didn't recognize him. She sat back, her heart beating rapidly. She'd been wrong. She twisted her pen. "Can they get him to take off his glasses?"

"They will, just relax." Bean could see that she was tense: she was frowning, cocking her head first to one side, then to the other. No one spoke in the adjoining room. It was eerie: the silence, the waiting.

"Would you please remove your glasses, Mr. Janklow?" It was the quiet voice of Bickerstaff.

"If you require my client to look at any evidence, he will need to use his glasses. They are not decorative but prescription. I'm sorry but your request is denied."

Bickerstaff opened his file. "Take off your glasses, please, Mr. Janklow. When it is required you may replace them."

Janklow slowly removed them. Lorraine felt chilled for the first time. His eyes were pale blue, washed out, and he stared ahead as if straight at her. She caught her breath as he moistened his lips. His mouth had been tightly closed until this moment, but when he licked around both lips his face took on a different quality, as if his lips had come to life, wide lips, wide, wet lips. She scribbled on her notepad. This was the man who had attacked her, she knew it now. His lips had given him away.

"It's him," she said softly, barely audible. Bean stared at her and then back to the window as the interview began in earnest.

Bickerstaff, quiet and authoritative, first explained that he would require from Mr. Janklow his whereabouts on certain dates. He was aware that some were several years ago, but he should answer to the best of his knowledge. When the date of the first murder was given, Janklow frowned. "I have no idea."

His lawyer jotted something in his leather-bound notebook. The second date and Janklow was unable to answer, the third and still nothing—he was even apologetic at his memory failure. Bickerstaff persisted. As the more recent dates came up, Janklow gave alibi times and places. He mentioned his brother and his mother. Both, his lawyer said, would verify his client's whereabouts.

Bickerstaff then laid out the victims' photographs in front of Janklow. He studied each one intently, in silence, before shaking his head. "No, I don't know any of these people."

Lorraine watched every gesture he made, his hands, long delicate fingers, and she made a note of the ring on his right-hand pinky finger. She was sure that this was the man who had attacked her, even though she didn't recognize his voice, or remember the ring. It was his face and hands that convinced her: he was left-handed. Bickerstaff was unhurried, taking his time over each question, each photograph. He was saving Norman Hastings and Didi—or David Burrows—for last. When he presented Janklow with the picture of Hastings, Janklow said he knew him quite well. He described how Hastings had used his garage to park his car but denied any social interaction between them. When asked if he was aware of Hastings's transvestite tendencies he looked shocked, and when Bickerstaff asked if he knew Art Mathews he looked nonplussed. To his knowledge, he said, he had never heard the name. He was then asked if he knew Craig Lyall. This time he paused and touched his mouth. He started to shake his head and then changed his mind. "Craig Lyall? Um, yes, I think I've been to his studio. He's a photographer. I took my mother there to be photographed, but he was not as professional as I'd hoped and the session was terminated. My mother is very particular, and this refers back to her days in the movies. She was a film star when she was in her twenties."

Janklow's voice was affected, often overprecise, and yet he did not make many hand gestures. Bickerstaff let him talk, quietly turning pages, before he interrupted. "Were you being blackmailed, Mr. Janklow?"

Janklow sat back in his chair. "Blackmailed? Do you mean by Lyall?"

"By anyone," Bickerstaff replied.

"Absolutely not."

He now presented Janklow with the photograph of Didi. Again, Janklow spent a considerable time looking at it, shifting his glasses on and off. "No, I've never met this woman."

"It's a man." Bickerstaff waited. "She or he never made you up for a photograph?"

Lorraine saw Janklow's mouth snap shut. Then he licked his lips again and gave a humorless laugh. "No, I was never made up—I presume you mean in female attire—for any photograph."

Bickerstaff didn't waver but continued, eyes down, still nonchalant, as he asked if Janklow was homosexual.

"No, I am not," Janklow snapped.

"Are you a transvestite?"

"No, I am not."

"Have you ever in the past been charged with any homo-sexual crime?"

"No."

Kophch reached out and touched Janklow's arm. He was becoming agitated and he constantly licked his lips. Lorraine chewed her pen, willing Bickerstaff to push for more, but he remained composed, even apologetic, looking at Kophch and saying that he was sorry if some of the questions were dis-tasteful to his client but he must understand they had to be asked.

Kophch leaned toward Bickerstaff, his voice low. "Mr. Bickerstaff, please feel free to ask my client any question— that is what we are here for, to confirm my client's inno-cence—but please let me remind you, he is here of his own free will."

"I am aware of that, Mr. Kophch. The sooner we have completed all the questions, the sooner your presence will no longer be necessary."

Lorraine sighed. If anything, Bickerstaff seemed to be on Janklow's side. He was taking so long, pussyfooting around. His methodical approach was driving her crazy. She asked Bean when Bickerstaff was going to up the ante.

He made no reply but kept his eyes on the glass partition.

Bickerstaff presented Holly's picture next and Janklow de-nied any knowledge of her. Then Bickerstaff gave him Didi's photograph again.

"I have already said I do not know this person."

Bickerstaff pushed the photograph closer. "This person sometimes calls herself Didi."

"I don't know her—whoever it is. I don't know them."

"You have also denied knowing or meeting Art Mathews."

"I don't know him. You're repeating the same questions."

Bickerstaff was beginning to step up the pressure, just a little. "Now, Mr. Janklow, can we return to the dates and the alibis you have given. It seems convenient that both your brother and your mother are always your only alibi. You have no other witness to—"

Janklow's voice rose as he interrupted. "It happens to be the truth."

"Mr. Bickerstaff," Kophch intervened, "it is obvious that you are beginning to repeat yourself. If you have no further questions to ask my client, then perhaps we can close this interview.''

''I'm afraid not, Mr. Kophch, because your client has so far been unable to present to me any alibi for a number of these cases.''

''But they took place some years ago. If we are given time we will attempt to present you with the whereabouts of my client on those specific dates.''

Kophch stood up but was ordered by Bickerstaff to remain seated.

Lorraine clasped her hands tightly together. This was more like it.

''Mr. Janklow, you've stated that you are not homosexual.''

''Yes.''

''You are not a transvestite.''

''No, I am not.''

''Is your brother?''

''No, that's ridiculous.''

''And you have never at any time in the past eight years been arrested on a homosexual-related incident.''

''No, I have not.''

''You have stated that on the night of Norman Hastings's death you were not in Santa Monica, you were not—''

''I was with my mother.''

''Is this your mother, Mr. Janklow?''

Bickerstaff placed one of the photographs Lorraine had removed from the Thorburn house before him. Janklow looked at his lawyer, then looked back at the photographs. He was visibly shocked. ''Is this your mother, Mr. Janklow?''

Kophch frowned and looked at the pictures. He seemed confused as Janklow sat tight-lipped with fury.

''Is this a photograph of your mother, Mr. Janklow?''

''Yes.''

''Are you sure?''

''*Yes.*''

Bickerstaff extracted a picture of Mrs. Thorburn from one of the stacks and placed it on the table. ''Do you notice any difference, Mr. Janklow, between this photograph of Mrs. Thorburn and the one I am now placing in front of you?''

The two photographs lay side by side, one of Mrs. Thorburn, the other, everyone was certain, of Janklow himself.

He picked up the photographs and stared at them. "Where did you get these?"

"Would your client please answer the question?"

Janklow was becoming agitated, and for the first time began to twist his hands, threading his fingers, releasing and locking them again. Lorraine stood up. Bickerstaff should go for him now. *What was he waiting for? Why didn't he push Janklow now?* Kophch requested a few moments alone with his client. As they were led out, Lorraine slapped the table. "I don't believe this. *I don't believe it!*"

The door opened; Bickerstaff walked in and asked quietly if she had anything to tell him.

"You bet I have! It's him, it's him! If you want me to I'll walk in there and confront him."

"No, you won't," Bickerstaff said firmly, and left.

They waited over half an hour before Janklow and Kophch returned. Janklow was calm again. Kophch opened the interview this time.

"My client and I would like to know how you came by these photographs."

Bickerstaff kept his head down as if studying his papers. "I am afraid, Mr. Kophch, I am unable to give that information to you. We feel we are required to place your client under oath and that anything he subsequently says—"

"If you have any charges related to my client, I want to hear them. If any relate to these murders, then we will not, at this interview, discuss or refer—"

Bickerstaff snapped, "You will not, Mr. Kophch, tell me what I can or cannot do. I am more than aware of the law and I am now ready to charge your client with assault."

"What?" Mr. Kophch's studied calm cracked. He had been unprepared for an assault charge.

Bickerstaff continued, "I wish formally to charge your client that he did, on the night of the seventeenth of May of this year, assault a woman, whose identity I have every right at this stage of my inquiry not to disclose."

"You never at any time told me my client was suspected of an assault," Kophch interjected. "You have brought my client and myself here on false pretenses."

Bickerstaff and Kophch argued for more than ten minutes. Lorraine was becoming impressed with Bickerstaff, who had remained in control. Kophch was aware of every legal loophole, but Bickerstaff was one jump ahead. He had wanted, from the outset, to force Janklow to talk under oath but without Lorraine's verification of his identity he had not had sufficient evidence. Now he did, and at seven o'clock that evening Janklow was sworn in and charged with assault. As yet there was still not enough evidence to charge him with any of the murders. All were more than aware that when Kophch received Lorraine's statements and was allowed access to the evidence against Janklow, they would be in trouble. But they had enough to hold him for another twenty-four hours.

At nine o'clock that evening, after an hour's break, Janklow was brought back into the interview room. He and Kophch had spent the time alone in a cell. Some supper had been sent out for and served to them there.

Lorraine had sat in the incident room with Bickerstaff over sandwiches and coffee.

"I think you should put more pressure on his homosexual activities."

"The blackmail's a strong murder motive and if he and Hastings ever discussed the blackmail—"

Lorraine leaned close, excited. "Of course he was being blackmailed. What about all the missing jewelry belonging to Mrs. Thorburn? We don't know if it was sold with her permission, but it's a good area to get Janklow to talk about— even more so as Mrs. Thorburn is his only alibi for the night I was attacked. Is anyone questioning her?"

Bickerstaff carefully wiped a crumb from his lips with his paper napkin. He was getting irritated, but he listened—he felt obliged to. "Don't tell me what I should and shouldn't do, Lorraine, I'm quite capable of interrogating a suspect." Finally, he asked her if she felt that Janklow was the killer.

"Yes, I do," she stated. "He has the motive, heavy blackmail and possibly over a long period of time."

"But you don't have any proof of that, it's just supposition and we don't have a motive for each of these women."

Lorraine looked at Bickerstaff, her head on one side. "What about Kophch? He's not as tough as I expected—he seems to be taking a backseat. Couple of times he could have gotten Janklow off the hook but he let it ride. Why?"

Bickerstaff grinned. "We got him. Here, read this. That retired cop has spilled the beans, and that hot-shit lawyer's in it up to his neck." He waved a neatly typed statement in Lorraine's direction, and said triumphantly, "Steven Janklow had been arrested for soliciting in a red-light district. He was given a warning, but three nights later was arrested again in the same area. This time they took him down to the station to book him. His lawyer subsequently bought off the vice charges against Janklow and paid the cop to pull his arrest sheet. Kophch would be disbarred if it was known that the client he bought out went on to kill eight women. But don't let his understated style fool you, he's a vicious little shark. His prowess is in court—you'd be surprised what he's like and what he can do. For the moment he's nervous—but don't think he's a pussy, because he's got razor-sharp claws."

The break was over. Janklow was being led back into the interview room. The session began again. Bickerstaff repeated almost every question he had asked earlier, and Janklow repeated himself virtually word for word. He denied any knowledge of the victims and confidently repeated the same alibis. It was only when he was asked about his sexuality that he became hesitant. He was quiet, subdued; then he admitted that he was homosexual but was now celibate; he had not had a relationship with any man for ten years. He was near tears when he admitted that he did, on occasion, wear women's clothes, but only his mother's. He had never been outside his home dressed as a woman. The photographs Lorraine had found were taken a long time ago.

"Who took these photographs, Mr. Janklow?"

Janklow became distressed. He sniffed, then took out a freshly laundered handkerchief and blew his nose. "Art Mathews, or one of his assistants."

"Where, Mr. Janklow?"

Again he sniffed, wiping his nose. "Santa Monica."

"Are you or were you being blackmailed by Mathews, Mr. Janklow?"

"No, and I haven't seen that wretched man since that session."

"Who did the hair and makeup for it?" Bickerstaff pressed, repeating the question.

Janklow wriggled in his seat. "It might have been David."

"David?"

"Oh, stop this! You know who I mean. That David Burrows—Didi."

"So was David 'Didi' Burrows blackmailing you, Mr. Janklow?"

"*No*. Why do you keep asking me this? I've told you I'm not being blackmailed. Not by that Art, or Burrows, or anybody. I haven't seen them since that session years ago."

Bickerstaff doodled with his pencil. "And you have not dressed as a woman for, as you said, many years?"

"*That is correct,*" he snapped back.

Bickerstaff now placed onto the table a brown manila envelope. He took his time opening it and with a slightly triumphant little smile, he withdrew the photograph from the envelope. Janklow was now confronted with Rosie's photograph. He stared at it, pursing his lips. He seemed disgusted by it. "*That* isn't me."

"Please look more closely, Mr. Janklow. Is that person in the photograph you?"

"No, it is not. It's my mother."

"Your mother?"

Janklow blew his nose again. His eyes watering, he moved his body restlessly, constantly entwining his fingers and licking his lips. He let out a short gasp of breath, and then whispered, "It's me." He had already lied—and under oath. Bickerstaff started in on him again, demanding to know just how deeply entrenched he was in the world of transvestites and transsexuals, swinging his questioning around to prostitutes—whether Janklow had ever picked up transsexual prostitutes. "No, I have not."

"You sure about that, Steven? You never picked up other men like yourself, dressed like this . . ." He pushed the photo of Janklow forward again.

"I do not pick up any of the filth from the streets."

"Tell me about David Burrows."

"I don't know him."

"Didi. Come on, Steven, you've admitted he made you up, fixed your hair for the photographs, and now you're saying you didn't know him. You're lying."

Janklow looked helplessly to Kophch, who examined his nails, refusing to meet Janklow's eye.

Bickerstaff leaned back. "Okay, Steven, you didn't know Didi, you didn't know Art Mathews. So tell me about the jewelry you've been selling off. It's a lot of money and it belongs to your mother."

"You leave her out of this." He was now on the defensive.

"But, Steven, if you've been selling it without her permission, then we'll have to discuss it with her."

"Leave her alone. She's not well."

"I can't do that, Steven, because she's also your alibi for the night of the assault and the night of Norman Hastings's murder. We're going to have to bring her in, you must know that."

Janklow slapped the table next to Kophch, who had no choice but to look up at him. "Tell them they can't do that."

"They can, Steven."

Janklow put his head in his hands. When Bickerstaff asked him again about the jewelry, he began to sob. This was not what Bickerstaff wanted: if he became too distressed, by law Kophch could take a break. Bickerstaff switched the subject away from Mrs. Thorburn.

Lorraine was furious. "What the hell is he doing? He's got him sobbing his heart out. Why doesn't he push for more about the jewelry? I don't believe it."

Rooney walked in and saw her angry face. "Mrs. Thorburn has just told us that she gave her son permission to sell all her jewelry and that he was, on the night he was supposed to have attacked you, with her. . . . I got to tell Bickerstaff."

"Shit." Lorraine looked at him. "Somebody must have gotten to her—like Brad."

"According to the nursing staff she's had no visitors, just one phone call. Late last night. From Kophch. But as her legal adviser he has every right to call her, and I'm telling you, she's a tough old broad and she's got all her marbles—told me to get the hell out." He leaned against the wall stuffing his hands into his trouser pockets. "She's in that old movie stars' home. I wouldn't mind movin' in there, supposed to be pretty cushy." Lorraine gave him a scathing look.

"Just making conversation. D'ya notice it's gone pretty quiet in there?"

There had been a long, almost ominous silence as Bickerstaff thumbed through his file, but now he was back on the subject of Janklow's relationship with Norman Hastings, asking him how close they were, and when was the last time they'd seen each other. Janklow seemed to ignore the questions and then he shrugged, becoming petulant. They had no relationship, he said, absolutely none, it was ridiculous. Bickerstaff sighed, looked to Kophch.

"Please answer the questions, Steven," Kophch said.

"He was a fool, a stupid idiot." Janklow was no longer tearful. He was getting angry, and both Lorraine and Rooney listened intently. It was eerie watching him, his face twisted, his lips wetter and shinier. "Stupid, boring, fat, bloated fool." Kophch gave a warning touch to Janklow's arm. "Get off me, don't *you* touch me, you're a useless waste of money. This is *your* fault, all your fault—you should never have brought me in here. I'd be better off on my own. I don't want you here anymore."

Bickerstaff continued, determined to push Janklow to the limit, now swinging the questions around to sound on familiar terms with him, asking Janklow why he didn't like Hastings, a man he had said he hardly knew. Janklow half rose out of his chair and pointed at Bickerstaff. Kophch attempted to calm him but he swiped him aside. "You have nothing to keep me here! You've been fishing around for hours and I know you have not one shred of evidence against me."

"What about a witness, Steven?"

"Lies. There was never any witness." Janklow sat back down. Pulling at his jacket and smirking now, he began rocking back and forth in his chair.

"We have a witness, Steven, someone you attacked on the same day Norman Hastings was killed."

Janklow laughed. "Oh, yes? You think I don't know who she is? She'd never stand a chance coming up against me. She's an ex-cop, ex-drunkard with a string of vice charges against her. She killed a kid when she was on duty. I know who you're protecting! I know—and it's a joke."

Kophch was white, his face rigid with anger as he watched his client blowing it. It was fatal for him to have admitted what he knew about Lorraine. Kophch rose to his feet. "I insist we take a break now."

"Sit down," Janklow leered. "I'm beginning to enjoy myself. This is fascinating. Go on, ask me anything you want."

Bickerstaff said evenly, "Listen to me, I don't care if we scooped a witness off the streets. All that matters to me is that she's a witness, you tried to kill her, you used a claw hammer. We have ascertained that there are a number of similar hammers to be found in your workplace, at S and A garage. I am quite prepared to let you go, Mr. Janklow, but I will need a blood test. You see, you made a big mistake with the assault. She attacked you as well, didn't she? She made you bleed, didn't she? And, Mr. Janklow, we have a sample of blood taken from the vehicle, the same vehicle into which you stuffed Norman Hastings's body. We have what I think is your blood. And now would you open your shirt.''

Janklow had become still, his face drawn, his hands clenched in front of him.

"Unbutton your collar and remove your tie."

Lorraine clutched Rooney as Janklow slowly loosened his tie, slipping it away from his neck, and undid his shirt, one button after the next. It was horribly sexual—he was flicking glances to each of the men in the room and then he pulled away his shirt, revealing his white neck.

Bickerstaff got up, hiding Janklow from Lorraine and Rooney as he peered at the man's neck. He stepped back. "You've got a mark on the right side of your neck. Where did you get it?''

Janklow shrugged his shoulders. "I have a German shepherd. He bit me a few weeks ago, maybe a couple of months. You can ask my brother, he was there, he saw it."

Bickerstaff returned to his seat. He asked the other officer to contact Brad Thorburn. Janklow did up his shirt.

"Did you ever use Norman Hastings's car, Mr. Janklow?"

"Oh, I might have—yes, I did . . . well, not drive it. I sat in it once, and—oh, I remember it very well. I was sitting talking to Norman, and I had a dreadful nosebleed because I have a weak septum.''

"What date would that be?"

"I borrowed his handkerchief to stem the blood flow. Brad saw it, because I looked dreadful, very white and shaking. So I have a witness to that as well.''

Janklow buttoned up his shirt and then unbelted his trousers as he tucked in the shirttails, giving more flirtatious glances around the room.

"I did not kill anyone, I did not attack anyone, I am an innocent man, and now I would like to go home. I'm tired.''

Bickerstaff would not let up. He asked again where exactly Janklow had had the nosebleed, and on what date. Janklow yawned and said in the front seat of Hastings's car—he'd been parking it for him in the garage.

"What date would that have been?"

"I have no idea, around the sixteenth of May, I suppose. That was why I didn't come into work the following day, the seventeenth, because I didn't feel well. I spent the day with my mother instead."

Bickerstaff began to collect his files. "I think, Mr. Janklow, you can leave. We will, of course, have to check all this information, make inquiries to verify your alibis, both with Mr. Brad Thorburn and Mrs. Thorburn. I would also like you to furnish us with further details of your whereabouts on the other dates you were unable to recall where you were."

Janklow gave a triumphant smile to Kophch as if to say he hadn't even needed him there. He stood up. "Yes, of course. I'll check back in my diaries, give the relevant information to Mr. Kophch, and, as they say in the movies, I'll get back to you."

Lorraine looked at Rooney in disbelief. "He's going to walk! They're going to let him walk out of here."

"Looks like it," Rooney said bluntly.

"But it's obviously him! You know it, they must know it."

"We're not through with him yet."

Lorraine slapped the table with the flat of her hand. "What about me? Don't I count? I've said it was him, I *know* it was him—he did *this* to me!" She showed Rooney the scar at the back of her head and then slumped deep in her chair. "Jesus Christ, I even feel like some of the women I used to take statements from, the whores beaten within an inch of their lives. They always used to say to me, 'Nothing will happen, nobody cares about us, nobody cares if they beat us to a pulp, because we don't matter.' Are all those dead women of no consequence? Because you know, Rooney, if he walks now he'll never be brought back in."

As if to confirm what she was saying, the chairs were scraping back in the interview room, Kophch assisting Janklow to the door. They were chatting and joking now.

Lorraine pushed past Rooney and made for the door. He grabbed her. "No, don't do it, Lorraine, you don't go out there."

She wrenched her arm free. "He's *walking out*, Bill! I swear before God I'll make a citizen's arrest! I'm not going to let him get away with this—"

"He just did. Now sit down."

When Janklow and Kophch had departed, the atmosphere in the interview room was of exhaustion and depression. Bickerstaff looked at Lorraine and lifted his hands in a gesture of defeat. Lorraine's hands were on her hips. "Get me a wire— get me a setup. I'll get him to incriminate himself. I swear to God I'll bring that piece of shit in."

Bickerstaff was worn out, but he grinned at her. "That's what I hoped you'd say. Go home and get some rest. We'll talk in the morning."

Bean was instructed to once again drive her home and remain with her. He'd been expecting to spend the night sleeping in the patrol car, but Lorraine invited him in. She said he could sleep on the sofa and she would sleep with Rosie. Bean thanked her, but it was Bickerstaff who had warned Lorraine that she should be kept under watch day and night. Janklow knew who she was, maybe even knew her address. The following morning she was to get some decent clothes before Bean brought her back to the precinct. Now she was all they had and everything depended on her. Bean was not to let her out of his sight for a moment.

Lorraine cuddled up to Rosie, resting her head against her shoulder, and Rosie gently stroked her head.

"You okay, darlin'?"

"Nope, it was a long long day and watching that piece of shit act up made my blood boil."

"You think he'll get away with it? Do you? Because of who he is?"

"I don't know, maybe. But I'm sure gonna fight it." Lorraine sighed and rolled onto her back. "I'm going to be wired up tomorrow, to try and entrap Janklow . . ."

"Oh, my God, that's dangerous, isn't it?"

"I don't know, could be."

"What'll you do?"

Lorraine laughed softly. "I know one thing I'm gonna do, and that is hit Rodeo Drive. Maybe take whatsit out there on the sofa to Armani. They're paying for the clothes, so I'm not going to walk away with nothing. Plus new shoes, purse, blouse . . . mmm."

Rosie laughed softly. "That's our girl, and if you can slip in a size eighteen or so for me, we'll make a great show in court."

Lorraine fell silent, and then whispered, "You just pray,

Rosie, that they never have to put me on the stand. They'll destroy me."

Rosie felt Lorraine move away, only a few inches, but she somehow knew she didn't want to be touched. She was scared, Rosie could feel it, and she whispered softly, "Goodnight, I'll pray for you at the meeting tomorrow."

Lorraine closed her eyes and she prayed in silence. "Dear God, let me pull this off tomorrow, please . . ."

Lorraine, accompanied by Bean and Rosie, set off early for Rodeo Drive. First they went to Saks, Bean trailing Lorraine from one makeup counter to the next; she was choosing perfume.

"Er, Ms. Page, I dunno if the department said anythin' about cosmetics and perfume, some of this stuff is expensive."

Lorraine went for Paloma Picasso: a good, strong, positive scent. She assured Bean it was all part of the plan; she didn't just have to look good and exceptionally smart, she had to have all the accessories as well.

Rosie sprayed herself with every available perfume tester. "She's right, Josh. Can I call you Josh?"

He nodded and blushed a bright pink when they went to the lingerie department; again he tried to halt the purchases.

"Ms. Page, shouldn't you just get some pantyhose? I mean, do you need all this?"

Bean was referring to an array of lace panties, matching bra, garter belt, and fine pale stockings.

"Josh, it's all part of the scam. I mean, to get what I want you never know how far I have to go . . . understand?"

His mouth opened and closed and he pulled at his tie. "If you say so, but all I was told was to get you a nice sort of outfit."

"Well, that is just what we are going to do, Josh. Next, the outfit, as you call it."

Josh Bean, carrying all the purchases, waited at a crowded crosswalk along Rodeo Drive. He was beginning to think he should call in to the station to check this all out, even more so when Lorraine and Rosie stopped to look into the window of Cartier. "Oh no, no, Ms. Page, you can't go in there."

Lorraine smiled and kept on walking. She and Rosie were stopping at most of the elegant shops, looking at clothes in the window, and then they'd both shake their heads.

"Ms. Page, we should watch the time, you know. They said to be back in the station at . . ."

Lorraine nudged Rosie, they were getting closer to Armani.

"Twelve, Josh, I'm watching the time, don't you worry, because I've got to have my hair done, and a manicure . . ."

Before Bean could reply both women had done a quick right turn into the store. An elegant sales clerk approached Lorraine. She was wearing one of the designer suits, an overpleasant smile, spoke with a possibly fake French accent, and had a deadeyed stare that took in Lorraine and Rosie's appearance in one swift appraisal. Lorraine went straight to a rack at the rear of the showroom, but it was Rosie who gasped when she saw the price tag dangling from one garment displayed on a dummy.

"Five hundred dollars!" she hissed.

Josh raised his eyebrow; that didn't sound too bad. Then he realized the tag was just for the string of beads around the neck of the dummy. The price tag he succeeded in tracing to the sleeve was three and a half thousand dollars.

"Oh, God, I'm gonna have to call Captain Rooney."

Rooney was in his office when Josh Bean called to say Ms. Page was spending an awful lot of money going shopping.

"She's gotta look good," Rooney said, lighting a cigarette.

"Well, this suit, I mean, she looks great, Captain, but it's over two thousand dollars. And then there's all the accessories . . ."

Rooney closed his eyes. "Look, Josh, don't tell me, take it up with the chief, okay? All I know is she's gotta be very confident and back here by twelve so cut the shopping expedition short."

"I'm trying to, but now she's in this plush hair salon getting a blow . . ."

"A what?" Rooney barked into the phone.

"She's getting her hair done! I'm callin' from the salon, they're doing the alterations to the suit and . . ."

Rooney closed his eyes. "Take it up with the fuckin' chief. I've got to get her wire and a surveillance vehicle sorted out." Rooney replaced the receiver. He gave a half-smile and then let rip with a bellow of a laugh: gotta hand it to the lady.

Lorraine was wearing an elegant new Armani suit with a tight, pencil-slim skirt with a thigh-high slit and a loose jacket with a soft creamy silk blouse beneath. She chose high-heeled shoes with matching clutch bag. Conscious that she was to be wired, she also bought a fitted, slightly padded bra and matching panties. Her hair had been streaked, cut, and blown dry, she'd had a manicure and a facial, and then her makeup applied by an expert. It was after twelve by the time she arrived at the station.

Already warned by Bean, Rooney still gaped at the bill and even more when he saw her. He blushed with embarrassment. She had always been one hell of a looker, but now she was stunning. But then he blew it when he said, intending a compliment, "Holy shit, they sure done a hell of a job on you."

Rooney was not the only one taken aback by Lorraine's appearance. Bickerstaff's jaw dropped and the chief, who'd had a screaming fit when he had seen the cost, also had to compliment her. Lorraine found it almost amusing the way they suddenly pulled out chairs for her, jumped to light her cigarette. She loved the feel of the soft kid leather handbag, containing new lipstick, powder compact, silk handkerchief, calf leather wallet, silver lighter, and cigarette case. The chief checked down the list of her accessories; he didn't know how he was going to explain the calf leather wallet, let alone the lighter. Rooney had suggested, as they were no longer using Andrew Fellows, they could maybe add it to his fee. The chief had given him a scathing look.

"How am I supposed to off-load these expenses on Fellows, in particular the lingerie and skirt?"

Rooney grinned. "Well, it's a case involving transsexuals, put him down as one!"

"I dunno why you're in such good humor," Berillo snapped.

Rooney suddenly went quiet. "Because maybe I know she could get herself hit over the head with a fucking claw hammer!"

Lorraine was to wear a small pickup mike disguised as a decorative pendant attached to a gold chain around her neck. It was in the shape of a heart and could record from a five-mile radius. She was impressed by its sophistication: she had half expected the old box in a belt strapped to her waist that she'd been used to in the past. Even if she was stripped naked, Rooney said half in jest, it would be hard to find. She had flicked him a look, wondering if they were all aware she had been to bed with Brad Thorburn. It seemed likely, since she was specifically warned that the only time she would lose contact with the radio surveillance truck would be if she took a shower.

Lorraine was then closeted with Bickerstaff and his team, Rooney standing glumly to one side as they discussed her approach to Janklow. They knew he was at home and they also knew that Brad Thorburn was with him, but a telephone tap had revealed that Thorburn was intending to leave for France and had been arranging his flight. Janklow had returned straight to the house after leaving the precinct but had made no phone calls. Mrs. Thorburn had been interviewed again and repeated the statement she had made. Brad Thorburn had also verified everything his brother had said. Two calls had been recorded from the tap on the Thorburn home, both from Alfred Kophch, requesting that Janklow visit him in his office at his earliest convenience. Kophch had also said that on no account should Janklow make outgoing calls, but speak to him only personally at his office.

As Bickerstaff and Lorraine discussed the new developments, a report came in that Mrs. Thorburn had just called Brad and asked him to visit her. She had refused to speak to Steven.

"That's good," Lorraine said. "The only time I saw Janklow really upset was whenever you made any reference to her, and if she's not talking to her nasty little pervert son, he might be even more on edge."

"You're very confident, Lorraine. How can you be sure you'll get into the Thorburn house?"

"I'm sure."

Bickerstaff was beginning to like her. He patted her shoulder. "Well, you take care—and I mean it. Use your backup and scream the fuckin' place down if you feel any kind of threat."

Bickerstaff looked up as Rooney returned, tapping his wristwatch. It was really time for Lorraine to leave. She tried to make light of it—they were all so concerned for her—and asked if Andrew Fellows was still working for them. Rooney dismissed him out of hand: the last thing he had suggested was that the killer might be a woman. They had all joked that she had even been under suspicion, and Lorraine laughed out loud.

She was presented with a clean driver's license, and a Mustang, also wired to the surveillance truck, was ready in the garage. The only thing she did not have was a weapon.

Rooney walked her to the car. He opened the driver's-side door, winking to warn her not to say anything because she was wired. Then he took his gun from his shoulder holster and stashed it in the glove compartment. "We're all with you and we'll be on hand. You know what to do?"

Lorraine nodded. They had given her the code word "Rosie." If she mentioned it the backup cops were to stand by; it meant she was heading into deeper trouble than she could handle. If "Rosie" was coupled with "partner" they were to come in no matter what else she said. This was an old scam she and Lubrinski had worked, just the name of someone they could start to talk about, someone who would pose no threat to the suspect but which was, in fact, a signal. Lorraine shut the glove compartment. "Thanks, Bill."

Rooney blushed, turning away from her. "Fuck off, and get a move on." He'd always said that and it touched her, but she quickly slammed the door and started the engine. She didn't look back but headed for Beverly Glen. It would take an easy hour and a quarter. She knew Brad and Janklow were home, and that no further outgoing or incoming calls had been made. The housekeeper and gardener were there, but Lorraine knew they left about four. From then on, it would just be the brothers.

Moving way behind Lorraine was a dry-cleaning truck with two overalled police officers up front. In the back were Bickerstaff, Rooney, and another FBI agent. Lorraine's car bleeped on the grid up ahead of them, but they made no effort to sit on her tail. They didn't need to—they knew where she was going and even if they were miles back they could still monitor the car and her personal microphone.

Lorraine parked right outside the gates, clearly visible from the house, and rang the doorbell by the intercom. The dry-cleaning truck parked a good distance down the tree-lined street.

"Who is it?"

Lorraine recognized Brad's voice. "Let me come in—it's Lorraine."

"Are you alone?"

"No, I got surveillance trucks and a couple of uniformed cops. What the hell do you think, Brad? Let me in."

The gates opened and Brad came out onto the porch. He watched her as she walked up the path, then frowned. "What have you done to yourself?"

She did a slow turn, hands out, one holding her purse. "I've spent all day at the beauty parlor. How do I look?"

"What do you want?" he asked abruptly.

"To talk." He stared at her and she laughed. "What are you so suspicious of? Here, you want to check my bag?" She tossed it to him and remained standing on the pathway.

He caught it in one hand but didn't open it. "I don't think I've got anything to say to you."

She moved closer. "You'll let me in, though. How about some coffee?"

He looked back to the hallway and then down at her as she remained on the lower step. "I'm going away; this isn't a good idea."

"Why don't you just hear me out, hear why I've come? I have a reason."

"I gathered," he said, as he turned and walked into the house.

She followed him, eyes flicking upward to the bedroom above. Was he there? Was he watching her? She saw nothing; no curtain moved aside; it was very still.

In the kitchen, Brad gestured for her to sit down, then opened her purse, tipping out the contents. He flicked a look to her as he sorted through her wallet, compact, cigarette lighter, laying each item out, obviously suspicious.

"Satisfied?"

He went to the fridge and took out a bottle of chilled wine, held it up to read the label, and then slammed the fridge door. He poured himself a glass as she perched on a stool and began to put everything back into her purse. He switched on the coffee machine and leaned against the sink.

"Don't you ever wear shoes?" she asked, smiling.

"What's this, a rerun of the other night?"

"I know they took your brother in for questioning."

"They also released him."

"So I gather."

He sipped his wine, leaning against the sink.

"Where are you going?"

"France."

"For how long?"

"I don't know. What do you want?"

She opened the cigarette case, held it up as if for his permission. He got out a cup for her coffee. She still found every move he made attractive, even just pouring coffee. He had such a great body, but his ease was what made him so sexy. When he moved close to give her the coffee he smelled of soap. "You just showered?"

"Yeah, I had a game of tennis. I was going to play squash with Andrew but he refused to speak to me."

"Why?"

He smiled. "Maybe his wife told him about her fantasy, that she and I were a hot number, but it's all in her head."

"Did she make it up, or did you fuck her?"

He passed her an ashtray. "You like to talk dirty? What does it mean to you if I screwed her or not?"

"It was just a question. I like her . . . he's okay, too."

Brad picked up his glass, tilted it toward her, and then drank the wine in two swallows. "What do you want?"

"Money."

He ran his glass under the faucet in the sink. "So what's your hourly rate?"

She chortled. "Oh, this isn't *hourly!* This is going to cost you and Steven a lot, lot more."

"*Steven?*"

Lorraine blew on the hot black coffee, looking at him over the rim of the cup. "Let's not waste any more time playing games. I want money, Brad. Your brother may have walked, but you take a good look at me. Now put me in court in front of a jury. You think they're gonna say, 'Oh, she's just a hooker, oh, she's just a fucked-up piece of shit, an ex-cop who killed a kid.' You take a good look at me, Brad, because I think I look pretty good. I look good enough to sway a jury, make them doubt all that shit about me, make them look at me, see the scar on the back of my head. They'll listen real good when I say it with tears, and I can conjure up tears, Brad. I'll have them running down my cheeks when I tell them what he did to me."

He couldn't deal with her at all. It was as if she'd become two, even three people. This hard, sophisticated woman was not the same woman who had wept in his arms.

He looked so confused that she felt suddenly guilty, wanting to comfort him. It was stupid. She lit a cigarette, blowing the smoke out high above her head. "I'll have your brother charged with assault and then they'll think again about the murders, same blow as the one to the back of my head. He wanted to kill me—he *tried* to kill me—and you may say in court that he was bitten by your dog, big Mr. Brad Thorburn, but wait till I tell them, weeping, holding my head in my hands, that when he struck me with the hammer I fought for my life. I bit him in the neck and I hung on until my teeth broke his skin, until he screamed like a stuck pig. . . . It was Steven who attacked me, Brad. Why don't we stop all the bullshit and get down to just how much you'll pay me to keep my mouth shut?"

He looked at her with open hostility. She revolted him.

"Okay, I'll give you more. I had a tooth missing. They get a match on those marks on his neck, they'll be able to verify it was my teeth—not your dog's but mine."

He wouldn't look at her.

"You don't like hearing me talk this way? Well, why don't you get Steven down here? Why don't the three of us discuss just how much it'll take to buy me off, maybe send *me* to France to forget I was ever attacked."

"You'd do that?"

"Sure. You wanted to know why I was here, well, now you do." Brad was so obviously out of his depth she felt almost sorry for him, sorry to have to be so hard, but she had no option. In some ways she wanted him to throw her out, wanted him to be straight and honest because she liked him so much.

"How much?" he said gruffly, his eyes lowered.

She inhaled and let the smoke drift out slowly, then rested her chin on her hand. "A million. You can afford it. But I want it in cash, used notes."

He made a sound that was half laugh, half sob. "A million."

"And I guarantee that I'll disappear, any charges will be dropped. Suddenly he didn't look like your brother, suddenly I guess I was just mistaken. He'd never even have to go to court."

"I doubt if he will, anyway," Brad snapped.

"You want to bet? Because if they don't press charges, then I will take out a citizen's complaint. I'll have every feminist group backing me up. You wouldn't believe the stink I could create. You and your precious brother and your beloved mother would be hounded by the press. You won't buy out of that, but you can buy me out now. Go talk to Steven. Is he home?"

Brad made it to the doorway, his fists clenched. He wanted to grab her by her hair and throw her out bodily. He had never felt such loathing for another human being—let alone a woman.

"Oh, I can see I got you real angry. Well, it's up to you, I think I'm being fair and square. What's a million to you, rich boy?" He moved so fast, one moment in the doorway, the next at her side. He slapped her face hard. She held her cheek. "That make you feel better, rich boy? It's just gone up another ten grand. Touch me again and, so help me God, I'll walk out of here and start screaming my fucking head off. Now go talk to your sick pervert of a brother—better still, bring his ass down here. Let's hear what he has to say."

He walked out. Lorraine was shaking all over—he had really hurt her. She rubbed her aching jaw and checked her face in her compact mirror. Her cheek was bright red and already getting swollen, but otherwise she looked better than she had in years. She snapped the compact shut, and moved cautiously, silently to the hall and looked up. Brad was nowhere in sight. She listened but could hear nothing, so she made her way into the empty drawing room.

"He's gone upstairs, I'm now in the drawing room." She said it softly, tilting her head down to the tiny gold heart.

Lorraine heard footsteps and leaned against the piano, as if she were looking over the framed photographs. "I'm in here, Brad."

He appeared in the doorway.

"He's agreed, a million, but he can't get it for at least a couple of months."

Lorraine propped both elbows on the piano. "No deal, I can't wait that long. I want it today. Why don't you pay me? You got the dough, haven't you?"

"This has nothing to do with me. I wouldn't pay you a cent."

"No, but you'd stand up in court and tell a jury that your

dog bit him on the neck, your mother would say under oath
that her son was with her all day and all night on the night he
nearly killed me. You're sick, you know that? Well, fuck you
and fuck your brother. I'm getting out of here, I can make
enough selling my story to the press.''

Brad blocked the doorway. ''He doesn't have that amount
of cash and neither do I. Everything's tied up in property, trust
funds. I can't get that amount of money released in a day, it
would be impossible.''

''I don't believe you and I want to talk to your brother.
You're a pain in the butt. *Steven!*''

She heard footsteps; he was coming down the stairs. She
saw Brad tense up, step back, and turn. She licked her lips
nervously. She wanted to make sure they knew exactly what
was happening outside in the surveillance vehicle.

''Is that Steven coming down the stairs, Brad? Is he in the
hall?''

Brad said nothing but he was turned toward the stairs and
looking up. Lorraine slowly walked out from the drawing
room, her heart was banging in her chest. She made sure Brad
was slightly in front of her but not blocking her view of Janklow in any way.

Steven Janklow was midway down the stairs. He was wearing light blue slacks, a blue-and-white-striped cotton shirt, and
velvet embroidered bedroom slippers. Seen from below, he
appeared taller, more threatening. His lips were clenched together, his eyes were very pale behind his gold, rimless
glasses. Slowly, stair by stair, he came down, lower and lower,
until he stood on the bottom stair, never taking his eyes off
her. It was unnerving, the silence, and also because his left
hand was held behind his back.

''Hi, you remember me, don't you, Steve? You said you
needed to be sucked off in a public place, twenty dollars. We
drove to the Glendale shopping mall. Sure you remember.
Look at him, Brad, he remembers me. Maybe it's my scar.''

Janklow's face twisted in rage. ''I don't know you. Throw
her out of here, Brad.''

Lorraine remained where she was. She felt safer with Brad
between her and Janklow. ''Fine, Brad, you throw me out, but
first fill him in, tell him what the deal is. If you don't have
the cash, then I'll take a couple of items belonging to your
mother. Art Mathews said he was getting good prices for the

stuff in Europe.'' Janklow looked as if he would attack her, spittle collected at the corners of his mouth, but Brad stepped right in front of him.

"Just calm down, Steven. Have you ever seen her before?''

"No, I don't know the bitch, and don't you tell me to calm down.''

Brad looked to Lorraine. "Go and sit down, let me talk to him.'' Lorraine backed into the drawing room as Brad moved closer to his brother. She was out of sight of both of them for a second and managed to whisper into the microphone that she was in the drawing room.

Lorraine had to hold on to the piano top, her legs were shaking so much. She could hear Janklow still in the hall with Brad, insisting that he did not know her, that she was lying. Suddenly furious instead of afraid, she stormed out and confronted both men. "I'm lying, am I? Right, you'll see, and I'll see you in court.''

She strode into the kitchen and picked up her bag. She was about to walk past them to the front door, when she heard Brad's low voice, "Give that to me! Give it here.''

She turned around just in time to see Janklow with the gun, but he hadn't even gotten it to waist level before Brad had taken it from him. Then he sank onto the bottom stair. Brad slipped the weapon into his pocket. He spoke softly to Lorraine.

"You'll get your money as soon as I can arrange it.''

"Well, what about the jewelry? Don't you have any left? Art seemed to think you had more'n the Queen of England.''

Janklow's head was in his hands, but he said, "He was a thieving piece of shit.''

Lorraine sniggered. "Yeah, no doubt about that, but you got no worries about him talking.'' She was on firmer ground now, testing how much she could say. "They had him arrested for the murders, didn't you know? Apparently he even admitted to a couple, then he got scared and killed himself—cut his wrists on his glasses.''

Janklow looked at her with his pale, expressionless eyes. Lorraine held his gaze. "You shouldn't have hurt Didi, though. She was a friend of mine. I know she was into the blackmail with Art, but he forced her to do it.''

Janklow looked up at his brother. "There's nothing left, Brad. I've got no money—I can't pay her.''

"What about your mother? She's sitting on a load, isn't she? How would you think she'd feel if I paid her a visit? It's all the same to me. Look, I don't want to walk away empty-handed. If Art and Didi cleaned you out, then why not—"

"You don't go anywhere near my mother." Janklow's temper surfaced.

"Then I'll just walk out of here. But I warned your brother—you ask him—I'm not gonna let you off. I'll sell my story to the papers and then she'll wish she could get up and run because they won't leave her alone. They'll dig up every inch of dirt on her, on this family—"

Janklow shoved Brad away and dived at Lorraine, but again Brad caught him before he managed to reach her. He pushed him up against the wall. "Tell me the truth, Steven. Was it you who attacked her?"

He screamed and tried to wriggle out of his brother's grasp, but Brad thumped him in the stomach so hard he buckled over. Then Brad yanked him up against the wall by his hair. "You'd better tell me, Steven, because if what she says is true, then we've got to pay her off."

She eased around to a better position, still making sure Brad was between her and Janklow. "He attacked me and he murdered the others. He did it, Brad! Ask him. *Go on, ask him!*"

"*Yes! Yes! Yes!*" screamed Janklow.

Brad released his hold but was still too close for his brother, who was gasping for breath, to try anything on her. Brad looked at Lorraine, then at Janklow. "Okay, we'll pay. I'll pay you whatever you want."

Janklow pulled at Brad's arm. "You fool, you pay her and she'll be back like that other bitch. They'll never leave you alone. You let her walk out of here and she'll be on your back like a leech. She's a leech, a bloodsucker."

"What you gonna do, Steven? Kill me like the others?"

Lorraine spat it out and Janklow tried again to reach her. Again Brad dragged him back, shoving him hard against the wall. He was frothing at the mouth with impotent fury, but Brad was too strong for him to escape. "They deserved it! And even if he's stupid enough to pay you off, I'll find you, wherever you are, no matter how long it takes. I'll bite out your eyes, claw them out with my hands, I'll never let you go, never. Never."

She pointed at Janklow and then back at Brad. "You did

hear that, didn't you? You're gettin' off real light. He's killed eight women and all I'm doing is asking for a million dollars. I could push for a lot more.''

Brad looked first at her, then at his brother as the implication sank in. His face was drained. Janklow was beginning to lose his anger and his mouth twisted like a child's. "Ah, no, don't let them take me, Brad, please, you'll take care of me? Brad, Brad, *don't look at me like that!*"

He began to sob, sliding down the wall, until he curled up, blubbering, his face in his hands. Brad bent down to him and Steven must have thought he was going to hug him, because he lifted his arms up to him. But Brad hauled him roughly to his feet by his shirt. "Is this true, Steven?" Brad shook him so hard his head cracked against the wall. *"Is it true?"* He gripped his brother's face in his hands. *"Is it true?"*

Deflated, Janklow was half pleading with Brad to hold him, not to hurt him anymore. He started crying again, his wet lips hanging open as he sobbed. But he did not deny it, he seemed only to want Brad to hold him.

"I'm taking him upstairs to his room. You stay down here."

Lorraine watched as Brad half carried, half dragged his brother upstairs. He sounded like a little boy, begging Brad not to smack him anymore. He had become pathetic, begging his brother to be nice, not to hurt him. She wondered how many of the wretched women he had hammered to death begged in the same way, like poor little Holly. "Brad," she said flatly. Halfway up the stairs, he stopped. "You'd better stay with him. Will you put the gun down that you took from him?"

They both looked toward her, as different as Dilly Fellows had said. It was impossible to believe they were brothers. Brad took the gun out of his pocket and for a split second she thought he was going to fire it straight into her head, but she said calmly, matter-of-factly, "I'm wired up, Brad. Every word we've said has been recorded. Just put down the gun."

He leaned down and carefully placed it on a step and the two of them continued up the stairs. When she heard the bedroom door close she went to the intercom in the hallway and said they should come in and that he was in the top right-hand front bedroom. She pressed open the gates and went to wait on the porch. The truck was just pulling up outside. Rooney was first out and gave her a thumbs-up. Next out was Bickerstaff. Lorraine had turned away to look over the beautiful gardens, the flowers, the swimming pool, the tennis courts. It was so perfect, so incongruously peaceful. The sound of squad cars arriving cut through the silence. Lorraine joined Rooney. She removed the tiny microphone and asked if she could go home. She was told by Bickerstaff that she must return to the station.

Brad Thorburn was led out between two uniformed police officers followed by Steven Janklow handcuffed between another two. Janklow began to sob out a wretched, sickening confession inside the vehicle, and, two hours after he was arrested, admitted to five murders, but seemed vague about Holly and Didi, and one of the as yet unidentified victims. Two remained unidentified because Janklow didn't know their names but agreed when shown the photographs that he had killed them. He said one was called Ellen and the other something like Susanna, but he hadn't known their last names, of course. He was dismissive and arrogant. Looking over the horrific photographs he had shrugged and said bitterly that he had not done anything to any nice women.

"Bitches, you know, they were just whores, dregs of unwashed humanity."

Lorraine did not get home until late that night. Rosie was waiting expectantly to hear all that had happened. She gave her friend a bear hug and was disappointed when Lorraine didn't want to go out for a celebration dinner.

"But it's all over, isn't it?"

Lorraine sighed, exhausted. "Yes, I guess it is, but I don't feel like celebrating."

The next few days were long and drawn out. She was asked to be on call should they require her at the station. Something nagged at her but she couldn't figure out what. In the end she put it down to the possibility that she still might be used as a prosecution witness.

The good news came at the beginning of the following week. Janklow would plead guilty, which meant Lorraine would not have to take the stand, to seven counts of murder.

A month after his brother's arrest, Brad Thorburn left Los Angeles to escape media attention, but remained in touch with his brother via their lawyer. Lorraine followed the progress of

the case through Rooney, or by dropping by the station. Money
was tight, and Rosie kept up her daily check of want ads, but
their financial situation made the prospect of starting up their
own agency a moot point.

Rooney was the one to tell Lorraine that her theory had been
wrong, although so had everyone else's. Further interviews
with Steven Janklow elicited that he had been blackmailed by
Art Mathews for much longer than they had thought—almost
nine years—but he had only met Art once. Didi had made the
calls and collected the money and the jewelry. Janklow had
always liked Didi, he said, because she fixed his wigs and
makeup. The other women had been murdered because they
were like his father's whores, dirty hookers he had brought
home to flaunt in front of Janklow's beloved mother. There
was no blackmail link to the dead women, only Didi. Norman
Hastings had been killed because, as he was being blackmailed
himself, he felt that he and Janklow could help each other out,
even go to the police to press charges. Janklow had not wanted
anyone to know about his private life; he was disgusted that
a fat, middle-aged man like Norman Hastings could ever think
that they were alike, so he killed him. When pressed for further
details on the murder of Angela ''Holly'' Hollow and David
''Didi'' Burrows, he said that he couldn't remember and he
supposed he must have killed them.

Janklow also admitted attacking Lorraine, again saying that
she was just like his father's whores and he had been right to
attack her as she was now his brother's whore. His obsessive
love for his mother had so twisted him that half the time he
believed that he was her, and, when he eventually admitted
everything he had done, did not hold it against her that she
had not come to see him.

To his surprise Rooney was called in to see Chief Berillo
and given a big bonus; contributions from all the officers had
paid for a gold travel clock and leather case. He hated the
thought of retirement, but his part in tracking down Janklow
had made good press coverage, and he grudgingly thanked
Lorraine but then said that if truth be told she should thank
him.

Lorraine's part in Janklow's arrest was not leaked to the
press. The only thing she got out of it was the few bucks from
Rooney, the clean driver's license, and the new clothes. She
had to hand back Rooney's gun because he had to return it

with his badge. She and Rosie were flat broke.

"The bastards! Don't you get a reward?"

Lorraine laughed. "No! But I got my self-respect, Rosie."

"Well, it ain't gonna pay the rent, sweet face, so now what do you do?"

She was looking good, she knew it; she was back in form and she knew that, too. Working again had filled in her days, her nights, and yet somehow she wanted or expected more. She studied her reflection in the bathroom mirror: so much for respect. If they really thought she was something, how come they didn't offer her a job? How come, at the end, she was still broke, and worse, back at square one? She gripped the basin and bowed her head.

"Tea's ready," Rosie yelled out.

Lorraine looked up at herself; it wasn't over, she hadn't beaten it. "Jesus Christ, I want a drink."

Rosie cut a thick slice of banana bread and poured tea for each of them. "It's homemade—got it at the deli near the corner." Lorraine choked suddenly. "What's the matter? Don't you like it?" Rosie watched as she grabbed the file from the Janklow case and began to thumb through it. Half an hour later she looked up. "I got to go out. If you want something to do can you find out who we contact to rent that place Art Mathews had as a gallery, and how much? I'm gonna see if I can raise some dough, then we'll open up Page Investigation Services. I'll be back or I'll call in, okay?"

Rosie followed her onto the steps outside the apartment. "Where are you going?"

Lorraine ran down the stairs, turning at the bottom to look back at Rosie. She waved and called back something about the banana bread, then she formed her right hand into the shape of a gun, and pretended to fire it. Rosie went back inside and glanced at the papers, wondering what Lorraine had been so excited about. The file was open to Didi's autopsy report. Rosie grimaced in distaste and went back to her bread. It didn't taste so good. The pathologist's findings stated that David Burrows's last meal had been banana bread.

NINETEEN

Ed Bickerstaff had been in a heavy meeting all morning discussing Janklow's mental deterioration. His family, via their lawyers, was insisting he be declared insane and therefore incapable of standing trial.

Bickerstaff had spent many hours with Janklow since his arrest in mid-August, during which he talked compulsively, almost with pride, about what he had done. He showed no guilt or remorse, but the reverse; he gloated in detailing how the women had died. He was still sketchy when it came to Didi and Holly, but was adamant that he had killed them. He was constantly smiling, always polite and cheerful, and continued to talk freely, even when he was alone in his cell.

It was now the second week of September. The last meeting Bickerstaff had had with Janklow had been two days earlier. Janklow's head was bruised from self-inflicted injuries and he was wearing a white gown with ties at the back, having just been for a brain scan. He sat on the bed dangling his feet, and midway through the interview he started to sing some long-forgotten song. He could only remember the chorus, and repeated the same words over and over. "If you say you love me, do you care? If you say you love me, do you care?"

•   •   •

When Bickerstaff was told that Lorraine Page was asking for him, he agreed to see her. He hadn't liked the way she'd been hanging around the station, so he intended on making this meeting short and sweet. She was ushered into his office— Rooney's old one. He got up as she entered and shook hands. She was still looking good and had gained a little weight— not fat weight, but working out and training now on a regular basis had gotten her body toned up and really back in shape.

"Is he insane, then?" she asked without any preamble.

"Well, they're certainly trying to prove it."

"What do you think?" she asked.

"Well, he may be putting up one hell of a performance, who can tell? I don't know."

Bickerstaff rested his chin in his hands. "That was one hell of a performance you gave at his place. Class act, but then Rooney said you were good. What he never said was just how good. You mind if I ask you something personal?"

"Go ahead."

"That shooting incident—the one with the kid—how come you fired six times when you could have brought him down with one shot?"

She hadn't expected him to bring up the shooting and it caught her off guard. "I'd had a few drinks. I didn't see the boy, just his jacket. It had this yellow stripe down the back. . . . I had a partner I was fond of. He was in a shootout. The man that killed him had a black sweater with a yellow stripe and I didn't see the boy—it wasn't him I was firing at but somebody else."

He stood up and, just as Rooney used to do, flicked at the blind. "I'm sorry, Ms. Page, but I should really be getting back to work unless there was another reason for your visit?"

Lorraine reminded him about the investigation agency. She caught him looking at his watch and knew he wanted her to leave. The Bickerstaffs of this world may remark on how good an officer she had been but they also would never have any tolerance or forgiveness for a checkered past. "And yeah, there is another reason I'm here beyond the fact I need money: I'm broke."

He frowned. She lit a cigarette and kept it between her lips as she spoke. "I don't think Janklow murdered David Burrows or Holly."

Bickerstaff sat again and leaned back in his chair, his face tightening with anger. He was a real control freak, this one, Lorraine surmised, and she picked up his hostility immediately. "He's admitted both."

"Way it sounds, he's admitting to any stiff we had in or around L.A. since 1965." He laughed and she took the cigarette out of her mouth. "How much if I get you proof that it was Art Mathews? You wouldn't look so dumb about his suicide. As it stands now, Janklow said he killed them, which makes Art Mathews look as if he was put under so much pressure he killed himself . . ."

"You want me to hire you?" he said with a sarcastic smile.

"You can call it what you like. I just need cash to get cards printed, a word processor, pay a little rent."

"You withholding further evidence, Ms. Page?"

"No, and maybe I'm wrong, but I think Art Mathews killed both Holly and Didi. And if he didn't, I'd like to find out who did. And, if you don't have Janklow on the stand, maybe you'll have somebody else, because I'm sure Art didn't do the murders alone."

"You gonna give me a name?"

"I don't have one yet, but I'm working on it. Come on, I know there's a kitty for informers—you can call me that if you like. It's not as if the FBI's broke, and it might be useful to you, Mr. Bickerstaff."

He smarted at her audacity. "How much?"

She stubbed out her cigarette. "Ten grand, in cash, in an envelope."

He sucked in his breath, stood up, and stuffed his hands in his trouser pockets. "Make it five and you've got a deal—if you get us proof that Art Mathews did the murders."

She tossed the hair out of her eyes. "You've got a deal, Mr. Bickerstaff. I'll be in touch."

When the door closed behind her, he could still smell her perfume. He liked it, but he was unsure about what he had just agreed to do. Then he shrugged it off—probably be able to pass her over the cash from his own expenses and if she did come up with something worthwhile then it would be a plus for him. He quite honestly no longer gave a damn about Lorraine Page.

• • •

Lorraine took a bus to West Hollywood and headed off to the clubs in search of Curtis. She found him in a bar with a blond Holly look-alike on his arm. When he saw her he whistled and she pivoted for him like a model.

"I want to talk to you, Curtis, someplace private." She swore she was on the level and they headed into a back room. They were only there for about ten minutes before they returned to the bar.

"You want a drink, Lorraine?"

"I'm not drinking today, but thanks for the offer." She banged out of the bar into the brilliant afternoon sunshine. She hadn't thought he'd bite but he *had* cared for Holly and what was a couple of grand? His girls were making that in a night for him. She caught the next bus home, taking out the dirty used notes Curtis had passed over. They were all in tens and twenties, but he'd been straight, there was two grand. It was enough to last for a while.

Rosie was waiting, immediately asking where she'd been. Lorraine would only tell her that she'd done a deal with Ed Bickerstaff. Rosie tried to get more information out of her but she was too busy taking a shower and changing. An hour later they left together with an overnight bag. They rented not a wreck but a decent car. They had a long drive ahead of them, maybe seven or eight hours: they were heading for San Francisco.

Rosie did most of the driving while Lorraine map-read. They only stopped for gasoline and coffee. It was after midnight when they arrived in San Francisco and booked into a cheap motel on the outskirts. Rosie was hungry and went out for a takeout hamburger and french fries, bringing one back for Lorraine, who was sound asleep, so Rosie ate it herself. She couldn't sleep, and tossed and turned, her bed creaking ominously, but Lorraine slept on. Rosie propped herself up on her elbow and looked over at her friend. In the blue light from the parking lot that broke through the motel's thin curtains, she studied Lorraine's sleeping face. The transformation from when they had first met was astonishing. She was a different woman in every way—less aggressive, more content within herself, more confident, more womanly.

Lorraine woke early. Rosie was dead to the world so she slipped into the bathroom and took a shower. As she soaped herself she thought about Brad Thorburn. She heard the way she had spoken to him, saw him so hurt, so bewildered. They would probably never meet again and he would never know just how much he had meant to her, what he had done for her. He had made her feel loved, wanted, had made some dead part of her revive. Brad Thorburn had woken her as a woman.

After breakfast, Lorraine took a street map of San Francisco, marked their destination with a cross, and passed it over to Rosie. "You're the driver. That's where we got to get to."

"Who we seeing?"

Lorraine hesitated. In all fairness Rosie should know why they had come here. "I *don't* think Janklow killed Holly or Didi. Nula lied to me. She said that she and Didi were working together the night Holly was killed, but Holly's pimp said Nula was on her own. I think it's got something to do with Art. Also, I think Nula lied about where Didi was the night she was murdered. It's Nula we're going to see. Curtis gave me the address and loaned me some cash. Funny guy, you know he really cared for Holly. I didn't think he'd cough up the cash, but he did. I left him the lighter and wallet the cops bought me as collateral." Lorraine laughed, quite pleased with the fact she had screwed so much out of the cops. She'd have taken the suit back and tried for a refund but it had been altered to fit her.

"I don't want to scare Nula off. I just want her to tell me a few things."

"Are you gonna get paid for this?"

"Five thousand dollars from Ed Bickerstaff, and Curtis said he'd forget the repayment of his two grand if I got Holly's killer, so we'll have enough to open the agency."

Lorraine called Nula's number. A sleepy voice answered and she hung up. She recognized Nula's voice.

She and Rosie left the motel. It was cooler here than in L.A. and quite foggy. They bought a morning paper and, following their map, headed into the city. They were hemmed in by traffic and the streets were a confusing mass of one-way systems, but they eventually reached the Tenderloin district located near the Civic Center in the central part of town. They passed through the area's wide, run-down streets, down which a few prostitutes even at this hour were wandering, maybe not working but probably on their way home. Lorraine surmised that this was a heavy drug hangout area. Big five-story brick buildings; a lot of Asian families and kids visible on the streets and grouped on the corners. They cruised past sleazy bars and closed-up sex shops with signs advertising live shows, past shabby hotels. More drug dealers' areas, more liquor stores per block than grocery stores. They continued on, passing old derelict theaters, when Lorraine tapped Rosie.

"Slow right down, real slow," Lorraine said. "Let's check the streets from here on. We pass Eddy Street, Jones Street, Ellis, and, okay, the one we want is Leavenworth Street, and it should be coming up on the left, number one eighty-two. There it is!"

Rosie pulled up outside a dilapidated four-story building. There was hardly a soul around and very little traffic. Cars were parked all along the street as none of the houses had garages or porches but big locking gates on the front entrances. Lorraine opened the car door. "I'll be about half an hour. Sit tight." Rosie picked up the newspaper and prepared herself for the wait. Lorraine checked the names on the apartments. She was looking for number twenty-three but most were broken or graffitied over. But she was in luck because the main gate to the apartment building was open. Lorraine made her way up an old stone staircase littered with garbage to the top floor. She knocked hard on the door of apartment twenty-three and waited.

"Who is it?"

"Surprise, Nula, open up, it's me."

The peephole slid back, and bolts and chain locks were removed. Nula opened the door. "Jesus Christ, how did you find me?"

"Curtis said you were here. Since I was passing, I thought I'd visit."

Nula opened the door wider and Lorraine stepped inside. Nula was wearing her scruffy kimono and she was barefoot. She had an old dirty terry cloth turban on her head, and no makeup. "It's only nine o'clock, for chrissakes."

Lorraine apologized and followed her into the apartment's single room. It was a mess, crammed with dresses and bags, cases half unpacked and old takeout cartons. "I just moved in, pretty depressing comedown, but I'm not gonna be here permanently. It used to belong to a friend and they're on tour in a big show so I've got it for a few months. Sit down." Nula folded her arms and looked over Lorraine. She pursed her lips. "Looking very chic, dear, come into money? That's a very expensive suit." She sat at her dressing table, fiddled with one of her wigs, and checked her face. "I look like a piece of shit but I was working nearly all night. Girl's got to do what a girl's got to do to earn a living, but, Christ, this is a shit hole. The pay isn't half as good as in L.A."

Lorraine told Nula about Janklow, how he had admitted to all the murders, including Didi and Holly. Nula closed her eyes. "Thank God. I've been praying they get the bastard and I know about Art. I cried my heart out, but he took his own life, so I guess that's what he wanted. Those bastards pushed him, the shits, and he was innocent. But why are you here?"

"Work. I'm with an investigation agency."

Nula shrieked with laughter, then pointed at Lorraine. "You were a cop, weren't you? Well, I hope you haven't come to arrest me." She brushed her wig, looking at Lorraine in the mirror. She was getting uneasy, Lorraine could sense it.

"What *do* you want?" Nula asked.

"Well, I'm trying to piece a few things together. You said on the night Holly died Didi was with you, that you both saw her cross the road, but Curtis said Didi wasn't there, you were alone." She paused.

Nula gestured for her to continue. She eased off her turban and slipped on the wig; it was one of Didi's—dark, straight, and silky. Lorraine remembered it as the one Didi had been wearing the first time she had met them both. Nula now began to carefully glue the netting to her forehead, all the time watching Lorraine in the mirror.

"Nula, I think Art killed Holly *and* Didi, but I got to have evidence to prove it. Whatever you tell me won't be used against you—I'll keep your name out of it and it won't hurt Art because he's dead. It'll really help me. It's Mrs. Thorburn's jewelry I'm interested in—or what pieces you've got left."

Nula blinked rapidly and swiveled around. "I don't know what you're talking about."

Lorraine got up and walked toward Nula. "The last meal Didi ate was homemade banana bread. She was at home, wasn't she? Not, as you said, out working. Curtis said she didn't show that night because her foot was still hurting. You said she'd been out all day with a regular, but that wasn't true, was it? Now, did Art come by that night?"

Nula began to paint her nails. "Bullshit, dear. She went out, and then I was told she'd been murdered. You even called the apartment.''

''The ring on Didi's finger, the one you said she couldn't take off, was Mrs. Thorburn's, wasn't it? Well, I'd never seen her wearing it before, so she must have been able to get it off. So I think it has something to do with that ring. Is that why Art killed her? Because of the ring?''

Nula painted the last nail of her right hand and began on the left with studied concentration. Lorraine moved closer. ''Didi and Art were blackmailing Steven Janklow. Art was cleaning up, wasn't he? He used Didi to make contact and to pick up the jewels. Where did she pick them up from? Janklow's garage? Was that where they did the exchange?''

Nula continued to paint her nails. ''Listen, dear, why don't you go and do your Perry Mason someplace else? Didi was my closest friend, we adored each other and we both loved little Holly—neither of us would hurt her. Whatever she was doing with Art . . . she never let on about it to me.''

''Maybe not, but Art might have gotten angry with her. Maybe it was Art that picked Holly up?''

Nula wafted her nails in the air to dry them. ''To be honest, dear, I don't know what you're getting at. You've had a wasted journey.''

''Come on, Nula, I know you have to be in on it. Janklow listed a lot of Mrs. Thorburn's jewelry, but he didn't sell it. Did he give it to Art?''

''I don't know,'' Nula snapped.

Lorraine shrugged. ''Fine, I'll go, but I won't keep quiet. You must know something; you had to be in on it.'' She tried a different tactic. ''Look, I don't like to do this, but I'm broke. Maybe I'll keep quiet if you give me a cut. I want money to keep my mouth shut, Nula. I lied about the agency crap— who's ever gonna employ me?''

Nula began to shake a bottle of foundation cream furiously and started to make up her face. ''Obviously I have so much money that I get some perverse kick out of living in this shit hole and getting twenty dollars a blow job if I'm lucky. I don't have any dough, all right?''

Lorraine walked slowly to the door. ''Well, if you won't help me, Nula, I'll go to the cops—see if they'll dole me out a few dollars for the information.''

Nula smirked and then said loudly, "Craig, why don't you come in and say hello to Perry Mason, dear?"

Lorraine pressed her back against the door as Craig Lyall walked in from the bathroom. Nula started to gather her clothes, relaxed and seemingly no longer interested in Lorraine. She held up a dress, checking herself in the mirror, while Lyall moved closer to Lorraine.

Nula giggled. "Sit down, sweetheart. We're going to have a little party, just the three of us. Well, *you* are. Open the bottle, Craig dear, she won't be able to resist." She minced out into the bathroom.

Lorraine's heart thudded. How long had she been in the apartment? Ten, fifteen minutes? Would Rosie do anything? Did she even know which was Nula's apartment?

Lyall produced a bottle of vodka.

"Listen, Craig. I just wanted a cut of the jewelry, nothing more, and Janklow's already admitted the murders. I won't go to the cops, I promise, it was just a threat. I didn't mean it—all I wanted was some dough."

Nula shrieked from the bathroom, "What do you think we are? What are you so scared about? All we're going to do is have a little party."

She reappeared, wearing a black silk slip and stockings. She held out a pair of shoes. "If you think your shoes are nice, look at these, three hundred dollars, handmade." She slipped on first one, then the other.

Lyall opened a bottle of vodka and poured a tumblerful. "Have a drink, Lorraine, dear. *Go on, drink it!*"

She swiped Lyall's hand away. The glass smashed against the wall.

"Hold her down and pour it down her throat." Nula had opened a suitcase full of new clothes. She selected a smart navy dress with a white collar, very demure, very respectable. She didn't want to be obvious, not anymore, not for a while. Lyall gripped Lorraine's wrist and dragged her toward the bed. She struggled and Nula smacked her hard across the face. "Listen, you'd better do what we want or we'll mark your other cheek. Is that what you want, Miss Goody Two-Shoes? I knew you were a cunt the moment you ripped us off at the gallery. You blackmailed Art. Now *drink*."

Lorraine was trying to locate the fire escape. Did the apartment face the street? How long had she told Rosie she would be? She'd fouled up so badly. Had she really felt so sure she'd be able to confront Nula, get the information she needed, and return to Bickerstaff? She'd been so off the wall, she'd lost her touch. She almost needed a drink she was so angry with herself.

"Drink," Lyall said, but she still hadn't taken the glass.

Nula moved to his side. "Pour it down her throat! What are you waiting for? Few glasses and she'll be begging for more. Go on, do it."

Lorraine looked up into his scared face. "Don't do this to me, Craig. I promise I won't tell anybody you've got the jewelry—"

He gripped her cheeks and forced the glass to her lips. Nula grabbed her hair and held her head back, screaming at Lyall to get on with it.

Rosie had read the entire newspaper. She tossed it aside and checked her watch. She looked at the front entrance, drumming her fingers on the steering wheel. Then she got out of the car, trying to remember the name of the person Lorraine was seeing. She looked down the row of names by the intercom but most were scratched out or blank. She pushed open the main door, walked into the corridor, which stank of urine, and climbed the stairs to the second floor. Halfway up she stopped when a door opened and two kids ran out. She had to flatten herself against the stairwell as they charged past her. A woman came to the door and Rosie hurried toward her. "Have you seen a tall blond woman?" The door slammed in her face.

She continued up to the third floor, where a male voice demanded to know what she wanted. She turned to face an elderly black man wearing overalls and carrying a broom. "You live here? What you doin' here?" Rosie explained she was looking for someone. "What apartment?" he demanded.

"I dunno. She came in about half an hour ago to visit a friend—Nula. You know anyone called Nula?"

He shook his head and shoved the broom at her feet. "Get out, go on, get out. This is private property."

She got to the car in time to see the kids who had pushed past her breaking one of its side mirrors. The window on the driver's side had been smashed. Rosie kicked at the glass in fury as the kids ran off shrieking. She carefully removed the glass from the seat. Where the hell was Lorraine? As she straightened up she saw a man walking out of the building with two suitcases. He was in one hell of a hurry and she was about to shout to him when he turned into an alley alongside the old building. Rosie followed. The alley led into a parking area strewn with a few old wrecks, old sofas, and broken furniture. As Rosie reached the entrance of the lot the man was throwing suitcases into the trunk of a car. Just as she was about to cross toward him, a woman shouted and he looked up to the fire escape.

Nula was leaning over the railings. "Get another bottle, and hurry up."

Lyall got into his car and started the engine. Rosie stared hard at Nula, sure it was the right woman. She didn't know what to do. If Lorraine was with her, maybe they were just talking and she'd go nuts if Rosie suddenly barged in. On the other hand, if Lorraine was in trouble and Rosie did nothing, she'd be just as mad. "Think like a detective, Rosie, come on," she muttered. "What would Mrs. Super Sleuth Lorraine Page do?"

Standing on an old crate, she managed to drag the ladder of the fire escape loose and started to climb upward. One or two rungs snapped off as she put her weight on them so she almost fell back to the ground. Halfway up she wondered what the hell she was doing, but by then she was almost at the first landing. She grabbed the railings and ducked under the railing to stand on the first escape. She was scared that if someone saw her they might push her off, so she picked up a garbage bag and tried to look like a resident dumping it. She passed one window after another, peering in, looking for Lorraine. The apartments were run-down and squalid, and she saw no one until the fourth window revealed a couple eating. She dodged back the way she had come and headed up toward the second floor. Suddenly, the bag caught and split and refuse clattered down the fire escape. She froze. The landing window opened below. "What the fuck's goin' on up there?" The window banged shut again and Rosie held on grimly, heart pounding. She nearly fell off again when another of the rusted steps gave way and she felt her arm wrench almost out of its socket as she hung on. It was only her anger with Lorraine that kept her climbing.

• • •

It took Lyall just a few minutes to get to a liquor store, buy
two more bottles of vodka, and return to the apartment house.
This time he parked on the street right behind Rosie's car, ran
up the stairs two at a time to the fourth floor, and banged on
the door for Nula to let him in.

Lorraine was on the bed, her feet tied together with a pair
of Nula's tights and her hands bound in front of her. The
empty bottle was on the bed beside her. Nula was dressed and
everything was packed ready to leave. Lyall locked the door
and tossed the bottles onto the bed beside Lorraine. He was
sweating with nerves. "There's a car smashed up outside, a
rental from L.A.—that hers?"

"Why don't you ask her yourself?" Nula snapped.

Lyall picked up the cases. "I'm not hanging around, Nula.
I'm getting out now with or without you. If that bitch could
find us so can the cops. She's probably workin' for them."

Nula was unscrewing the cap of a fresh bottle, glaring at
him. "You'll do just what I tell you and so will she." Nula
pushed the bottle between Lorraine's lips, tilting it. The vodka
dribbled down her chin, soaking her new blouse. "Drink it,
Lorraine! *Swallow it!*"

The vodka hit the back of Lorraine's throat. She had to
swallow but she turned her head away. Nula slapped her face
hard and pinched her nose so that when she forced the bottle
between Lorraine's lips she had to swallow. The liquor made
her body feel as if it were on fire and the room began to blur.
"That's a good girl, come on, let's see you finish the bottle."

Lyall was frightened. "Christ, you'll kill her."

Nula laughed. "What the fuck do you think I'm trying to
do? Get those bags down to the car." He opened the door and
suddenly Nula sprang off the bed and ran toward him. "No!
I don't want you pissing your pants and driving off. We'll go
together. Open the other bottle."

"I'm not doing it!"

Nula punched him and pushed him up against the wall. "We
got to do this, we have no choice. She knows enough to get
them sniffing around us, and if they pick me up I swear to
God you'll go down with me."

Nula sat astride Lorraine pouring the vodka down her throat.
Lorraine heaved as if to vomit and Nula withdrew the bottle

and again slapped her hard across the face. Her eyes closed and her body went limp, and Nula poured the rest into her slack mouth. The liquid dribbled down her face, into her hair, saturating her. Nula got off the bed. Lorraine was motionless. "Let's go," Lyall urged. "We'll miss the plane, Nula! *Come on!*"

Rosie, meanwhile, had reached the fourth floor, and was edging along the fire escape, peering into one window after another, as Nula and Lyall got into their car and drove off. Her legs were shaking, her hands cut from the rusted railings as she inched toward the landing window. She'd break the glass if necessary—she was not going to climb back down. Now she didn't even care if she was arrested for breaking and entering. She got to her knees and began to crawl the last few yards. It was then she saw Lorraine.

She banged on the window. Lorraine half turned her head but then went back to untying her legs. She kept flopping over and she was giggling. Rosie banged on the window again but Lorraine seemed oblivious. Rosie attempted to open the window but it held firm. She pressed her face closer as Lorraine tried to stand, lurching into the wall, then into the dressing table. She rolled around laughing and then she saw the bottle of vodka that had fallen off the bed.

Rosie kicked at the window. The glass cracked but only after she had used both feet was there a hole big enough for her to undo the lock.

Lorraine paid no attention to her. She was trying unsuccessfully to drink from the bottle. Rosie heaved her bulk through the window. The glass cut her leg and she was gasping for breath from the effort. She reached Lorraine as she lifted up the bottle to drink and grabbed it. Lorraine screamed and tried to hold on to it but Rosie wouldn't give in. She tore the bottle from her, ran with it into the bathroom and poured the contents down the sink. She was heaving and panting for breath. She looked at her reflection in the old cracked bathroom mirror—her face was red and shiny with sweat, her clothes were filthy, her hand bleeding. As she gasped for breath, she became aware of an ominous silence from the other room and dropped the bottle. Lorraine had passed out. She looked green, her breathing rasping, rattling. Rosie was terrified that she was choking and dragged her to the bathroom, hung her over the edge of the tub, then ran water over her,

pushing at her lungs. Lorraine heaved and coughed, then vomited. Rosie forced her under the cold water tap. She was like
a pitiful rag doll, unable to fend Rosie off, unable to do anything as she retched.

Rosie got her to her feet and forced her to walk up and
down. Her head lolled on her chest; she couldn't speak; her
eyes were unfocused and she didn't seem to know who Rosie
was. She mumbled incoherently and then slithered to the floor.
''Lemme sleep.''

Rosie dragged her up again, walking her up and down. She
was crying—she was so afraid. She didn't know if she should
call an ambulance and she kept asking Lorraine her name but
she couldn't reply, just kept saying that she wanted to sleep.
It wasn't until she had been violently sick again that Rosie
helped her to the bed. She stripped off Lorraine's clothes and
drew back the sheets, rolling her naked body farther onto the
bed.

''Lorraine? It's Rosie.''

Lorraine's eyes drooped and she gave a weak smile. Rosie
went into the filthy kitchen in the corner of the room, enclosed
by a grease-splattered curtain half hanging off its rail. She
brewed some coffee, able to keep her eyes on Lorraine as she
was doing it, then went back to the bed and shook her. Lorraine moaned and swatted at Rosie to leave her alone. But
Rosie persisted, made her sit up and tried to get her to drink
the coffee. After half an hour, Rosie could tell she was coming
around. She asked where she was and Rosie said they were in
San Francisco, but it didn't seem to sink in. She closed her
eyes again but Rosie still wouldn't let her sleep: she pressed
ice cubes wrapped in a pillowcase to Lorraine's head. ''Rosie,
I have to sleep. Leave me alone.''

Finally, Rosie lost patience. ''*Right.* I'm going to leave you.
You disgust me—just as you got everything going for you.
Why did you do it?''

Lorraine threw aside the sheet. ''I got to have a drink, Rosie,
I'm going crazy, my head aches. Just get me a drink.'' She
held her head in her hands. ''I got to make a call—got to call
Bickerstaff. Is there a phone here?''

''The state you're in you can't call anyone.''

Lorraine squinted up at her. ''They forced it down me.''
She tried to stand but the room spun and she had to sit down
again. ''Nula, you got to get her arrested, she's with that pho-

tographer Craig Lyall. I got to call Bickerstaff.''

Rosie didn't know whether to believe her or not. She stood with her feet planted like a solid oak. "Well, you can't do nothin' about that now. They've gone."

"Shit." Lorraine picked up the ice pack and rested it against her head. "You saw them leave?"

"Yeah."

Rosie poured more coffee and a glass of water. "Start drinking this and as much water as you can take—go on, take it."

Lorraine did as she was told but when she attempted to get up off the bed she felt faint. "Rosie, start looking in the garbage. See if they left anything that might tell us where they're heading."

Rosie found nothing in the disgusting kitchenette, but moving around the bed she spotted a small trash can by the dressing table filled with cotton balls and tissues smeared with makeup. She tipped them out onto an old newspaper and poked around. She found nothing and wrapped up the mess in the newspaper—then opened it again. There were marks around the air-flight ads. "There's this. What do you think?"

Lorraine forced herself to look at the paper: two airlines had been underlined and their phone numbers circled. "Call Delta and American airlines, see if any flights are leaving this afternoon with a Mr. Lyall on board."

"They won't tell me. They never tell you what passengers are boarding—that's a law, isn't it?"

Lorraine craved a drink, her whole body screamed for one, but she gulped the water. "Say it's an emergency, something to do with kids. . . . Anything, just find out which airline they're on." Lorraine hung on to the headboard as she stood up. She inched her way into the bathroom, where she saw the vodka bottle and reached out for it. A single drop remained in the bottom and she drank it before she retched again, clinging to the washbasin. She saw herself in the mirror: her face was pale green, her eyes red-rimmed, and her lips swollen.

Rosie stomped in. "Two seats booked by Mr. Lyall for the four-fifteen flight to Las Vegas. Now what?"

Lorraine's eyes were closed. "Did they go off in a cab?"

"No, Lyall had a car. So, now what do I do?"

She told Rosie to call Ed Bickerstaff. "This is what you say to him. Tell him you're my partner—Jesus, just tell him anything—that it's to do with the murders of David Burrows and Holly, you got that?''

Rosie reached for the phone as Lorraine crashed to the floor.

Ed Bickerstaff hung up. He wondered if he could trust the information. He would have been happier if it had been Lorraine herself who had called—she had never made any mention of a partner. He decided there was nothing to lose, so he put in the call to send agents in Las Vegas to arrest Craig Lyall and his companion. He then arranged for a search warrant to look over Lyall's studio. As he was leaving his office, he received the phone call he had been half expecting: Steven Janklow's plea would stand as guilty on seven counts of murder, but his mental state had been scrutinized and eight doctors and four psychiatrists had declared him criminally insane and medically unfit to stand trial. He would be held in a secure mental institution for life, with no hope of release. Mrs. Thorburn had still not made any contact with him. Brad Thorburn continued to monitor his brother's welfare via the family lawyers but did no more than that.

The subsequent arrest of Lyall and Nula would be welcome as a show of the FBI's thoroughness, but Bickerstaff was wondering if he had made a mistake. He called Rooney to double-check on Lorraine but he was away, and although he'd already ordered that Nula and Lyall be brought in, he was nervous enough to want to run it by the chief. Bickerstaff embroidered the facts a little, pointing out that Lyall's arrest might further clarify Janklow's guilt. It might also confirm that Art Mathews had instigated the murders of Angela Hollow and David Burrows. It sounded so good in the telling that he felt more confident.

''Who's the informant, Ed? And how come you haven't discussed this with anyone else from my department?''

Bickerstaff blushed. ''It's Lorraine Page.''

The chief gave a fish-eyed stare. He rubbed the stubble on his chin and took a deep breath. As usual his shirt buttons seemed about to pop as his chest expanded.

''Lorraine Page? You'd better hope to Christ that it pans out as well as the Janklow tapes she did.'' He hesitated. ''Has she got something else on Janklow?''

''I'll get back to you as soon as I hear anything.''

The chief glared. "So you'll be staying on? What you doing, Ed, taking up permanent residency in Pasadena?"

Bickerstaff seemed fazed. "Of course not, and you know as well as I do I can't walk away from this until I see if it's connected. I mean, if it ties in with the original investigation . . ."

"You sure it's not tied in with you trying to whitewash your fuckup with Art Mathews?"

Bickerstaff stood square-jawed in front of the desk, retaining his composure. "I'm just trying to do my job. Nothing has been whitewashed and I'm not making any excuses for the Art Mathews fuckup, but I would like to check any new evidence that may come to light."

"How much did Page hit you for?"

Bickerstaff smiled but it was totally without humor. "She doesn't get a cent." He closed the door behind him silently. He had not added that Lorraine's payout depended on her providing evidence that proved Mathews's part in the hammer murders. If she did bring in the goods, five thousand dollars was not much to pay for the FBI coming out smelling like roses.

As Bickerstaff was about to enter his office he was handed a fax informing him that Lyall and Nula had been arrested in Las Vegas. Lyall insisted they were there to get married. Bickerstaff requested they be brought to L.A. for questioning in connection with a homicide investigation and a possible accessory to murder charge.

He'd received no reply to his calls to Lorraine's apartment, and was getting impatient. Nula and Lyall were on their way to Pasadena from Las Vegas and he hadn't the slightest idea what he was going to question them about. What had they overlooked in previous interviews? Or was it possible that Lorraine Page had, yet again, withheld vital evidence? If she had, she was now in dangerous waters, and Bickerstaff would damned well make sure she drowned.

Rosie and Lorraine hardly spoke during the long drive back to L.A. It took all of Lorraine's willpower not to beg Rosie to buy a bottle. The need to drink was stronger than her headache and sickness. She felt despairing and, worse, inadequate. It was the end of the agency, the partnership—she was back at square one and it hurt. But nothing was stronger than the urge to drink. She had not beaten it. She felt it had beaten her, that it would always beat her; that was what really hit home hard and made any thought of a future a hopeless dream.

The phone was ringing as they opened the front door. It was Bickerstaff. Rosie asked him to call back, and hung up before he could remonstrate. She then called Jake, who said he'd be right over. When he arrived Rosie had cooked some spaghetti and set the table. Jake put his arm around her shoulder. "How you doing?"

"Fucked! I had a future and a job yesterday but today, well, I dunno. You got to talk to her—this guy Bickerstaff keeps calling."

Jake nodded and went into the bedroom. Lorraine was awake, sitting on the edge of the bed. She had on a bathrobe and looked pale, sickly. She gave that look of hers, tilting her head, that slight squint. "It's no good, Jake, I'm not going to make it. I blew it so badly. I got overconfident, arrogant. You know, I thought I was so damned clever, and if it wasn't for Rosie I'd probably be dead."

He squeezed her hand. "It'll always be a part of your life. You can never have one drink. Even if you think you're strong enough to deal with it you won't be because it's an illness, Lorraine."

Lorraine was crying. "All I want is a drink, Jake."

He stood up. "Lemme tell you something. I want one. Rosie wants one. We all want one. You're no different. We all feel like you do, so get your ass off that bed and come in and eat."

He walked out and she got up slowly. When she joined them at the table, he pulled out her chair.

"Thanks for helping me out this afternoon, Rosie."

"Think nothing of it, partner, but next time you tell me to wait outside, I want to know how many minutes, who you're going to see, and why."

Lorraine doubted if there would be a next time. The phone rang. Rosie answered and handed it to Lorraine. "You better talk to him, it's Bickerstaff."

Lorraine took a deep breath. "Hi, Ed. We just got back. It was a long drive. . . . Yeah, yeah, no problem. I'll be there. . . . Sure, thanks." She hung up and sighed, completely deflated. "They want me at the station. They're sending a squad car. I can't think straight—I can't even see straight. They're going to take one look at me and they're gonna know. I'm still plastered, look at my hands, I've got the shakes so bad.''

Jake took off his jacket and rolled up his sleeves.

''Let's get that shower running.''

Lorraine looked at them deadeyed. ''Oh, God, not again . . .''

TWENTY

Nula had been separated from Lyall on the way to Pasadena but the flight to Las Vegas had been long enough for them to get their story straight. Lorraine had not yet arrived at the station when their lawyer angrily confronted Bickerstaff, insinuating that he was wrongfully holding them on the word of a known drunkard, a woman who had arrived at his clients' apartment in San Francisco attempting to blackmail them. He doubted if Bickerstaff would be able to make any sense of what Ms. Page had leveled against his clients as she had been so drunk when they had last seen her that they had left her in the apartment. Time was against Bickerstaff—without strong evidence implicating them he could not hold Lyall and Nula longer than twenty-four hours. He was in a hot seat of his own making and could ask for no help from the LAPD. This had been an FBI arrest and Bickerstaff was on his own.

Jake and Rosie were still plying Lorraine with water and coffee. She had no hangover now but her confidence had gone. She was afraid to confront Bickerstaff, and Rosie knew it.

The doorbell rang, and Lorraine jumped. Bickerstaff stood on the steps, his shirt sticking to him, his tie loosened; he knew he could lose his job over this latest development. Having been told about Lorraine's condition he wanted to see her for himself, and was immediately relieved to see she was looking sharp, well dressed, and sober.

"I was just on my way," Lorraine said lamely.

"Let's move it. We've got them for twenty-four hours and time's running out. You'd better have a fucking good reason for setting this scene up. I got Berillo and their lawyer at me and the entire department wondering what the hell is goin' on and they aren't the only ones."

Lorraine followed him down the stairs. She stepped into the back of the patrol car, he slammed the door, and got into the front.

"They both said you were drunk."

"They poured a bottle of vodka down my throat, so I guess I was."

"You okay now?"

"Just a bit shaky."

"You should have told me who you were going after, and more important why. You wanna fill me in before we get there?"

Lorraine took a deep breath. "I wasn't sure, I knew Nula was possibly involved. What I didn't know was that Lyall was, too."

Ed started the engine. "I've given them both a tough grilling and they stuck to their story. They were in Vegas to get married, or whatever kind of ceremony you'd call it in their case. They got preachers there who'll marry anybody. They also maintain they don't know a thing about Holly's or David Burrows's murder, but they do know that Janklow's admitted to killing them. They also said you were drunk when you visited them and that they told you if you needed them they'd fly back after they got hitched."

There was silence for a moment. Then Bickerstaff asked bluntly, "How do you want to work this?"

Lorraine was desperate for a drink. She didn't dare take out a cigarette as her hands were shaking so much. "Maybe talk to Lyall first, break him. I don't think he killed anybody. He's dominated by Nula, maybe even scared of her, so go for him first."

Bickerstaff was uneasy. His brain ticked like the small hand on his watch as he tried to assimilate what she had just said.

"It's something to do with Mrs. Thorburn's jewelry," she added. "I need to look at the lists Janklow made out and I want to see the morgue shot of Didi—David Burrows."

Lorraine followed Bickerstaff through the maze of sterile corridors, stopping off at his office. In just a matter of weeks, all evidence of poor old Bill Rooney had disappeared: his big creaking swivel chair had gone, the desk was devoid of anything but telephones. Bickerstaff gestured for her to sit down, reaching for a phone. She looked around, sniffed, and guessed they'd even given the office a quick paint job. No wonder Rooney had hated the new precinct, there was something so anonymous and characterless about the vast building.

Bickerstaff dialed an internal number and asked for Lyall to be brought up from the cells and taken to one of the small interview rooms with a one-way mirror. He replaced the phone and looked at his watch.

"We'll give it five minutes, then go down."

"I wonder if we can keep him waiting for a few minutes. I need a few things typed up—is there a clerk I could use? One that works with a Dictaphone so we can cut down the time?"

Bickerstaff looked puzzled and she smiled. "I want to make a statement!"

Lorraine worked with a young clerk for fifteen minutes and then Bickerstaff returned, saying he couldn't wait any longer.

Lorraine nodded and licked her lips. Her mouth felt bone dry, and she felt worse as they took the elevator down to the basement level. Her stomach lurched as the elevator stopped. When Bickerstaff looked at her, she was very pale.

"You okay?"

"I'll need a glass of water."

Bickerstaff nodded as the elevator doors opened. They passed through the security checkpoints and into the interview areas, stopping when they saw an officer standing by an open door. Bickerstaff tapped Lorraine's arm.

"In here, we'll watch him being brought in."

"Okay, um, I need that glass of water." She was tensing up, clasping and unclasping her hands, her mouth thick and dry, as if she had eaten sawdust.

"You'll have it." He turned to the officer standing by the door.

"Make sure there's a pitcher of water for Ms. Page."

Lorraine stood in the small, barren viewing room and stared

at the glass partition in the room beyond. Lyall was being ushered in, nervous and repeatedly asking for his lawyer. He sat with his hands splayed out on the small bare table, his face set, his mouth a rigid line. Watched by Lorraine and Bickerstaff, he stared around the small windowless room and then looked directly at the one-way glass.

"You want to go in?" Bickerstaff asked softly.

Lorraine could feel the tension disappearing. She coughed again, lightly clearing her throat, rereading the freshly typed pages. "Just let him sweat a few more minutes. I'll need some kind of official-looking file; good photographs of the dead women, lot of documents, pens, notepad—and keep his lawyer out for as long as you can. And for chrissakes, is somebody getting me some water?"

"They'll be here right away, and so will the water."

Bickerstaff glanced at his watch, constantly monitoring the time as it ticked away. A female rookie officer appeared with a thick file, passing it to Bickerstaff, who then handed it over to Lorraine. She began checking down Janklow's list of jewelry. More copies of files were brought in, the photographs of the murdered women, two dummy files and she began stacking them in order, making notes on a notepad. She looked through the glass partition at Lyall, watching his every move, the way he clenched and unclenched his hands and kept running a finger around the inside of his collar. They could see him crossing and uncrossing his legs, his shoes scuffing the floor. Ten minutes later Bickerstaff was still waiting, Lorraine was now staring at Lyall, the files stacked neatly in front of her. She patted her pockets to make sure she had the cigarettes and lighter; she was no longer shaking but was feeling a buzz beginning inside her. She was almost ready. An officer appeared with the water and two glasses at long last. She poured half a glass and gulped it down, then passed it back to the officer.

"Okay, take it in, but you are not to say a word, even if he asks a question."

She watched him enter the room. They heard Lyall asking how long he was to be kept waiting but the officer didn't even look at him.

Lorraine nodded to Bickerstaff. "I'm ready."

As she left the room he murmured "Good luck," but she didn't turn back.

When Lorraine walked in, Lyall covered his surprise fast, turning away as she sat in the chair opposite. She paid no attention to him but opened the dummy file first and her notebook, carefully laid out her pens, cigarettes, and lighter. Then she reached over to the pitcher and poured herself a glass of water.

Lyall cleared his throat and tapped his foot. Bickerstaff waited. Watching as she sat down, she then turned to the officer on duty.

"Could you please bring me an ashtray? Thank you."

Lorraine slowly got out the photographs of Holly and placed them in front of Lyall. The officer slipped the ashtray onto the table, hovering until she told him he could leave the room.

The officer nodded and walked out.

"Please look at the photographs, Craig."

He turned away.

"She was only seventeen and she was beautiful, wasn't she? Take a look at her pretty face."

He glanced at the ten-by-six photograph. Then Lorraine pointed to the morgue shots, which showed the injuries that virtually obliterated her face, broken nose, eye sockets filled with blood, and the gaping mouth with the front teeth smashed.

"Someone hammered her face, broke her skull, her nose, even her teeth. What kind of person do you think would do this? What kind of *madness* did this?"

Lyall wouldn't look at the photographs, instead keeping his eyes on the wall.

"I keep on telling them that you couldn't have done it, but they won't believe me, you know why? Because—"

"I didn't do that. I'm innocent." His voice was high-pitched, bordering on hysterical.

"I know you are, of course you are. All you were involved in was blackmail. I know that but—"

"Janklow did it, he admitted it—so why don't you piss off and leave me alone? I want my lawyer here." He sounded less hesitant now, his voice lower and more steady.

"Your lawyer will be here, Craig, but he's just finalizing Nula's release. She's going, so I hope you've made arrangements for your share of any money you had, because she . . ."

Bickerstaff covered his face. She was really pushing it.

"I don't believe you," Lyall said sullenly.

"Believe what? That she's being released?" Lorraine

flicked through the dummy documents. "This is her statement. You can read it if you like, but you won't be released, Craig, because Nula has stated that you were involved in murdering this girl and David Burrows."

Lyall sneered, "I know you're lying."

Lorraine pushed forward Didi's photographs, the before and after shots. "Am I? That's naïve of you, Craig. You know Nula killed Didi, even though she insists that you did it—that you drove her to their apartment, sat and drank tea, even shared her banana bread of hers, didn't she? Anyway, according to Nula, the three of you started to argue because Didi had kept a ring, one of Mrs. Thorburn's pieces. You'd all agreed to get rid of everything because the items could be traced, but Didi kept a ring. This one. Look at this picture, Craig—that's the ring, isn't it? On the third finger of her right hand."

Bickerstaff had no idea what Lorraine was talking about. What ring? Was it in the files? He turned to his backup. "Get someone to bring me the original files down here, will you? And fast." His backup turned to the young rookie and repeated Bickerstaff's request. She whispered back to him, very flustered, and the agent turned to Bickerstaff.

"Um, what exact file would that be? She, uh, Ms. Page has got . . ."

"Copies, I want the file on the Thorburn jewelry. Now get out, go on, the pair of you."

He turned his attention back to the interview room.

Lyall's fists were clenched so tight the knuckles stood out white. Lorraine placed the full-length morgue shot of Didi in front of him. All she was wearing was the ring.

"Just nod if it is the ring, Craig. You don't have to say anything. I'm only trying to help you, you must know that. I'm not even pressing charges about your part in trying to kill me."

"What are you?" he snapped.

"I'm a private investigator, not even attached to the station or the FBI, but because I was there in San Francisco they're allowing me to talk to you. You both tried to kill me and you almost succeeded, but what you didn't know was that I was wired, so everything you said in that apartment has been recorded. That's why you were both arrested in Las Vegas."

He still didn't believe a word.

"Nula knew that she had to frame somebody to get herself released and that was you, Craig, because as soon as she saw me with the FBI agents she knew the game was up. She's been talking since they brought her in. Look at these statements. Don't you think it's strange your lawyer isn't here?"

Bickerstaff could feel sweat running down his back. He was relieved no one else was privy to what Lorraine was saying as none of it was fact. She was making it up as she went along, coming out with one lie after another. None of it was confirmed evidence, all of it was supposition, and he knew that what was going on in that small enclosed room was illegal.

"I never killed anybody," Lyall snapped, but his hands were shaking now.

Lorraine sipped her water. "I know that, Craig, but let me read you a section of Nula's statement . . ."

Lyall was sweating even more than Bickerstaff, who couldn't believe Lorraine's audacity—Nula's statement was what she'd just had the clerk type up for her. He watched the way she took her time sifting through the dummy documents, and continued to talk quietly and calmly. She then pulled a page toward her and started to read it aloud.

" 'It started as an argument between the three of us. Didi wouldn't give the ring back, she said she couldn't get it off her finger so then Craig said he would cut it off and she started to get hysterical.' "

"That's not true," he interjected. Lorraine held up her hand as if to tell him to be patient, then continued reading in the same steady voice.

" 'Craig became more and more angry because Didi could get us all into trouble. We'd been selling Mrs. Thorburn's jewelry for years, in bits and pieces. Art would find the buyer and we would just collect, but because of the killings it was dangerous for Didi to walk around showing off this big ring. It was a topaz with a row of diamonds around it and it was worth a lot of money.' "

Lorraine had made it all up, unsure herself. All she knew, or had pieced together, was that according to Janklow's lists and description the ring belonged to Mrs. Thorburn and it was possibly the ring Didi was wearing. She looked at Lyall. "I presume when she says Art she is referring to Art Mathews, is that correct?"

"Why are you asking me these questions?"

"I used to be a cop, now I'm freelance, insurance claims, that kind of thing. Before they charge you I want to get my facts straight and until your lawyer is available they can't talk to you. There's nothing illegal about it—there's nobody else here, we're not even being taped."

He was really sweating now. "You mean it's true? They're releasing Nula?"

She nodded, tapped the dummy file. "She's given her statement and all I want to do is get on to her for my clients and before she skips the country. I don't care who did what to whom just so long as I do my job."

Lyall tried to fathom how she was sitting in front of him. He knew she'd been dead drunk. How in hell had she gotten herself together?

Bickerstaff shook his head, even more impressed. Lorraine was giving to him, piece by piece, a section of the jigsaw puzzle, the stolen jewelry, the blackmail scam, but Lyall had not as yet implicated himself in any way.

Lorraine asked, "You took the photographs of Janklow, didn't you?"

Lyall sighed. "Art did. Well, some of them, years ago when he had a studio in Santa Monica. Janklow had this thing about looking like his mother, you know, all dragged up. At first Art didn't know who he was—he'd used some false name, they all do—and then he saw him at some Society dinner with his mother, years ago, and started milking him. That's all I know. I swear to God, I honestly had nothing to do with it. I didn't even know it was going on . . ." He trailed off. "I don't know what to do," he said suddenly, helplessly.

"Maybe tell me the truth. Then I'll tell you what I think, as a friend, you should do, and in return, you tell me about the whereabouts of the stolen jewelry. I'm not interested in the murders. If you did them with Nula that's not my problem."

"I didn't," he said flatly. "I'm so confused, I don't know who I can trust and I don't believe a word you're telling me."

Lorraine snapped the file closed. "If that's the way you feel I'll just go. All I wanted to do was get my insurance claims sorted out. There's more than three million dollars' worth of gems missing. Mrs. Thorburn's son Brad asked me to look into it. They've let me talk to you because they aren't quite ready to charge you." Bickerstaff's mouth was bone dry. She was fishing in dangerous waters again: actually naming people—that could get him into real trouble.

"They can't charge me with anything," Lyall said shrilly.

Lorraine slapped her hand hard on the table and Lyall jumped. "Don't be so fucking stupid. Nula's named you as Holly and Didi's killer. You're crazy if you think they're not going to lock you up for a very long time. Art Mathews is dead so she's only got you to blame. Now, if you're saying you didn't have any part in those murders then you'd better have a good alibi, because she's given them evidence to prove you killed them both. Because you were in Didi's apartment, weren't you? If you didn't kill her then Nula did, right?"

He sniffed. "I didn't touch her."

"So who did?"

"She did, of course. Nula."

Lorraine felt as if she had been punched. She'd expected him to say Mathews, not Nula.

Bickerstaff muttered to himself, "Fuck me . . ."

"You saw her?" Lorraine asked, keeping her voice steady.

Lyall put his head in his hands. "Yes, she said she pushed Didi and she fell and hit her head against the coffee table. We couldn't find any pulse and she began to panic. Well, she had reason to."

"Because of Mrs. Thorburn's jewelry?"

"Yes. And then I panicked, it was just all confused and terrible. We couldn't get it off her finger, the ring . . . we couldn't get it off."

He broke down and started to sob.

"So who decided to make it look as if it was one of the hammer murders?"

"She did. She said no one would believe it if they just found her, especially not after Holly."

He sobbed, pleading with her to believe it wasn't him, he hadn't done anything.

Lorraine reached across the table and touched his hand. "Craig, what do you mean 'after Holly'? What about Holly?"

Lyall flapped his hands wildly. "Oh, Christ, this is terrible, it isn't right, I know it."

"Come on, Craig, get it off your chest, tell me."

He steadied himself. "Holly had somehow found out about the blackmail—God knows how but she had. She'd been picked up by some john, taken back to his place, and—"

"Do you know who it was?"

Lyall chewed his lip. "I think it was—you said his name before—Thorburn."

Lorraine couldn't believe what she was hearing. "*Brad Thorburn?* You mean he's involved in all this?"

"Yes, inasmuch as he picked up Holly and took her back to his house. I dunno what happened, but she somehow figured out what we were all doing—maybe she saw Janklow there—but she started pushing Nula and Didi for money. They got on to Art—they were really worried—and next thing I read she was murdered. I don't know which one of them did it, but they got away with it because they made it look like this serial killer had done it. I think Art was involved. But I swear to God I don't know. I was caught up in it all because I'd taken photographs of that Norman Hastings and he was a friend of Janklow's, but I didn't know that. It was just, well, I knew *they* were doing it and it seemed so easy."

Lorraine was trying to absorb what he was saying and then it clicked. "Were you blackmailing Norman Hastings?"

"Yes, but then he went to Janklow and asked him what he should do about it. I suppose the two of them discussed it together. I've told you all I know. I had nothing to do with any of the murders. All I did was a little blackmail."

Bickerstaff checked his watch, crossed to the phone, and dialed. Even though the room was soundproofed, he spoke very quietly. Josh Bean answered.

"This is Bickerstaff. I want Brad Thorburn brought in for questioning."

Bean hesitated. "I think he's still in France, Mr. Bickerstaff."

"I don't give a shit if he's in Outer Mongolia, get him in." He replaced the phone, feeling elated, and couldn't wait to get his own hands on Lyall. And he couldn't wait to lay it all before the chief for the sheer pleasure of seeing his face.

Lorraine continued to question Lyall as he sobbed out his part in the blackmail racket. She made only a few notes, knowing that Bickerstaff would go over everything. She didn't even feel self-congratulatory. She couldn't stop Brad Thorburn's face from drifting into her mind, and she only half listened as Lyall talked, freely now, as if relieved it was all out in the open.

Lyall had used Didi to make up the men who came to him

for secret photographic sessions. They had met through Mathews when they worked together in Santa Monica. When they met again in Los Angeles they continued their old tricks and Mathews let Didi and Nula use his apartment for photo sessions. He moved out, leaving them there. Didi continued to pass on potential blackmail victims. Janklow was paying first Art, then all three to keep silent. None had any indication that he was also a killer. He had always paid up without argument, regaining one negative after another, until he began to get edgy, saying he had no more money, no more jewelry.

Lyall asked for water, sipped it, and then nervously kept tracing the rim of the glass with his finger. "Hastings didn't have much cash but he paid up, fifty bucks here and there. But when Art found out he went crazy." The rim of the glass squeaked as he ran his finger around and around.

"Did you kill Norman Hastings, Craig?"

"No, I didn't. And I had nothing to do with any of those others."

Lorraine leaned forward. "What about Didi?"

Lyall closed his eyes and sighed. "I saw her—she was already dead, she was at their apartment. Nula called me. She was lying on the floor. I never touched her. I think they had something to do with that girl Holly, but I don't know what—they knew something, I'm sure of it."

"What about Mathews? Was he involved in Holly's murder? That's what you're suggesting, isn't it? That Nula and Didi had something to do with Holly's death?"

His voice was quiet, almost a whisper. "Yes, but I don't know if Art was involved." He started to cry, biting his bottom lip to stop the tears. "I swear all I'm guilty of is helping Nula to—" He broke down, and Lorraine waited until he had composed himself. "I helped move her body, carry it to the stolen car."

"When you carried Didi, did she have these injuries?" Lorraine brought out the photograph of Didi's hideously beaten face again and he straightened up.

"No. When I last saw her her head was covered in a black plastic bag, I never saw her face, and after she was put in the car, I went home."

When he had finished Lyall seemed more relaxed. He had stopped crying and seemed resigned. As Lorraine gathered her notes and files together, he gave her a weak smile. "I loved her, you know, really loved Nula. We were going to be married in Vegas—that's why I helped her. It wasn't anything but that, I didn't do anything."

Lorraine walked across to the door. "They'll want a statement from you, Craig, and I think you'd be wise to tell them everything you know, just as you've told me. Don't let her get away with it."

Bickerstaff didn't congratulate Lorraine. He almost grabbed her notes from her while directing his men to begin the detailed requestioning of Craig Lyall. Lorraine sat in his office, Rooney's ex-office, completely drained, as the atmosphere around grew charged with excitement. She felt ill, her head thudded, but all she could think of was Brad Thorburn. Had she been wrong? Could he be implicated in the murders? Had he always known more than he had let on?

"What about Thorburn?" she asked Bickerstaff quietly.

"We're having him brought back from France." He hesitated and leaned over her. "How involved do you figure the smooth bastard is?"

"I just don't know."

"You mean there's something you *don't* know about this business?" Bickerstaff didn't mean it to sound quite so sarcastic; he was actually trying to pay her a compliment, but she was not amused.

"I didn't think Brad Thorburn was involved."

Bickerstaff looked directly at her. "We'll find out soon enough."

Bickerstaff was by now moving like a man on speed, talking nonstop, firing instructions right, left, and center. Lorraine remained sitting in his office, thinking about Brad Thorburn, until they were ready for her.

Nula was not brought up from the holding cells until four P.M. that afternoon. She had refused to be interviewed without her lawyer present, so they had been forced to wait until Craig Lyall's statement was completed. Bickerstaff was given permission by Chief Berillo to allow Lorraine Page to watch the interrogation of Nula from the adjoining viewing room. She was taken from his office, back down to the basement level.

As Nula was being ushered from the cells, she was aggressive and abusive, and had to be half dragged along the corridor, kicking and spitting. Bickerstaff might not have intended Lorraine and Nula to meet. It could have been coincidence that the two met in the corridor coming from opposite ends. Only when Nula saw Lorraine did she quiet down, visibly shocked into silence. As the door closed behind her, Lorraine entered the adjoining room. Nula had become outwardly calmer and asked for a mirror in order to check her makeup and wig. Sitting at the table, her lips a deep dark vermilion with a sheen of gloss, she asked for a tissue to wipe her teeth as small flecks of the lipstick had stained her front teeth.

"Well, I'm ready, are you?" she smirked, looking at the one-way mirror.

Bickerstaff stood by Lorraine, both looking at Nula. He didn't turn to her when he asked if she wanted to sit in on the interrogation rather than watch it from the viewing room. She nodded, he then turned to face her and smiled. "Good, I hoped you'd agree."

First Bickerstaff then two uniformed officers followed by Lorraine entered. Nula turned slowly to face her and then laughed. "I underestimated you," she said, completely relaxed, and apparently unconcerned by the formidable lineup. If anything, she seemed almost to be enjoying the attention. Her lawyer waited to speak until everyone had been seated and the tape recorder turned on.

Nula was facing two separate charges: blackmail and extortion, and first-degree murder. She stated that her birth name was Nicholas Simmons. Her lawyer now turned to Bickerstaff. "My client categorically denies any part in the charges leveled at her and she has the right to remain silent. She has been made aware of certain statements by Craig Lyall, implicating her in these said crimes, and again denies playing any part in the said crimes but will, if required, be prepared to stand trial for the prosecution and to implicate Craig Lyall as being solely responsible for the crimes."

There was a short pause before Bickerstaff began by asking Nula directly if she had been involved in the blackmail of Steven Janklow.

No comment.

Had she struck David "Didi" Burrows during an argument and then, with the assistance of Craig Lyall, carried his body to a stolen car and deposited it?

No comment.

Bickerstaff asked detailed questions for almost half an hour. Each one was answered with "No comment."

Throughout, Nula sat checking her nails, fixing her skirt, straightening her frilled blouse. She sometimes looked at Lorraine, raising an eyebrow, and then, as if bored by the proceedings, yawned, crossing and recrossing her legs. When the photographs of Didi were displayed, she averted her face and stared at the wall. When she was asked again to look at photographs, she sighed and glanced down, then looked at her lawyer.

Holly's pictures were laid in front of her. This time her lawyer asked her to look at the photographs as requested. She picked one up, glared around the room, and then let it drop back on the table, drumming her nails on it.

"No comment."

"Are you saying you do not recognize her? Or that you do not know her?" Bickerstaff asked impatiently.

"My client refuses to answer that question in case it may interfere with her request to act as a prosecution witness."

Bickerstaff turned toward Lorraine. He gave a brief nod and they requested a break in the interview to enable them to confer. Both left the room.

Bickerstaff shoved his hands into his pockets. "This could go on for days. You want to have a try, see if we can hurry it up in there?"

"Okay. Is it legal for the same lawyer to represent both parties?"

"Lyall has already given his statement. It'll be up to him to hire someone else. I would, if I was him, but that's not my main concern right now."

They went back into the interview room and the tape was turned on again. The date and time repeated. Lorraine pulled her chair up close. Nula giggled and leaned across the table. "Your turn now, is it?"

Lorraine ignored her remark. "She was just seventeen, Nula. Why did you have to kill her? What harm had she ever done you?"

Nula conferred with her lawyer and then sat back.

"My client wants to know why Ms. Page is present at this interview. She is aware that she is not attached to the FBI or the police Homicide Division. She is also aware that Ms. Page is a chronic alcoholic. I would also like to lodge my own formal complaint as to such a woman being present.''

Bickerstaff leaned back in his chair. "No comment."

"Is she some kind of witness?" the lawyer asked tersely.

Nula smirked. "They couldn't put her on a stand in any court of law, she'd be laughed off. She's a drunkard, she's a whore, and she's even been paid for working with Art Mathews. She more than likely instigated the blackmail—she was certainly paid enough to keep quiet. Ask her! Has anyone asked her how much Art Mathews paid her? I never touched Holly, nor did I hurt my best friend. She's making it all up, probably with that pervert Lyall. I can even smell the booze on her—it's coming out of her pores. Look at the way her hands are shaking."

Lorraine refused to be goaded but she was blushing, not, as it would appear with embarrassment, but anger. She turned to Bickerstaff and got a steely stare back, as if to say "back off me." He hesitated, as if he was going to say something, but then looked away.

Lorraine leaned back and imitated Nula's smiling face. "I'm as sober as she is and she's lying. I was never paid a cent by Art Mathews."

"You lying cunt," Nula spat out.

"Takes one to know one," Lorraine snapped back. "But then you don't have one. Is that your problem? Is that why you had to kill little Holly? Because she was young, beautiful, everything you wanted to be but—"

Nula stood up, pushing away the restraining hand of her lawyer.

"She was about as innocent as my ass!"

"Taking your clients away, was she?" Lorraine shot out and Nula swiped at her from across the table.

Lorraine was on her feet. "That's it, Nula, come on, show what you're really like. Show just what a mean bitch you are—and you are mean. The way you hammered poor Didi's face after all she'd done for you."

No one in the room acknowledged what was going on. They sat stony-faced as Nula and Lorraine shouted at each other. At one point, an officer half-rose but Bickerstaff glared. He wanted this catfight to continue.

Nula snarled, "It was *me* that did everything for *her*. Don't you know anything?" She pointed a red-tipped talon at Lorraine. "She doesn't know what she's talking about."

"Without Didi you were nothing. She had to tout you around—you couldn't even pick up a john without her."

"Fuck you, that's bullshit." Nula's hands were on her hips. Her lawyer tried to make her sit down but she stepped away from the table.

"She told me, said you were a useless piece of garbage."

Nula swiped at her again.

"And then when you found out she'd kept a ring, you just snapped, didn't you?"

Nula looked at them all smugly. "I know what you're trying to do. Well, I'm not saying another word."

She sat down and smoothed her skirt as Lorraine walked to the side of the room and propped herself against the wall. "Nobody's asking you to, Nula, because we know. We know that you tried to get the ring off her finger—even threatened to cut it off—but she wouldn't part with it. She told you to piss off, so you punched her, like the man you really are. All this makeup and wig, all the fancy clothes, you're just a heavy-handed man underneath it all, aren't you, Mr. Simmons? But Didi, she was really beautiful, wasn't she? She was curvaceous, petite, not a big ham-fisted bastard like you. She had tiny delicate hands. . . . Look at your hands, Nula."

Nula elbowed her lawyer. "Tell her to shut the fuck up. This isn't legal. I want to leave."

Bickerstaff calmly looked at the lawyer. "Tell her she won't be leaving here for a long time."

Nula stood up again and lunged forward. "You're all jerks, all of you, you've got nothing on me, nothin' but what that wimp Lyall has told you and he's full of shit."

"Then why don't you tell us what really happened?" Bickerstaff asked.

"No fucking way, you asshole, I'm not sayin' another word. I know my rights, I don't have to tell you anything because I know all you've got is his word against mine. That's *all* you've got and until we make a deal and make me a prosecution witness, I'm not talking."

Lorraine was still standing by the wall, arms folded. "Tell us about Holly. Why did you kill Holly?"

Nula shouted, "I never touched her, I never touched Didi, I never did anything and I know you got nothing on me, nothing. Janklow killed them, just like he killed all the others—

it's in the papers. It's Janklow. I've got nothin' to do with anything.''

"But he didn't kill Holly and he didn't kill Didi."

"Yes, he did." Nula was red in the face with fury. "He was a sicko, everybody knows it, he's nuts, can't even stand trial. Don't you follow what's going on with your so-called investigations? I know what you did. You put poor Art in prison and you killed him. You gave a big press conference, 'We got the killer,' and you were wrong. How come nobody is standing trial for that? He was innocent. I'm innocent."

Getting no reaction from anyone she turned back to Lorraine, pointing at her. "I'll scream it all out to the papers about you, Lorraine Page, about what's going on in this room. Janklow has admitted to killing Holly and Didi, Janklow is a sicko, a pervert and—"

"So are you," Lorraine said softly.

"Get her out of this room or I'll—"

"You'll what, Nula? Kill me like you did Holly?"

"This isn't right, she shouldn't be allowed to do this to me, she's saying things to get me going. Well, I'm not gonna say another word. If you got the evidence, then arrest me, charge me. Go on, let's hear you do it."

Nula put her hand out to her lawyer, who looked confused. "I wanna tissue, it's so fuckin' hot in here, gimme a tissue." She snatched the paper tissue her lawyer held up to her and dabbed her face. Her makeup was starting to run, her mascara smudged, and a section of the front of her wig gauze had broken loose. She tugged at it with annoyance.

Bickerstaff checked his watch. It was almost six-thirty. He suggested they take a break and continue the interview the following morning.

"Does that mean I can go?" Nula asked.

"You will be held in custody pending further inquiries."

"But you haven't charged me," she said. "Can they do this?" she asked the lawyer.

"Yes, I'm afraid they can, with Craig Lyall's statement against you and . . ."

"Bastards," she muttered.

"You'll meet plenty of them, Nicholas," Lorraine said quietly. "How many will be in her cell with her? Three or four?" she asked Bickerstaff. He made no answer.

"I want to be put in the women's section," Nula demanded.

"That won't be possible," Bickerstaff said flatly and turned to the lawyer. "Please explain to your client that as she is listed as male on her birth certificate she cannot be placed in a female wing."

For the first time, Nula seemed frightened. She clung to her lawyer. "But I'm a woman. They can't do this to me." He whispered to her and she looked at Bickerstaff, then Lorraine, lunging at her, knocking over the table. "You bitch! *You did this to me!* You know what'll happen to me in with those animals."

Lorraine ducked and sidestepped Nula as an officer grabbed her. "Then talk, Nula. At least they can segregate you. Tell us the truth about Holly."

"Shut up, you schmuck."

Bickerstaff and the officers straightened the table and replaced all the documents that had fallen to the floor. They straightened Lorraine's chair back into position and it looked as if they were packing up ready to quit for the day.

"Tell the truth, Nula. It was an accident, wasn't it? You never meant to kill Didi, did you? She was your best friend—I know that, I've seen you two together." Lorraine saw the change sweep over Nula in her body language; suddenly she lost all the fight.

"Yes, she was," Nula said softly, and then averted her face. Her eyes filled with tears. "Best friend I ever had."

The room fell silent as if everyone knew it was coming. Nula looked up at the ceiling, her eyes brimming with tears, and Lorraine moved silently back to her own seat. Nula blew her nose on a tissue and then began plucking at it. "Oh, all right, there's no point, is there? You'll find out, I suppose. She fell and hit her head on the side of the glass coffee table. Craig started to panic because we couldn't find her pulse. We thought she was dead and what with—"

"The blackmail? You were worried about that, were you?" Lorraine asked softly.

"It was all getting out of hand. We suspected Janklow was doing these killings because he was a real crazy fucker. He always paid up like it was a joke, like he got off on it. He never argued or nothing but paid up once a month regular as clockwork. But Art began to get greedy, kept pushing him for more, and what was so sick . . . we were blackmailing him because of all his drag pictures but he still wanted more of them. We all kinda knew he was going to crack someday. Maybe that was why Art kept asking him for more money, more jewelry, like he knew he was gonna break.''

''But why did you think it was him murdering these women?''

Nula was tired; she supported herself on her elbow, her wig askew. ''Art put it all together, don't ask me how. He always was an intuitive shit, but instead of backing off he asked for more. We were against it but he wouldn't listen to us. I mean, we were doing okay, we had dough and then we opened that gallery. There was no need to be so greedy, we even had the other business, the photo sessions. We'd all never had it so good . . .''

''How did you collect the money?''

''We'd just go to his garage, one or other of us, pretend we were looking for cars. Art used to drive an old Bentley. He'd bought it from S and A, so he was able to go in and out of Janklow's place. We wouldn't go in dragged up, anything like that. We were pretty cool, changed into straight gear.'' She laughed, a humorless, deep sound.

''You know, sweetheart, without my dresses I can be so butch. I bind my beautiful tits and hey presto, it's me again!''

Nula pulled off her wig as if to prove it. It was horrible, the outline of the glue, her thinning short-cropped hair.

''How did Hastings fit into it?'' Lorraine asked, ignoring Nula's theatricality.

Nula sighed. ''Well, Art and Didi saw him at the garage. Didi recognized Hastings because she'd been doing his wigs and makeup at Craig's studio. Well, this panicked Art for a while, then he discovered that Craig's at it, like he's picked up our tricks and he's doing Norman Hastings himself. Craig's such an oaf, he couldn't even pick a guy with dough. Art was furious—it could've all come out—and what got him worried was that Janklow and Hastings knew each other, and could put two and two together, cause trouble.''

''But Janklow must have known who you were?'' Lorraine said.

Nula shrugged. ''Maybe, but if he did he never contacted the cops. Like I said, he seemed to get off on it, like it was punishment. Anyway, we thought we should just back off. Besides, Art had plenty more, not as much dough as Janklow, but he did all right . . .''

"So, did Hastings talk to Janklow about the blackmail?"

Nula sighed. "I don't know, but when he was found dead, we freaked. Then fucking Janklow appeared and said he needed Art to cover for him, like say he was someplace when he wasn't. He'd done something."

Lorraine asked if Nula remembered the date. She thought for a moment and then said it was the sixteenth or probably the seventeenth of May. It was the date Lorraine had been attacked. She flicked a glance to Bickerstaff, who'd written the date and made a deep circle around it on his notepad.

"Go on, Nula, can you go on?"

Nula nodded, cried for a few moments, and then sniffed, wiping her cheek with her hand. "This wig was Didi's favorite, it's real hair, you know? Anyway, Janklow said he'd pay well for Art to cover for him. He couldn't get cash so he handed over a box of jewelry, said it was all he had left."

"Did you sell it?"

Nula blew her nose. "In the past, when we'd gotten a few things, we'd used Curtis to fence it for us. We didn't say where we got it and he wasn't going to ask." Nula sighed. Everyone hung on her every word. "Curtis gave away one of the pieces we were selling off—a ring—like it was an engagement ring, you know? He gave it to Holly and she used to wear it, showed it to everyone. It was the big topaz, with diamonds around it. It's unbelievable really, small fucking world, because Holly gets picked up by a john who takes her back to his place and asks where did she get the ring 'cause his mother had one like it but—"

"Who was it?"

"Janklow's brother. Anyway, Holly puts two and two together and comes up with sixteen. She asks us about the stuff we fenced to Curtis and then tells us about this john, Brad Thorburn. We tell Art and he's going fucking ape-shit because he knows it's goddamn Janklow's brother, and that Curtis, if he smells a good racket, would want in on it, and Curtis would cause trouble. It was just a fucking mess. I mean, of all the johns to screw Holly it hadda be Janklow's fuckin' brother, I mean . . ."

Lorraine lit two cigarettes and passed one to Nula. She inhaled deeply for a while and then bowed her head. "We had to do something about the ring—we could all have been implicated, know what I mean? She showed it off to everyone—

not that Curtis would have ever married her. He's got a wife and kids anyway.'' She sucked at the cigarette. ''We knew we had to get rid of Holly. We figured she hadn't said anything to Curtis. He never came on to us, but we were all worried—me, Didi, and Art. Art was working the night we decided to do it at the gallery. It was him that said for us to handle it between us, remember that night, Lorraine?''

Everyone in the room looked at Lorraine. She turned to Bickerstaff.

''The art gallery, I worked there.''

Bickerstaff nodded, again making a note and drawing circles around and around it. Nula looked at Lorraine, trying to recall the night.

''Well, you left, right? What, about ten-thirty or so? We worked on sort of thinking about how we would do it. Art made a few crass suggestions. I think it was him who came up with the idea, I dunno, but me and Didi went back to the apartment and Didi got into men's gear. We nabbed a car and parked it not far away from the apartment. Didi left, then I left. I went to my corner and waited for Holly to arrive.''

She sobbed and was given a clean tissue. Everyone waited, hanging on her every word. She suddenly put the wig back on, smoothing it into place, then lit another cigarette. ''Holly, well, she was always jumping into johns' cars. We knew if she saw a decent car she'd find her way to it. Didi pulled up across the road and sort of waved toward Holly and, sure enough, she shot across the road so fast I had a tough time following her. Course, soon as she got into the car she knew something was up, but by that time I'd gone over, opened the back door, and gotten in; then Didi drove off. We wanted just to get the fucking ring off her, warn her, but she was like a wildcat. We didn't even drive far—we couldn't, she was screaming and shouting so much. I think Didi hit her first, then me, but we never meant . . . We didn't mean to hurt her. She was suddenly just like a rag doll, it was awful, so we stuffed her into the trunk. Didi was supposed to dump it, leave her in it, and get back to work, meet up with me. I went back on the streets, to sort of give us an alibi, you know, saying Didi had gotten a john and I was to talk to Curtis.''

''So where did Art come into all this?''

Nula stubbed out the cigarette. ''That stupid bitch Didi, she didn't turn up. We'd agreed to meet in the Bar Q, but she never showed because she went back to the gallery. She was hysterical because, as she was driving around, Holly must have come to. She started banging on the trunk, screaming again, and Didi just drove around and around, faster and faster. She was scared someone on the street'd hear the silly cow screaming and kicking in the trunk.'' Nula rested her head in her hands. ''Art was mad as hell that she'd gone to the gallery with Holly in the car, plus Didi's face was scratched and bruised and she was screechin' and shoutin'. Holly was a tough kid; she put up a fight. If she hadn't we'd never have hurt her.''

''So what happened at the gallery?''

Nula licked her lips. ''I'm not sure, but Art said he'd check on Holly, and he went out. Then he came back in and got a hammer. Didi knew what he was gonna do and tried to stop him and it fell on her foot. Anyway, Art did it and came back and told Didi to dump the car. He gave her the ring—he'd taken it off Holly.'' Nula stared vacantly ahead, sitting low in the chair, her shoulders slumped.

''So Didi got back in the car, knowing Holly was dead in the trunk. Then what?'' Lorraine waited a beat. ''Nula?''

''All the stupid cow had to do was dump it and piss off, but she gets into a terrible state. Her foot swelled up, and she drove the car home because she said she couldn't have walked and she was scared of anyone seeing her. *I* had to dump it. I gave it a good cleaning in case there were any prints. It wasn't so bad because there was no blood or anything. In fact, it wasn't until I got out and was walking past it that I saw this piece of cloth sticking out and then I freaked. I just ran like hell back home.''

Lorraine sounded friendly and understanding. ''It must have been really hard for you.''

''It was, but then it was un-fucking-believable. Didi started wearing the ring. And she wouldn't part with it, it was like some kind of obsession, as if she wanted to be caught. She was always crying and she couldn't sleep. Nothing I said made any difference. She wouldn't listen to me and that's why we had this huge fight. I was trying to get it off her but she went hysterical, saying it was hers after all she'd had to do for it, she wasn't going to let anyone else have it.''

''So you had to get the ring away from Didi, is that right?''

''Course I did, but she wouldn't give it up and so we had

this argument. She pushed me, then I pushed her and she fell.
I thought she was dead, but when . . . It was like Holly happening all over again.''

Nula started to cry, her shoulders shaking, and Lorraine
reached across the table for her hand. ''It's okay, everything's
going to be okay. After she fell what happened?''

Nula's lipstick was smeared, her mascara was running down
her face. ''I called Art and he came over. He said we should
make it look like this serial killer had murdered her, like we'd
done with Holly. But he said since he'd fixed it with Holly, I
should do Didi, that he was having nothing to do with it and
then he left . . .''

''And?'' Lorraine asked.

Nula's face twisted as she tried to stop crying. ''Oh, Jesus,
she was still where she'd fallen. And I got some newspaper
and put it under her head. I hit her with the hammer and it
must have been just like Holly because she moaned. She was
still alive, just like Holly. I could hear her voice, telling me
about Holly, and I just kept on hitting and hitting her until she
was quiet.'' Nula accepted another cigarette, inhaled deeply,
and then sipped some water. Her hand was shaking, the water
dribbling from her mouth as she gulped two or three mouthfuls. ''After I'd done it, I didn't know what to do next. I
couldn't lift her by myself, so I called Craig. I got a black
plastic garbage bag, tied it around her face so he wouldn't see
what I'd done. All he did was help me get her to the car.''
She fell silent. No one spoke. She smoked the cigarette down
to the filter, then looked at it, began to roll it back and forth
between her fingers.

Lorraine took the stub from her and tossed it into the ashtray. She stood up, her back straight. For a moment she stood
with her hands on her hips, breathing deeply. All the men
looked at her, a little puzzled, then she smiled at Bickerstaff.

''Where are you going?'' Nula asked.

''They can charge you now.''

Nula watched fearfully as Lorraine walked briskly to the
door. She didn't even look back; she just walked out.

It was after midnight. Ed Bickerstaff was jubilant. Lyall's and
Nula's statements were signed and they had been taken to their
cells. He passed a small white envelope to Lorraine. ''Five

thousand dollars in used notes. You did good. I didn't think she'd crack.''

"I won't be needed at the trial, will I?''

"Not unless she changes her plea, but I don't think she will.''

"What about Brad Thorburn?''

"I figure the only thing he was guilty of was screwing a prostitute, but we'll need him for questioning. He's on his way back from France.''

Bickerstaff guided her to the door, then paused. "If I ever need you again . . .''

Lorraine smiled. "I'll send you my card. I can set up an office now.''

"Just one more thing, if you don't mind me asking. You seemed pretty friendly in there with Nula.''

"Just doing my job. She's scum—she almost killed me.''

"You don't want to press charges, though, do you?''

She gave him a wry look and one of her rare laughs. "No, I sure as hell don't.''

Rosie was sitting on the sofa watching TV when Lorraine got home. Lorraine looked at her and grinned. "You're a good friend, Rosie.''

"Bed's all made up. Tonight I'm on the sofa.''

Lorraine winked. "Thanks.''

Just as she walked into the bedroom, the phone rang. "If that's for me, I'm not back yet.'' She turned on the shower and couldn't hear what Rosie was calling through the door. She had to turn it back off.

"That was Brad Thorburn. He said he'd call again tomorrow morning.''

Lorraine stripped off the clothes she'd been wearing for the last twenty hours and stepped beneath the cool water, tilting her face up to the jet spray. She was unnerved by his call; she hadn't expected to hear from him again.

"Is he back in L.A.?'' she shouted.

Rosie appeared in the doorway again. "On his way, be here in the morning. He said he was at the airport in Paris. Did you want to speak to him?''

Lorraine wrapped the towel around herself and frowned. Brad had picked up Holly, taken her back to that house, had probably screwed her in the same bed he'd fucked her in, little seventeen-year-old Holly. Brad Thorburn would probably always pick up the wrong kind. As much as she wanted to see him, she thought he was probably calling to find out if she knew why the police wanted to talk to him.

"If he calls again, I'm out. He's no good . . . well, not for me."

"Okay, whatever you say. You want a cup of tea?"

"Sounds good."

Lorraine lay down on the bed. Tomorrow she would open up the agency, get cards made, get a word processor. By the time Rosie came in with the tea she was fast asleep. Rosie didn't wake her but gently draped the bedspread over her. Lorraine didn't stir. The last item on her to-do list had been blurred by sleep, only half considered, but it was the first thing she thought of in the morning. Rosie looked up sleepily from the couch when Lorraine walked in.

"What did you say?"

"Let's go to a meeting this morning."

Brad Thorburn stared around the empty house with all its furnishings covered in dust sheets. He walked out, slamming the front door. He drove to the police station and was introduced to Ed Bickerstaff. The interview was formal and he gave a detailed statement of the night he had picked up a young blond hooker. He couldn't recall her name; he admitted she was just one of so many. Bickerstaff questioned him as to what time of night, how long she had stayed, and then asked if on the night in question he had noticed anything unusual about her. Brad shrugged, he couldn't remember clearly.

"How about an item of jewelry?"

Brad thought, and then it dawned on him. "She was wearing a large ring. I only remember because it was similar to one my mother used to wear, but she took it off and slipped it into her purse and I never gave it much thought."

"Was this it?" Bickerstaff held out the ring taken from Didi's finger.

Brad stared at it. "Yes, well, it was similar."

"Could this be your mother's ring?"

"Possibly. It's similar, but whether it's hers or not I couldn't say. She had a large collection of jewels—she was a collector.

Some of them were worth thousands, others cheap replicas. She was always terrified of being mugged. I'm sorry not to be of more help.''

Bickerstaff didn't bother to explain how important the ring had been in so many people's lives—and deaths.

Brad left and returned to his car. He drove to the Melville and Thompson real estate agents on Rodeo Drive, signed over the documents for the contents of the house to be sold along with the property, said the property as from that afternoon would be vacated and he wanted his personal possessions put into storage. The sale notices already hung outside. Brad collected the items he wanted to take with him and put little red stickers on the rest so the storage men would know which articles were to be removed.

He walked from room to room in the shrouded house. There was little he needed or wanted, it was mostly his personal belongings from his own quarters. He did, however, stick red dots on all the silver-framed family photographs. He found it difficult to look at the faces of his brother and mother but went about his work as fast as possible. Steven's room was more difficult than he had anticipated, with his precious collections of shells and snuffboxes, and the banks of photographs of their mother. He closed the door, refusing to allow himself to think about Steven. Not until he was in his own room did he relax, as he checked his book and record collections, his sports equipment. There was so little with which he had any emotional ties—everything could easily be replaced. All he knew was that he would never come back to this house and its memories.

Brad arrived at his mother's nursing home in the late afternoon. He had called Lorraine's number four times but received no reply. He decided he would try once more before he left. He didn't know why he wanted to see her; he was not infatuated or in love with her, but he couldn't shake off the memory of how gentle he had felt toward her, how good it had been to hold her in his arms.

Mrs. Thorburn was seated by the windows overlooking the elegant gardens. The nursing home was not far from the horrific L.A. County Medical Center but very different. This was the Motion Pictures Home for ex-stars or anyone connected to show business. Mulholland Drive was on one side, Cabon Avenue on the other. The private rooms with dining areas and small kitchens looked out onto a spacious garden and beyond the gardens was Mirasol Park. Mrs. Thorburn was there out of choice. She was not incapacitated or infirm, but she said she liked the company. She was sitting in one of the bright communal lounges, reading *Vogue*, the arthritic hands with their perfectly manicured nails gliding over the pages, pausing to tap a particular photograph and then ripping off a yellow sticker from a pad and carefully applying it to a page. She still bought lavish clothes, sometimes an entire collection, which were delivered to the home.

Brad watched her for a few more minutes. Everything about her was immaculate: her wig, false eyelashes, and pale powdered skin drawn tightly over the high cheekbones. The many face-lifts had given her a surreal look so she could, at a distance, be taken for a thirty-year-old woman; only close up did one see the stretched, taut, aging skin. He called her name softly as he approached and bent to kiss her cheek. As always she averted her face.

"Be careful of my hair, darling."

He pulled up a chair, sitting to one side. She closed the magazine and held it out as if to an unseen butler. Brad took it and pushed it into the side of her wheelchair. She was wearing a lilac silk draped blouse with four rows of pearls at her neck and large matching pearl and diamond earrings. There was a soft cashmere lilac shawl across her knees and her skirt was a deeper tone. He could see her delicate feet encased in soft handmade cream shoes, her pale white legs and still shapely ankles resting on the wheelchair step.

"How are you?"

"Dreadful. How do you expect me to be?"

Her perfect lips, dark crimson, her overlarge, overwhite false teeth, grimaced in a sneering smile. "I hear you're selling the house? I always hated it. Will we get a good price?"

"I think so."

"Where are you going to live?"

"South of France."

"Always loved Cannes but it's not what it used to be. Your father took me there often in the early days, but we had problems with the staff, probably because he was fucking them."

Brad smiled at the way she dropped in the word "fucking"

as if to shock, but he was used to it. She could swear better than any man he'd ever met and he felt something akin to fondness for her, which surprised him. Suddenly she pointed one frail, red-nailed finger toward the gardens. "They're putting in a new border and a fountain. I just hope it's not some awful cherub pissing. I hate those little penises spurting water. I'm always surprised how many people choose them, very distasteful, nasty things, penises—uncircumcised ones in particular. I made sure you were circumcised—much more attractive, especially if you're being sucked off." She gave a shrill laugh, and placed her hands over her lips like a naughty schoolgirl, her diamonds glinting in the sunlight. He gave a small tight smile; she had often disgusted him when she'd said something similar in company, especially in front of his college friends. She'd always delighted in being crude, offensive, and overtly sexual, enjoying the embarrassed blushes she caused.

"Mother, do you remember that big topaz ring? It had diamonds all around it, very large, set in platinum," he said quietly, surprised at himself for even bringing the subject up.

"Hard to forget. Your father would always give me something extravagant when he was screwing somebody else. The more expensive it was the higher the chance of it being a close friend. The topaz was good quality and they were rose diamonds, excellent carat. Why do you ask?"

"No reason."

"Ah, my darling, there's always a reason. I suppose it was one of the items Steven stole or sold or whatever they wish to call it. Well, it was a beautiful ring but too ostentatious for my taste." She turned to face Brad, her eyes still china blue.

"Why did he have so many other women? My father. It's always struck me as odd. You must have loved each other at one time?"

"Love never came into it, sweetheart." He wanted to hold her clawlike hand, but she was turning to one of the other residents, waving like royalty.

"We worked together. She's very infirm, poor dear. We were having such a good gossip the other day, she told me a marvelous story about Irving. It was on a Mickey Rooney movie . . . now there was a talent, pity he was so short and . . . um . . ." He saw her mouth tighten, then she plucked at her cashmere shawl.

"No, love never came into it, that was why he hated me so much and tried to hurt me in every way possible. He hated me because I could not find him attractive. I married him for his money. I told him at the time but I don't think he believed me."

He leaned back slightly. He wanted her to be lying, needed her to say there had been some love. He felt like a helpless young boy; had he been born out of hatred?

"Is that true, Mother?"

She turned back to face him, her blue eyes like ice chips. "What do you think?"

"I don't know and I have to go." He stood up. She waved again across the elegant room and murmured that it was tea-time. "Will you write to Steven?" he asked.

He was astonished by the venom in her voice when she replied.

"He's dead to me. I can't bring myself to write or make any contact. He does not exist. I've already changed my will. You'll get everything. Everyone here has been so, well, understanding, but I won't discuss it. Ah! Yes, I remember what I was going to tell you, it was a movie with Judy Garland and Mickey Rooney, and Irving came to my dressing room and . . ."

He touched her shoulder. He had heard all her movie stories many times, knew they were mostly lies. "I'll write, and then, as soon as I'm settled, you'll come visit me."

"That would be very pleasant, dear." Both knew the other was lying; there would be no visits. There was no antagonism or reprimand in her bright eyes. She held out her hand and he kissed it gently. How often had he smelled that sweet floral perfume? How many times had he as a child wanted this woman to hold him and kiss him? He felt it even now: he wanted some sign that she cared for him. But she gave none, dismissing him by withdrawing her hand.

He walked away across the polished wood floor, then turned back, half hoping she would still be watching him. But she was already flipping through the pages of *Vogue* again, positioning a yellow sticker on a long cream evening gown worn by a doe-eyed model.

She hadn't worn an evening gown for more than thirty years but she hadn't wept for much longer. Tears ruined her makeup, made her false eyelashes unstick. It had taken many long years of practice not to weep. She could remember the last time she had cried herself to exhaustion. It had been when she had found her husband in bed with her closest friend. The two of them naked, moaning with orgasmic pleasure. She had never had an orgasm in her entire life; she was frigid; she was, as her husband had called her, the "Ice Maiden." Only little Steven had broken through to her heart. Only Steven had known how to love her, seemed to know intuitively the fear she had of allowing herself to be loved. He had known how to kiss her without pawing or fumbling. Only Steven knew how delicate she was—and now even he had betrayed her. He had been as brutal as every man she had ever encountered, selling off her precious things without even asking, going with disgusting lowlife, whores, filthy disgusting unwashed pieces of humanity. Sitting trapped in her wheelchair, she remembered his slim, delicate body; his sweet, tender kisses; his perfect circumcised penis that she had loved to kiss awake and then to rub his semen over her skin, because it was better than any of her expensive creams. They had discussed its therapeutic powers endlessly, lying together in her overheated bedroom. She had never believed that what they were doing was wrong—it was only natural. She bore no blame for what he had subsequently done: that had nothing to do with her. The women he had murdered were whores, just like the bitches her husband had brought home. They had meant nothing to her, and she refused to feel any remorse for the women her beloved son had killed. She would not forgive him for stealing from her, not forgive him for bringing the terrible-smelling police officers to interview her, showing her photographs, terrible photographs of Steven pretending to be her. She could not understand why he had subjected her to such awful humiliation, such scandal, when she had managed to live her entire life without so much as a hint of gossip surrounding her. It was unforgivable because she thought, of all people, Steven understood; she had only ever loved Steven. She started to sing softly to herself, snatches of a song she'd sung in a chorus someplace a long time ago.

"If I say I love you, do you mind,
   If I shower you with kisses, if I tell you, honey . . . this
   is . . ."

but she could no longer remember all the lyrics.

Steven Janklow was being led from his neatly made bed in the white-walled room. He liked nighttime. Every night on the way to the bathroom with his guard, he passed a window. He always stopped in his tracks when he saw his reflection in his white cotton institution gown. "Oh, hello, darling," he whispered, before he was led into the bathroom. He never spoke to anyone else, only to the image in the dark windowpane, but he was always smiling. He seemed happy and contented, often singing the same few lines from some half-remembered song.

"If I say I love you, do you mind,
If I shower you with kisses . . ."

Brad Thorburn returned to France. He made one last attempt to contact Lorraine but received no reply. "If I say I love you, do you mind . . ."

Rosie and Lorraine had worked hard all week. They had bought some cheap office furniture, a bookcase, and filing cabinets. They had arranged for the phone to be connected and delivery of a word processor. Lorraine dropped by the gym to see Hector and explained that she was taking over the office next door. The proximity of the gym would make it very convenient for workouts.

They did not hire a sign painter as no good agency wants its work broadcast. They would keep a low profile and advertise in newspapers and magazines. Lorraine would require a license and a permit to carry a weapon, but she felt she should give Bickerstaff a few weeks before she asked a favor. She'd left her number and the address in case he wanted to talk to her but he hadn't called.

She and Rosie were surveying their handiwork when there was a thump on the door. Lorraine turned. "I thought you were doing Europe."

Rooney took off his hat. "The wife still is. They called me back for the Craig Lyall business."

She tilted her head to one side and he gave an odd, rueful smile.

"Okay, I'm lying. I called Josh to see what was happening and, well, in case they needed me I thought I should come back."

"Do they?" she asked, wanting to give him a hug but deciding against it. Rooney was not really the kind of man you hugged.

"Nope, they didn't, but, man, are they all very pleased with themselves, and now there's no nasty smears about the Art Mathews suicide, which makes the FBI happier."

Rooney was wearing a big T-shirt, baggy pants, and a loud checkered jacket. He somehow even managed to take his bad taste right down to odd two-toned shoes. He edged farther into the new office and looked around. "You won't get a license, you know," he said flatly.

She shrugged. A lot of agencies were working without one.

"Won't get the good clients. You won't even get a weapon license."

"I'll take it day by day, Bill."

He sniffed and looked around, twisting his hat. "You got my home number?" he asked. He had something on his mind but was too embarrassed to come out with it, so he merely shrugged his shoulders. "I might go and have some of that raw fish. I've missed it. I don't suppose you're in the mood for some?"

"Not right now, but thanks for the offer." She let him plod all the way to the door before she took pity on him. "Bill . . ."

He turned, plonking his hat on. "Yep?"

She walked slowly toward him, arms folded. "I know you're retired and looking forward to sitting back and enjoying a life of leisure, but I was just wondering . . ."

He couldn't hide it: his face lit up as he looked at her expectantly.

"Well, as you said, I couldn't get an investigator's license or a weapon permit. I've only got my driver's license thanks to you. What would you say to helping me out—not full-time, I wouldn't ask that of you, but maybe just a couple days a week?"

She let him do a lot of frowning and head scratching but then he smiled. "I'll put in the license application today. I've got a lot of contacts—we could make a go of it."

She put out her hand and he shook it and then he pulled her toward him. The big man that nobody dared hug clasped her tightly, his voice was hoarse with emotion. "Always said you were one of the best. I'm proud you pulled yourself back up. I'm proud of you, Lorraine."

Rosie watched him walk off before she snapped, "I thought I was your partner!"

"You are. We need him, Rosie, he's got his retirement bonus, he's got contacts. It's all to do with contacts and he'll be a good front man." She put her arm around her fat friend's shoulders. "I'm feeling good, Rosie, positive. How about you?"

Rosie was as tickled as old Rooney had been. Lorraine had this ability to draw you to her, make you want to please her— kill her at times, too—but more than that, you felt if she was happy then you were part of that happiness.

"I'm feeling good, partner. I know we'll make a go of it, I just know it."

Rosie and Lorraine went on to an AA meeting. They both went regularly twice a week. Jake was waiting for them to join him. He was the greeter at the door as they took their places in front of the small informal platform. This meeting was important because Lorraine was going to share her story. Rosie glowed with pride. She herself was not ready yet to stand up and be counted, as Jake called it, but she was closer than she'd ever been before, and she felt she owed it to her friend Lorraine. Rosie had a future. It wouldn't all be smooth sailing, she knew that—she was no fool—but at least she was in a far better position than she had ever dreamed possible. She was thankful that she'd taken that crazy chance on the strange skinny woman minus a front tooth, because they'd both come through. To see Lorraine sitting up there, elegant, strong, and vital, made the long, hard journey they'd traveled together worth every minute.

Jake took out a big square handkerchief. He couldn't stop himself: Lorraine was making him cry, not because of what she was saying—he knew most of it by now—but because, like Rosie, he was so proud of her, and it was hard for him to believe that the wretched creature Rosie had brought back from the institution was now facing the demon head on. She had fought it, and almost been beaten, but now he was sure she was on her way to recovery. You could almost feel her energy, her optimism.

"My name is Lorraine and I'm an alcoholic. Eight years ago, I was a police lieutenant. I was also a drunk. I committed a terrible injustice. I mistakenly took a young boy's life because I was drunk. There is no excuse. Nothing will ever take away the guilt I felt, still feel, will always feel." Lorraine continued the story of her life, how she had lost her children and her husband, how she had sunk into prostitution, how she had fallen downward to every kind of depravity simply to earn enough money to drink herself into oblivion. She talked about meeting Rosie. When she said that was in April, it made her pause, realizing it was not so long ago. Then she continued about her introduction to Jake, how she came to be here, and finally that on the first of October she had opened her own business and was hoping she would make a success of it. She then thanked everyone for listening to her story, and said she felt she was living proof of how far down someone could go and how, in only seven months, climb back again.

"I don't want oblivion anymore. I want my life. I want to live my life and I want to live it sober. I will always be indebted to AA and to my friends. At last I feel more at peace with myself and with God. Because for a while, I thought he'd abandoned me. But he didn't, he hasn't. I'm Lorraine again, and she's been missing for a long long time. Thank you."

ABOUT THE AUTHOR

LYNDA LA PLANTE started her career as a television actress, then turned to scriptwriting, where she made her breakthrough with the phenomenally successful British television series *Widows*. In the United States, she is best known for her television miniseries *Prime Suspect*. She has won two Emmys, the 1993 Edgar Allan Poe writers award, and top British awards. La Plante lives in East Hampton, N.Y., and London.

7. 11. 19.20.22 (1)